Praise for Elizabeth Chadwick

"An author who makes historical fiction come gloriously alive."
—*Times of London*

"Elizabeth Chadwick is a gifted novelist and a dedicated researcher; it doesn't get any better than that."
—Sharon Kay Penman

"The best writer of medieval fiction currently around."
—Richard Lee,
founder of the Historical Novel Society

"The reader is well aware on every page that this is life as it was lived eight hundred years ago, yet the characters are as fresh and natural as if they were living in the present time."
—*Historical Novels Review*

"Elizabeth Chadwick knows exactly how to write convincing and compelling historical fiction."
—Marina Oliver

"A stunning grasp of historical detail...her characters are beguiling, the story intriguing and very enjoyable."
—Barbara Erskine

"There's no better writer of medieval fiction than the marvelous Elizabeth Chadwick."
—*Lancashire Evening Post*

"Elizabeth Chadwick is to Medieval England what Philippa Gregory is to the Tudors and the Stuarts, and Bernard Cornwell is to the Dark Ages."
—*Books Monthly, UK*

The Greatest Knight

THE UNSUNG STORY OF
THE QUEEN'S CHAMPION

ELIZABETH CHADWICK

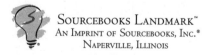

SOURCEBOOKS LANDMARK™
AN IMPRINT OF SOURCEBOOKS, INC.®
NAPERVILLE, ILLINOIS

Published by Sourcebooks Landmark, an imprint of Sourcebooks, Inc.
P.O. Box 4410, Naperville, Illinois 60567-4410
(630) 961-3900
Fax: (630) 961-2168
www.sourcebooks.com

Originally published in 2005 by Time Warner Books

Library of Congress Cataloging-in-Publication Data

Chadwick, Elizabeth.
  The greatest knight : the unsung story of the queen's champion / by Elizabeth Chadwick.
    p. cm.
  Includes bibliographical references and index.
  1. Pembroke, William Marshal, Earl of, 1144?-1219—Fiction. 2. Eleanor, of Aquitaine,
Queen, consort of Henry II, King of England, 1122?-1204—Fiction. 3. Great Britain—
History—Henry II, 1154-1189—Fiction. 4. Great Britain—Courts and courtiers—Fiction.
5. Knights and knighthood—Great Britain—Fiction. 6. Favorites, Royal—Great Britain—
Fiction. I. Title.
  PR6053.H245G74 2009
  823'.914—dc22

                                2009022444

        Printed and bound in the United States of America.

          VP 10 9 8 7 6 5 4 3 2

KINGS OF ENGLAND

THE CONTINENTAL DYNASTIES
1066–1216

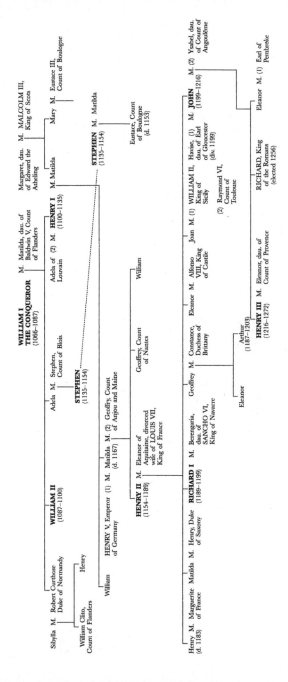

MARSHAL FAMILY TREE

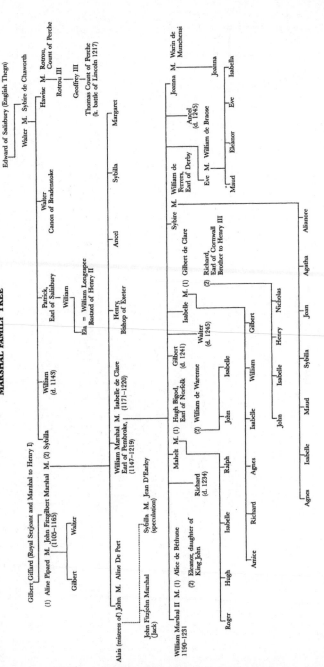

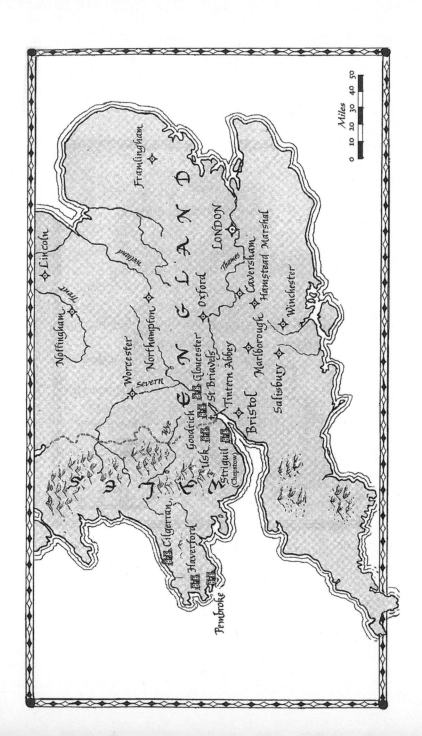

ENGLAND

WALES

Framlingham
Lincoln
Trent
Nottingham
Welland
Northampton
Worcester
Severn
Oxford
London
Thames
Caversham
Hamstead Marshal
Winchester
Goodrich
Usk
St Briavels
Gloucester
Tintern Abbey
Strigoil (Chepstow)
Bristol
Marlborough
Salisbury
Cilgerran
Wye
Haverford
Pembroke

Miles
0 10 20 30 40 50

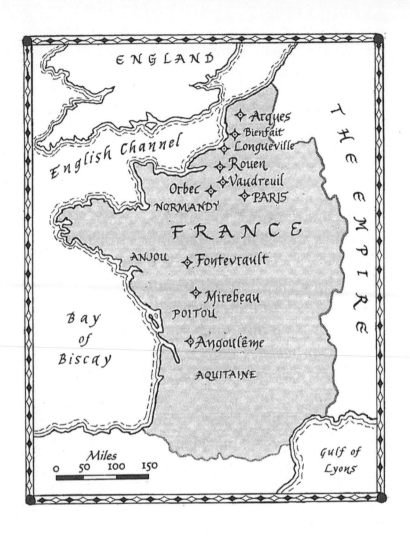

"Car en nostre tens n'ot il unques
En nul liu meillor chevalier"

"For in our time there was never
A better knight to be found anywhere."
—*Histoire de Guillaume le Mareschal*

One

FORTRESS OF DRINCOURT, NORMANDY, SUMMER 1167

*I*N THE DARK HOUR BEFORE DAWN, ALL THE SHUTTERS IN THE great hall were closed against the evil vapours of the night. Under the heavy iron curfew, the fire was a quenched dragon's eye. The forms of slumbering knights and retainers lined the walls and the air sighed with the sound of their breathing and resonated with the occasional glottal snore.

At the far end of the hall, occupying one of the less favoured places near the draughts and away from the residual gleam of the fire, a young man twitched in his sleep, his brow pleating as the vivid images of his dream took him from the restless darkness of a vast Norman castle to a smaller, intimate chamber in his family's Hampshire keep at Ludgershall.

He was five years old, wearing his best blue tunic, and his mother was clutching him to her bosom as she exhorted him in a cracking voice to be a good boy. "Remember that I love you, William." She squeezed him so tightly that he could hardly breathe. When she released him they both gasped, he for air, she fighting tears. "Kiss me and go with your father," she said.

Setting his lips to her soft cheek, he inhaled her scent, sweet like new-mown hay. Suddenly he didn't want to go and his chin began to wobble.

"Stop weeping, woman, you're unsettling him."

William felt his father's hand come down on his shoulder, hard, firm, turning him away from the sun-flooded chamber and the gathered domestic household, which included his three older brothers, Walter, Gilbert, and John, all watching him with solemn eyes. John's lip was quivering too.

"Are you ready, son?"

He looked up. Lead from a burning church roof had destroyed his father's left eye and melted a raw trail from temple to jaw, leaving him with an angel's visage one side and the gargoyle mask of a devil on the other. Never having known him without the scars, William accepted them without demur.

"Yes, sir," he said and was rewarded by a kindling gleam of approval.

"Brave lad."

In the courtyard the grooms were waiting with the horses. Setting his foot in the stirrup, John Marshal swung astride and leaned down to scoop William into the saddle before him. "Remember that you are the son of the King's Marshal and the nephew of the Earl of Salisbury." His father nudged his stallion's flanks and he and his troop clattered out of the keep. William was intensely aware of his father's broad, battle-scarred hands on the reins and the bright embroidery decorating the wrists of the tunic.

"Will I be gone a long time?" his dream self asked in a high treble.

"That depends on how long King Stephen wants to keep you."

"Why does he want to keep me?"

"Because I made him a promise to do something and he wants you beside him until I have kept that promise." His father's voice was as harsh as a sword blade across a whetstone. "You are a hostage for my word of honour."

"What sort of promise?"

William felt his father's chest spasm and heard a grunt that was almost laughter. "The sort of promise that only a fool would ask of a madman."

It was a strange answer and the child William twisted round to crane up at his father's ruined face even as the grown William turned within the binding of his blanket, his frown deepening and his eyes moving rapidly beneath his closed lids. Through the mists of the dreamscape, his father's voice faded, to be replaced by those of a man and woman in agitated conversation.

"The bastard's gone back on his word, bolstered the keep, stuffed it to the rafters with men and supplies, shored up the breaches." The man's voice was raw with contempt. "He never intended to surrender."

"What of his son?" the woman asked in an appalled whisper.

"The boy's life is forfeit. The father says that he cares not—he still has the anvils and hammers to make more and better sons than the one he loses."

"He does not mean it…"

The man spat. "He's John Marshal and he's a mad dog. Who knows what he would do. The King wants the boy."

"But you're not going to…you can't!" The woman's voice rose in horror.

"No, I'm not. That's on the conscience of the King and the boy's accursed father. The stew's burning, woman; attend to your duties."

William's dream self was seized by the arm and dragged roughly across the vast sprawl of a battle-camp. He could smell the blue smoke of the fires, see the soldiers sharpening their weapons, and a team of mercenaries assembling what he now knew was a stone-throwing machine.

"Where are we going?" he asked.

"To the King." The man's face had been indistinct before but now the dream brought it sharply into focus, revealing hard, square bones thrusting against leather-brown skin. His name was Henk and he was a Flemish mercenary in the pay of King Stephen.

"Why?"

Without answering, Henk turned sharply to the right. Between the siege machine and an elaborate tent striped in blue and gold, a group of men were talking amongst themselves. A pair of guards stepped forward, spears at the ready, then relaxed and waved Henk and William through. Henk took two strides and knelt, pulling William down beside him. "Sire."

William darted an upward glance through his fringe, uncertain which of the men Henk was addressing, for none of them wore a crown or resembled his notion of what a king should look like. One lord was holding a fine spear though, with a silk banner rippling from the haft.

"So this is the boy whose only value to his father has been the buying of time," said the man standing beside the spear-bearer. He had greying fair hair and lined, care-worn features. "Rise, child. What's your name?"

"William, sir." His dream self stood up. "Are you the King?"

The man blinked and looked taken aback. Then his faded blue eyes narrowed and his lips compressed. "Indeed I am, although your father seems not to think so." One of his companions leaned to mutter in his ear. The King listened and vigorously shook his head. "No," he said.

A breeze lifted the silk banner on the lance and it fluttered outwards, making the embroidered red lion at its centre appear to stretch and prowl. The sight diverted William. "Can I hold it?" he asked eagerly.

The lord frowned at him. "You're a trifle young to be a standard-bearer, hmm?" he said, but there was a reluctant twinkle in his eye and after a moment he handed the spear to William. "Careful now."

The haft was warm from the lord's hand as William closed his own small fist around it. Wafting the banner, he watched the lion snarl in the wind and laughed with delight.

The King had drawn away from his adviser and was making denying motions with the palm of his hand.

"Sire, if you relent, you will court naught but John Marshal's contempt…" the courtier insisted.

"Christ on the Cross, I will court the torture of my soul if I hang an innocent for the crimes of his sire. Look at him…look!" The King jabbed a forefinger in William's direction. "Not for all the gold in Christendom will I see a little lad like that dance on a gibbet. His hellspawn father, yes, but not him."

Oblivious of the danger in which he stood, aware only of being the centre of attention, William twirled the spear.

"Come, child." The King beckoned to him. "You will stay in my tent until I decide what is to be done with you."

William was only a little disappointed when he had to return the spear to its owner who turned out to be the Earl of Arundel. After all, there was a magnificent striped tent to explore and the prospect of yet more weapons to look at and perhaps even touch if he was allowed—royal ones at that. With such a prospect in mind, he skipped along happily at King Stephen's side.

Two knights in full mail guarded the tent and various squires and attendants waited on the King's will. The flaps were hooked back to reveal a floor strewn with freshly scythed meadow and the heady scent of cut grass was intensified by the enclosing canvas. Beside a large bed with embroidered bolsters and covers of silk and fur stood an ornate coffer like the one in his parents' chamber at Ludgershall. There was also room for a bench and a table holding a silver flagon and cups. The King's hauberk gleamed on a stand of crossed ash poles, with the helmet secured at the top and his shield and scabbard propped against the foot. William eyed the equipment with longing.

The King smiled at him. "Do you want to be a knight, William?"

William nodded vigorously, eyes glowing.

"And loyal to your king?"

Again William nodded but this time because instinct told him it was the required response.

"I wonder." Sighing heavily, the King directed a squire to pour the blood-red wine from flagon to cup. "Boy," he said. "Boy, look at me."

William raised his head. The intensity of the King's stare frightened him a little.

"I want you to remember this day," King Stephen said slowly and deliberately. "I want you to know that whatever your father has done to me, I am giving you the chance to grow up and redress the balance. Know this: a king values loyalty above all else." He sipped from the cup and then pressed it into William's small hands. "Drink and promise you will remember."

William obliged, although the taste stung the back of his throat.

"Promise me," the King repeated as he repossessed the cup.

"I promise," William said, and as the wine flamed in his belly, the dream left him and he woke with a gasp to the crowing of roosters and the first stirring of movement amongst the occupants of Drincourt's great hall. For a moment he lay blinking, acclimatising himself to his present surroundings. It was a long time since his dreams had peeled back the years and returned him to the summer he had spent as King Stephen's hostage during the battle for Newbury. He seldom recalled that part of his life with his waking memory, but occasionally, without rhyme or reason, his dreams would return him to that time and the young man just turning twenty would again become a fair-haired little boy of five years old.

His father, despite all his manoeuvring, machinations, and willingness to sacrifice his fourth-born son, had lost Newbury, and eventually his lordship of Marlborough, but if he had lost the battle, he had rallied on the successful turn of the tide. Stephen's bloodline lay in the grave and Empress Matilda's son,

Henry, the second of that name, had been sitting firmly on the throne for thirteen years.

"And I am a knight," William murmured, his lips curving with grim humour. The leap in status was recent. A few weeks ago he had still been a squire, polishing armour, running errands, learning his trade at the hands of Sir Guillaume de Tancarville, Chamberlain of Normandy and distant kin to his mother. William's knighting announced his arrival into manhood and advanced him a single rung upon a very slippery ladder. His position in the Tancarville household was precarious. There were only so many places in Lord Guillaume's retinue for newly belted knights with ambitions far greater than their experience or proven capability.

William had considered seeking house room under his brother's rule at Hamstead, but that was a last resort, nor did he have sufficient funds to pay his passage home across the Narrow Sea. Besides, with the strife between Normandy and France at white heat, there were numerous opportunities to gain the necessary experience. Even now, somewhere along the border, the French army was preparing to slip into Normandy and wreak havoc. Since Drincourt protected the northern approaches to the city of Rouen, there was a pressing need for armed defenders.

As the dream images faded, William slipped back into a light doze and the tension left his body. The blond hair of his infancy had steadily darkened through boyhood and was now a deep hazel-brown, but fine summer weather still streaked it with gold. Folk who had known his father said that William was the image of John Marshal in the days before the molten lead from the burning roof of Wherwell Abbey had ruined his comeliness; that they had the same eyes, the irises deep grey, with the changeable muted tones of a winter river.

"God's bones, I warrant you could sleep through the trumpets of Doomsday, William. Get up, you lazy wastrel!" The voice was accompanied by a sharp dig in William's ribs. With a grunt of pain, the young man opened his eyes on Gadefer de Lorys, one of Tancarville's senior knights.

"I'm awake." Rubbing his side, William sat up. "Isn't a man allowed to gather his thoughts before he rises?"

"Hah, you'd be gathering them until sunset if you were allowed. I've never known such a slugabed. If you weren't my lord's kin, you'd have been slung out on your arse long since!"

The best way to deal with Gadefer, who was always grouchy in the mornings, was to agree with him and get out of his way. William was well aware of the resentment simmering among some of the other knights who viewed him as a threat to their own positions in the mesnie. His kinship to the chamberlain was as much a handicap as it was an advantage. "You're right," he replied with a self-deprecating smile. "I'll throw myself out forthwith and go and exercise my stallion."

Gadefer stumped off, muttering under his breath. Concealing a grimace, William rolled up his pallet, folded his blanket, and wandered outside. The air held the dusty scent of midsummer, although the cool green nip of the dawn clung in the shadows of the walls, evaporating as the stones drank the rising sunlight. He glanced towards the stables, hesitated, then changed his mind and followed his rumbling stomach to the kitchens.

The Drincourt cooks were accustomed to William's visits and he was soon leaning against a trestle devouring wheaten bread still hot from the oven and glistening with melted butter and sweet clover honey. The cook's wife shook her head. "I don't know where you put it all. By rights you should have a belly on you like a woman about to give birth."

William grinned and slapped his iron-flat stomach. "I work hard."

She raised a brow that said more than words, and returned to chopping vegetables. Still grinning, William licked the last drips of buttery honey off the side of his hand and went to the door, bracing his arm on the lintel and looking out on the fine morning with pleasure. The peace of the moment was broken by the sound of shouts from the courtyard. Moments later the mail-clad Earl of Essex and several knights and serjeants raced past the open door towards the stables. William hastened out into the ward. "Holà!" he cried. "What's happening?"

"The French and Flemings have been sighted on the outskirts!" a knight panted over his shoulder.

The words hit William like a bolt of lightning. "They've crossed the border?"

"Aye, over the Bresle and down through Eu. Now they're at our walls with Matthew of Boulogne at their head. We'll have the devil of a task to hold them. Get your armour on, Marshal, you've no time for stomach-filling now!"

William sprinted for the hall. By the time he arrived his heart was thundering like a drum and he was wishing he hadn't eaten all that bread and honey for he felt sick. A squire was waiting to help him into his padded undertunic and mail. Already dressed in his, the Sire de Tancarville was pacing the hall like a man with a burr in his breeches, issuing terse commands to the knights who were scrambling into their armour.

William pressed his lips together. The urge to retch peaked and then receded. As he donned his mail, his heartbeat steadied, although his palms were slick with cold sweat and he had to wipe them on his surcoat. Now was the moment for which he had trained. Now was his chance to prove that he was good for more than just gluttony and slumber, and that his place in the household was by right of ability and not family favour.

By the time the Sire de Tancarville and his retinue joined the Earl of Essex at the town's West Bridge, the suburbs of Drincourt were swarming with Flemish mercenaries and the terrified inhabitants were fleeing for their lives. The smell of cooking fires had been overlaid by the harsher stench of indiscriminate burning and in the rue Chaussée a host of Boulonnais knights were massing to make an assault on the West Gate and break into the town itself.

Eager, nervous, resolute, William urged his stallion to the fore, jostling past several seasoned knights until he was level with de Tancarville himself. The latter cast him a warning glance and curbed his destrier as it lashed out at William's sweating chestnut. "Lad, you are too hasty," he growled with amused irritation. "Fall back and let the knights do their work."

Flushed with chagrin, William swallowed the retort that he *was* a knight and reined back. Glowering, he allowed three of the most experienced warriors to overtake him but as a fourth tried to jostle past, William spurred forward again, determined to show his mettle.

Roaring his own name as a battle cry, de Tancarville launched a charge over the bridge and down the rue Chaussée to meet the oncoming Boulonnais knights. William gripped his shield close to his body, levelled his lance and gave the chestnut its head. He fixed his gaze on the crimson device of a knight on a black stallion and held his line as his destrier bore him towards the moment of impact. He noticed how his opponent carried his lance too high and that the red shield was tilted a fraction inwards. Steadying his arm, he kept his eyes open until the last moment. His lance punched into the knight's shield, pierced it and even though the shaft snapped off in William's hand, the blow was sufficient to send the other man reeling. Using the stump as a club, William knocked the knight from the saddle. As the black destrier bolted, reins trailing, William drew his sword.

After the first violent impact, the fighting broke up into individual combats. Nothing in his training had prepared William for the sheer clamour and ferocity of battle, but he was undaunted and fed upon the experience avidly and with increasing confidence as he emerged victorious from several sharp tussles with more experienced men. He was both terrified and exhilarated: like a fish released from a calm stewpond into a fast-flowing river.

The Count of Boulogne ordered more troops into the fray and the battle for the bridge became a desperate crush of men and horses. Armed with clubs, staves, and slingshots, the townspeople fought beside the castle garrison and the battle swayed back and forth like washing in the wind. It was close and dirty work and William's sword hand grew slippery with sweat and blood.

"Tancarville!" William roared hoarsely as he pivoted to strike at a French knight. His adversary's destrier shied, throwing his rider in the dust where he lay unmoving. William seized the knight's lance and urged the chestnut towards a knot of Flemish mercenaries who were busy looting a house. One man had dragged a coffer into the street and was clubbing at the lock with his sword hilt. At a warning shout from his companions, he spun round, but only to receive William's lance through his chest. Immediately the others closed around William, furiously intent on dragging him from his mount.

William turned and manoeuvred his stallion, beating them off with sword and shield, until one of them seized a gaff resting against the house wall and attempted to hook William from his horse. The gaff lodged in his hauberk at the shoulder, the lower claw tearing into the mail, breaking several riveted links and sinking through gambeson and tunic to spike William's flesh. He felt no pain for his blood was coursing with the heat of battle. As they surrounded him, trying to grab his reins and drag him down off the horse, he pricked the chestnut's loin with his spurs and the stallion lashed out. There was a scream as a shod hind hoof connected with flesh and the man dropped like a stone. William gripped the stallion's breast strap and again used the spur, forward of the girth this time. His mount reared, came down, and shot forward so that the soldiers gripping the reins had to let go and leap aside before they were trampled. The mercenary wielding the hook lost his purchase and William was able to wrench free and turn on him. Almost sobbing his lord's battle cry, he cut downwards with his sword, saw the man fall, and forced the chestnut forwards over his body. Free of the broil of mercenaries, he rejoined the bulk of the Tancarville knights, but his horse had a deep neck wound and the reins were slippery with its blood.

The enemy had forced the Drincourt garrison back to the edge of the bridge. Smoke and fire had turned the suburbs into an antechamber of hell, but the town remained unbreached and the French army was still breaking on the Norman defence like surf upon granite. Bright spots of effort and exhaustion danced before William's eyes as he cut and hacked; there was no longer any finesse to his blows. It was about surviving the next moment and the next…holding firm and not giving ground. Every time William thought that he could not go on, he defied himself and found the will to raise and lower his arm one more time.

Horns blared out over the seething press of men and suddenly the tension eased. The French knight who had been pressing William hard disengaged and pulled back. "They're sounding the retreat!" panted a Tancarville knight. "God's blood, they're retreating! Tancarville! Tancarville!" He spurred his destrier. The realisation that the enemy was drawing off revitalised William's flagging limbs. His wounded horse was tottering under him but, undaunted, he flung from the saddle and joined the pursuit on foot.

The French fled through the burning suburbs of Drincourt, harried by the burghers and inhabitants, fighting rearguard battles with the knights and soldiers of the garrison. William finally ran out of breath and collapsed against a sheepfold on the outskirts of the town. His throat was on fire with thirst and the blade of his sword was nicked and pitted from the numerous contacts with shields and mail and flesh. Removing his helm, he dunked his head in the stone water trough provided for the sheep and, making a scoop of his hands, drank greedily. Once he had slaked his thirst and recovered his breath, he wiped the bloody patina from his sword on a clump of loose wool caught in the wattle fence, sheathed the blade, and trudged back to the bridge, suddenly so weary that his shoes felt as if they were made of lead.

His chestnut was lying on its side in an ungainly way that told him—even before he knelt at its head and saw its dull eyes—it was dead. He laid his hand to its warm neck and felt strands of the coarse mane scratch his bloodied knuckles. It had been a gift at his knighting from the Sire de Tancarville, together with his sword, hauberk, and cloak, and although he had not had the horse long, it had been a good one—strong, spirited, and biddable. He had expended more pride and affection on it than was wise and suddenly there was a tightening of grief in his throat.

"Won't be the last you'll lose," said de Lorys gruffly, leaning down from the saddle of his own dappled stallion which had several superficial injuries but was still standing, still whole. "Fact of war, lad." He extended a hand that, like William's, was bloody with the day's work. "Here, mount up behind."

William did so, although it was an effort to set his foot over Gadefer's in the stirrup and swing himself across the crupper. The cuts and bruises that had gone ignored in the heat of battle now began to strike him like chords on a malevolently plucked harp, especially across his right shoulder.

"Wounded?" Gadefer asked as William caught his breath. "That's a nasty gash in your mail."

"It's from a thatch gaff," William replied. "It's not that bad."

De Lorys grunted. "I won't take back the things I've said about you. You're still a slugabed and a glutton, but the way you fought today…well, that makes up for everything else. Perhaps my lord Tancarville has not wasted his time in training you after all."

That night the Sire de Tancarville held a feast to celebrate a victory that his knights had not so much snatched from the jaws of defeat, as reached down the throat of annihilation, dragged back out, and resuscitated. Badly mauled, the French army had drawn off to lick its wounds and, for the moment at least, Drincourt was safe, even if the neighbouring county of Eu was a stripped and pillaged wasteland.

William sat in a place of honour at the high table with the senior knights who fêted him for his prowess in his first engagement. Although exhausted, he rallied beneath their camaraderie and praise. The squabs in wine sauce and the fragrant, steaming frumenty and apples seethed in almond milk went some way to reviving his strength, as did the sweet, potent ice-wine with which they plied him. His wounds were mostly superficial. De Tancarville's chirurgeon had washed and stitched the deeper one to his shoulder and dressed it with a soft linen bandage. It was sharply sore; he was going to have the memento of a scar, but there was no lasting damage. His hauberk was already in the armoury having the links repaired and his gambeson had gone to the keep women to be patched and refurbished. Men kept telling him how fortunate he was. He supposed that it must be so, for some of the company had left their lives upon the battlefield and he had only lost his horse and the virginity of his inexperience. It didn't feel like luck though when someone inadvertently slapped him heartily on his injured shoulder in commendation.

William de Mandeville, the young Earl of Essex, raised his cup high in toast, his dark eyes sparkling. "Holà, Marshal, give to me a gift for the sake of our friendship!" he cried so that all those on the high table could hear.

William's head was buzzing with weariness and elation but he knew he wasn't drunk and he had no idea why de Mandeville was grinning so broadly around the trestle. Knowing what was expected of him, however, he played along. The bestowing of gifts among peers was always a part of such feasts.

"Willingly, my lord," he answered with a smile. "What would you have me give to you?"

"Oh, let me see." De Mandeville made a show of rubbing his jaw and looking round at the other lords, drawing them deeper into his sport. "A crupper would do, or a decorated breast-band. Or a fine bridle perchance?"

Wide-eyed, William spread his hands. "I do not have any such items," he said. "Everything that I own—even the clothes on my back—are mine by the great charity of my lord Tancarville." He inclined his head to the latter who acknowledged the gesture with a sweep of his goblet and a suppressed belch.

"But I saw you gain them today, before my very eyes," de Mandeville japed. "More than a dozen you must have had, yet you refuse me even one."

William continued to stare in bewilderment while a collective chuckle rumbled along the dais and grew in volume at William's expression.

"What I am saying," de Mandeville explained, between guffaws, "is that if you had bothered to claim ransoms from the knights you disabled and downed—even a few of them—you would be a rich man tonight instead of an impoverished one. Now do you understand?"

A fresh wave of belly laughter surged at William's expense, washing him in chagrin, but he was accustomed to being the butt of jests and knew that the worst thing he could do was sulk in a corner or lash out. The ribbing was well meant and behind it, there was warning and good advice. "You are right, my lord," he agreed with de Mandeville. The shrug he gave made him wince and brought a softer burst of laughter. "I didn't think. Next time I will be more heedful. I promise you will receive your harness yet."

"Hah!" retorted the Earl of Essex. "You've to get yourself a new horse first, and they don't come cheaply."

On retiring to his pallet that night, William lay awake for some time despite his weariness. His mind as well as his body felt bludgeoned. The images of the day returned to him in vivid flashes: some, like his desperate fight with the Flemish footsoldiers, repeating over and over again; others no more than a swift dazzle like sharp sun on water, there and gone. And through it all, running like a thread woven into a tapestry was de Mandeville's jest that wasn't a jest at all, but hard truth. Fight for your lord, fight for his honour, but never forget that you were fighting for yourself too.

Two

THE CLOAK THAT WILLIAM HAD RECEIVED AT HIS KNIGHTING was of Flemish weave, felted and thrice-dyed in woad to deepen the blue, and edged with sable. The garment was designed to cover the wearer from throat to ankle in a splendid semi-circular sweep of fabric. Brushing his palm over the expertly napped cloth, William's heart was heavy with reluctance, regret, and shame.

"I will give you fifteen shillings for it," the clothes-trader said, rubbing his forefinger under his nose and assessing William with crafty eyes.

"It's worth twice that!" William protested.

"Keep it then, messire." The trader shrugged. "I've a wife and five children to feed. I cannot afford to give charity."

William rubbed the back of his neck. He had no choice but to sell his cloak because he needed the money to buy another horse. The Sire de Tancarville had shown no inclination to replace the chestnut. A lord's largesse towards his retainers only went so far and it was up to the individual knight to account for the rest. William was not at fault for losing a valuable warhorse in battle; his blame lay in his omission to recoup that loss from the men he had defeated. His problem was compounded by the fact that the Kings of England and

France had made peace and Lord Guillaume no longer needed so many knights in his retinue—especially inexperienced ones lacking funds and equipment.

"Being as it's never been worn, and it's a fine garment, I'll give you eighteen," the merchant relented.

William's gaze was steel. "No less than twenty-five."

"Then find another buyer. Twenty-two, and that's my final offer. I'm robbing myself blind at that." The trader folded his arms, and William realised that this was the sticking point. For a moment he nearly walked away, but his need was too great and although the taste was bitter, he swallowed his pride and agreed to the terms.

Leaving the stall he hefted the pouch of silver. Twenty-two Angevin shillings was nowhere near enough to buy a warhorse. It might just pay for his passage home across the Narrow Sea with his light palfrey and pack beast, but arriving at his family's door in such a penurious state would be tantamount to holding out a begging bowl. It would have been difficult enough were his father still alive, but now that William's older brother John had inherited the Marshal lands, he would rather starve than receive his grudging charity.

Forced to a grim decision, he used the coin to buy a solid riding horse from a serjeant's widow whose husband had been killed in the fight for Drincourt. It was a decent beast, well schooled and, although a trifle long in the tooth, had plenty of riding left in it—but it wasn't a destrier.

Having stabled the beast, he visited the kitchens and availed himself of bread, cheese, and a pitcher of cider, hoping that the latter would wash away the sour taste of what he had just been forced to do. The cloak was the thin end of the wedge. Next it would be his silk surcoat and his gilded swordbelt. He could see himself trading down and down until he stood in the leather gear of a common footsoldier or became his brother's hearth knight, undertaking petty duties, living out his days in ennui, and growing paunchy and dull-witted.

The cook tossed a handful of chopped herbs into a simmering cauldron, stirred vigorously, and glanced round at William. "I thought you'd be in the hall," he remarked.

"Why?" William took a gulp of the strong, apple-scented cider.

"Ah, you haven't heard about the tourney then." The cook's eyes gleamed with the relish of the informed in the presence of the ignorant.

William's expression sharpened. "What tourney?"

"The one that's being held in two weeks' time on the field between Sainte Jamme and Valennes. The herald rode in an hour since with the news. Lord Guillaume's been invited to take part." He pointed his dripping spoon at William. "It'll be a fine opportunity to build on your prowess."

A spark of anticipation blazed up and died in William's breast. "I don't have a destrier," he said morosely. "I can't ride into a tourney on a common hack."

"Ah." The cook scratched his head. "That's a pity, but surely my lord Tancarville will give you a warhorse for the occasion at least. He's taking as many knights as he can muster. Why don't you ask him?"

The spark rekindled, making William feel queasy. If he did ask and was refused, he would have no option but to return to England, his tail between his legs. To ask at all was humiliating, but he had little alternative. Besides, his pride had already taken a fall; it couldn't sink much lower. Gulping down the cider and leaving the food, he hurried to the hall.

The news of the tournament had created a festive atmosphere. William stood on its periphery, his emotions finely balanced between hope and despair. Going to his sleeping space, he sat on his pallet and began checking over his equipment: his mended mail shirt, his neatly patched gambeson, his shield and spear and sword. The squires sped hither and yon on errands for the knights as if their legs were on fire.

Men came up to him, slapped his back, and spoke excitedly of the tourney. William laughed, nodded, and worked at concealing his anxiety. Buffing his helmet with a soft cloth, he wondered if he should have spent the coin from the sale of his cloak on a passage home instead of a horse. His mother would be overjoyed to see him, and perhaps his sisters, but he harboured doubts about his brother John. The latter had been furious that William and not he had been chosen to go for training to Normandy. Instead John had remained at Hamstead, his likely fate that of service to their two older brothers, Walter and Gilbert, from their father's first marriage. As it happened, Walter and Gilbert had both died, leaving John to inherit the Marshal lands, but that did not mean John would forget old jealousies and resentments.

Their younger brother Henry would not be at Hamstead as he was training for the priesthood and like William was expected to have fledged the nest for good. Ancel, the youngest, a wiry, freckled nine-year-old when William had last seen him, would be of squiring age now, although his training would probably be at John's hands, God help him.

William polished his helm until it glittered like a woman's hand mirror. He didn't want to return to his kin in an impoverished state, but he very much desired to see them, even John. And he wanted to pay his respects to his father whose funeral mass he had been too far away to attend.

"You look troubled, William."

He raised his head and found Guillaume de Tancarville standing over him, hands at his hips and amusement crinkling his eye corners. He was sensitive about his receding hairline and concealed it with a brightly coloured cap pulled low at the brow and banded with small gemstones.

William scrambled to his feet. "No, my lord, just deep in thought."

"And what does a lad of your age have to think deeply about, hmm?"

William glanced down at his reflection, distorted in the polished steel of his helm. "I was wondering if I should return to my family in England," he said.

"A man should always keep his family in his thoughts and prayers," de Tancarville replied, "but I expected your mind to be on the tournament. Everyone else's is." He smiled and gestured around the bustling hall.

"Yes, my lord, but they have the equipment to take part, and I do not." He made himself hold the Chamberlain's gaze.

"Ah." De Tancarville stroked his chin.

William said nothing. He wasn't going to tell his lord that he had been forced to sell his knighting cloak in order to buy a common rouncy.

De Tancarville allowed the moment to stretch beyond comfort and then released the tension with a sardonic smile. "You displayed great courage and prowess at the fight for Drincourt, even if you were a rash young fool into the bargain. You'll be a fine asset to my tourney team. I've arranged for a horse-coper to bring some destriers to the tourney field on the morrow. You weren't the only knight to lose his mount in the battle. Since you've been taught a lesson, I'll replace your stallion this time. The rest is up to you. If you capture other knights and take ransoms, you'll be able to redeem your finances. If you fail…" De Tancarville shrugged and let the end of the sentence hang. He didn't need to put it into words.

"Thank you, my lord!" William's eyes were suddenly as bright as his helm. "I'll prove myself worthy, I swear I will!"

De Tancarville grinned. "You're a good boy, William," he

said, slapping him on the shoulder. "Let us hope that one day you'll make an even finer man."

William managed not to wince despite the lingering tenderness from his wound. It was a small price to pay; everything was suddenly a small price to pay. He would show de Tancarville that he was a man, not a boy, and capable of standing on his own two feet.

William eyed the stallion that two grooms were holding at the de Tancarville horse lines. Its hide was the colour of new milk, its mane and tail a silver cascade. Spanish blood showed in the profile of its head, the neat ears, the strong curved neck, deep chest, and powerful rump. It should have been the first to be chosen, not the only one left. William had been busy erecting his pavilion and whether out of spite, oversight, or heavy-handed jesting, no one had told him that the horse-coper had arrived and that the new destriers were being apportioned to their owners.

"We left you a fine horse, Marshal!" shouted Adam Yqueboeuf, a belligerent, stoutly set young knight who disliked William and baited him at every opportunity. "Only the best for our lord's favourite relative!"

Pretending indifference to Yqueboeuf's taunt, William approached the stallion and saw from the sweat caking the line of the saddle cloth and breast-band that the others had probably had their turn at it. Like a new whore in a brothel, he thought. Used and overused on the first night until of no use at all to the last man in line. In dismay he took in the laid-back ears; the tension in the loins; the way the grooms were holding tight to the restraining ropes.

"He's wild, sir," one of them warned as William approached side-on to the horse's head so that it could see him. Its hide shivered and twitched like the surface of a pool in the rain. He reached out to pat the damp, gleaming neck and for a while quietly soothed the stallion, letting it drink his scent and grow accustomed to his presence.

"Wild?" he questioned the groom in a soft voice. "In what way?"

"He's a puller, sir—bad mouth. No one's been able to manage him."

"Ah." William glanced at his jeering audience and continued to stroke the destrier's quivering neck and shoulder. After a time, he set his hand to the saddle bow, placed his foot to the stirrup, and swung astride. Immediately the stallion lashed out and sidled crabwise. "Whoa, softly now, softly," William crooned and gingerly set his hands to the reins, exerting no pressure. Its ears flickered, and it continued to prink and dance. William applied firm pressure with his heels and the destrier sprang across the ward towards the watching knights. When William drew on the rein to pull him round the stallion fought the bit, plunging, sawing his head, and swishing his tail. The audience scattered amid a welter of curses. William had no time to laugh at them for he was too busy trying to stay astride a dervish. Dropping the reins he grabbed the mane instead, gripped with his thighs, and clung like a limpet. As soon as the pressure on its mouth relaxed, the horse quietened and after a moment, William was able to leap down from its back.

"Let's see you win a tourney prize with that!" sneered Yqueboeuf from the corner into which he had leaped. Stone dust and cobwebs streaked the shoulder of his tunic.

William's open smile was belied by the narrowness of his eyes and his swift breathing. "How much would you wager?"

"You're a pauper, Marshal," Yqueboeuf scoffed, dusting himself down. "What have you got that I could possibly want?"

"My sword," William replied. "I will wager my sword. What will you put up?"

Yqueboeuf laughed nastily. "If a sword is what you want

to lose, then I'll put my own up against it—even though it's worth more."

William raised his brow but managed not to comment that half a sword's value lay in the fist that wielded it. "Agreed," he said curtly, and turning back to the horse set about removing the bridle and examining the bit.

The morning of the tourney dawned fine and bright and the Chamberlain's company was up early.

"Where's Marshal?" de Tancarville demanded, for the young knight's tent was empty and his bed roll neatly folded up. The Chamberlain had half expected to find William still sleeping, as was his wont.

"Probably breaking his fast at one of the bakers' booths," said Gadefer de Lorys with a knowing roll of his eyes.

"No, my lord," said a squire. "He's been working half the night on a new bridle for his horse, and he's gone to try it out."

De Tancarville quirked a brow at the information. "Which horse did he take yesterday?" he asked de Lorys.

"The Spanish grey," said the knight in a neutral tone. "He was late to the choosing and it was the only one left. It has a ruined mouth."

De Tancarville frowned and hitched his belt in an irritated gesture. "That's unfortunate," he said. "I wanted to give the boy a chance." Glancing down the rows of striped tents and pavilions, he saw William striding cheerfully towards them and shook his head. Predictably the young knight's right hand was occupied by a large hunk of bread and his jaw was in motion. He was wearing his padded undertunic so was at least part dressed for the joust and his expression was one of almost child-like delight. Stopping short when he saw de Tancarville and de Lorys outside his pavilion, he hastily swallowed the mouthful he had been chewing and his gaze grew anxious.

"My lord, is there some trouble? Did you want me?"

"Only to wonder where you were, but I've been told you were tending your horse. I understand you had some difficulty with it yesterday?"

"Nothing that can't be solved," William replied enthusiastically. "I have let out the bridle by three finger-widths so that the bit's lower in his mouth and not resting on the part that hurts him."

"You'll not have the control," de Lorys warned, folding his arms.

"At least I'll have a rideable mount. I've been out practising, and the change seems to work."

De Lorys raised a sceptical brow and turned his mouth down at the corners, but held his peace.

"I did not mean for you to receive a bad horse," de Tancarville said gruffly.

"It isn't a bad horse, my lord," William answered, smiling. "Indeed, it is probably the best of all those given out." He hesitated as he was about to duck inside the tent. "I would ask you not to say anything to Adam Yqueboeuf about that. He has wagered his sword that I won't win a tourney prize on Blancart, and I want to surprise him."

De Tancarville gave a snort of reluctant amusement. "William, you surprise us all," he said. "I won't say anything; it'll be evident soon enough. Make haste now, or you'll not be ready to form up with the rest of the mesnie."

"Yes, my lord." William crammed the last chunk of bread into his mouth, moistened it with a swallow of wine from the pitcher standing on his campstool and, chewing vigorously, beckoned a squire to help him arm.

Compared to William's baptism in battle at the desperate, bloody fight for Drincourt, the tourney was a jaunt. Death and injury were hazards of the sport, but the intent was to capture and claim ransom, not to kill. His stallion was fiery and unsettled, but William could deal with that. It was a matter of remembering to go lightly on the reins and do more work than usual with the thighs and heels. When he lined up in close formation with the other Tancarville men, his heart swelled with pride. He had chosen a place in the line well away from Adam Yqueboeuf, but each knight was aware of the other's presence. William did not allow himself to think of failure. He would make gains today; his honour and his self-esteem depended on it, and he would rather die than yield his sword to a conceited turd like Yqueboeuf.

Their opponents were a medley of French, Flemish, and Scots knights, as eager for the sport as the Normans, English, and Angevins. De Tancarville stayed at the rear of his mesnie. For him the tourney was a place to meet friends and peers and display his largesse and importance through the number and calibre of knights fighting for him. The sport was for the young and reckless whilst he and the other sponsors looked on.

At the trumpet call from a herald, the two opposing lines spurred towards each other. William felt Blancart surge under him, the motion as smooth and powerful as a wave in mid-ocean. He selected his target: a knight wearing a hauberk that glittered silver and gold like the scales of a carp, his warhorse barded in ostentatious saffron and crimson silk. As the two stallions collided like rock and wave, crashing, recoiling, crashing again, William wrapped his fist around the knight's bridle and strove to drag him back to the Norman pavilions. "Yield!" William's voice emerged through his helm in a muffled bellow.

"Never!" The knight drew his sword and attempted to beat William off, but William held on, ducking, avoiding blows, striking back in return, and all the time drawing his intended prize towards his own lines. A second French knight who tried to help his companion was beaten off by Gadefer de Lorys. William saluted in acknowledgment, ducked another assault by his now desperate adversary, and spurred Blancart.

"Yield, my lord!" he commanded again, dragging his victim far behind the Norman line.

The knight shook his head, but at William's single-mindedness and bravado rather than conveying refusal. "Yielded," he snarled. "I am Philip de Valognes and you have my pledge." He gave a lofty wave. "You were fortunate to catch me before I had warmed to the sport." His tone suggested that William's vigorous assault and grim determination to hold on were not quite chivalrous. "Release me and have done…and I would know to whom I have yielded the price of my horse."

"My name is William Marshal, my lord," William replied, his chest heaving, his fist still tight around the knight's bridle. "I am kin to Guillaume de Tancarville, nephew to the Earl of Salisbury, and cousin to the Count of Perche."

"And by the looks of you, one of de Tancarville's young glory hunters without a penny to your patrimony," growled de Valognes.

"Not until now, my lord," William said pleasantly.

De Valognes acknowledged the quip with a snort of reluctant humour. "I will have my attendant bring the price of my horse and armour to the sharing of the booty," he said.

With a bow, William released the bridle, letting de Valognes spur back into the tourney like a carp reprieved by an angler and returned to the river. "Hah!" cried William and, urging Blancart into the fray, went to net more fish.

A muscle working in his cheek, Adam Yqueboeuf unbuckled his swordbelt and handed it across to William. "You win your wager," he muttered gracelessly. "I've never seen anyone with so much luck."

William had gained the price of four warhorses in the tourney and half the price of another which he had shared with Gadefer de Lorys. The amount might be no great sum to the likes of Philip de Valognes and Guillaume de Tancarville, but to William it was a small fortune and proof of his ability to provide for himself. Smiling at Yqueboeuf, he inclined his head. "Some would say that a man makes his own luck, but what do they know?" He studied the swordbelt and the attached scabbard, but did not draw the weapon. "A man's blade is made to suit his own hand. I gift it back to you with my goodwill." Bestowing a courtly bow, he returned Yqueboeuf's sword, his smile becoming a grin.

If Yqueboeuf had been struggling to swallow his mortification before, now it was choking him. Uttering a few strangled words of insincere gratitude, he closed his fist around his scabbard and, turning on his heel, strode away.

"You make enemies as well as friends in life, remember that, lad," said de Tancarville, drawing William aside for a quiet word before the carousing started. "You've a rare talent there and lesser men will resent it."

"Yes, my lord," William said. He looked troubled. "Yqueboeuf's sword would have been of no use to me. I thought about asking him for its value in coin, but it seemed more courtly to return it to him."

De Tancarville pursed his lips. "I cannot fault your reasoning, but high courtesy will not protect you from malice."

"I know that, my lord." William's eyelids tensed. "I have endured the years of being called 'Guzzleguts' and 'Slugabed.' Perhaps some of it is deserved, but as much stems from being your impoverished kin as from the truth. At need I can go without food and sleep."

"I'm sure you can." The Chamberlain cleared his throat with unnecessary vigour. "What will you do now?"

The question shook William, for he understood what it presaged. Whatever his skill, de Tancarville was not prepared to continue to furnish his helm. The tourney had been a great success, but it was over and now he had a surplus of young knights. William was being as good as told he was too trouble-some to keep.

"I have been thinking about visiting my family," he said, swallowing his disappointment.

"You have been many years away; they will be glad to see you again." De Tancarville showed his discomfort by rubbing his forefinger over the jewelled band on his cap.

"Perhaps they won't recognise me," William said, "nor I them." He looked thoughtful. "Tourneying is not permitted in England, and Gadefer told me that there is another contest three days' ride away. I thought I might try my fortune there first—with your permission."

The last three words gave de Tancarville a way to make a graceful and formal ending to the obligation that had tied him to William and William to him for the past five years. "You have it," he said, "and my blessing." He clasped William's shoulders and kissed him soundly on either cheek, then embraced him hard. "I have nurtured and equipped you. Now go out and prove your knighthood to the world. I expect to hear great deeds of you in the future."

William returned the embrace, heat prickling his eyes. Guillaume de Tancarville had never been especially paternal towards him, but he had given him the tools with which to make the best of his life. "I will do my best, my lord," he said, adding after a hesitation, "There is one last boon I would ask of you."

"Name it and it is yours, and let there be no talk of 'last boons' between us," said de Tancarville, although his mouth quirked as he spoke the words. *Within reason*, said the look in his eyes.

"I ask that you send a messenger to the Earl of Essex with this." William produced a fine jewelled breast-band and crupper off one of the horses he had claimed in the tourney. "Bid him say that William Marshal pays his debts."

De Tancarville took the gilded pieces of harness and suddenly he was laughing. "It's a good thing you were not taken for ransom today," he chuckled, "for I doubt you have a price."

William grinned. "Does that make me worthless, or worth too much?" he asked.

Three

Hamstead Marshal, Berkshire, Autumn 1167

REPLETE WITH SPICED CHICKEN AND SAFFRON STEW SERVED with fresh wheaten bread and washed down with a satisfying quantity of mead, William leaned back from the trestle and gazed at his surroundings. Hamstead was small and humble when compared to Drincourt, Tancarville, and the other great Norman donjons where he had trained to knighthood. There were no chimneys and the fire blazed in an old-fashioned stone-ringed hearth in the centre of the room, but it didn't matter. Hamstead, on its hill above the Kennet, was the core of the family patrimony, and it was home.

"So," said John, his elder brother, his smile not quite reaching his eyes, "you're a great tourney champion now." The beard he had cultivated since inheriting their father's title two years ago edged his jaw in a closely barbered line. Their father had always gone clean-shaven, saying that a man should not be ashamed to bare his face to the world, but John thought that a beard lent his youth gravitas and dignity.

William shrugged. "Hardly that." His own smile was diffident. "But I've had some good fortune at the few I've attended."

"More than that to judge from the horses you have brought with you." John's voice was envious. Against William's courtly dazzle, he was conscious of looking like a poor relation rather than the head of the Marshal household.

"They're recent gains. At the end of the summer I had naught but a common rouncy to my name." Amiably, William regaled his fellow diners with the tale of the battle for Drincourt and his subsequent impoverishment. His tone was self-deprecatory and he was careful not to boast but even so, John looked away and fiddled with his eating knife while fourteen-year-old Ancel hung on William's every word, his eyes as wide as goblet rims.

"A thatch gaff?" his mother said faintly.

William unpinned the neck of his tunic and dragged his shirt aside to show her the narrow pink scar. "I was lucky. My hauberk saved me. It could have been much worse."

Her horrified expression disagreed with his statement. His sisters, Sybil and Margaret, craned to look.

"Didn't it hurt?" asked Alais, a damsel of his mother's chamber. William had known her since her birth, which had caused something of a scandal at Hamstead. She was the result of an affair between one of Sybilla's women and a married knight in the service of the Earl of Salisbury. Her father had died in battle before her birth, and when Alais was nine years old, her mother had succumbed to a fever. Sybilla Marshal had taken Alais beneath her wing, raised her with her own daughters, and given her a permanent place in the chamber as a companion and attendant. When William had left for Tancarville she had been a skinny little waif, still in wan mourning for her mother, but she had certainly blossomed in the interim.

"Not when it happened," he said, "but after the battle when I had time to notice it burned like a hot coal. It's still sore when my shield strap rubs on it."

Her hazel eyes widened with admiration. "I think you were very brave."

He chuckled. "Some of the others thought I was foolish."

"I don't." Alais rested her chin on her hand and gave him a melting stare.

Amused, William thanked her and from the corner of his eye caught the brooding look that John was directing at the girl. He suspected that his older brother's emotions were more involved than mere amusement, and that if their mother noticed, there would be trouble.

"I don't either," Ancel said with more than a hint of hero-worship in his cracking adolescent voice.

"Why have you come home?" John asked abruptly.

William's survival in the Tancarville household had depended on his ability to read expressions and voices. "Aren't you pleased to see me?"

"Of course I am." John flushed. "You're my brother."

Which said everything, William thought. "And that makes you obligated."

John shifted uncomfortably in the fine, carved lord's chair, its arms polished from the wear of their father's grip. "I was wondering if you were still with Guillaume de Tancarville, that is all." He spoke as if it didn't matter, but they both knew that it did.

William looked down at his cup. "He has chosen not to retain me in his household. It was a mutual leave-taking, but done while it could still be counted that."

His mother made an indignant sound. "Surely he could see the advantage of keeping you as one of his mesnie?"

"Yes, but he could also see the disruption it might cause. Some of the knights believed that he showed me too much favour because of our kinship."

"Then he should have dismissed them."

William shook his head. "Not when I was his youngest and least experienced knight. He took a commander's decision and, likely, in his shoes I would have done the same. Don't worry," he said to John, whose taut expression bristled with hostility, "I'm not going to ask you to retain me as a hearth knight when you already have Ancel in training." He sent a wink towards his youngest brother and managed to keep his tone light.

"I wouldn't have you," John replied. "Keeping those horses in oats and stabling would beggar me in a season, and there are no tourneys in England where you could play to earn your silver. Besides," he added defensively, "you would find life as my knight dull after Normandy. If you can stomach the advice of your older brother, you'll go to Uncle Patrick at Salisbury. He's hiring men to take to Poitou."

The point was made with little finesse—there was no place for William at John's hearth—although William had known as much ever since their father's death. It would not have harmed John to make some provision for him out of their father's revenues, but he had chosen not to. "That was indeed what I was intending to do," he said evenly, concealing his hurt.

"And what if his knights think that he is showing you favour because of your kinship?" his mother wanted to know.

He shrugged. "At least I will come to my uncle's household with horses and armour to my name and some experience of war. He won't have to provide my equipment, nor have I ever served his knights as a squire and been taken for granted by them. It's a clean slate."

It was very late when William finally retired, for there had been many years of catching up to do on both sides. His mother and sisters retired to the women's chamber, their way lit by Alais bearing a lantern. William marked how John's eyes lingered on the latter's slender form.

"Our mother will kill you if she sees you," he said. His tongue fumbled the words for the mead had been strong and he had been drinking it slowly but steadily for most of the night. John was in a similar case and the candle flame inside the lantern he was holding wavered and guttered with the unsteadiness of his footsteps.

"Kill me if she sees me what?" John slurred.

"Looking at Alais the way a fox looks at a goose."

John gave a contemptuous snort. "You're imagining things. Must be your debauched life at Tancarville." He staggered along the passage and into the lord's bedchamber. A string-framed bed and feather mattress had been set up for William in the corner and his gear was deposited around it: sword, shield, hauberk, helm.

"Chance would be a fine thing," William retorted. "The lady de Tancarville guarded the women of her chamber like a dragon coiled on a hoard of gold and the household whores weren't interested in a lowly squire."

"The Sire de Tancarville kept whores?" Ancel asked, eyes agog.

"A few." William licked his finger and stooped to rub at a mark on the surface of his shield which still bore the Tancarville colours. "They were hand-picked by my lord."

"Hand-picked?" John guffawed as he set the lantern down precariously on a chest. "Are you sure he didn't use anything else?"

William laughed. "I meant that they were either barren or knew how to avoid getting with child. That way the place wasn't overrun with bastard brats." He looked hard at John. "She's a maid of Mother's chamber. If you touch her there'll be hell to pay, especially when you consider the circumstances of her birth."

"I don't need a lecture from you," John flashed, "riding in here with your fine horses after years away and telling me how to conduct my life. You're no saint of chivalry, so don't pretend you are." He threw himself down on his bed. "There's no harm in looking and you're a liar if you say you didn't look too. I saw you."

William abandoned the argument with a wave of his hand and turned to warn Ancel against leaving sweat prints on the sword the lad had just drawn from its scabbard.

"I've begun my training," Ancel said indignantly. "I know how to care for a blade."

"Never a good idea to draw one in your cups though." William gestured to him to sheath the weapon.

"Why? Do you expect brotherly love to degenerate into a drunken brawl?" John's tone was sardonic.

"I do not know what I expect of brotherly love, or what brotherly love expects of me," William said with a bleak smile. He ruffled Ancel's light brown hair. "On the morrow you can take my sword on to the practice ground and try it out full sober in the daylight. For the nonce, I'm for my bed."

Although he was tired when he lay down, his brothers' snores were raising the rafters before William finally relinquished his grasp on consciousness, his last waking thought being that "brotherly love" was a sword that needed to be oiled, sharpened, and treated with the utmost respect and caution if it was to be of any use at all. And it had two edges.

Four

SOUTHAMPTON, DECEMBER 1167

WILLIAM STOOD ON THE DOCKSIDE IN THE GATHERING winter dusk and watched the sailors loading the supplies on to the vessels riding at anchor. He was not fond of sea crossings and silently prayed that the good weather would hold for the voyage to Normandy. The thought that all that lay between him and untold fathoms of icy green sea were a few flimsy spars of wood held together by caulking and nails was one that brought cold sweat to his armpits.

He had bidden farewell to his family several days ago at Bradenstoke Priory where a mass had been said for his father and William had been wished Godspeed. There had been a brief reunion with his brother Henry, now in the service of the Archbishop of York. The twelve-year-old to whom William had bidden farewell five years ago was now an earnest young priest with a precisely clipped tonsure, a small mouth, pursed as if holding secrets, and a pedantic air. He made it clear that living by the sword was an acceptable occupation, but nowhere near as worthy as making one's mark through the Church. He made much of his ability to read and write in Latin. As he pompously held forth, William and John had exchanged glances, the tension between them thawed by mutual opinion. Having a priest in the family was useful—but, in Henry's case, preferably at a far distance. "God help anyone who has to listen to his sermons," John had muttered from the side of his mouth and William had responded with an irreverent chuckle. Still, since Henry was family and the fraternal ties existed for the benefit of all, they let him boast. Who knew when they might need his learning?

William's mother had given him a cross set with beryls of cat's-eye green to wear around his neck, saying that it would protect him from injury, and the women had found time to stitch him two new shirts for his baggage. Alais had presented him with a pair of mittens and a kiss on the cheek—much to John's ire. William smiled, remembering, and turned at a shout to face his uncle who was striding along the dockside, accompanied by his household knights and retainers.

Patrick FitzWalter, Earl of Salisbury, had florid good looks running to flesh at the jowls. His paunch strained against his Flemish woollen tunic, but he moved easily and he was solid rather than flabby. For seven years, he had been the King's commander in Aquitaine and was a trusted, competent soldier. He had the approval of both King Henry and Queen Eleanor, which, William had discovered, was something of a novelty in the Angevin household these days.

"I wondered where you had gone," his uncle said.

"I wanted to watch the loading, my lord." William smiled ruefully. "If I had stayed any longer in that alehouse I'd have been tempted to drink myself into a stupor."

Earl Patrick grinned, exposing even white teeth marred by a missing incisor. "I take it that you dislike crossing the water."

"Yes, my lord," William said, adding hastily, "but I do at need."

"So do we all, young man. There's not many of us born sailors. Your horses boarded all right?"

William glanced towards one of the transports riding at anchor. "Yes, my lord. One of the destriers baulked at the gangplank, but a groom tempted him aboard with an apple."

Earl Patrick cupped his hands and blew on them. The vapour of his breath was wine-scented, revealing that he too had fortified himself for the night crossing to come. "Sounds like its owner," he said.

William laughed. He had developed an immediate rapport with his uncle who was at home both in the battle-camp and the court. Patrick of Salisbury knew how to roister and how to be refined. Despite rivalry in feats of arms being encouraged among his knights on the practice field, and the existence of a hierarchy, the atmosphere in his household was comfortable and the jesting largely without malice. Not that Patrick FitzWalter was an easy lord. Like Guillaume de Tancarville, he expected to be served with alacrity. He kept long hours and he required his men to do the same. Earl Patrick had been highly entertained to hear that William's nicknames in de Tancarville's mesnie had been "Guzzleguts" and "Slugabed."

"You'll have no time for either in mine," he had promised. "The more so because you're my nephew. Favouritism is out…unless you earn it in front of all."

Knowing where he stood, William had settled with gratitude and pride to the task of being his uncle's knight and bearing the Salisbury colours on his shield.

Although he had spoken of not favouring William above the other knights of his mesnie, Patrick of Salisbury had taken a keen interest in his nephew. For one so young he had started trailing glory early—if the stories were to be believed. William himself had been dismissive of the incidents, but his mother, who was Salisbury's sister, had written a fiercely proud letter to recommend her son, filled with details of his achievements thus far. Salisbury thought that the truth lay somewhere in between. The young man must have talent. No knight of his tender years and means would have been able to afford the warhorse and palfrey that he was shipping to Normandy unless he had won them in battle or tourney. Even William's squire had a Lombardy stallion. Being a good fighter was an excellent start, but Salisbury wanted to mentor William further and see if he had the intelligence to partner his brawn.

"There's a hard task ahead," Salisbury said to him as they sailed out of the harbour on a high tide and a strengthening wind. The silver light of a full moon capped the jet glitter of the waves and the pale linen sail resembled a slice of the moon itself, raked down and lashed to the mast.

"Yes, my lord."

Watching his nephew clench and unclench his fists inside a pair of sheepskin mittens, Salisbury was struck anew by how much the young man resembled his father in looks: the eyes and nose, the stubborn set of the jaw. Pray God that if he had inherited John Marshal's nature too, the traits were tempered by FitzWalter caution and common sense, otherwise he was a lost cause from the start. "How much do you know about Poitou and Aquitaine?" he asked.

The young man shook his head. "Not a great deal, my lord. I have been no further than the Chamberlain's castles and a few tourney grounds on the French border. I know that the lands belong to the Queen and they are the source of much discord."

Salisbury laughed sourly. "You have a way with understatement, William." He folded his arms beneath his thick, fur-lined cloak. "I sometimes think that not even the Devil would want to dwell in Poitou. Queen Eleanor's vassals see every petty complaint as reason to rebel, especially the lords of La Marche and Lusignan. They have to be brought to heel, which is what

I am being sent to do. The Queen is to accompany me, as is the lord Richard, since he is her heir."

William looked interested.

"Ten years old," said Salisbury "and a handful, but he shows promise. Already he excels at arms practice and he's a good scholar too. He's going to be a capable ruler for Aquitaine and Poitou, but first he has to grow into the role and we have to buy him that time." He flashed William a vulpine smile. "Your sword won't sleep in your scabbard once we arrive there." He watched William touch his hilt for reassurance and chuckled. "Don't worry, you'll have the pleasures of the Norman court and the Christmas feast at Argentan to break you in before we reach Poitou. After that, a pitched battle will seem easy by comparison, I promise you." He was silent for a moment then asked, "Have you ever met the Queen?"

"No, my lord, although I have heard tell of her beauty."

"And the tales are not wrong. I would tell you to guard your heart, but it would be a useless warning. She will take it anyway and all other women will lack savour after that."

His nephew's gaze flickered to him and then away to study the moon-white sail.

Salisbury smiled. "What is it?"

"I was going to ask if you were smitten, my lord, but then I thought you might consider me impertinent."

Salisbury threw back his head and laughed. "I do, and ignorant too, but I will tell you anyway. Any man who is not smitten would have to be made of stone, and even then, the resisting would crack him down the middle."

William hesitated then said, "King Henry must be made of stone then, for the rumour is that he has forsaken the Queen for a mistress."

"Where did you hear that?"

"My mother told me when I first came home. She said that

it was a scandal that the King should be so openly consorting with the daughter of Sir Walter de Clifford and fêting her with all manner of gifts."

Salisbury sighed. "I fear it is more than rumour. The King has taken the Clifford girl to his bed and to his bosom. He's always had occasional whores but they have never lasted longer than a week, but this is different. He's as smitten as a mooncalf and de Clifford's daughter is no common harlot. He's given her a household of her own and pays her serious court while shunning his wife, and for that, Eleanor will never forgive him. It's half the reason she's returning to Poitou after Christmas." He studied the sky. "It's calm out here tonight, nephew, but there are stormy waters ahead."

William swiftly settled into life at King Henry's court. In many ways it was similar to the time he had spent in the Tancarville mesnie with the same constant bustle of officials and messengers, clerks, priests, soldiers, servants, and hordes of supplicants, their pouches draining of silver as they sought to bribe their way through ushers and stewards to the King's ear. William was still a small grain in a great mill. His sleeping quarters remained little more than a straw pallet either on the floor of the great hall, outside Salisbury's chamber, or sometimes in a tent pitched on spare ground in the bailey of whatever castle the court was currently occupying.

Unlike de Tancarville's orderly household, where William had trained, the royal court functioned in an atmosphere of organised chaos and the food was atrocious. Henry's impatient palate was not a gourmet's. As far as he was concerned, bread was bread and if a trifle burned or somewhat gritty, it didn't matter. Complaints were met with raised eyebrows and short shrift. In Henry's lexicon, fit for a king was fit for everyone else. The same went for his household wine, which had a reputation throughout his lands. "Like drinking mud," Salisbury warned William. The Earl had prudently brought his own supply and a servant who knew how to care for it.

Henry was also impatient with ceremony and careless of his clothes. They were always rumpled and there was usually a thread dangling where some of the seed pearl embroidery had torn loose, or been snagged by a dog's paw. Henry forgot to pass messages on to his ushers and stewards, or he would change his mind after having done so with the result that the court would be ready to move on a morning when the King was still lazing abed, or caught napping while the King sprang to the saddle and hastened off at dawn.

"They say the Angevins come from the Devil!" the Bishop of Winchester spluttered one rainy morning when this had happened for the third time in a row and he was trying to mount his circling, braying mule. "I can believe it, because following the King around is like being at the court of hell, and God in his mercy alone knows if we'll all have beds tonight!"

The great lords and bishops would send outriders ahead to secure sleeping space and stabling and fodder and there were often undignified squabbles over the most unsavoury of hovels. William learned to take it all in his stride. His genial, easy-going nature meant that he counted having to bed down with his horse less of an earth-shattering disaster than it was to others more tender of their dignity.

The court came to Argentan for the Christmas feast and a great gathering of vassals from all parts of the Angevin lands. The Queen was due to arrive any day with the children, and the servants hastily prepared quarters to house them. Rooms were swept and fires laid. New rushes were strewn on the floors and sweetened with herbs and dried flowers. The damp December cold was further kept at bay by braziers placed in the draughty areas near window splays and doors. Seldom noticing the heat or cold unless they were extremes, Henry cared little for such touches, but with small children expected, additional warmth was a necessity.

On the day the Queen arrived, William was schooling Blancart in the tiltyard. Bleached winter sunshine lit the day, but imparted no warmth. William's breath smoked in the air and mingled with the stallion's as he leaned over to pat its muscular arched neck. Mindful of the horse's tender mouth, he had further adjusted the bit and rode with the lightest of curbs.

Collecting a lance from the stack at the end of the tiltyard, William turned the destrier to face the field and the quintain. A squire was standing beside the upright pole and cross bar and at William's signal he hooked a small circle of woven reeds on to the end of the latter. William nudged Blancart into a short, bouncing canter and the stallion's ears twitched and then pricked as he settled to his task. William encouraged Blancart with thighs and heels and the stallion increased speed, galloping in a straight, smooth line. William hooked the ring neatly on to the end of his lance and rode round to the start again, by which time the squire had placed a second, smaller ring on the end of the post.

William continued tilting at the ring, using the smallest diameter garlands and rowing them down the shaft of his lance with each successful pass. He was aware in his peripheral vision that he had an audience, but the sight of knights at their training was always guaranteed to draw spectators and his concentration was such that he paid little heed. However, as he drew rein and slipped the rings down his spear into the squire's hands, he happened to glance across and noticed that the numbers were unusually large.

A woman wearing a wine-coloured cloak detached herself from the crowd and began picking her way delicately across the churned ground towards him. An embroidered blue gown flashed through the opening of the cloak as she walked and her veil was edged with tiny gold beads. William had not seen her about the castle before but knew that several great lords had brought their wives to court for the Christmas feast. She had three boys in tow; the tallest one brown-haired and slender, striding confidently beside her. On her other side, also striding out, was a strikingly attractive lad with hair of auburn-blond and a fierce smile blazing across his face. The smallest of the three hurried along behind, dark-browed and a determined jut to his jaw. Looking beyond the woman, William took in the conroi of armed knights and a throng of richly clad ladies. A nurse was holding an infant that was squalling its head off at being restrained in her arms. Two little girls, one with dark hair, the other reddish-gold, clung to her skirts. There was an older, plump girl too, in a blue dress. A thick braid of bright brown hair tumbled over her right shoulder.

The woman reached William and looked up. Beneath arched dark brows, her eyes were the colour of woodland honey, neither brown nor gold. Her nose was thin, her cheekbones sharp, her mouth wide. Not a beautiful face in the aesthetic sense, but so filled with charisma that William's senses reeled. He stared, and she gave him a smile that contained the brimming mischief of a girl and the allure of an experienced woman.

"Madam," he croaked and, dismounting from Blancart, knelt at her feet and bowed his head. Even if his senses had been bludgeoned, his wits had not. From the moment his eyes had fallen upon her guards, he had known who she was.

"I pray you rise," she said with a soft laugh. "I am accustomed to men falling at my feet, but I prefer to bring them to their knees by means other than my rank."

Her voice, deep and husky, sent a ripple down William's spine that reached all the way to his loins. She was old enough to be his mother, but there the resemblance ended. "Madam," he said again, all his eloquence deserting him. As he stood, he caught her scent—a combination of winter spices and summer rose garden.

"My sons were admiring your prowess at the quintain," she murmured, "and so was I."

William reddened with pleasure and embarrassment. "Thank you, madam. I have not had the horse long and I work with him as much as I can."

"You would not think it to look at the pair of you. You are…?"

"William Marshal, madam, nephew to my lord the Earl of Salisbury."

Her smile grew less wide, although it remained. "Ah yes," she said in response to the latter statement, but did not elaborate on whether the news was to William's advantage or detriment.

"Can I ride him?" The bright-haired boy pointed to Blancart, his hand already reaching for the reins in a way that told William the child was confident and accustomed to getting his own way.

In spite of his awe for the boy's mother, William shook his head and held him off. "He would run away with you…sir," he replied. "He's a difficult horse to handle."

"I've ridden warhorses before." The boy thrust out his lower lip. "My mother's knights always let me ride theirs."

"But you know your lady mother's knights and their horses," William replied. "You do not know me or mine."

The older boy smirked at his brother, plainly delighted at William's rebuff. "I've ridden destriers too," he bragged, puffing out his chest.

"So have I," piped up the youngest one, not to be outdone. "Lots of times."

Their mother fought a smile. Her hand ruffled the red-haired child's head in a tender gesture. "Enough," she said. "Messire Marshal is right to deny you. A warhorse is no toy and skill like

Messire Marshal's does not come of the moment but is won by long hours of training."

William looked at the upturned faces and remembered himself and his brothers as children watching their father and his knights at practice. He recalled the desire, the longing, the bright, starry feeling in the gut—and the frustration, and saw it mirrored in these three boys who could have been himself and John and Henry. "Perhaps another time," he said. "I have a second stallion who is quieter than this fellow."

"I don't want to ride a quieter stallion," the bright-haired boy declared, his fair skin flushing. "I want the best."

"Richard." Eleanor's voice sounded a warning. "Where are your manners? You are no longer a small child, so do not act like one."

"But I am a prince," the boy replied, casting his mother an oblique look through long lashes, plainly testing the boundaries.

"Even more reason to mind your manners."

"My father doesn't."

"Your father is not always the finest example of a prince," she retorted waspishly.

"I only said I wanted the best."

Eleanor's lips twitched and William saw the glow of affection in her eyes. He suspected that this particular son could wrap her around his little finger.

"Blancart wasn't the best to begin with," William said. "In fact no one wanted him because he pulled too hard on the bridle. Sometimes you have to work long and hard to fashion the raw material into the best."

The Queen tilted her head and gave William a feline stare. "And is that what you are, Messire Marshal?" she asked huskily. "The best?"

William cleared his throat. "I fear I am still very rough around the edges, madam."

"And I fear that you are too modest. Deeds may speak more compellingly than words, but I believe that words have their place too. A man who has both is gifted indeed." Inclining her head, she turned away to her waiting attendants and retainers. The boys followed her, both of the older ones looking over their shoulders, the red-haired one in particular with calculation in his blue-grey eyes. He hadn't given up yet.

William placed his hand on Blancart's withers and leaped to the saddle. There was a starry feeling in his gut just now, but it was more concerned with the Queen of England than his jousting. Why on earth, he wondered, would Henry want to flirt with mistresses when he was wed to a woman like that?

That night, Eleanor appeared formally in the hall with her husband. She and Henry sat side by side and performed their public duty as two halves of one whole. For once Henry's dishabille had been tamed into order. His hair had seen the teeth of a comb and his new tunic of mulberry-coloured wool was immaculate—not a dog hair or torn cuff in sight. Eleanor wore mulberry too, the fabric looking as if it had been cut from the same bolt of cloth, and her own hair was bound in a net of jewelled gold. To watch them formally greeting the earls, barons, and bishops gathered for the occasion, no one would have guessed at the rift in their relationship.

In soft candle and torchlight, Eleanor looked much younger than her forty-five years. The colour of her gown enhanced her skin tones and brightened the tawny glint in her eyes. If William had been smitten by her that afternoon, now the feeling inside him grew until he was drunk on it. She drenched his senses and made rational thought difficult. Now he understood why his uncle Patrick had said that any man not smitten by the Queen of England would have to be made of stone—although she could certainly turn specific parts of a man's anatomy to rock.

William had a place at one of the side trestles for the duration of the feast. His uncle Patrick sat at the high table in a
place of honour close to King Henry's right hand. A cloth of
embroidered linen adorned the marble top and the places were
set with platters and cups of silver gilt, green glass, and gold-
embellished horn. The rock-crystal flagons were honoured for
once by wine that was smooth and rich, for Eleanor had had
fifty casks delivered from Poitou rather than trust to Henry's
notorious provision.

Where William sat, the tableware was more prosaic. The
board was of wood, not marble, and the cloth bereft of embroidery. Instead of silver-gilt platters, the food was set upon thick
trenchers of bread, but since this was the usual mode—indeed
the cloth was a refinement—William felt no lack. The finery
on the dais was the Queen's doing too. Normally the King
would drink out of the nearest vessel, which often as not was
a wooden cup. Eleanor, however, appreciated and enjoyed a
more sophisticated style. William watched her sip from a silver
goblet, its base encrusted with amethysts. Salisbury spoke to her
and she turned her head as gracefully as a swan to answer him.

William had learned the language and conventions of courtly
love in the bower of de Tancarville's wife, but until now it had
all been lip service. The notion of being desperately in love
with an unattainable lady far above his rank, of suffering unrequited pangs and of performing heroic deeds in order to receive
a single indifferent glance from her eyes, had been a diverting
whimsy; a game to play in the bower on a wet afternoon to
please the women with no real heartache involved. Now,
suddenly, he understood both the pleasure and the pain.

The formal feast ended, but the evening was not over.
Eleanor retired to her chamber, summoning a select party
to join her, including Patrick of Salisbury. Henry elected to
stay in the hall, and although he and the Queen were civil to

each other on parting, the air between them was glacial with unspoken words. As Salisbury followed in the Queen's train, he crooked his finger at William. "Join me," he commanded. "I need attendants."

William's eyes widened. "Join you, my lord?" Even as he questioned the words, he was rising to his feet, dusting crumbs from his tunic, and tugging the folds straight beneath his belt.

Salisbury's eyelids crinkled with humour. "If you are to serve me in Poitou you must become acquainted with the Queen's household." He laid his hand on William's shoulder. "Besides, you have a fine singing voice." With a nod and a smile he moved on, leaving a bemused William to step free of the dining trestle and bow out of the King's presence.

Although he was accustomed to the trappings of wealth, William was astounded by the transformation Eleanor's arrival had wrought on apartments that this morning had been bare. Detailed embroideries in rich hues of red and gold blazed upon the walls while chained lamps hung from the roof beams and were augmented by candelabra alight with clear-burning beeswax candles. Oak benches strewn with plump cushions lined the sides of the room, as did several brightly painted coffers. Thick woollen curtains decorated with exquisite stitchwork and tassels of gold silk enclosed the Queen's great bed. Heavy scents of incense and musk drugged the air. At a sideboard scaled with silverware, a squire poured wine into silver goblets. Eleanor herself sat on a curved chair near a brazier, attended by her women and surrounded by a cluster of devoted men, including Salisbury.

William took a cup of wine from the squire, but was hesitant to join the others for he was afraid that they would see how Eleanor quickened him, and laugh at his gaucheness. Instead, he wandered into the antechamber which was populated by a few stray courtiers and ladies of the chamber. Two minstrels leaned over their instruments—harp and lute—playing practice rills of notes. A nursemaid was jiggling a crotchety infant, trying without success to shush him. The child had a quiff of dark hair and bright hazel eyes, their amber hue intensified by the redness of his face as he bawled.

"He's always crying."

William glanced down at one of the boys he had met that afternoon and whom he now knew to be Prince Henry, the King's eldest son. The lad was almost thirteen years old and well proportioned. His hair was the same deep brown as William's own and his eyes the blue-grey of woodsmoke.

"He's my brother." The curl of the youth's lip informed William that the Prince was not enthralled by the relationship. "His name's John."

"I too have a brother called John," William said, "and one called Henry."

The boy studied him with a frown while he decided if William was teasing him or speaking the truth. "Do you have one called Richard?" If there had been a grimace for John, there was a telling hostility in the way the boy said "Richard" and flicked his glance towards the main room where his flame-haired brother was sitting at their mother's feet.

"No, just Ancel. I had two other brothers who died, but they were Walter and Gilbert."

"One of my brothers died," the boy said. "His name was William. He would have been my father's heir if he had lived. Are you your father's heir?"

William shook his head. "I have no lands to call my own, which is why I am in service to my uncle of Salisbury."

"John has no lands either." Prince Henry jutted his chin at the red-faced baby whose roars were beginning to make folk in the antechamber wince. He raised his voice. "I'm to have

England and Normandy, Richard's to have Aquitaine, and my father says Geoffrey's going to get Brittany."

The instinct was to move away from the source of the racket, but William gestured to the nurse, who was beginning to look as flustered as her wriggling charge, and plucked young John out of her arms. The noise ceased in mid-bawl, the wriggles stopped, and in a silence almost as loud as the din that had preceded it, the infant stared at William with eyes stretched in shock. William laughed, tossed the baby in the air, caught him, and tossed him again. A squeal erupted, this time of utter delight.

"He likes you," Henry said, surprised. "John doesn't usually like anyone."

"Babies are just babies," William replied. "My father used to do this to us…except in a wilder fashion, and my mother would be frantic at him." He chuckled at the memory, although he must have been older than this, and it was probably his youngest brother Ancel he could recall being tossed and caught like a ball.

"If you are not careful, he will repay you by being sick all over your fine tunic," said Queen Eleanor, her voice husky with amusement.

It was a good thing that William was not in the throw part of the game, or he might have missed his catch and dropped the youngest royal on his head. He spun round, John in his arms. "It doesn't matter, madam," he said, and thought how foolish the words sounded.

Her laughter caused his stomach to wallow. "I am sure that it does," she replied, "unless you are like the King and do not care about appearance."

"A tunic can be cleaned, madam," William responded, seeking a diplomatic path through the dilemma she had created—whether to admit to being vain or slovenly, of which he was neither. "I was more concerned with comforting the Princeling."

"He is a young man of many talents, madam," chuckled Salisbury, standing by her shoulder. "Even I did not know he had this particular one, but I'm sure it will come in most useful."

Eleanor pursed her lips. "Indeed," she said softly, looking William up and down. "I am sure it will."

Later in the evening there was singing and dancing and as the candles burned down, they were replaced by new ones. The Queen had no intention of retiring early and seemed determined to prove that although she was a decade older than her husband, her energy was more than a match for his. She flirted with the men both young and old, but was careful never to step outside the bounds of propriety, sharing her favours in equal measure, never lingering with a particular man unless he was old enough to be her grandfather. Twice she danced with William and her hand, cool at first touch but warm beneath, pressed to his damp one as she moved lightly to left and right.

"Not only a skilled horseman and nursemaid, but a fine dancer too," she complimented him with a smile. "What other talents do you hide I wonder?"

"None that you would find worthy, madam," William said, trying not to sound callow.

"And how do you know what I would find worthy?"

He hoped the question was rhetorical, for he did not have an answer. Their hands met and parted on the diagonal: right to right, left to left.

"Perhaps in Poitou we'll find out."

She moved on to the next man in the line in a swirl of heavy woollen skirts, a flash of gold, and a smile over her shoulder, leaving William bemused, his senses reeling. If the musicians hadn't been playing their instruments, his swallow would have been audible. Since the dance was progressive, he found himself partnering a plump, pale-faced child, chestnut-haired, brown-eyed, gowned in a dress that was lavishly embroidered with tiny silver daisies. Princess Marguerite was Prince Henry's nine-year-old wife and daughter of King Louis of France by Constance, his second queen. The children had been married since infancy, a papal dispensation having been granted to permit the nuptials. William could remember his father laughing about the event at the time and admiring the way King Henry had manipulated the Church and outmanoeuvred Louis, who had handed his daughter to the keeping of Henry's court expecting many years of betrothal. Instead there had been a rapid marriage, thus enabling Henry legally to appropriate little Marguerite's dower lands on the Franco-Norman border.

William solemnly danced with the child and bowed formally to her when she moved on, treating her as he would one of the grown women. Marguerite too cast a glance over her shoulder as the Queen had done, but her eyes and her smile were as innocent as the flower for which she was named. Her look, her broad, toothy grin, relaxed William's tension and enabled him to recover his equilibrium. By the time he had danced with Eleanor's small daughters, their nurses, and then a couple of Eleanor's ladies, he felt much more at home in the company.

Between the dances, there was singing, a pastime that William loved. He might not be able to read or write, but he had an excellent memory for tunes and lyrics, and his voice was clear, strong, and wide-ranging. Modest in the exalted company, he let the other knights and ladies take their turn, but when Salisbury clapped him on the shoulder and pressed him forward, he took up the challenge, choosing a lay written by the Queen's famous and infamous poet grandsire Guillaume, Count of Poitou: a song of springtime after winter and the frustration and pain of unrequited love. Lest folk think him too bold, he sang then of the virtues of the Virgin Mary and finally a child's ditty for Marguerite and the little ones, which involved hand-clapping at certain parts. Throughout the singing, he was aware of Eleanor's eyes on him, watching, assessing, peeling back the layers until he felt as exposed and vulnerable as a newborn infant.

"No talents that I would find worthy indeed!" she said to William, teasing laughter in her eyes as she finally chose to retire and bade goodnight to her guests. "Either you do not realise your own skills, or you are a shameless liar."

William's face burned. "Madam, I have never been called upon to sing in such exalted company before. I would not presume to know what you deem worthy, but if I have entertained you, that is the most I can hope."

"Oh yes," Eleanor murmured. "I have been most diverted, and who knows what hope might bring you, Messire Marshal."

With a parting smile, she moved away to bid farewell to the next guest. William bowed, straightened, and then bowed again as Princess Marguerite held out her hand for him to kiss.

"I'm glad you came," she said, "and I liked your songs. Will you sing again tomorrow?"

"If you command it, my lady." He brushed his lips against the back of her small, soft hand, playing the role of courtier to the hilt for her amusement.

Returning to the great hall, William lay down on his pallet, his head light with wine and his thoughts whirling. The restless stirrings of the other sleepers in the hall, the coughs and snores, the wandering of dogs, the drunks lumbering for a piss in the corner, prevented him from falling immediately into slumber even though he was tired. The image of the Queen of England lingered in his mind's eye. Behind his lids, he pictured her turning from the barred door, gesturing to servants, dismissing the children into the care of their nurses. He envisioned her maids removing her veil, unbraiding her hair, and combing it down around her shoulders in a heavy dark waterfall.

He did not for one moment believe that Eleanor had

singled him out for special attention. She had spoken to her other guests in similar wise; she had laid her hand on his uncle Patrick's sleeve and smiled at him as if he were the only man in the room. William knew there was a difference between play and pragmatic reality. Queen Eleanor was inhabiting the role of the lady worthy of courtly love for her own diversion and amusement, and the men she attracted, himself included, were her victims, albeit willing ones.

His imagination took him to her bed. How big it was for one person, and how small she looked inside the shadows of the wool brocade hangings. She was lying on her side, facing towards him, her elbow bent, her head propped on her hand, a beguiling smile on her lips. He swallowed, his throat dry and his heart pounding. His body was light except for the area of his groin which was beating like a lead drum. Eleanor continued to smile, but she beckoned him no closer and he was aware of a reluctance to go forward. It was as if a line were drawn on the floor, and he knew that if he crossed it and approached the bed, he would be destroyed.

William twisted restlessly on his pallet and opened his eyes, trying to banish the image. He was met by the sight of the man beside him copulating with one of the castle whores. They were rolled in the knight's cloak; there was little to see, but the stealthy sounds they made and the increasingly rapid movements told their own tale. William turned over and clenched his jaw. There was always a lack of privacy for hearth knights and servants and at a great gathering like this where even breathing space was at a premium, the sight of couples furtively swiving was commonplace. Everyone knew it happened and if close to the activity, pretended that it didn't—except for those who gained salacious pleasure from watching.

The woman made a different sound, almost a yelp, and the knight's breath caught, held, and then shuddered out of him. There was silence, then a long sigh. Coins clinked softly together and the woman left, an anonymous dark shape picking her way between the pallets of the sleeping men until moments later she stooped by one of them and lifted his blankets. Muffled by a greater distance, the sounds began again, while beside William, the knight began to snore.

Thinking of the transaction that had just taken place and the new one in progress, William realised what that line on the Queen's bedchamber floor had symbolised, why he wouldn't cross it, and why she would never invite him to do so. The realisation relaxed his thoughts and he closed his eyes. The tension in his groin remained though—a dull, persistent surge that was not eased by the moans emanating from further down the line of pallets. Priests advocated will power and prayer to battle the lusts of the flesh. The Sire de Tancarville, of a more worldly and practical mind, had provided whores for his men, like the one going about her business now. For the soldiers lacking funds or fastidious like William, he had baldly suggested the common remedy. William resorted to this now, quickly and quietly. He was young and aroused and it took no time. There was guilt after the swift pangs of pleasure, but not as much as there might have been given other circumstances, and there was relief too. Soon he was as soundly asleep as his companions, and since his dreams had arrived early and troubled his waking mind, they did not disturb his slumber.

Five

Lusignan, Poitou, March 1168

ELEANOR'S THREE SONS HAD BEEN RIDING THEIR PONIES ALL morning, practising at the quintain with blunted lances fashioned to their size and playing at jousts with the sons of the knights and lords billeted at Lusignan. The quintain post had been lowered to take account of the stature of the children and their mounts. Richard was proving more adept than Henry, although both lads possessed natural ability. There was intense rivalry between them. Resenting being younger than Henry, Richard had set out to prove that age was no indicator of skill. Henry was enraged at being defeated by Richard because it undermined his natal superiority and made him look less glorious in the eyes of the other children and their nurses who were watching from the sidelines.

"That's twelve to me and nine to you," Richard declared, returning to the start of the quintain run, his teeth bared in a triumphant grin, a withy ring decorating the end of his lance. His pony was sweating hard, its sides working like bellows.

"Ten." Henry thrust out his lower lip. "I hooked the last one."

"Yes, but it dropped off, so it doesn't count."

"Yes it does."

"I'm still winning," Richard scoffed. "I bet I could beat you at swordplay too. William Marshal says I'm good," he added, as if that clinched the matter.

Henry glared at Richard. Praise from William Marshal was an accolade sought by Eleanor's sons—not the courtly sort provided by William's ready smile, but the approbation that sometimes showed in his eyes when one or all of them had been particularly good during battle practice. Not that William was their tutor or involved in any aspect of their training, but Henry, Richard, and Geoffrey often contrived to be around when William was honing his skills. They became his shadows; they tried to emulate, and sometimes, if he had the time and his mood was right, he would give them an impromptu lesson. "He says I'm good too," Henry declared haughtily. He didn't particularly want to fight Richard. His brother's pure aggression made him a difficult opponent. Henry had the advantage of two years' growth and a longer reach, but he preferred things that came easily; that did not have to be fought for quite so hard. Richard had been a lot worse since the skirmishing in Poitou and kept talking about becoming Duke of Aquitaine and riding to war himself instead of following in the army's tail. Henry couldn't wait until he was King of England, Duke of Normandy, and Count of Anjou, but that was different.

"Not as good as me."

Henry's jaw tightened. "He didn't say that."

"No, I did." Leaping from his pony, Richard drew his practice sword from his belt. It was made of whalebone and the grip was bound just like a true knight's with overlapping layers of buckskin. "Come on—or are you afraid?"

The words goaded Henry. He always swore that he would not rise to Richard's bait, but he always did. Giving his pony to a groom, he drew his own whalebone sword and prepared to do battle. Richard came at him like a fury, as if it were a fight to the death. Henry parried and tried to hold his ground, but Richard pressed him back towards the watching children, his eyes glowing with relish. With a thrust and a flick, he struck Henry's sword from his hand. The suddenness of the blow stung Henry's palms and fingers, but not as much as his pride. He made a sideways lunge for his dropped blade, but Richard got there first and brought the tip of his play sword to Henry's throat.

"Yield." The gleam in Richard's eyes was almost incandescent.

Henry glowered at him. To complain that it wasn't fair would only allow Richard to prove again and again that it was. "Yielded," Henry muttered. Richard made his point by keeping the weapon at his brother's throat an instant longer than necessary, then withdrew it and smugly sheathed it through his belt.

"Just remember that you'll have to kneel to me in homage when I'm King of England," Henry snarled, fighting the shameful heat of tears.

"I won't 'have' to do anything," Richard retorted. "And you won't be able to make me."

"I will. You'll only be a duke, after all." Flinging away from Richard, Henry snatched his pony from his groom and heeled it towards the stables.

The farrier had been reshoeing some of the castle horses and an acrid stench of hot metal and burning horn filled the air. Several animals were tethered to a hitching bar, awaiting collection and return to their stalls, among them William Marshal's two stallions, Blancart and Fauvel. The latter was plucking in desultory fashion at a net of hay and resting on one hip, eyes half closed. Henry had ridden him several times. For a destrier he was good-natured and indolent. It took a sharp dig in the flanks to remind him that he was a warhorse at all. Blancart, however, was gazing around with pricked ears and flaring nostrils, every inch the stallion. Now and then, he sidled, giving a flash of his new iron shoes, and his tail swished like a fly whisk. He was saddled which meant that Sir William intended riding him before he was returned to his stall. Henry gazed at the horse, his winter coat now grown out and his hide the colour of damp cream silk. Richard kept talking about riding him; he had tried to do so several times but had been thwarted by a mingling of circumstance and the vigilance of others. Henry glanced around; the horses were momentarily unattended, the opportunity was God-given and it would be a sin not to take advantage. It would counter the recent humiliation tenfold and wipe the smug expression off Richard's face.

William was in the armoury having his hauberk mended and altered. Some links had been broken during a skirmish with the Lusignan rebels a fortnight ago. The damage had been simple enough to repair, but William had put on weight and muscle during the months since his knighting and the garment was now too snug across his chest.

The armourer sat on a bench outside his workshop, making the most of the good March light. His tools were laid to hand and a shallow wooden bowl contained a coruscation of several hundred mail links. Another dish held masses of tiny rivets the size of pinheads. The armourer had been painstakingly inserting new links into the garment and closing each one by hammering in a rivet. Finished, he rose to his feet, shook out the mail shirt, and requested that William try it on over the quilted tunic he was wearing.

"Much better." William nodded his approval as he flexed his arms and peered at the mended links in his armpit. The new rings were a shade darker than the old ones. There was another small patch of a different hue across the shoulder of the garment where the gaff had caught him at Drincourt. He wondered how much of the original would remain by the time he died. You could always tell the hardest fighters by the dappled patches of repair on their hauberks…the most fortunate too. Now all he had to do was wear it for a while to grow accustomed.

"I swear you live in that thing," Salisbury remarked, pausing by the armoury on his way elsewhere.

William looked rueful. "I have to, the amount of battle we have seen these past few months."

Salisbury nodded and turned his mouth down at the corners to show that William had a point. "You've earned your keep of late, I'll give you that," he admitted. "If you need new rings in your hauberk, it's due to hard work, not gluttony." His glance flickered to a platter occupied by a half-eaten pie and a substantial chunk of bread. William noticed the direction of his uncle's gaze and said sheepishly, "I didn't have time to dine in the hall."

"You need make no excuses to me," Salisbury laughed. "As long as you perform your duties to my satisfaction, what you eat and when is your own business. Do as you will."

William drank a mouthful of wine from the cup beside the platter and turned sharply as a groom's lad burst upon them.

"Messire Marshal, come quickly! Prince Henry's up on Blancart in the tiltyard!" the youth panted.

William and Salisbury looked at each other and, with one accord, sprinted towards the sward, arriving in time to see the heir to England and Normandy white-faced, grimly determined, cantering Blancart towards the quintain. A lance wobbled under the boy's arm. Through his anger and alarm, William noted that the Prince had about as much control of horse and weapon as a drunkard did of his senses. The wonder was that Blancart had not yet bucked him off into the mud. To run out and stop the boy on his approach to the quintain would cause more harm than good and William halted at the front of the gathering crowd. Princess Marguerite looked up at him, her expression filled with fear and guilt on her boy husband's behalf.

"Don't be angry," she pleaded anxiously. "Henry didn't mean to do it."

"If Henry hadn't meant to do it, Princess, he would not be riding at the ring on a warhorse worth a hundred marks without seeking my permission," William said grimly.

Her voice continued to twitter and he shut it out, watching the lad, willing him not to make a mistake and bring both himself and the horse to grief. It was an act of God rather than any human design that Henry stayed on Blancart's back as the stallion thundered towards the quintain post. Henry's eyes were squeezed shut and his seat in the saddle was appalling. The stallion's new-shod hooves churned clods of turf and his tail was swishing with that mingling of eagerness and irritation that William recognised with foreboding.

By rights, Henry should have missed the ring entirely, but the miracle continued as with more than his lifetime's share of divine providence he succeeded in spearing the withy ring and riding on. As the stallion turned away from the tilt, Henry's eyes opened and a beatific expression spread across his face. Features ablaze with triumph, he sought Richard in the crowd—a victor gloating at the vanquished.

William started forward and Henry's attention turned. Fear and defiance constricted the elation, but it didn't vanish entirely. The lad fixed William with an imperious stare, which William ignored. He would kneel to the King and the Queen and yield deference to the royal children in a formal situation. But this wasn't a formal situation and young Henry had just broken the code of chivalry and needed teaching a lesson. However, before he could reach horse and boy and secure them both, Blancart gave an irritated buck. Henry was flung backwards, his spine striking the hard wood of the cantle. He dropped the lance, grabbed the reins in panic, and yanked on them. The stallion went wild, twisting, kicking, plunging. Prince Henry tried to hold on but he stood no chance for he was straddling a whirlwind. The inevitable moment arrived when he lost his grip, sailed from the saddle, and hit the ground with a breath-jarring thud. Blancart bolted, punctuating his gallop with a series of violent bucks and kicks.

Salisbury ran to the Prince who was bleeding from the nose and mouth. William chased after the agitated stallion and managed to seize the trailing rein before the horse could put his hoof through the loop, fall, and break a leg. Speaking firmly and slowly, standing side on, William slid his hands up the rein until he was close enough to grip the cheek strap. He laid his palm to the sweating, trembling neck, grabbed a fistful of mane, and swung into the saddle. Blancart shuddered, but with a familiar solid weight across his back rather than a child's flimsiness, he steadied. Using knees and thighs, putting no pressure on the reins, William rode over to the fallen prince, his heart filled with dread. "*Christ, let him be all right,*" he prayed, crossing himself. A crowd had gathered around the boy, including the senior royal nurse, Hodierna, who was weeping and wringing her hands.

Salisbury looked up as William arrived. Henry was sitting up, hugging his body, his face twisted with pain. Closer now, William could see that the blood in his mouth was from a bitten lip and the nosebleed had already stopped.

"Bruised ribs, I would say," Salisbury said. "He bounced well. Is the horse all right?"

"Hard to tell, my lord. It hasn't done his temper much good." William rubbed his hand reassuringly along Blancart's neck and crest and felt the horse shiver under his touch.

"Stop panicking, woman, he's not dead," Salisbury snapped at Hodierna as she continued to wail. He gripped Henry's shoulder and squeezed hard. "What do you think you were doing?"

The boy gasped. His eyes were glassy with the tears he would not let fall. "I wanted to ride a real destrier. Richard said I couldn't do it, but I did." He raised his chin, suddenly defiant.

"And might have died. If that horse is injured through your stupidity, you will owe Messire William the price of its tending or replacement. A King's heir or not, you're a young fool!"

Henry compressed his lips. Clearly in pain, he rose to his feet and gingerly turned, clutching his ribs, to face William. "I am sorry, Messire Marshal. He is such a fine horse that I could not help myself."

"Then you have much to learn about self-discipline," growled Salisbury.

William's heart was still pounding in reaction to the incident, but something about the lad's manner, the look in the eyes, the set of the mouth, softened his anger. He understood the emotions: the need to prove oneself before one's peers and siblings; the need itself when one was thirteen and raised among sharp swords and valuable horses. "Lord Henry has learned from his prank the painful way," William said with a warning look at the boy. "I don't think he'll be attempting it again?"

Henry stared at William through his fringe and mutely shook his head.

Salisbury grunted and looked severe. "You're getting off lightly," he told Henry. "Best go and get your bruises seen to." He gave the boy to Hodierna, which was in itself something of a humiliation, for Henry saw himself as being almost too old for a nurse these days, especially one who was making as much fuss as an old hen. The Earl dispersed the crowd with a wave of his arm, but with a sudden lunge caught Richard back by the scruff. "You saw what happened to your brother," he warned, shaking him like a terrier with a rat. "Don't ever think of doing the same."

"I won't." Richard put his hands together like an angel. However as soon as Salisbury released him he added cheekily, "For a start, I wouldn't fall off." He was gone in a duck and a rapid flash of heels.

Salisbury dug his fingers through his hair. "Young devil," he muttered, but there was reluctant humour in his eyes.

"You let him off lightly too," William said.

"True," Salisbury replied, "but they've still got to run the gauntlet of their mother, and there'll be no mercy from her."

"Lame," announced the groom with the relish of the eternal pessimist proven right. "Said yesterday afternoon that foreleg looked dicey."

William laid one hand to Blancart's shoulder, and ran it firmly down the affected leg. The knee was hot to the touch and the destrier flinched and shied with a grunt of pain.

"Strained it good and proper, the lad has," the groom continued. In this instance, the "lad" referred to was Prince Henry, not the stallion. "Horse'll not be carrying you anywhere for a sennight at least. I'll get a poultice put on it straight away but…" He clucked his tongue, shook his head, and rumpled his hair. "A sennight," he repeated.

William cursed. The stable yard was busy as Salisbury's knights mounted up and prepared to escort the Queen to a neighbouring castle. Eleanor had not yet arrived, but the moment she did, the troop would depart and Salisbury would only have sharp words for laggards.

Beckoning to his squire, William collected his bridle and saddle from the tack room at the side of the stables and set about harnessing his second destrier. Fortunately, Fauvel was as dozy as a gelding and saddling him only took half as long as it did with Blancart. William buckled the bridle and fastened the breast-band while his squire cinched the girths. By the time he led Fauvel out to join the escort, the Queen was just entering the yard with two of her women. Eleanor wore a riding gown of blue wool and a light cloak of leaf-green edged with silver braid and fastened with a magnificent cloisonné clasp. Silver spurs glinted at her heels. Her bright gaze settled briefly on William and Fauvel before she nodded to Salisbury.

"The Princes are not accompanying you, madam?" the Earl enquired as he boosted her into the saddle of a dappled Barbary mare.

"No," she said, "they are not, although perhaps I should have made Henry ride with us and suffer in the saddle for yesterday's folly. As it is, I have allowed my sons the pleasure of a day's extra tuition in Latin and on the subject of the responsibilities of kings."

Salisbury gave a laconic grin. "I am sure they will benefit, madam."

"Then you are more certain than their mother," Eleanor replied with exasperation.

The company rode out into the bright spring morning. Initially William was morose at having to ride his second destrier, but the fine weather and the festive atmosphere soon lightened his humour. He was the only man wearing his hauberk. The other knights had brought their mail and weapons, but carried them on sumpter horses or rolled behind their saddles—as William would have done had he not been testing the fit of the repaired garment.

"If my son has caused injury to your stallion by his prank, then I will have him reimburse you," Eleanor said, joining William as the party rode along a rutted cart track. Sunlight dappled through the new leaves, the hawthorn sprays were in bud, and the breeze was as warm as a lover's breath. Hidden amongst the trees a cuckoo sent its throaty call in search of a mate.

"In truth, madam, I believe that he has paid his debt," William answered. "I doubt he will be as hasty to repeat the trick. My groom tells me that Blancart will need to be rested for a week, but that there is no lasting harm."

"You are generous." Eleanor's smile curled her mouth corners in a way that shortened William's breath. Three months on from the Christmas feast at Argentan, he had grown more accustomed to Eleanor's powerful sexual charisma, but her flirting still caused him to be deliciously disturbed.

"Madam, if you had spoken to me earlier, I might have been less amiable," he admitted ruefully.

"But you are not one to hold grudges, William?"

He shook his head. "Not over trifles, madam."

She tilted her head at him as if considering a puzzle. "You are perhaps the most good-natured man I have ever encountered. Promise me that you will not let the passage of time sour your temper or your temperament."

William smiled. "Depending on what the morrow holds, I promise."

Eleanor threw back her head and laughed. "Oh, very diplomatic, sir!" She leaned across to slap him lightly on the arm. "You will go far."

"I sincerely hope so, madam." William bowed in the saddle, delighted to be bantering with her. And yet, beneath the banter, what was being said had a serious core. The Romans said that there was truth in wine—that men and women spoke their inner feelings when the grape loosened their tongues. But there was also truth in things cast lightly into a conversation: the sort of gossamer to be snatched as it passed, and then examined later in the open palm.

The party stopped at a wayside stream bordering a hedged field to water their horses and refresh themselves with wine. Some of the men, including his uncle, dismounted, but William remained astride Fauvel, lowering the rein to let the stallion dip his muzzle in the swift running water while he himself drank from his leather travelling costrel.

A squire, who had wandered a little away to take a piss in the bushes, suddenly yelled a warning and William looked round to see a conroi of knights galloping out of a copse a hundred yards away and thundering down on their own small troop. The squire ran, his legs a blur. William threw down the costrel. Reining Fauvel out of the stream, he was already unslinging his shield from its long strap at his back and thrusting his left arm through the shorter grips. He seized the lance that he had propped against a tree trunk while he drank and, couching it, spurred forward to engage the enemy.

Salisbury grabbed Eleanor and bundled her back on to the Barbary mare. "Go, madam!" he shouted urgently. "Ride hard for Lusignan and don't look back!" He struck the mare hard on the rump and Eleanor, after one shocked glance at the fast-approaching knights, lashed the reins down on the mare's neck and took off with the speed of a storm wind.

"Go with the Queen!" Salisbury commanded the closest knights. "Make sure she reaches safety…with your lives if you must!" With the enemy almost upon them, Salisbury drew his sword, threw himself on to his palfrey, and spurred towards his groom and destrier.

As the knights closed in, William recognised the blue and silver shields of Geoffrey and Guy de Lusignan, with whom King Henry had been in dispute these long months. They were formidable warriors and it was plain that this was no chance meeting but a planned ambush. One of their number rode wide, clearly intending to intercept the Queen. William urged Fauvel across his path and bowled the knight from the saddle with a driving thrust of his lance. The warrior struck the ground with a jarring thud and his horse careered off, stirrups hammering its belly. William pivoted Fauvel, brought down another would-be pursuer, and then spurred to defend his uncle.

Reaching his destrier, Salisbury leaped from the palfrey's saddle and reached to his stallion's bridle. As he set foot to his stirrup, Guy de Lusignan bore down on him at full gallop and pierced his spine with his lance. William saw the bright, sharp point punch into his uncle's body, saw his uncle slam into his destrier's flank and recoil, mouth open, arms sailing wide and sword falling from his hand. For a moment the lance held him upright and then de Lusignan was wrenching it out and Salisbury was buckling, crumpling, his expression one of utter astonishment. He hit the ground, landed hard, rebounded on to his side, and stared at William with blood in his mouth and the soul already gone from his eyes.

"No!" William's bellow clogged his skull with red fury, obliterating reason. "Treachery!" he roared, and rammed his spurs into Fauvel's flanks, intent on reaching de Lusignan, but his path was blocked by more enemy knights. He brought the first one down, and the second. Then he lost his lance and had to draw his sword which meant fighting at close range. The battle cry of "Lusignan!" rang in his ears and there were no voices to counter it except his own, and soon he had no breath to shout for aid and no hope of rescue.

A knight clad in a sumptuous silk surcoat ran a lance into Fauvel's breast. The stallion went down, legs threshing. William kicked free of the stirrups and rolled away. Scarred shield held before him, sword edge red to the hilt, he backed from his attackers until he stood against the hedge bordering the field. His breath burned in his chest and his arms were on fire. He knew his situation was desperate, but rather than felling him, that desperation kept him strong. He fended off their probing assaults, keeping his shield tight in to his body and his sword poised. At the back of his mind was the spark of hope that they would tire of trying to cut down one man and ride away. After all, his death was mere chopped straw compared to the harvest they had reaped by killing his uncle. The thought of Salisbury's shameful murder goaded him to continue fighting, even when Geoffrey de Lusignan shouted at him to surrender.

"I do not yield to cowards and traitors who would strike an honourable man from behind!" he cried, his voice somewhere between a sob and a snarl.

"You're a purblind fool," retorted de Lusignan. "This is war, not fair combat on a tourney field." He spurred forward, but William struck his horse a hard blow to the head with his shield and the stallion shied, almost unseating him. Two knights engaged William, but although they were mounted and he was not, he held them off, for neither knight wanted to lose his warhorse to a slice from William's all too skilful sword and he was holding his shield in such a way that they could not reach him without endangering their mounts.

Instead of tackling William head on as the others were doing, Guy de Lusignan set his destrier at the hedge and jumped his stallion into the field of new spring wheat. He cantered along the hedgerow to the point where William stood with his back to it, and once more used his lance from behind.

The pain was as sharp as the steel tip and William was unable to suppress the cry that fled over his larynx before his breath caught on the agony of the wound. Brought down at last like a stag at bay, his shield was dragged off his arm and cast aside and his sword torn from his hand. Geoffrey de Lusignan stood over him and laid his blade to William's throat. "You should have yielded when given the chance," he said.

William glared up through an explosion of red stars. His wound and the sight of his uncle being cloven from behind like a carcass in a town shambles had splintered the courtly shield he usually presented to the world and left him naked. "You're baseborn murderers!" he gasped, tears of grief and rage running down his face. "You butchered my uncle without honour or chivalry. Now do the same to me too and finish it."

Geoffrey's blade nudged William's windpipe but did not bite. "You are a green fool if you expect to find much courtesy in true battle," he growled. "Patrick FitzWalter received his just deserts." Withdrawing his sword, Geoffrey snapped his fingers to his men. "Find him a mount and bring him with us. He's FitzWalter's nephew and worth a few pounds of silver if he lives. Make haste. The sons of whores will have a full troop out after us soon enough."

William's awareness dissolved in pain. The lance was still embedded in his flesh and his captors were not gentle when they pulled it out. The ground reddened under him, for although a flesh wound, it was deep and his blood soaked his braies and hose. A knight thrust some coarse linen at him to plug the wound and he had to bind the material in place with the garters from his hose. They seized his hauberk and thrust him on to the pack animal that had been carrying his uncle's accoutrements. William clung to the wooden hoop at the front of the pack saddle, knowing that he was probably on the swift road to death. Even if he survived his wound, his captors were unlikely to treat him well, especially when they discovered that despite being Patrick of Salisbury's nephew he had no wealth at his disposal and neither did his family. There was no one to pay his ransom and, sooner or later, they would tire of him, cut his throat, and dump him in a ditch.

That night they camped in a wood and William was thrown down at the fire's perimeter. The crude bandages he had been given were sodden with blood, but his requests for fresh bindings and water to wash the wound went ignored, apart from the occasional kick or sneer. Once the horses had been tended, a squire did bring him a cup of wine, a hunk of dry bread, and a blanket stinking of horse sweat, but the youth refused to meet William's eyes and returned swiftly to the company of the other men.

Excluded from the enemy's camp fire, William lay shivering

in the darkness. The pain in his thigh was like a continuous scream from which there was no respite and his mind was screaming too as time upon time he relived the moment when Guy de Lusignan had struck down his uncle. He clenched himself around the image, using the rage and grief it generated to fuel his determination to survive and wreak his revenge. Later in the night, unsleeping, racked by pain, he heard the brothers arguing around the embers.

"We should have taken FitzWalter for ransom," Geoffrey growled. "He's more of a threat to us dead than he ever was alive. He'd have made a rich prize with which to barter. As it is, without Eleanor, we've got less than nothing; it's all been a waste of time." Sparks flared skywards as he angrily cast a dry branch into the grey-red glow.

"I wouldn't call it a waste that Patrick FitzWalter is dead," answered Guy. "We were hunted before, so nothing changes in that respect. They'll have to choose FitzWalter's successor before they turn their attention to us, and that'll take them a while. Besides," he added, his tone aggressive as he attempted to justify his action, "I wasn't to know it was FitzWalter. He had neither shield nor armour to mark him out."

"But it never occurred to you that a man dressed in a tunic of embroidered silk might be worth a decent ransom?" Geoffrey snapped. "You still never thought twice about spearing an unarmed man through the spine."

"He would have been armed in another moment. What else was I to do?"

Geoffrey made an impatient sound and sat down on the fallen log that the brothers were using as a bench.

"No corpse was ever resurrected by wishing a thing undone," Guy said with brutal practicality. "I still say we're well rid of him. He's been a scourge to us for far too long."

William eased awkwardly round, turning away from the

sparking camp fire and the men discussing the murder they had done. His wound throbbing, he faced the darkness of the woods and remembered Eleanor's husky amusement of that morning, now a lifetime ago, as they rode along a sunlit path and she asked him if he ever bore grudges. He had answered lightly, but then, a lifetime ago, he had not understood what a grudge was.

Six

THE DE LUSIGNAN BROTHERS APPROACHED THE CASTLE through a quickening spring dusk and William gazed at the pale walls and red-tiled turrets with a mingling of relief and despair. Whilst he welcomed a respite from the jolting of the horse and the rubbing of the pack saddle against his wounded thigh, he knew that his likely destination was the damp bowels of the donjon. He had no delusions; he was going to die here among his enemies with no one the wiser to his fate.

Having satisfied the castle guards that they were allies, the brothers and their troop clattered beneath the gate arch and into a dusty bailey filled with an assortment of timber sheds and workshops. A ratcatcher watched them from a bench while he ate a bowl of stew, his latest victims dangling by their tails from the wheeled pole at his side. A grubby child was poking at the dead rodents with a stick and making them swing about while two women, fussy as hens themselves, cooped up the castle poultry for the night. As the soldiers were dismounting, William noticed a woman watching their arrival from a spinning gallery that spanned the upper storey of the stone hall. She was olive-skinned and slender, her gown a startling saffron-yellow that blazed in the encroaching dusk. Her gaze lit on William and lingered a moment in curiosity before she left the gallery rail and disappeared from sight into the room beyond.

Without consideration for his wound, William was hauled off the pack beast and manhandled into the hall. The lord of the castle, whose name was Amalric, greeted his visitors with a smiling mouth and wary eyes and William gleaned that he was either a vassal or a castellan of one of the brothers.

The latter were ushered to the dais table at the far end of the hall and promptly served with wine. William was thrown into the straw in the corner of the hall near the door. The stink of urine filled his nostrils, for this was where men came to piss at night rather than go outside to the midden pit or seek the garderobe. He eased himself away from the fouled straw, but each movement caused him excruciating pain and dewed him in cold sweat. His "bandages" were filthy with blood and grime and he knew that he was in mortal danger of contracting the wound sickness. It wasn't as bad as the donjon, but by a degree that made little difference.

Several women entered the hall, among them the one in the yellow gown whom he had seen on the spinning gallery. Ingrained courtliness and his knowledge of the potential tenderness of women made William incline his head when they glanced his way. They twittered to each other like sparrows confronted by a cat and hastened into the body of the hall, except for the young woman in yellow, who paused to accost a servant. Even from a distance, William could tell that her tone was peremptory. The man bowed to her, went to the flagons on the sideboard, poured wine, and brought it to William, his manner nervous and reluctant.

William's hands were shaking so badly that he could barely hold the cup. "Thank you," he croaked, then somehow trembled the rim to his lips and drank. The wine was little better than the poison served up at Henry's court, but it tasted ambrosial as it slipped down his parched throat and he had to stop himself from gulping. He made a point of toasting the woman in yellow as if they were dining partners at a formal feast. She returned his gesture with an infinitesimal dip of her head and turned away.

"My lady asks if there is anything that you need," the servant muttered. His eyes darted about and he looked briefly over his shoulder, plainly worried at being seen talking to William.

"Thank your mistress," William replied, his throat tight with emotion, "and tell her that apart from my freedom, my most pressing need is for clean bandages. If I can have them, I will be in her debt for ever."

The servant hovered until William had finished the wine and, without another word, snatched the cup from him and hastened away.

William fell into a feverish doze. The servants erected trestle tables and the Lusignan party was served with a hastily assembled meal. William's patroness sat with the other ladies at a side table, attending studiously to her food. Not once did she glance in his direction and no one brought him food.

Having eaten, the de Lusignan brothers and their host retired to the private solar on the floor above, the ladies accompanying them. The one in the yellow gown paid no attention to William, but followed the men, her gaze modestly downcast.

William's part of the hall grew quiet. No one ever settled near the piss corner unless forced and with the weather being fine, folk were content to relieve themselves outdoors. The dining trestles had been stacked against the walls and men began laying out their pallets, ready to retire. William tugged his stinking, louse-infested horse blanket over his shoulders and sought sleep, but his pain and discomfort were too great to grant him that blessing.

"Messire..."

The voice was soft yet vibrant. William turned over and struggled to sit up, his wound pounding. The woman in the yellow gown stood before him. Bound with ribbons of gold silk, her jet braids fell to her waist and her eyes were as dark as polished obsidian. "My lady," William acknowledged in a voice hoarse with pain. "I must thank you for your kindness earlier."

"I would offer any wounded man the same," she said. "To see you thus treated makes me ashamed but I cannot go against the will of our overlord."

"I understand, my lady."

"Do you?" She smiled cynically and shook her head. "You said you needed bandages." Stooping, she placed a large loaf in his hands, so fresh that it was still slightly warm. For a moment, the stench of his surroundings was overlaid by the homely aroma of the bread and the spicy scent emanating from her garments.

William had to swallow before he could speak. "Thank you, my lady," he said huskily. "I will not forget your charity."

"Perhaps," she murmured, giving him a sceptical look from her great dark eyes. Gathering her skirts to hold them clear of the soiled floor rushes, she left the hall. William looked down at the loaf. The golden crust was cracked in several places and it was from these that the appetising smell was leaching. He broke a piece off one particularly damaged end and saw that the middle had been hollowed out and replaced with several tight rolls of linen bandage. His vision blurred and he had to cuff his eyes. So small an act of compassion, yet beyond price. He meant what he said; he would not forget.

At dawn, they left the castle and headed deeper into the Limousin with its numerous hidden forests and gorges. William had cleaned his wound with water begged from one of the hall wenches, and bound it with a strip of new bandage. The girl had told him that the lady's name was Clara, and he consigned it to his memory so that he could light a candle for her soul next time he was in a church.

William was young and strong; fortune was with him and his injury healed cleanly, except for a slight limp when he was tired. With his flair for being sociable good company, he steadily eroded his enemies' hostility, whilst keeping an essential rein on his own, and by high summer, they had almost accepted him as one of their own.

As the Lusignan brothers rode between their allies, claiming sporadic succour and support, news came to them that Guillaume de Tancarville, Chamberlain of Normandy—and also William's kin—had replaced Patrick of Salisbury as governor of Poitou. The Lusignans grilled William for details of de Tancarville's character, his methods and his men and William cheerfully fed them a complex, subtle concoction of half-truths and lies, telling them much and giving them nothing.

One evening in late July four months after the ambush, the de Lusignan brothers returned to the castle where they had first brought William. Amalric's greeting was strained and it was plain that while he would do his duty and aid his overlords, he was fearful too. De Tancarville had brought fire and sword to Poitou and prudent men were keeping their heads below their battlements.

Under the watchful eye of a Lusignan serjeant, William was unsaddling the spavined nag they had given him to ride, when a youth stuck his head round the stable door to say that William was summoned to the great hall. "There's a messenger arrived on the business of the Queen Eleanor," the lad announced, wiping his nose on the back of his wrist before loping off.

"Hah!" declared the serjeant. "Looks as if someone's finally decided you're worth something."

William's heartbeat quickened. He tethered his horse, avoiding the snap of its long yellow teeth, and headed for the hall at a swift limp.

The messenger he recognised as Father André, one of

Eleanor's chaplains. As a priest, his spiritual calling gave him a certain (although not guaranteed) immunity and he was more easily able to venture where a sword-wearing man could not. The chaplain's eyes widened and William became conscious of the sorry vision he must present. Four months of continuous wear had rendered his garments so filthy that they could have stood up by themselves. His hair was overlong and matted, his beard thick, and both were infested with lice; his braies were held up by strips of leather and frayed string.

"My son…" he said, shaking his head. "My dear, dear son…" Pity and concern creased his blunt features.

Falling to his knees, William bowed his head. "Thank God." His voice cracked as he fought not to weep. "Tell me that you are here to ransom me?"

"Indeed, my son, that is my purpose." The priest's tone was gentle with compassion. "Queen Eleanor has redeemed your price in full. On the morrow you are free to leave."

The words were the sweetest that William had ever heard. The lump in his throat made speech impossible. Father André set his hand to William's sleeve and gently raised him to his feet. "Although not as free as you might choose," the priest added with a smile. "The Queen desires words with you on your return."

William stepped into the steaming bathtub and hissed at the scalding heat. A swift command from the lady Clara hastened a serving girl to the tub with an extra half-pail of cold water. Now that he had been ransomed and was no longer a prisoner, the laws of hospitality declared that he must be treated as a guest—perhaps not a welcome one, but the courtesies still had to be observed. Since Eleanor herself had paid his ransom, William's importance had suddenly risen dramatically and neither the Lusignans nor Amalric were about to return him to her clad in filthy rags and looking like a scabrous beggar. He had been brought to the domestic chambers above the hall and the women instructed to tend him and find him fresh raiment.

The bathwater was already turning a scummy grey. Clara brought a jar of soap and some stavesacre lotion to deal with the lice. Sitting on a stool to the side of the tub she set about ministering to him, efficiently barbering off his beard and cutting his hair before rubbing the pungent stavesacre lotion into his scalp.

William was embarrassed. "You do not need to do this, my lady, I can see to these things myself."

Her lips curved in a half-smile. "I do not need to, but I wish to."

"May I look a gift horse in the mouth and ask why?"

She slowed kneading his scalp. "Because I was angered and ashamed by the way they treated you," she said. "I do not like to see suffering. I would have done more for you if I could, that first time."

"I am very grateful, my lady, for what you did do."

"It was little enough." Her breathing hesitated, but when he tried to look round, she tipped a jug of water over his hair to sluice it clean.

She provided him with clean garments from the chest containing clothing that had been made as gifts for the household knights. The linen shirt was a little too short but fitted well across the shoulders; the braies could be made to fit any waist by adjusting the drawstring tie; and she found some good woollen hose for him that were sufficiently long in the leg. When she enquired if his wound needed dressing, he answered swiftly that it did not. The thought of her long, slim fingers anywhere north of his knees sent a flood of heat to his groin. If she caught his turmoil, she was sufficiently tactful to ignore it and presented him with a tunic of green linen, a light woollen cloak and a leather hood.

"My lady, you have my thanks," he said as, finally, clean and spruce for the first time in four months, he prepared to go down to the hall and take his place among the knights instead of in the piss corner. "If ever there is anything I can do to repay you, then you need only send word and I am at your service."

Mischief lit a gleam in her dark eyes. "Anything?" she said, and then laughed. "Thank you, messire; I will bear it in mind. For the moment, you can best repay me by staying alive lest I should need you to fulfil your promise."

He bowed over the hand she extended to him. "I will do my best, my lady," he said.

When William entered the Queen's chambers in Poitiers, he was immediately struck by the familiar scents of cedar and sandalwood and by the opulent shades that Eleanor so loved: crimson and purple and gold. He drew a deep, savouring breath; he was home. Eleanor had been standing near the window talking to Guillaume de Tancarville but, on seeing William, she ceased the conversation and hastened across the chamber.

Somewhat stiffly, William knelt and bowed his head. Clara had shorn his hair close to his scalp to help rid him of the remainder of the lice and the air was cold on the back of his neck.

"William, God save you!" Eleanor stooped, took his hands and raised him to his feet, her tawny eyes full of concern. "You're as thin as a lance, and I was told that you had been grievously injured."

"A spear in the thigh; it is almost healed, madam," William replied, not wanting to dwell on his injury. "I am for ever in your debt for ransoming me."

Eleanor shook her head. "There will be no talk of debt

unless it is on my part. You and your uncle sacrificed yourselves for my freedom and I can never repay that. Patrick of Salisbury was my husband's man, and did his bidding first, but he was honourable and courteous and I grieve his death. His murderers will be brought to justice, I promise you that." Behind Eleanor, de Tancarville made a sound of concurrence.

"Yes, madam," William agreed, his mouth twisting. He had sworn an oath on his sword on the matter. Until the Lusignan brothers had taught him the meaning of hatred, he had harboured strong grudges against no man. Now he had that burden and it was as if something light had been taken from him and replaced with a hot lead weight.

"You have no lord now, William." Eleanor drew him further into the room and bade him sit on a cushioned bench. He did so gratefully for his leg was paining him and he had yet to regain his stamina.

"No, madam." William glanced at Guillaume de Tancarville, who was watching him with an enigmatic smile on his lips. William had half expected the Chamberlain to invite him to rejoin his household, but the older man remained silent. "It is the tourney season, and I still have Blancart. I can make my way in the world."

De Tancarville's smile deepened. "Are you sure about that? You seem to have an unfortunate skill for losing destriers and putting yourself in jeopardy."

"I would have done the same for you, my lord, were you in my uncle's place," William replied with quiet dignity, thereby wiping the humour from de Tancarville's face.

"I'm sorry, lad. I should not have jested. Perhaps it's because I know more about your future than you do. You won't need to ride the tourney roads or accept a place in my mesnie."

"My lord?" William gave him a baffled look; Eleanor shot him an irritated one, as if de Tancarville had given too much away.

"What my lord Tancarville is saying in his clumsy fashion is that I am offering you a place among my own household guard," Eleanor said. "I will furnish you with whatever you need in the way of clothing and equipment…and horses should the need arise," she added with a twitch of her lips. "It is more than charity. I would be a fool of the greatest order not to take you into my service. My children adore you, we have missed your company, and you have proven your loyalty and valour to the edge of death."

Her compliments washed over William's head in a hot wave and he felt his face burning with pleasure and embarrassment.

"Lost for words?" she teased, her voice throaty with laughter.

William swallowed. "I have often dreamed of such a post but I never thought…" He shook his head. "It is an ill wind," he said and suddenly a sweeping feeling of loss and sadness overtook his euphoria. He put his right hand over his face, striving to hold himself together. He had managed it for four months under the most difficult of circumstances. He wouldn't break now, not in front of the Queen.

"William, I understand," Eleanor said in a gentler voice than was her wont. "Take what time you need and report to me as soon as you are ready. Speak to my steward. He will see that you are provided with anything you lack. Go to." She gave him a gentle push.

"Madam." William bowed from her presence. On the threshold, just as he was almost free, Princess Marguerite came skipping into the chamber with her nurse. Her face lit up when she saw William. Producing the puppy that had been tucked under her arm, she thrust it at him. "This is Diamond," she announced. "She's my new dog. I'm glad you're back."

"So am I." William dutifully tussled the pup's silky ears. It opened its little jaws and nipped his finger with its milk teeth. The word "rat" came to mind but he kept it to himself.

"Are you crying?" Marguerite asked, some of the pleasure leaving her face as she prepared to pucker her chin in sympathy.

William's nostrils filled with the smell of the pup—a mingling of mild urine and baby fur. "No, Princess," he lied, forcing the shield of his control to remain even though it was damaged beyond repair. "I have a cold, that is all." Suddenly he was very glad that it was only Marguerite on the stairs and not Eleanor's demanding, boisterous sons.

Holding on to the storm had its price. Like summer lightning, it flickered on the horizon, clouding his head, building painful pressure behind his eyes, refusing to break because he had stopped the natural order of things. He avoided as many folk as he could, replying in monosyllables to those who attempted to speak to him.

He came to the church of Saint Hilaire shortly after vespers with the sun mellowing at his left shoulder and casting long shadows over a landscape wearing the dusty, faded green of midsummer. He had thought of nothing as he walked, because that had been the easiest thing to do—exist in his own company with a blank mind. It took him a moment to respond to the porter on duty and the words fumbled out of him as if he had been drinking, causing the monk to look at him with disapproval.

William drew himself together and in a firmer voice repeated who he was and why he had come. The porter summoned another monk to lead William to Patrick of Salisbury's tomb. Their footsteps echoed in the vault of the nave and the evening light spun through the arches and gilded the walls and floor in soothing, quiet gold.

In silence the monk indicated the tomb, currently devoid of embellishment save for a pall of red silk fringed with gold, candles burning in sockets at each corner of the cover. The formal effigy was still in the process of being carved. William nodded his thanks and knelt beside the tomb. The monk's footsteps whispered away, leaving William to his vigil. As the sun set, blue dusk followed by deep night covered the church in successive layers. Shrine lamps glimmered in the darkness and candles made pools of light. William heard the monks at their compline service and then again at matins. A deep hush fell, as profound as the darkness between the islands of light. Alone, William leaned his forehead against the shroud and willed himself to weep for the proud man struck down from behind, but the tears would not come. Somewhere between Eleanor's chamber and the church, they had dried up and the storm had rumbled off to some fasthold at the back of his mind.

Seven

SOUTHWARK LONDON, JUNE 1170

William had often heard about the stews that populated the suburb lining the south bank of the Thames, but until today, he had never set foot in the notorious district of brothels, bathhouses, and cookshops that served the city across the river. That he was here at all was the fault of Eleanor's kitchen clerk, Wigain, who said that no man had lived until he had tasted Emma's roast goose with sage and onion frumenty. Predictably it had been the description of the food that had lured William to the Southwark side, together with a need to escape the tangles of court intrigue and ceremony for a short while. William might be a workhorse, but tonight he had cast off the yoke and was a young man of three and twenty, set on enjoying himself with his friends and family. The company consisted of Wigain, Walter Map, who was also a royal clerk, Baldwin de Béthune, who, like William, was a knight in the royal household, and William's brothers John and Ancel.

William's first shock was discovering that "Emma" was a man—over two yards tall and hairy as a bear. Dangling around his neck was a startling array of gaudy glass necklaces, beads and pewter tokens, one of which portrayed an enormous winged phallus in a glorious state of erection. Wigain laughed at William's stunned expression. "Don't worry, he likes other men, but not unless he's invited."

"Well that's a relief," John Marshal said acidly. "I don't suppose he gets many offers."

"You'd be surprised." Walter Map smiled broadly behind his ink-stained fingers. He was forever writing down his observances concerning life at court and the people in positions of authority. "I know of at least one baron who comes here for more than the goose and he's not interested in wenches."

As he spoke, the men turned to observe two young women emerge from the bathhouse that was situated beyond the eating room. They were bearing piles of damp towels and giggling to each other, their faces flushed, hair escaping their veils, and their gowns clinging to their bodies. Before they closed the door the sound of a client's voice bantering with another, unseen bath maid could clearly be heard. Wisps of herb-scented vapour wafted across the dining space.

"I can see why you might think life at Hamstead too staid for your appetite these days," John muttered to William.

William laughed at his brother's prim expression. "Despite what you think, we don't lead a life of debauchery, do we, Baldwin?"

De Béthune's dark eyes sparkled. "Not yet, but I'm hoping our luck's going to change."

They leaned back to allow "Emma" to place the roasted goose on the trestle. A succulent aroma oozed from its crisp golden pores. Amber droplets trembled down its flanks and pooled on the salver. The scent of sage and onion frumenty rose in heavenly waves. There was a jug of verjuice and raisin sauce to offset the richness of the meat and good white bread in quantity to soak up the juices.

"You won't taste anything better, even on the morrow," announced Wigain as he cut into the bird with alacrity. "The kitchen sheds are piled to the rafters with swans and peacocks and God knows what else. If you and Baldwin want feathers for your caps, I can get you plenty." He speared a piece of breast on the tip of his knife and directed the meat to his mouth. A look of pure bliss crossed his face and he gave a lecherous moan.

John leaned towards William and said with an edge to his jesting, "After the morrow your head will be too big for any kind of hat to stay on it."

"I trust you to shrink it to size," William retorted amiably. "I'm well aware of how fortunate I am."

"Aye, you've always had the luck, even when you were a snot-nosed brat," John growled. "We all thought we'd never see you again when you were given as a hostage to King Stephen. Gilbert and Walter taunted me that you had been hanged and our father beat them for it."

"I didn't know that…"

John shrugged. "No reason why you should. I bawled my eyes out for you, God knows why."

"Perhaps because you didn't know how lucky I was going to be," William suggested, to which John replied with a grunt that might have been amusement but was probably something darker.

As William dined on the succulent roast goose, he pondered the nature of that luck. Being in favour at court was a two-edged sword, and the court itself was a constant battlefield of wits, where the wrong word or an unwise alliance could destroy a man and one's enemies were never met face to face, for, as often as not, the killing blow was to the defenceless back.

During the past two years in the Queen's household, William had been developing the diplomatic survival skills learned under Guillaume de Tancarville. At the outset, he had been just another hearth knight, beholden to Eleanor for his daily bread, but even so he had been noticed and marked for attention. He had heard it muttered that he was a favourite because his face fitted, but if so, he had worked hard to ensure that it did. His reward had been a change of households and additional responsibility.

Tomorrow Prince Henry was to be crowned and given the title of king in his own father's lifetime. There would be two King Henrys—the "Old" one who was but seven and thirty, and the "Young" one who had turned fifteen in February. The crowning of the heir while the father still lived was traditional in the French royal family but had never been undertaken in the English one. However, the elder Henry, scarred by the inheritance wars of his own childhood, had decided to ape French custom and crown his eldest son and pronounce him heir to England, Normandy, and Anjou. Richard had been made Count of Poitou the previous year and betrothed to Alys Capet, Marguerite's sister. Geoffrey had been given Brittany. All business of inheritance was being tidied and made certain.

Since Prince Henry was to be a king and was surging rapidly through adolescence towards manhood, his parents had deemed that he should have his own household. William and Baldwin had been amongst the young knights chosen to enter his service and William had particular responsibility for Henry's military training. It was a task he had been casually undertaking for the last two years, but this set it on a formal basis and raised his position to greater prominence. The one fly in the ointment was the appointing of Adam Yqueboeuf, his rival from his Tancarville days, to the Prince's household too. William could have lived very happily without that particular friction.

The women returned bearing fresh towels. Before re-entering the bathhouse, one of them slanted an inviting glance over her shoulder at the dining men.

"You think they'd entertain six of us?" Wigain asked, rubbing his hands.

William rolled his eyes. The little clerk reminded him of the fearsomely lecherous terrier belonging to the royal nursemaid,

Hodierna. William had lost count of the times he had booted it across the room for trying to futter his leg. "I prefer my pleasure to be less of a mêlée outside tournaments," he replied, "and I've certainly no desire to watch you take yours."

"They have private arrangements if you'd rather."

William opened his mouth to say that any arrangements would be of his own making, not theirs, but the words went unspoken as the client emerged from the bathhouse. His sleeked-back hair was a deep chestnut that would be fox-red when it dried and his angular features were dappled with freckles. He rapidly assessed the occupants of the main room out of pale grey eyes, his hand hovering close to his sword hilt. Two squires who had been drinking quietly in a corner rose to attend him.

"It's Richard de Clare," muttered Walter Map out of the side of his mouth, adding when Baldwin looked blank, "Lord of Striguil. He's not long returned from escorting the Princess Matilda to her marriage in Saxony and he's seeking the King's permission to go to Ireland and fight for King Dermot of Leinster." He leaned forward like a conspirator. "The rumour is that King Dermot's offered him his daughter, the Princess Aoife."

"If I wanted to know my future, I'd not ask heaven, Master Map, I'd enquire of a court clerk, because their breed appears to know more than God," said de Clare, bending over the table to speak in Walter's ear. He slapped him on the shoulder, thereby sending the clerk's cheek into the greasy goose carcass. "I have sharp hearing and you have a loud whisper." He looked around the table. "I have no need for clerks where I'm going, gossips and spies the lot of them, but it is true that I am bound for King Dermot's court on the next ship to Ireland, and I have need of good knights." His gaze ranged over the swords worn by William, John, and Baldwin. "If any of you has a mind, I'm recruiting followers. I can't promise riches, but likely you'll acquire them."

"It is generous of you to offer, my lord," William replied, wiping his hands and lips on a napkin. "If we did not already have places with King Henry and his sons, we would be glad to consider your proposal." He indicated the table. "Will you join us?"

De Clare eyed the glisten-cheeked Walter and smiled sourly. "Thank you, but I have already eaten," he said, "and I'm not sure that sharing company would aid my digestion or yours." Saluting them, he departed with his squires. The odour of herbs and costly scented oil lingered in his wake.

"I don't think he approved of you, Master Map," chuckled Baldwin.

"Well, King Henry doesn't approve of him," Map retorted, on his dignity. "He'll be glad to be rid of him to Ireland and hope that some Hibernian with an axe puts an end to his ambition. He's a brawler and a troublemaker."

William said nothing. The brief exchange had given him an impression of a strong, charismatic personality. A man of plain speaking who did not suffer fools gladly and was short of patience, but who had the ability to mock himself and laugh at the world. A man to follow, except that William already had his feet on another path and his allegiance was to a young lord of a very different kind.

Emma came to clear the table of the remnants of the goose and receive ardent compliments concerning his culinary expertise. A smile appeared within the thicket of black beard and he simpered. Wigain and Walter chose to partake of the pleasures offered by the adjoining bathhouse, while William, his brothers, and Baldwin paid for their meal and headed out into the warm spring evening in search of a boat to row them back to the respectable side of the city.

William's and Baldwin's eventual destination was the White Tower where their duties would begin long before dawn, but first they accompanied John and Ancel back to their lodging near Billingsgate and the rest of the Marshal family.

Their arrival caused a flurry of delight. William's sisters were wild with excitement to be in London for a coronation, especially when their brother was one of Prince Henry's chosen knights. Not having seen William for more than two years, they flung themselves upon him. Sybilla Marshal was laughing as she called them to heel like two half-trained puppies. Glowing with pride herself, she embraced William tenderly then stepped back to look at him.

"The Young King's tutor in arms and his marshal," she declared proudly. "You have travelled far in a short time. If your father could see you..."

"He would praise me with one hand and fist me down to size with the other," William answered merrily. "Mother, this is Baldwin of Béthune, who is to serve with me in the new King's guard."

Sybilla greeted him with warm words of welcome and insisted that both young knights take a cup of wine before they left for the Tower. Baldwin's eyes lingered on the maiden who served them, as did William's. In the two years since he had seen Alais, the last softness of childhood had melted away, defining the lines of cheekbone and jaw. She appraised him and Baldwin with clear hazel-green eyes and her full lips parted in an uninhibited smile that turned her from pretty into strikingly beautiful.

"It is good to see you again," she said warmly to William.

"And you." He returned her smile. "That colour suits you." He was adept at the trivial talk and flattery that smoothed the way underfoot at court. Not that he needed to flatter in Alais's case. The soft moss-green of her gown lit similar lights in her eyes and contrasted well with her fair skin.

Alais blushed and giggled nervously. John cleared his throat and gave William a ferocious glower. William had often received such looks at court, generally from anxious fathers, brothers, or husbands who disliked the ease with which he formed rapports with their womenfolk. Their alarm amused William for it had no substance. He enjoyed the company of women, and it was a delight to flirt with them, but he was no poacher and there was plenty of legitimate game should he choose to pursue it. John's glare was definitely neither paternal nor filial as he moved to stand protectively in front of Alais. Every bone in his body said "mine."

"Pretty girl, your mother's chamber lady," Baldwin said with speculation in his eyes as he and William took a barge downriver to the Tower to snatch what sleep they could before dawn.

"Don't go harbouring ideas," William replied, a note of warning underlying the good humour in his voice. "She's not for tumbling."

Baldwin grinned. "Your brother was certainly being as protective over her as a dog with a marrowbone. The look in his eyes, I don't think I'd want to fight him for her."

"It wouldn't be my brother you'd be facing if you damaged Alais, but my mother, and you'd die."

Baldwin laughed and then sobered. "So what are her circumstances? I take it your brother is not for marrying her or he'd have had six children out of her by now and another in her belly."

William shook his head and studied the oar bench between his spread knees. "He's the heir and Alais has neither dowry nor high family connections. A man of his standing has to select his wife for her estates and the importance of her kin."

"And there was I thinking from the chivalrous way you behave towards women that you were a romantic soul who believed in wedding for love alone," Baldwin mocked.

William curled his lip at Baldwin's jesting to show that he thought it in poor taste. "That won't comfort an empty belly," he replied. "Should I ever marry, I would hope to love my wife for herself as well as her lands, but if I'm being practical, it won't happen. Hearth knights like us seldom take wives or have the opportunity to settle down and beget sons and daughters."

"And that disturbs you?" Baldwin eyed him curiously for it was not often that William allowed a glimpse beneath his good-natured composure.

William frowned. "Not for the moment, but it might when I'm older. Does it not disturb you?"

Baldwin shook his head. "We take what we're given and make the best of it. Even without lands there is nothing to prevent a man from taking a mistress…or a wife, save perhaps his ambition in the second case. The right offer has to come along."

"Then, like my brother, I must be an ambitious man," William said with a smile. "And I have seen no woman yet with whom I am tempted to share a bed beyond a night…except perhaps the Queen," he added with self-mockery. "And that's not a temptation that's ever likely to be fulfilled."

"One to dream about though," Baldwin said.

"Dreaming's best. You can't get into trouble for dreaming, and it costs less."

"Indeed," Baldwin laughed. "I wonder how Wigain and Walter are enjoying their bath!"

Westminster's great hall was packed to the rafters with nobility celebrating the coronation of the royal heir. Now two King Henrys, their crowns identical, sat side by side on the raised dais beneath a banner of snarling red and gold leopards. Queen Eleanor, wife to one and mother to the other, wore her crown too and everyone's garments shone with the gleam of silk and glittered with gemstones and thread of gold. William thought that it was like looking upon a river as it flashed with coins of dazzled light at sunset. He too was a part of the majestic flow in his court tunic of blue silk with red linen undergown. As a bodyguard to the Young King, he wore his sword in the hall and his scabbard was laced to his ceremonial swordbelt of embossed and gilded leather. The one he usually wore, wrinkled and polished with constant use, was stored in his baggage roll awaiting the end of the formal festivities.

Although William was on duty, he had still managed to sample many of the courses of the coronation feast. He had decided that swan was overrated, that cooking a peacock did not improve it, but that the chicken pasties and spiced almond wafers were delicious, as were the honeyed, fried pork trotters.

A stocky young priest joined him, his brown fringe neatly clipped and his river-grey eyes bright with pleasure. "The crowning went well, don't you think?" he asked, his smile pursed and smug.

William turned to his younger brother. Henry had taken his monastic vows and was forging an ecclesiastical career in the service of Roger de Pont L'Évêque, Archbishop of York. "Indeed," William said. "Everyone played their part."

"The Archbishop was magnificent." Henry's voice was belligerent. He folded his arms and stood firmly planted as if to resist a buffet, his posture very reminiscent of their deceased uncle Patrick.

"Yes, he was," William agreed. Even had he thought otherwise, he would have been diplomatic for his brother's sake. The Archbishop of York had performed the crowning because Thomas Becket of Canterbury was currently in exile at the French court, having quarrelled with King Henry over several issues of Church and State. Most of the barons thought that the quarrel was Becket's fault for being so stubborn and determined to thwart Henry's will at every turn. The senior churchmen were divided as to who should take the blame—Henry or Becket—but all agreed that it was a great pity that Becket, who had been the Prince's boyhood tutor, was not here to crown his pupil. Roger of York had filled Becket's empty space but such a choice had always been bound to cause dissent, especially amongst the Canterbury faction who had been heard to mutter that it wasn't a "real" coronation.

William had small interest in the dispute for it impinged little on his daily life. Prince Henry had other tutors now and his days with Becket had already been finished when William had entered Eleanor's service.

"You've heard the grumbles from the French?" his brother asked.

William nodded. "They expected the Princess Marguerite to be crowned beside the Prince and they are bound to be angered that she has not." He frowned, remembering Marguerite's bewilderment at being left behind in Normandy. The gift of a gold circlet and a new gown had not consoled her, for the child cared little for such things; he felt sorry for her.

"I've heard that she is to be crowned at a later date," his brother said. "The King seems to think that Becket won't be able to resist the opportunity to officiate and that it'll bring him to heel."

"I've heard that too," William said neutrally. The King wanted to push the argument with Becket aside like detritus into a midden pit. William had the notion that King Henry's midden pit was already overflowing, and that a cautious man would do well to watch his boots and know when to leap.

"York performed the first ceremony; that will always stand, no matter what Becket and Canterbury do."

William murmured agreement and looked towards the dais. King Henry had taken a flagon and napkin from a passing attendant. His face full of pride, a smile on his lips, he proceeded to fill the cup of his newly crowned heir. "It is a great and sacred occasion when a king is crowned!" he announced in ringing tones for everyone to hear. "I want all gathered here to mark this auspicious day for the house of Anjou and for my son!"

His words provoked roars of approbation from the gathering. Lacking cups in which to toast the speech, William and his brother raised their arms in the air and shouted the salute. Henry turned to his heir. His voice remained loud to include the company and it was bright with jest. "Few of you will ever have seen one king wait upon another, but you witness it now."

A dutiful chuckle circulated around the trestles. Graceful as a young stag, Prince Henry stood to acknowledge his father's words and lifted his cup. His crown gleamed at his brow: a wide gold band pronged with fleurs-de-lis and set with sapphires, rubies, and pearls. "Indeed it is"—he acknowledged his father with a bow and a quicksilver smile—"but less unusual to see the son of a count wait upon the son of a king." The riposte might have been amusing in the private chamber but in the great hall it caused a collective gasp.

The good humour left his father's face, which slowly reddened—always a sign of impending rage, but on this occasion he held it in check and retained his smile, even if it was more a baring of teeth than the genuine expression. "Clever," he half snarled, wagging his forefinger, "very clever, boy. Now all you need is the wisdom to go with your wit." There was emphasis on the word "boy."

William exhaled softly through his teeth, thinking that young Henry was fortunate not to have had that cup of wine dashed in his face. "Jesu," he muttered softly to his brother, "if we had spoken to our own father thus, he'd have whipped our backside to the bone."

"Yes, but none of us would have offered him such disrespect

in the first place," Henry Marshal said. He looked at William. "Are you certain that it's a good idea to seek your fortune in his service?"

William heaved a sigh. "It's like today's coronation, brother," he said. "We are stuck with it for better or for worse." Unconsciously he squared his shoulders as if bracing to meet a foe in battle. The Prince's crass comment had swept out from the dais and was spreading towards the far end of the hall with the speed of rampant bindweed through a field, as could be attested by the uneasy laughter and whispered conversation. Somewhere, he knew, Walter Map and his ilk would be making notes and writing it down for posterity, God help everyone.

Eight

RHYS AP MADOC, A MERCENARY ARCHER FROM GWENT, drew the string of his longbow back to the ear, marking a point of reference with his knuckle to the last molar in his upper jaw, his gaze never wavering from the target of stuffed straw. When he loosed the arrow, it flew as straight as a saint's word to God into the target centre. Before William could draw breath to speak, a second arrow was winging to split the first. The archer swore at the damage done to the flight, but there was a satisfied gleam in his dark brown eyes.

"You'll do." William strove to sound nonchalant, as if he saw such talent every day. He was actually in search of a new groom, but he wasn't going to cavil if that groom also happened to be deadly with a bow and a handy soldier into the bargain. "Go and find yourself a billet in the guardroom for now. Tell Master Ailward that I sent you."

"Yes, sir." The man touched the tip of his greasy leather cap and would have departed, had not William called him back, for his curiosity had been whetted. "You say you were with Richard de Clare of Striguil?" William thought of the red-haired lord to whom he had briefly spoken in the Southwark bathhouse two years ago. De Clare had made good on his promise; had carved his fortune out of the green Irish turf and taken to wife Aoife, daughter of Dermot MacMurrough, King of Leinster.

"Yes, sir, I was, but my wife's Norman and she was homesick. She's not one to complain but I could tell she was miserable, and a man doesn't need misery at his hearth. Besides, I'm not a man to baulk at a fight, but there was never any respite. I knew sooner or later I'd wind up dead in a bog or bleaching my bones on some riverbank."

"And what makes you think that you won't bleach your bones in my service?" William asked with a grim smile.

The Welshman gave a philosophical shrug. "I might do that, sir, but I reckon there's more chance of surviving in your retinue long enough to enjoy my married state."

William dismissed Rhys and watched him jog towards the guardroom. He wished Richard de Clare well of his marriage to the Princess Aoife. Men who had not been to Ireland listened to tales of its green-grey mistiness, its savage bearded chieftains, its place at the edge of the world and shuddered into their wine. William, though, had always felt drawn towards the country by his natural sense of adventure. Had he been a penniless younger son without prospects, he might have accepted a taste of life in de Clare's service—and perhaps an Irish wife. From what he had heard, de Clare had already had a child out of Princess Aoife, a daughter, and the lady was breeding again.

His smile was ironic as he thought of what the archer had said about living a strife-torn life in Ireland. William's existence might not be as fraught with daily danger, but that did not mean it was peaceful. Then again, such storms as beset Prince Henry's household would probably pass over the head of a groom.

As William entered Southampton Castle's great hall, Adam, one of the clerks, scuttled past him, pieces of a broken wax tablet in his hand. The look he cast at William glittered with venom. Glancing back at him in speculation, William continued into the room. Plainly spoiling for a fight, the Young King was pacing the rush-strewn floor, his grey eyes stormy and his chin, with its new sprouting of beard, belligerent. His fourteen-year-old wife was sitting over her needlework frame but she wasn't sewing and her lips were pressed firmly together. She was a queen now, having finally been given her own coronation three months ago at Winchester: nowhere near as grand as her husband's, but it served its purpose, which was to mollify her father.

"Is there trouble, my lord?" William enquired. He noticed that a trestle had been set up to one side of the room. The London merchant Richard FitzReinier, who supplied many of the Prince's requirements, was rolling up assorted bolts of fine cloth, aided by a nervous-looking assistant.

"Not of my making," Henry snapped.

William wandered over to the mercer's trestle, noting that the fabrics were mostly wool, softly teased and napped, and in muted jewel colours—the most expensive sort. There was some silk too, including a small bolt of the staggeringly costly imperial purple. FitzReinier flicked William a swift look from under his brows and gave an infinitesimal shake of his head.

"My father gives me a crown like tossing a bauble to a little child, and expects it to be enough," Henry snapped. He picked up the inkhorn that the clerk had left behind in his eagerness to be out of the room and ran his thumb over the ridges.

William marked the presence of Adam Yqueboeuf and the brothers Thomas and Hugh de Coulances, whose strategy was to agree with everything that Henry said and butter him with flattery. The Young King was no fool, but his head was easily turned by praise and other men's visions of the status he ought to command. "Your father thought long and hard about your coronation," William remarked in a tone that was deliberately mild and conversational.

"He only did it because he was afraid of the country falling into anarchy if he should die suddenly. He wanted to secure the succession."

William cocked an eyebrow. "Surely it is to your benefit as well as his?"

Henry scowled. "What use is a crown without the power behind it? He says I have to learn how to govern before he'll slacken the reins, but how can I do that when he won't give me the responsibility? When he was my age, he was leading armies!"

Henry had a point, William thought. The King desired him to be recognised as his heir, but refused to relinquish one iota of control to let him test his wings. At seventeen years old, Henry stood on the verge of manhood and it was dangerous to continue treating him as a juvenile.

"It's humiliating to have to answer to him for every penny I spend," Henry complained. "Am I supposed to clad myself in rags and freeze in the winter cold?" He gestured toward FitzReinier and his lad. "That idiot clerk Adam was beside me checking every ell of cloth I ordered, and now he'll tell my father who will complain that I spend too much. I am a crowned king, a duke, and a count, and it's all dross!" He hurled the inkhorn at the wall. It broke upon the plasterwork, splattering the limewash with blots and drips of oakgall brown.

"You are attending his Christmas court," William said. "Speak to him and tell him of your discontent."

"He won't listen. He never listens," Henry flashed. "Why do you think my mother no longer dwells with him? She hates him. Everyone hates him except his English whore and that's only because her brains are between her legs. Everyone knows that he was to blame for Becket's murder. It doesn't matter that the Pope has absolved him and he's done penance and promised money for a crusade. He'll always be stained by the shame of the blood spilled on Canterbury's altar."

William winced. The memory of that time was one he would rather put behind him. The King had grown furious at Becket's stubborn refusal to come to terms over the matter of clerical reform. A royal tirade against the Archbishop had been misinterpreted and four knights eager to secure the royal favour had ridden to Canterbury and murdered Thomas Becket on the steps of the altar. The dead Archbishop had become more popular and revered than the living one had ever been. His bloodied clothing, his hair shirt, his soiled, filthy braies were stored in a locked chest by the monks of the cathedral and periodically brought out to be soused in Holy Water. The cloudy results were then sold to an increasing number of pilgrims as a cure-all. Becket had been truculent when alive but dead he was more successful by far and had perhaps created more ills than his diluted essence would ever alleviate. There was a growing feeling of unease and discontent among the people of England, and here was a smooth-browed young man with fine looks and charm and a crown on his head. William knew how volatile the situation could become.

"You could govern better than him, sir," said Adam Yqueboeuf. "The magnates and barons love you, and so do the people. You should make your father listen to you, not just 'speak' to him."

William sent Yqueboeuf a quelling look to which the latter responded with a sneer. "And how would he do that? Threaten his father with force? Bring about the strife that the coronation was supposed to avoid?"

"Anyone would think you were on my father's side," Henry said irritably. "You're like an old woman sometimes."

"And does chivalry not tell you to respect old women, sire?"

Henry's scowl slowly gave way to reluctant humour. "That depends on whether or not they are senile," he retorted. "Are you senile, William?"

"I hope that I still have some reason left in my skull, sire. I am in your service, not your father's, and my loyalty first and foremost is to you."

Henry chewed his thumbnail. "I do respect my father—I have a care for old men as well as old women." He paused to give his sycophants time to guffaw their appreciation. "But he must respect me too. I am no longer a child and I won't be treated like one." His lips thinned mulishly. "I will speak to him at the Christmas feast, but he had better listen."

William said nothing because there was no point. Henry was too high on his pride to pay heed to other than his own desires. Turning away, William studied the bolts of fabric, now tidied on the trestle, noting that the purple silk had been set to one side, together with some fine linen chansil and a glorious gold and blue wool brocade.

"You know what will please," William murmured sardonically to the merchant.

FitzReinier shrugged. "My business would fail if I did not," he said. "The Young King wanted to see my choicest wares and it is my place to satisfy his need, not pander to his clerks."

William smiled. "Or perhaps to encourage his hunger."

FitzReinier returned the smile and clicked his fingers at his assistant. "If you're interested in silk but don't have the means for purple, I have some remnants of green and yellow that would make a surcoat...at a very attractive price," he added with delicate mischief.

A short while later, William stood on the dockside, marvelling at FitzReinier's skill in persuading otherwise sane and sensible men to part with their silver. He was now the owner of some green and yellow silk that he didn't really need, not to mention several ells of red wool for a tunic. He could hardly cavil at Prince Henry's extravagance when he was incapable of controlling his own.

Irritated and slightly bemused by his own folly, he watched porters load the furniture of Prince Henry's household on to the royal *esnecca*. The vessel was sleek and narrow, built to knife through the water and carry her passengers at speed across the expanse of sea separating England from Normandy. Brightly painted shields lined her strake and the leopards of Anjou fluttered from her mast. Men were busily erecting a deck shelter near her stern so that Marguerite and her ladies would have some protection from the flying spray and sharp sea wind. The young royal couple was bound for the French court to visit Marguerite's father, King Louis, and then for an Angevin family gathering at Chinon.

William strolled along the dockside, past the moored fishing vessels and two men mending nets by a brazier, their knuckles chapped and red with cold. William's new groom Rhys was standing with a group of soldiers, his bow stave horizontal across his shoulders and his arms propped over its length. Beyond them, a rider and his attendants were picking their way along the crowded wharf. William's gaze narrowed. "John?" His stomach lurched as if he were already on board ship, his first thought being that something had happened at home to bring his brother chasing down to Southampton. Ancel was with him too. His worry was compounded by John's strained expression, and did not diminish even when his brother found a smile as he dismounted.

"I hoped I would catch you before you sailed," John said as they clasped each other in a brief embrace.

"What's your news?" William turned from John to greet Ancel. The youth had grown again and his narrow frame was filling out with adult muscle. He wore a sword at his hip too, which meant that he was now sufficiently accomplished to use one. "It's surely not just brotherly love that brings you to Southampton?"

"That if you will," John replied with bluff unease, "but business too." A caustic note entered his voice. "I'm the King's

Marshal you know; I don't spend all my time mouldering like a rustic. I've letters for the King to be taken on ship and matters to discuss with the constable."

"Matters not for my ears?" Reassured that the news from home was plainly not that dire, and imparting it not John's sole purpose for being in Southampton, William relaxed and found a mocking smile.

John chose not to return it, his own expression officious and fussy. "Not that you've an imprudent tongue, I know you better than that; but the King's business is the King's business."

"And we're both loyal to the last drop in the flagon," William said. "It's cold here, and going to be even colder than a witch's tit once at sea. We can at least be warm while we talk." He indicated the alehouse standing back from the dockside, lazy smoke twirling from its louvres. "Unless you want to go straight to the castle?" His voice lacked enthusiasm. He had come from there to escape the tense atmosphere and FitzReinier's depredations on his purse.

John gave him a speculative glance. "No, the alehouse will do."

The establishment was already busy with sailors and passengers waiting to embark and who, like William and his brothers, were here to warm and fortify themselves in the interim. The brothers sat down at a trestle in a corner of the room and a woman brought them a pitcher of straw-coloured English wine, a basket of freshly baked bread, and another of raisin and chicken pasties. William eyed the food, his stomach rumbling. The pity was that anything he ate, he'd likely lose five miles out to sea. He didn't know which was worse, puking on an empty stomach or a full one. John was staring at the food too, but as if he were faced by platters of logs and sawdust. Only Ancel set to with a will.

William took a swallow of the wine which was dry and tart, but not sour. John echoed him, and then looked across his cup.

"You might as well know," he said with a grimace, "Alais is with child."

William stared at his brother for a long moment. "You couldn't keep your hands off her, could you?" he said with quiet disgust.

John reddened. "It wasn't like that." He plucked a loaf out of the basket and set about reducing it to crumbs with vicious digs of his thumbnail.

"Then what was it like? I think you were just biding your time."

"I didn't come here for you to judge me. God knows, you're no innocent yourself."

"I don't recall that I've ever seduced one of my mother's ladies, or any young virgins of the chamber," William retorted. He took one of the raisin and chicken pasties, deciding that he was going to eat and be damned.

"Christ!" John twisted the loaf in two. "I knew you'd react like a mealy-mouthed priest. I don't know why I thought that you might understand."

"I do understand," William said acidly. "I saw it in your eyes when I returned from de Tancarville's household, and again when we were in London for Prince Henry's crowning. You have ruined her—unless of course you are going to offer her the position of Lady Marshal and ruin yourself instead."

"I didn't seduce her; she came to me of her own free will. It was mutual."

"It's true," Ancel said between rotations of his jaw. "She did." He poured more wine into his cup.

The red in John's face darkened. "She wanted to learn to fly a hawk to the lure," he said. "I offered to teach her, and whatever you might think of me, it started off as no more than that. I held back...I..."

"But she is with child." William cocked a knowing eyebrow. "That doesn't sound like 'holding back.'"

"I'm not made of stone," John flared. "She's a woman grown with a mind of her own. Whatever you think, I didn't drag her into the woods and commit rape." He pushed his hands through his hair. "Ach, done is done, and no going back. She will want for nothing and neither will our child. Christ, it happens all the time. Old King Henry begot two sons before he was wed. His grandsire had more than a score. If it hasn't happened to you then you've been fortunate. Don't tell me you live like a monk."

William started on his second raisin pasty. "No, I'm careful," he said between rotations of his jaw. "But then I'm in no position to support a wife or a mistress and raise children."

"Yes, well, pulling out doesn't always work."

William swallowed. "I suppose Mother roasted you both over a slow fire?" he said after a moment.

Ancel grinned. "She made hell seem cold by comparison," he volunteered and received a hard nudge from John.

"She made her displeasure known," John said stiffly, "but we have come to an understanding. Providing Alais and I are not brazen about our relationship, she is willing to accept it."

"And when you take a wife?"

John sucked a hard breath over his teeth. "I'll cross that bridge when I come to it. I just wanted to tell you that you are going to be an uncle and I hope you'll wish us well and take an interest in the child."

It would have been pitiless to continue pointing out the trials that John and Alais were going to face. John must know them very well and, as John said, in truth, who was he to judge? There but for the grace of God...Relaxing, William refilled his cup and raised it in toast. "I'll be glad to do both," he said. "If you are pleased, then I am pleased for you too."

John's smile was as sour as sloes as he clinked his cup to William's. "So you should be," he said, "since it means that in law you will still be my heir."

Nine

CHINON, ANJOU, MARCH 1173

Spring was late coming to the Loire valley. An icy, rain-laden wind blustered outside the thick walls of the keep at Chinon, threatening to blow the new pale blossom from the cherry trees and spitefully assaulting the daffodils and celandines blooming tentatively in sheltered corners of the ward.

It wasn't just the weather that was making the winter bitter and delaying the spring, William thought as he and Baldwin de Béthune exercised their horses, taking the opportunity to practise the fighting skills they might soon need. The destriers' hooves churned the tilting ground to mud as the knights pounded down the line to the quintain. As usual, a crowd had gathered to watch, including Wigain, who was standing with Will Blund, the Young King's usher and Richard Barre, the keeper of his seal. William suspected that their presence here in the chilly March morning was an attempt to forget for a moment the storm that was brewing within the walls behind them. William punched the shield on the quintain with his lance, causing the cross bar to whip round at speed. Ducking to avoid the sandbag on the other end, he cantered on and drew rein to watch Baldwin do the same. On a normal day, Prince Henry would have been out with them, training under William's guidance, but this was not a normal day, and without a miracle, unlikely to turn into one. William slapped Blancart's neck and trotted the stallion back to the start of the tilt.

Baldwin joined him. "We shouldn't tire the horses." The neutrality of his tone was more eloquent than his words.

"One more time," William said, "lest we need to be as sharp as our lances."

As they ran a final tilt, more knights arrived on the field, plainly with the same intention as William and Baldwin, but these were King Henry's men and suddenly the atmosphere was tense. William relaxed his grip on the lance, but held it in such a way that it could be readied on the instant. The tip was blunt for it was only a practice weapon, but he knew how to make it effective should the need arise. The knights circled each other warily, but no one wanted to make the first move and Baldwin and William were able to leave the field unchallenged. Nevertheless, the tension was like a thread strung tight and vibrating with strain.

"This is their last chance to resolve their dispute," Baldwin said as they trotted into the stableyard and dismounted.

He was stating the obvious but William didn't stop him for the same thought burdened his own mind. "I pray that they do," he said. "I do not want to see father and son at each other's throats, nor do I want to fight men that I know and respect with weapons *à outrance.*"He thought of the field they had just left; the looks exchanged; the wariness. He didn't want to, but he would, because he had given his oath. He waved away Rhys when the small Welshman came to take Blancart's bridle. "I'll see to him myself," he said, leading the stallion towards his stall. Baldwin hesitated for a moment, not quite as keen as William to stable his own horse when servants existed for that purpose, but then he shrugged and followed suit. He suspected that William was deliberately eking out the time spent out of their young lord's presence. As matters stood, a warhorse was a deal more predictable.

"While the King refuses to give our lord the freedom to make his own decisions and rule his own lands, there's bound to be trouble," Baldwin said. "His father will never give up those lands while he lives, and he'll do with them as he chooses, even down to dividing them further and giving a portion to his youngest son."

William grunted as he unbuckled the girths and lifted the saddle on to a support tree. What Baldwin said was true, but it wasn't palatable. After crossing the Narrow Sea in November, Henry and Marguerite had sojourned with her father, King Louis of France. Louis had been only too glad to breathe on the glowing coals of his son-in-law's discontent. By the time Henry left the French court for his father's Christmas gathering at Chinon, the fire was burning steadily. It might have been damped down by a placation of additional funds to support the Young King's extravagant ways and by giving him a few charters to authorise to make him feel as if he were involved in government, had not the issue of John's inheritance suddenly fanned the flames to white heat. Not only was Henry's father refusing to give Henry any responsibility to accompany his crowned status, he was intending to remove chunks of his patrimony and bestow it on Prince John.

Enraged both by the manner in which her husband hoarded power to himself and his continued affair with Rosamund de Clifford, Queen Eleanor had encouraged the conflagration. Let her husband keep their youngest son and the bastards begotten on his whores. She had the sons that mattered: angry, fickle Henry; Richard, bright and sharp as a sword blade; Geoffrey, the deep thinker.

"How loyal are you?" she had asked William as he prepared to accompany the Young King to Chinon after the most recent argument between father and son. Her tawny eyes had been fierce as they sought his face.

"Madam, I swore my oath to your son," he had answered. "And it will hold unto death. I know of no other way."

"Then I love you for your chivalry. You must realise what is coming."

He had nodded. "I hope that it can be avoided, but if it comes to sword upon sword, I will defend my lord to the last breath in my body."

She had given him her hand to kiss, but as he bowed over it, she had angled his head with her other hand and instead, pressed her mouth to his—a hard, firm kiss, with lips closed, one of gratitude and salute, but bold nonetheless. "May God reward you," she said. "Certainly if it is ever within my gift, I will give you riches."

As he had fought to recover his equilibrium in the wake of such a gesture, the young Queen Marguerite had emerged from the women's chambers to bid him farewell too. Aping her mother-in-law, she had kissed him, but on the cheek instead, and given him a piece of boiled loaf sugar for the journey, for she set much store by such small tokens and gifts and had a loving, generous heart.

"Everything is going to be all right?" she had asked, her soft brown eyes filled with anxiety.

"Yes, my Queen," he had murmured, choosing platitude above uncertain truth. "Everything is going to be all right."

Now "everything" hung in the balance and William knew which side the scales were weighted. Young Henry and his father might have different characters, but in stubbornness they were alike.

William set about currying his stallion and soon the teeth of the comb were clogged with harsh white hairs, for Blancart was beginning to moult his winter coat. As William was plucking them out on the side of his hand and casting them into the straw, Prince Henry strode into the stables.

"What are you doing?" Henry's tone was high-pitched and incredulous. "Why are you skulking in here when you have squires and grooms to do such tasks?" He was breathing hard and flushed with temper.

"Sire, I would ask nothing of a squire or groom that I would not be prepared to do myself," William replied in a level tone. "A knight should be able to turn his hand to anything."

"Then turn it to your sword," Henry snapped, "and resaddle your horse. We're leaving."

"Now, sire?"

"Now!" Henry snarled. "While the gates are still open. The talking is over. What happens next is on my father's head, not mine."

William's heart sank but he received the news without surprise. The signs had been there to read since November. Sometimes the only way to cure a festering wound was to drain it, not lay on more bandages.

"Where are we going, sire?" asked Baldwin.

"To my father-by-marriage," Henry said. "To Chartres."

The stables flurried with activity as horses were swiftly harnessed. Men grabbed their weapons and stuffed belongings into their baggage rolls. William formed up the Young King's conroi and they left Chinon at a rapid trot. Only a few of Henry's clerical servants rode among the party, Wigain one of them, his legs banging against the flanks of his fat dappled cob. The others, including Henry's chamberlain, usher, and chancellor, chose to remain in Chinon with the King, thus adding more hurt to Henry's grievance with his father. The administrative servants were all obviously in his pay and their loyalties had never been given to their young lord.

Tears of rage brightened Henry's eyes. "He wouldn't listen," he fumed to William, his voice cracking with emotion as they rode. "He didn't want to hear. Is what I'm asking so much?"

"No, sire, it is not," William replied.

"My mother agrees with me." He cuffed his eyes impatiently. "She says that she will do all in her power to thwart him. He's not going to ride roughshod over us all."

For a while, they concentrated on putting distance between themselves and Chinon, the knights grim, the servants who had chosen to come absorbed in their effort to keep up. William sent outriders to the front and rear, the space between his shoulder blades prickling.

"He won't chase yet," Henry said bitterly. "He doesn't believe that I will really leave him. He thinks that this is just a fit of pique, that I'm a petulant boy who'll come running back to him because it's cold outside without my cloak. He doesn't realise that there are others ready and willing to offer me fur-lined mantles and all the comfort I want. He is the one who is out in the cold."

The brightness of Henry's tears gave way to a different sheen, one that was vindictive and glittering with ambition. "My mother is going to get Geoffrey and Richard away to safety and then she'll join us. We have allies only waiting the word to rise against him...in England too. The Earls of Leicester and Norfolk are with us, and the King of Scots and his brother."

Although he felt an initial shock at the revelation, William had been expecting something of the sort. Recently a steady trickle of messengers had been visiting the Young King's chambers, some at very unsociable hours. William could not read and wasn't a party to what their letters contained, but he had seen the way their contents set the Young King on edge and, even if he couldn't understand the written word, he well recognised many of the seals, including those of Leicester and Norfolk. There had been clandestine meetings with Eleanor too, to which he had not been a party, but of which he was well aware. Filled with misgiving, he kept pace with his young lord but wondered how this could end without all sides losing.

They reached Argentan, a blood-red sunset turning the trees to black behind them and the keep's great walls punching towards the dying light. The porter hurried to admit them, and the constable came in haste, taken by surprise at the sudden appearance of the Young King and his conroi. Servants were sent running to the kitchens and the laundry chests and a chamber was swiftly prepared. Questions filled the man's gaze, although he asked none and the look on Henry's face kept the constable's lips sealed except for the remark that it was always a pleasure to receive the King's eldest son.

"I hope that you'll remember those words," Henry said, looking round. "I'm expecting the arrival of some of my wife's kin. I want them welcomed and brought to me the instant they ride in."

"Yes, sire. May I enquire how many?"

Henry shrugged. "Probably half a dozen and their retinues."

The constable blenched, partly at the notion of having to cater for another host at short notice, partly at the fact they would be French and thus the natural adversaries of Normandy—even if they were Henry's kin by marriage.

"They won't be staying and neither will I," Henry snapped. "You need not concern yourself on that score."

He retired to the room that had been rapidly prepared for him and, touching the linen bedsheets, made a face. "Cold as a witch's arse," he said and turned to warm his hands at one of the braziers that had been kindled in an effort to banish the dank chill from the room. Having departed Chinon at speed, Henry was without the usual comforts of his baggage train— the hangings, the candelabra, his own sheets and bedcovers, silver-gilt cups and platters, and had perforce to use the equipment supplied by his host.

William set out his own kit by the side of his pallet and drew his sword to check the blade for nicks and rust. It was a comforting ritual; something to ground him when the terrain underfoot was shifting like grains of sand on a dry beach. The detail that Henry was expecting members of the French court had surprised him. The steps of the dance had quickened, and if he didn't want to fall by the wayside, he would have to pick up the pace at once.

Dismissing the constable's servants with a flick of his fingers, Henry paced over to William. "Marshal, I have a boon to ask of you," he said.

William sheathed his sword and propped his scabbard against the wall. Close now, he could see the smudged shadows under the Young King's eyes and the sheen of sweat in the hollow of his throat. In spite of his misgivings, William was swept by a wave of tender concern. "You have no need to seek boons of me, sire," he said, opening his hands. "Anything you command of me I will perform to the best of my honour and ability."

Henry nodded. "I know that, but this is not a command and I ask out of friendship and respect."

William could have said that it made no difference, that a request from Henry was as good as an order, but it would have been ungracious; and the way the young man spoke the words, the look of uncertainty on his face, the combination of reckless courage and charm, made William realise why, even through the exasperation, irritation, and impatience, he had taken an oath to stand beside him unto death. Therefore he remained silent, his expression solemn and filled with waiting.

"I cannot lead men in battle unless I am a knight." The tightness of Henry's jaw made hollows in his cheeks. "I...I want you to confer it upon me."

William inhaled sharply. To one side he was aware of Baldwin de Béthune and Adam Yqueboeuf staring with open mouths. "Me, sire? You want me to confer your knighthood?" For once, William's aplomb deserted him. "Would not the King of France be better, or one of his lords?"

Henry shook his head impatiently. "No, I want you to do it. Why should you be so surprised? You have the renown, and the respect of all your peers. My mother loves and trusts you." His complexion flushed. "It means more to me that you belt on my sword than any Frenchman, no matter his rank."

"Then I would be honoured to knight you, sire," William said hoarsely. He bent his knee and bowed his head, but Henry immediately bade him stand.

"I should kneel to you," he said. "You have trained me to arms, you have stood at my side even when I haven't deserved it. You show me what courtesy should be." He knelt before William, the gesture dramatic but sincere. William sought for something to say but this was new territory and he had no precedents to guide him.

"Sire, you imbue me with virtues that I am not sure are mine. Please." Stooping, William drew Henry to his feet and gave him the kiss of peace. For a moment the young man gripped his arm. To the others it looked like a soldiers' clasp but William could feel the desperation in the touch. Henry wanted to be considered a man, capable of ruling, a fledged knight, a fine general on the battefield, a king. All those things he might become in time, but, for the moment, he was borrowing the robes of such men to clad a fickle, untried youth. As his young wife had done, he was asking William for reassurance. Unqualified, shouldering his own burden of expectation, William borrowed a stranger's robes too—and gave it.

Ten

HAMSTEAD MARSHAL, BERKSHIRE, MAY 1175

THE TREES WERE IN FULL PALE GREEN LEAF AS WILLIAM RODE along the dust-whitened lane towards Hamstead. The twitter of birdsong, the soft plod of shod hoof, and the creak of harness and accoutrements were pleasant sounds, but to William they were an uncomfortable reminder of the day his uncle Patrick had been murdered by the Lusignans. That too had been a soft, spring day with everyone off their guard. Not that he expected to be attacked within sight of the family keep, but memory did not answer to reason and he rode in his hauberk with his sword belted at his hip and a mace pushed through his belt.

He had left the Young King at Westminster with his father, attending a synod convened by the Archbishop of Canterbury. Father and son had been on the best of terms, laughing at each other's jests, clapping each other's shoulders like old friends. No one would suspect there had been a deep rift between them, or guess that their quarrel had caused a vicious, bloody war. But William only had to see smoke rising from a burning midden pit to remember the villages in flames as the bitter dispute ravaged the land and plagues of mercenaries despoiled and plundered at will. The sight of a dead ox or sheep would clench his gut even before his nostrils drew in the stench. Every castle he passed left him pondering ways to besiege it and bring it to surrender. William was pragmatic; he had not flinched from deeds of fire and sword, but there was a price to pay and it lay heavy on him now.

Louis of France had welcomed Young Henry with open arms; had given him a seal of his own, generous funds, and together they had coordinated an attack on Henry's father. Richard and Geoffrey had arrived safely at the French court to join the rebellion but their mother had been captured as she rode to join them, disguised as a man, and was now under house arrest at Salisbury. The Young King had threatened to hew England to pieces in order to free her. Richard had been vociferous in his declarations to do just that, for the bond between him and his mother was particularly close. However, the practicalities had proven more difficult than the rhetoric and the English uprising had been left to the likes of the Earls of Leicester and Norfolk with aid from the Scots, who were always willing to stir the pot. The unrest had been widespread but the justiciar, Richard de Luci, had managed to contain it, the rebels had been routed, and their leaders captured. In Normandy too, despite modest successes and French support, the rebellion had failed. The best that could be salvaged was the King's concession that his eldest son should have an income of his own, rather than be dependent on begging at his father's purse strings. Young Henry had been given two castles in Normandy and an annual income of fifteen thousand Angevin pounds. Richard was to have half the revenues of Poitou and Geoffrey the same for Brittany. But the Young King had been forced to acknowledge his father's right to make provision for John as he deemed fit, and Queen Eleanor remained a prisoner in Salisbury.

As William approached Hamstead he tried to set aside thoughts of the war, but it was difficult since his brother had fought in it too—on the King's side. He hoped that John would understand, but a nugget of uncertainty caused him to pull back on the bridle even while he urged his palfrey onwards. Confused, the horse champed the bit and baulked. Rhys uttered a startled expletive as his horse collided with William's mount and he had to rein back to avoid the irritated lash of a hind hoof.

William apologised. "I was thinking back instead of going forward," he said.

"Never wise to do that," Rhys replied in his sing-song French.

"No," William agreed wryly. He looked at the small Welshman. Since his thoughts were on the recent war, it was a natural progression to mention Rhys's former lord. "Richard de Clare was in Normandy fighting for King Henry," he said. "Were you not tempted to return to him?"

Rhys screwed up his face. "I thought about it, sir, especially when things were going badly for us, but I knew that I'd be jumping out of the cauldron into the fire. Lord Richard came to fight for King Henry because he was ordered—because it was his duty and he's a man of honour. But he's back in Ireland now, and Ireland was the reason I left his service."

William nodded at his servant's reply. He had encountered de Clare briefly during the peace negotiations. There had been a few new scars, and the auburn hair had begun to salt with grey. Despite a leg wound that was slow to heal, the lord of Leinster and Striguil had been full of vigour. In some ways, Richard de Clare reminded William of his own father. There was that same incisive, ruthless streak combined with charisma and vision—and so much vitality that only the energy he threw into warfare seemed able to calm it.

"Lord Richard wouldn't want to be away from the Princess Aoife and his children for too long, especially now she's borne him a son and heir."

William raised an eyebrow. "You keep abreast of his doings then."

Rhys glanced over his shoulder towards William's modest baggage train and the quiet, dark-eyed woman straddling one of the pack horses. "My wife's like all women—no interest in men's disputes, but likes to know the cosy fireside details."

William laughed quietly at his groom's eloquent expression. His heart was lightened by Rhys's domestic observation and he urged his palfrey towards Hamstead with restored buoyancy.

William watched the toddler struggle out of his mother's arms and, squealing with joy, make a beeline for her pet mouser. The sleek tabby cat sprang from floor to sideboard and, curling its paws into its chest, regarded the infant disdainfully out of slanting golden eyes, the tip of its tail twitching. The squeals became less delighted. The infant reached upwards, fat fists opening and closing. "Cat," he shouted. "Cat, cat, cat!"

"He has our father's determination and the temper of the King," John Marshal said smiling with paternal pride.

William grinned. "You mean he bites the floor rushes when he is denied?"

"As near as makes no difference." John eyed William. "I never believed those tales about King Henry doing that. I've seen him in some rages this past year, but never rolling on the floor."

"Neither have I, but if true, he would do it for the effect it had on the witnesses, not because he was suffering from a fit of uncontrollable fury."

"Cat!" The toddler's scream was ear-splitting. Flushed with chagrin, Alais hastened to distract her son with a morsel of honeycomb but he was having none of it and continued to yell. William stooped to seize a fistful of his nephew's smock and swung him aloft. The infant stared at him in astonishment, pink mouth frozen open and the wail locked in his throat.

"If you are going to be my squire in years to come, you'll have to learn the meaning of courtesy," William informed his nephew, "and that some things are out of bounds, no matter how much you scream."

"You didn't teach your other pupil very well, did you?" John said acidly. "The tantrum he threw was beyond belief."

William swung his nephew up on to his shoulders and wrapped his hands around the chubby feet, which were encased in soft, sheepskin slippers. "I agree the Young King threw a tantrum, but it wasn't beyond belief and in part he was justified. Crowning him was like giving him a chest full of treasure and then telling him that he couldn't open it and have any of the contents."

John was unimpressed. "Yes, and what would he have done with those contents? We've heard about his extravagances. It is said that were he given all the revenues of Normandy, he'd find ways to spend them in a week."

"You shouldn't listen to every piece of gossip you hear." William swept the child down from his shoulders and swung him gently just off the floor. The baby laughed, exposing two rows of perfect white milk teeth. "He's a fine, sturdy lad," William said to Alais to change the subject.

She reddened with pleasure and smiled back. Childbirth had ripened her curves. A wimple respectably covered her chestnut braids and although she wore no wedding ring, several others adorned her fingers, including one set with a fine ruby. "He is a handful," she said, "a proper boy, into every sort of scrape and not yet two summers old." Her voice glowed with pride. She touched William's arm. "Whatever his father says, you will make a fine tutor for him when he's old enough to be a squire, nor will it harm him to have an uncle well placed at court."

John coughed. "I do not call being tutor to a fickle young spendthrift and protégé of an imprisoned queen being well placed," he said disagreeably.

"But things change." Alais squeezed her lover's arm.

"Don't be so crabby. William's not here for long and you are brothers."

"That's no recommendation for harmony," John growled but, at her glare, added, "I am pleased to see him, but that doesn't stop us having our differences, and I can still be concerned for the future."

William shrugged. "Plan for it by all means, but don't let it trouble your sleep."

"You say that after what happened last year?" John's voice filled with scorn. "England, Normandy and Anjou in flames, not to mention Poitou. The King and his sons at each other's throats and the Earl of Leicester landing an army of Flemings in Norfolk? Christ, you might want to dance in the mouth of hell, but I want to live to see my son grow up. I had to stop Ancel from riding off to join the Young King's party," he added darkly. "He was in his hot blood and ready to cross the sea and seek you out. I told him you'd not thank him and that finding a place in a lord's mesnie isn't just a matter of riding up and offering one's sword. I managed to command his loyalty, but he doesn't like me for it. He's at Wexcombe with Mother, letting the dust settle."

William felt sympathy, for both John and for Ancel: one having to give orders; the other forced to obey them; and neither benefiting. "I would take Ancel if I could, but I cannot afford to at the moment." William plucked at his rich tunic. "I may look prosperous to you, but I am beholden to my lord for the clothes I wear, the horse I ride, and the food in my mouth. However fine my equipment, when it comes to the crux, I am still a hearth knight."

"But an exalted one."

William twitched his shoulders, acknowledging the fact while making little of it.

Unable to contain their restlessness indoors, the brothers

went out of the castle and walked around the walls where they had played as children. Today, other small boys were engaged in a boisterous game of chase in the May sunshine, their laughter adding a layer to the echo of memory. William remembered mock sword fights on the sward: what it felt like to win; what it felt like to lose.

"So in truth, and ignoring the rumours," John said, "what sort of king will Prince Henry make? You are his tutor. What do you know of him?"

William gnawed his thumbnail and considered. "He is not like his father," he said slowly, "except perhaps he has the same determination to get his own way. If money trickles through his hands like water down a drain, it is indeed because he enjoys spending it and being generous to those in his service. He believes it increases his standing to be seen to have an open door and to scatter largesse as if silver were of no more account than ears of wheat."

John's mouth turned down at the corners. "Well, that accords with the rumours," he said.

William paused to look up at the high, narrow windows. There was a gallery at the top of the tower and someone had hung several shirts over the rail to dry. "He is still growing. You can argue that his father was a man before he was sixteen years old, but he matured early and from necessity. My lord is clever and sharp; he knows how to make people love him. The rest will come."

"Despite that remark about being the greater king because he is the son of a king, not the son of a count?"

William sighed. Henry's "witticism" seemed set to endure. Everyone had heard of it and he was growing sick of fending off adverse comments. "He was younger then and drunk on wine and excitement. He has more control these days. I do not know why he gets the reputation for being the one who's too clever with his words. Geoffrey is just as bad and Richard's tongue is so sharp he can make men bleed."

"But Richard is Duke of Aquitaine and unlikely to be our king," John said. "He's little known in England and Normandy—just another royal whelp…"

"…and Eleanor's favourite," William reminded his brother, but John was not persuaded.

"She is locked away in Salisbury and, as matters stand, unlikely to be given her freedom for a long time."

William conceded the point with a brief nod. "Perhaps not, but for the moment Richard is his brother's heir and the Queen has had the major hand in raising him. Richard is the child of her soul in the same way that John is King Henry's."

His brother looked alarmed and William's lips twitched. Men professed to love Eleanor, but it was an adoration tinged with fear and more than a hint of "God forbid." Perhaps they were right to be fearful, but William had long gone beyond that.

"Then I wish the Young King the wherewithal to grow up and mature," John said. "What of his wife? Does she show any signs of breeding?"

"You would have to ask her women about that," William said neutrally. He could have told his brother that the marriage between Henry and Marguerite had only lately been consummated and that the couple were dutiful rather than passionate when it came to sharing a bed. However, William considered the matter personal and, being protective of Marguerite and his lord, said nothing.

John took the hint, although he made a jest of wondering whether the Young King would have his own heir crowned in his lifetime.

"I doubt it," William said with a humourless smile. "Would you?"

John looked over his shoulder towards the castle doorway

and Alais who was dandling the baby in her arms. "Probably not," he said.

The following day William took his leave of John, and although their parting was cordial enough, the brothers were relieved to say farewell. John, no matter how he tried to hide it, was jealous of William's meteoric rise at court. To have a younger brother in the daily company of kings and queens, magnates and archbishops chafed his own sense of self-worth. Nor did he approve of William's extravagant lifestyle, although part of that disapproval was because he desired such for himself but would not admit it.

For his part, William was fond of John but found him staid and insular—although those traits would probably have been worse had he not had Alais and their infant son to lift him out of his rut. In spite of the stigma of having borne John a child out of wedlock and being his mistress, Alais seemed soft and content. It was that very contentment, the sight of her cuddling her son on her knee in a shaft of evening sunlight and smiling back at John that had given William his own moment of envy. He wasn't ready to settle down—might never be, and it might never happen—but seeing that moment of quiet pleasure was like standing in the winter snow and looking through a window at a torchlit golden feast to which he was a witness, but not a guest.

As he put distance between himself and Hamstead, William's envy evaporated and he brightened, glad to be on the road again, a knight errant with a glittering future before him. He paused at Wexcombe to visit his mother and Ancel, promising the latter that as soon as there was a place for him, he would take him on, rode on to Bradenstoke to pay his respects at his father's tomb, and then turned away from filial and domestic duty towards his other life. Loyalty, gratitude, and a deep affection brought him first to Salisbury and Eleanor.

❖ ❖ ❖

The Queen's chamber was more suited to that of a nun than a queen and her position as her husband's prisoner was unequivocal. The walls were devoid of hangings and her opulent bed coverings had been replaced by plain blankets. Instead of her beautiful flagons and goblets, there were heavy jugs and cups fashioned of crude local pottery. The painted coffers were gone and the usual pile of books was missing, although her chessboard stood rather forlornly on a plain wooden chest in the embrasure.

Eleanor herself sat near the open shutters, some sewing in her lap. When William was ushered into the room, she rose to her feet, her face brightening with pleasure. "William!" She came towards him, her hand outstretched and slightly trembling. He knelt and kissed her fingers, which were still adorned with a wealth of gold rings. Henry hadn't taken those from her at least.

"Oh, it is so good to see you; you cannot know!" She raised him to his feet and when their eyes met, William saw the new lines of suffering and experience dredging her face. The fine bone structure would always guarantee her beauty, and her eyes were still the same slanting bright gold, but the years did not sit as lightly as before.

"Madam, you look well," he said. It was the truth. Despite her tribulation, there remained a glamour about her, like the gilding on the wing of a dark butterfly.

"Do I?" She gave a sceptical laugh. "Well, I don't feel it. Jesu, even nuns have more freedom than I do. My gaolers think it a great concession to allow me to dine in the great hall or receive a visitor every once in a while." She glanced towards the castellan who had followed William into the room. He was looking uncomfortably at the ceiling, but still standing close enough to hear every word.

"I am deeply sorry, madam."

"Hah, so am I…to be caged at least. For the rest, not even the pincers of hell will wring a confession of remorse from my lips." She clapped her hand at a maid and gestured her to pour wine. "From Poitou," she said. "Henry may have given me cracked old cups to drink from, but at least I'm granted the boon of wine from my own province." Her eyes narrowed. "I would not drink his even if I were dying of thirst."

Knowing the King's wine, William didn't blame her. He took the cup from the maid and saluted Eleanor. The castellan too was grudgingly furnished with wine, but not invited to join the conversation.

"So," she said brightly, "tell me of the world outside."

William saw through the smile in her voice to the desolation beneath. To be shut away here on a frugal income, her visitors closely vetted and not encouraged, must be soul-destroying to the vivacious and intellectually hungry Eleanor. She loved to shine in company and to feed upon the dazzle she created. Indeed, she craved company for its own sake. He set out to entertain her with tales of the latest doings at court; the scandals; the political manoeuvring. He made her laugh and for a while forget her circumstances, and he gave her news of her sons. Here too he kept his tone light. Aware of the constable's stretched ears, he said nothing that could be passed back to the King and used to his or Eleanor's detriment. She was circumspect too but bade him greet her sons and tell them that they were held in her heart and her prayers.

"As you are held in mine, madam." He kissed her hand again. When he looked beyond her fingers, still fine, still manicured, but scattered with the brown mottles of age, and into her eyes, he saw that they were shimmering with tears.

William took his leave with a troubled and heavy spirit. He wished he could ransom Eleanor the way that she had once ransomed him. All he could do was watch out for her eldest son, who was in his charge, and do his best to honour that position of trust.

At Hamstead, John had said with a curl of his lip that Eleanor's plight was of her own making, but William had answered that rebellion was surely never in her mind when she had married Henry of Anjou and that her husband was as much to blame. It was the march of years and the slow, dark spiral into disillusion that had brought her to an edge and then tumbled her over it. How did one guard against that, he wondered? How did one hold on to one's loyalty when love was dead and fidelity betrayed? Perhaps one did so because it was the only light in the void and to let go was to fall for eternity. He shivered at his thoughts and clapping his heels to his palfrey's flanks picked up the pace.

Eleven

ANET, NORMANDY, SPRING 1177

THE TOURNEY AT ANET ON THE NORMAN BORDER HAD attracted competitors from far and wide: France and Flanders, Brie, Champagne, Lombardy, Brittany, Anjou, Poitou, Normandy, and England. There were great lords and their retinues, lesser barons with their squires and grooms, landless knights hoping to be noticed and employed by a patron. Supplying their needs were numerous traders and craftsmen, for without the armourers, smiths, farriers, horse-traders, saddlers, cookstall owners, and a host of others, the event could not have taken place. Clinging like carbuncles and galls upon this great tree of activity, the outcasts performed their parasitic role—the beggars, the thieves and cutpurses, whores and pimps, the men with loaded dice, the women who lured clients into dark alleys where accomplices robbed the victims of their silver.

Tourneys had their own particular scent that nothing else could replicate. William inhaled the mingled aromas with pleasure and anticipation as he walked among the tents and booths with the Young King, greeting old comrades and inspecting the goods. The scent of green turf, dust, and hot horses; the sour smell of anxious sweat that would later be intensified by the effort of battle; the waft of gruel and frying bacon from cooking pots and griddles.

"We're going to take a fortune in ransoms today," the Young King said, rubbing his hands. "I can feel it in my bones." He was posing in an embroidered silk tunic heavily encrusted with small gemstones and his cloak was collared with ermine tails. His retinue moved in front and behind, clearing a path, giving him a space in which to walk and be admired.

William grinned. "You probably will feel it in your bones by the day's end, my lord."

"Not if my mesnie is doing its job," Henry retorted.

A year ago Henry had gained permission from his father to cross the Narrow Sea with his entourage and take part in the tourneys that were held fortnightly across France and neighbouring territories. The King had been reluctant at first, for he had a personal hatred of the sport, seeing it as a waste of time and effort, not to say a breeding place for rebellion. He would like to have seen tourneys banned from all his dominions, not just England. However, worn down by young Henry's constant harassment and pleading, he finally capitulated, hoping that it would harness his heir's restless energy, concentrate his fickle brain, and imbue him with some of the discipline he lacked.

At first, the losses of Henry's mesnie on the field had been spectacular and embarrassing. William still cringed when he thought back upon those early days. Their failure had not been due to any lack of prowess, rather that their opponents were experienced professionals, some of whom had been riding the circuit for years and knew all the tricks, both honest and foul. It had been a matter of learning from their mistakes and learning fast.

William had taken it upon himself to fashion a decent tourney team out of a number of disparate abilities and personalities. He set the more cautious and solid men to hold the flanks and watch Henry. The fiery ones or those with the strongest destriers headed the line. The most versatile were in the middle, ready to attack or defend. He had the knights fight each other with every combination of weapon and he made them practise on their own mounts and other men's so that they became accustomed to a variety of horses. When Adam Yquebeouf complained that such antics were below his dignity, William remarked that there were plenty of other knights keen to join Henry's service who would not baulk at what was required. Henry desired to excel at the tourney; it was up to his men to ensure that it happened. Yqueboeuf had looked daggers, but had ceased to grumble—at least in William's presence.

The intensive training during the slack winter months had begun to bear fruit this new season. Knights who had once laughed at the callow efforts of the Young King's mesnie were now rubbing their bruises and polishing their respect. Henry basked in the adulation like a cat in warm sunshine and William's cachet within tourney circles had risen considerably.

Passing a pavilion belonging to a Poitevan knight, William and Henry heard a man and a woman heatedly arguing behind the closed tent flaps. A red-faced squire was checking equipment outside the pavilion and unsuccessfully pretending to be deaf. Several knights were chuckling to each other and exchanging knowing glances.

"You whoreson, you promised me!" The woman's voice was seething with fury.

"I said I would if I could afford it, and I can't."

"Hah, because you've swilled your coin away in gaming and dice with your cronies!"

"They're a better bargain than a carping bitch. Whores like you can be bought ten a penny in any town brothel." There was the sound of a slap, a scuffle, and a cut-off shriek.

"My parents used to scream at each other like that sometimes," Henry said, moving on and shaking his head. "My father once compared my mother to a Rouen fishwife, and she replied it was a good thing she wasn't, because she would have ripped him open with a gutting knife." He snorted down his nose. "Preferably before he begot John on her and took up with the Clifford slut." He looked at William, his mouth twisting with distaste. "I would never strike a woman. God knows, Marguerite irritates me on occasion but I'd never beat her for it."

William thought wryly that Marguerite was probably also irritated by her young husband, who could be difficult in his cups and was frequently inconsiderate. "How is the Queen this morning, sire?"

Henry made a face. "The same as yesterday—puking. Her women say that it'll stop in the fourth month. I hope so. I can't abide her company while she's heaving into a bowl every five minutes, even if she is carrying my heir in her belly. She says she's not well enough to watch me either." His tone verged on the petulant, for to Henry an admiring audience was crucial.

"It's a wide tourney field, sire," William said diplomatically. "She wouldn't see much of you anyway."

Henry made a disgruntled sound. "You're right," he said, but in a way that let William know that his words were a gracious concession and that his opinion had not changed.

The attractions of the booths explored and the opposition inspected, Henry repaired to his tent to don his armour. William followed suit, and while he waited for his squire to fetch his accoutrements, mentally prepared himself for the coming fray. Outside his pavilion, Rhys was carefully checking over the harness. His loyalty to William had solidified ever since the news had arrived of the death of Richard de Clare; not in battle, but of an infected leg caused by an old wound that had refused to heal. His children, a girl of six and a boy of three, were in royal wardship and for the moment their vast inheritance was being milked into the royal coffers. William had liked Richard de Clare from the little he had known of him and had attended a mass to honour his passing. Rhys had been deeply affected and it only took an extra cup of wine to make him maudlin with memories and regrets.

As William was adjusting his scabbard at his hip, Wigain arrived bearing slices of cold roast goose wrapped in lime leaves, a loaf, a handful of dried fruit, and a costrel of wine. "I've been making wagers with some of the other clerks," he said as he placed the items on the trestle, ready for William's saddlebag.

William raised an amused brow. "And what might they be?"

"That you and our lord Henry will win the most ransoms."

"And you think this a wise thing to do?" William shook his head at the clerk. "I hope you haven't put your shirt on it."

Wigain grinned. "More like two shirts. Now that we've started winning, I'm recouping the losses of last year."

"I don't know whether that speaks to me of your faith or your folly." William unwrapped one of the leaves and sampled a sliver of goose.

Wigain gave a cheerful shrug. "I was discouraged last year, sir, but then I saw the way you trained the knights every day, even when there was snow on the ground and they were complaining like a bowerful of old women."

William snorted at the image.

"It's made all the difference; there's no one to better us now."

"Your faith commends you," William replied, "but why should others accept your wager unless they thought you were going to lose?" He devoured another slice of goose then bade his squire remove it to his saddlebag before he was tempted to eat the lot.

"Because you've only just begun to be successful and they still remember how you were. Some say that the Young King is a cocky young wastrel and his mesnie a group of bored fops without a yard of steel amongst them." Wigain cleared his throat and looked apologetic.

"They're going to be disappointed then, aren't they?"

William dug in his own purse and thrust a handful of silver into Wigain's hastily provided palm. "Here, wager this too. Let's see what a cocky young wastrel and a group of bored fops with soft swords can accomplish."

The fighting was hard, fast, and at times almost as brutal as true war. The hooves of the destriers churned up the sweet spring grass and as the day wore on the horses began to slip in the mud. William changed mounts several times, always aiming to keep his stallion fresh and selecting the animal best suited to the ground.

Henry was fearless and led from the front—which meant extra work for William who had to keep pace with him and turn any blows that threatened his young lord's superiority. However, the hard training through the winter was paying dividends. Fighting as a tightly knit team, Henry's mesnie stormed the field. Henry was laughing as he led his team against a conroi of French knights who had just fought their way out of a conflict with another troop. The opposition resisted but William pushed forward, seeking their breaking point, knowing that it wasn't far away. A blow from his mace sent his opponent reeling and William grabbed the knight's bridle. "Yield!" he commanded, wrapping his fist around the rein, one eye on his prize, the other on Henry who was caught up in the thick of the brawl, but with Baldwin de Béthune and Roger de Gaugi close to hand. Reassured, William gave his full attention to his opponent who was trying to wrench his destrier away. By the time William had forced him to surrender, the rest of the French had scattered with the Young King's mesnie in hot pursuit, including Roger and Baldwin. Having been busy taking the ransom pledge of his adversary, Henry was left behind.

"More training, I think," William avowed, joining his young

lord. "What would happen in true battle if they all hared off like that?"

Muffled laughter emerged through the slits in Henry's gleaming new helm. "I've heard tales about you at Drincourt where you pushed forward with no thought for the outcome."

"It was my first battle and I was green," William retorted.

Henry leaned over to slap him on the shoulder. "You're being an old woman again," he teased. "If you're going to lecture them, we've to catch them first, and likely we'll catch a few Frenchman along the way too!" He spurred his stallion in the direction that the others had taken.

William and the Young King rode into the town of Anet and clopped their way downhill towards the centre. As they rode, William hunted in his saddlebag and brought out the goose and bread. Henry lifted his wine costrel off the saddle bow and he and William removed their helms and bolted their food and drink in companionable haste. Henry washed down a mouthful of goose with a swig of wine. "I love this life." He wiped his lips on the cuff of his gambeson, his eyes alight with pleasure.

William nodded vigorous agreement, for he loved it too: it was something that he and the Young King had in common. Troubadours sang of the joy of the breaking of lances on a fine spring morning, the boldness running as red as blood through men's veins, the hungry elation and desire for glory, and it was all true. Come cold rain, a lame horse, rusting armour, and a bad day at the tilt, a knight might wish to wring said troubadour's neck, but not now, not when one was living the song.

The main street was empty of combatants but the townsfolk were standing at their balconies and spinning galleries, hoping to see some activity. A few brave souls stood at the roadside, including a wine seller who had set up a trestle of jugs to take advantage of the thirsty knights. A gang of little boys were daring each other to dance in the roadway and then leap clear at the last moment.

"Which way?" William asked a freckled urchin, thumbing him an Angevin penny and a piece of the loaf from his meal. The child's eyes rounded at such largesse and he pointed down a street leading off to the right. "The knights went down there," he said. Keeping his fist tight around the precious coin, he bit into the bread and worried the crust like a dog.

Replacing their helms, William and Henry urged their destriers down the road the boy had indicated, but found their way blocked by a lord named Simon de Neauphle and a troop of footsoldiers brandishing fearsome glaives and spears. Henry swore under his breath and reined in so hard that his stallion leaned on its haunches. "What now?" he asked William, some of his confidence evaporating. "We won't be able to go through them, but we can't go back." He half turned in the saddle to gesture at their difficult retreat.

William studied de Neauphle's men through the eye slits in his helm. "They won't hold their ground if we charge," he said. "It's not true battle where it's our lives or theirs. Whatever he's paying them, it's not worth standing in the path of a pair of galloping stallions. De Neauphle doesn't have space to make a counter-charge. They won't defend him…trust me."

Henry made a noise within his helm that sounded like reluctant laughter. "I always have," he said. "Don't let me down now."

"Never," William said. "Remember, posture and attitude is more than half the battle. Those footsoldiers are seeing two knights on fledged warhorses. They are seeing iron-shod hooves that can shatter a limb with a single kick. They are seeing mail which cannot be easily pierced and facing the blankness of our helms while we are watching their fear."

Henry nodded, absorbing the lesson. "And what are we seeing?"

"Sheep," William replied with a low chuckle. "Panic one and the entire flock will run."

As one, they levelled their lances, tucked in their shields, and spurred their mounts. The horses' shoes struck sparks on the street cobbles; the silk barding of the destriers rippled as they galloped. William fixed his gaze on Simon de Neauphle who was roaring commands at his men to stand firm, but William knew they wouldn't. The majority were hirelings with no history of loyalty to glue them in place and withstand the power of two charging warhorses. Between one hard stride of his destrier and another, the nerve of the footsoldiers broke and they scattered like chaff on the wind. William nudged his bay with his thigh, turning a fraction so that he was able to seize de Neauphle's bridle and hold him fast.

"Marshal, you bastard, let go!" De Neauphle was wearing an open-faced helm and his brown eyes were ablaze with chagrin and fury.

"Gladly, if you yield me your pledge of ransom," William answered and laughed as de Neauphle let fly with several expletives aimed at his captor's ancestry. Henry following, William led his quarry down a narrow side street with low-hanging gutters, his destination a livery stable which had been designated one of the rallying points of the tourney. Captured knights were brought to make their pledges and combatants could take a rest, mend equipment, or change horses as their needs dictated. In the confines of the street, their horses' hooves raised an echoing clatter and the light was so poor that William's vision was reduced to a murky slit. De Neauphle ceased swearing and fell silent but this was compensated for by Henry who was singing loudly and somewhat tunelessly to himself.

At the livery stable, William dismounted and as he unlaced his helm, commanded one of Henry's waiting squires to take the captive knight into custody. "What knight?" Henry asked before the bewildered squire could speak. He had removed his own helm and set it before him on the pommel. His eyes were sparkling and his shoulders were shaking. "Certainly you have custody of the horse and its harness, but you seem to have lost your captive."

William slewed round and, now that he had full vision, stared at the empty saddle in astonishment. He handed his helm to the squire and untied his arming cap. "Where's de Neauphle?" he demanded.

Turning in the saddle, Henry pointed back the way they had come. "He took advantage of one of those gutters—swung up on to it without you seeing. Christ, it was funny." The mirth that he had been struggling to contain burst out of him and he bowed over his saddle, incapacitated by laughter.

Scowling, William strode back up the street. Simon de Neauphle was no longer hanging off a gutter, but capering on the walk of the spinning gallery belonging to the same house. A shocked matron was standing near him, clutching her distaff to her bosom as if it were a talisman against rape.

"I claim sanctuary, Marshal!" de Neauphle cried, showing William a taunting forefinger. "You enter this house and the good dame here will beat you to a pulp with her distaff!"

Hands on hips, William stared up at his escaped quarry. "Well, she couldn't be any worse at defending you than your men!" he retorted, and began to laugh himself as the humour in the situation overrode his annoyance at losing his quarry. "Enjoy your nuptials." He flourished a bow. "I'd serenade you, but I've a fine warhorse and harness to stow."

Predictably, de Neauphle dropped his braies and waggled his buttocks at William, who threw up his hands and returned to the stables to find Henry still convulsed. "If you had seen him, Marshal!" he spluttered. "What a trick, what a trick!"

William wasn't so sure the incident had been that sidesplitting, but he had the grace to laugh at himself and the good nature to enter into the spirit of the jest. Henry harped on about the matter to all who would listen and by the time they arrived back at the tourney field there was scarcely a contestant who had not heard the tale of de Neauphle's escape literally behind William's back. William endured the joshing and back-slapping and consoled himself with the knowledge that he had the ransom money due from de Neauphle's Lombard destrier and its fine Spanish harness. He was further mollified when a grinning, excited Wigain dropped a weighty pouch of silver into his cupped palm—profits from wagers won on the success of Henry's mesnie.

The great lords hosted feasts in their tents, vying to outdo each other in extravagance and largesse, offering the strongest wine, the whitest bread served on silver dishes, the most skilled tumblers, the most amusing jester, the best troubadour. The townspeople and farmers playing host to this vast locust plague prayed to be reimbursed for the supplies consumed and the crops trampled in the course of the contest. The presence of a tourney crowd was always enlivening and exciting, creating a spectacle amidst a fairground atmosphere, but although the silence was resounding when it moved on, the peace was a relief, especially to the older members of the community. Silly, smitten girls and young lads with the shine of armour in their dreams took longer to fall back into the monotonous daily routine.

The tally of injuries to Henry's mesnie included cracked ribs, broken fingers, and a dislocated shoulder, but nothing too serious, and the celebrations continued long into the night. William drank, but not to excess, and kept an eye on the men. There was to be more sport on the morrow and the winners would be those who were able to rise in the morning without heads as thick as thunderclouds.

Queen Marguerite appeared with her ladies and briefly joined her husband for the early courses of the feast. He regaled her with tales of the day's doings, and the story of William's escapee was repeated yet again. Marguerite laughed dutifully, but the laughter scarcely reached her eyes, which were shadowed with fatigue.

"Are you unwell, madam?" William enquired with concern, for she was as pale as a shroud.

She dabbed her lips with her napkin. "Just tired," she said, "but I thank you for asking, messire."

"You should eat a sliver of loaf sugar," William said. "I always do when I run out of strength."

"You do?" Her eyes lit with a moment of genuine warmth. "Do you remember when I gave you that piece at Chinon?" She leaned a little towards him, her gaze eager.

"Indeed, madam, I do. It was the best gift I have ever received, and I am not teasing you. Boiled sugar truly does lift your spirits if you are flagging."

"Then I will have some brought to my chamber. I wish..." She started to speak and then changed her mind.

"William, stop making love to my wife and tell my lord of Flanders about de Neauphle's escape!" Henry gave William an impatient nudge.

Marguerite flushed at her husband's words, but William read nothing more into them than Henry's impatient desire to have his captain's attention directed towards discussing the tourney rather than making small talk with a woman.

"I would rather talk to a beautiful lady than tell tales about de Neauphle's acrobatics," he retorted, but nevertheless obliged the impatient Young King with a repeat of the story. Marguerite begged leave to retire with her women, pleading the fatigue of her pregnancy. Henry managed to be solicitous to her for a moment, escorting her out, holding her hand, and kissing her temple, but he was obviously relieved to see her depart, and returned to the gathering, rubbing his hands and exhaling with anticipation. "Wigain says there's a pair of eastern dancing girls doing the rounds of the lodgings.

Rubies in their navels, so I'm told. Now the women have gone, I'll have them sent for."

William raised his brows. At least, he thought, Henry had waited until his wife had retired. He supposed that not every lord would have done so.

It was well past midnight before William finally made his way to his pavilion, his footsteps still reasonably steady. He had enjoyed watching the dancing girls perform, and they had indeed had jewels in some interesting places. One boasted a ruby, the other a pearl. Someone said that the latter was a symbol of her virginity. William doubted that any girl who was prepared to dance on a table clad in exotic nothings still had her pearl to give, but it was an entertaining fantasy—even if it would have to be admitted next time he sought the grace of confession.

Rhys was waiting outside his tent mending a piece of harness, but jumped to his feet when William arrived. "Sir, you have a visitor," he said.

"At this time of night?" William cast his glance towards the closed tent flaps. "Who is it?" Notions of a few decent hours of sleep fled.

"It is a lady, sir. She said she knew you and that you would not refuse to see her."

William looked severely at the Welshman. "If you have allowed a camp whore into my tent, I'll have you picking rust off hauberk rivets with your fingernails for a sennight. Did she give her name?"

"No, sir, but she said she was an old friend."

Mystified, William parted the flap and stepped inside his tent. Seated on the folding stool at his bedside, hands clasped in her lap, was a young woman of about his own age. She was wearing a cloak of good wool, although it had been patched near the hem, and her hair was properly concealed beneath a veil of fine, bleached linen. William stared. In the years since he had been a hostage to the de Lusignan brothers, he had had his share of dealings with women, most of them fleeting due to the peripatetic nature of the Young King's household and his own decision not to add the complication of a woman to his baggage train. Names, faces had blended into each other, but he had never forgotten the woman sitting before him. Her face was thinner, her bones more defined, but the wide dark eyes were the same, and the straight, fine nose. What she was doing in his tent without an attendant for decency's sake and at midnight was a mystery.

"Lady Clara," he said, and bowed.

She rose and came to him, a smile on her lips, but her eyes filled with caution. "You remembered my name," she said. "I did not know if you would."

He kissed her hand in formal greeting. "It is not so much a case of remembering, as never forgetting, my lady," he murmured. "Has my attendant offered you wine?"

She shook her head. "No, but do not rebuke him. I gained the impression that he was risking his life by allowing me to wait in your tent."

"He was indeed," William said. "You would not guess the number of subterfuges that some of the camp women perpetrate, and Rhys knows that my bed is usually a solitary one."

She lowered her lids and the light from the hanging lamp in the tent roof made fan shadows of her lashes. "I would not have to guess," she murmured, "because I am one of them."

William went to the pitcher standing on his coffer and poured wine into the cup standing beside it, making time to compose himself. One-handed, he unfolded a second stool for himself, and gesturing her to be reseated, gave her the cup.

"None for yourself?" she asked.

William shook his head. "I need a clear head for the

morrow," he said, "and perhaps for now as well. What do you mean, you are one of them?"

Her mouth twisted. "I am a whore...one of the women of the camp. You can put finer words on it—say that I am a courtesan and a concubine, but it amounts to the same thing. I belong to any man who has my price, and providing he pays it, I will do all that he asks." She took a sip of the wine.

Her words sent an involuntary shock down William's spine and into his loins. "How did you come to such a pass?" He leaned forward on the stool. "When last I saw you, you were lady of a castle." Looking closer he saw that the discoloration on one cheek he had taken for shadow and rouge was actually a bruise. He thought of the argument he and Henry had overheard earlier in the day as they walked through the camp, and wondered.

She gave a bitter laugh. "When last you saw me I was Amalric's mistress, not his wife—a concubine. My mother was the youngest daughter of a knight and my father a passing troubadour who duped her into lying with him. I was always going to be either a lady's maid, a whore, or a nun. I started off as the first, became the second when Amalric took me out of the bower for his own use, and some day, who knows, perhaps I'll repent and take my vows."

William's eyelids tensed as he thought of his brother and Alais. The stories ran parallel, save that Alais had the security of a roof over her head and had borne John a son upon whom his brother clearly doted.

"Amalric was killed in a skirmish with the troops of Guillaume de Tancarville," she continued, "and the keep was seized. I gathered what I could, saddled up Amalric's palfrey, and fled to the tourneys. I've been following them for four years now, finding 'protectors' when I have been able."

"That is a sorry tale, my lady."

She shrugged. "I do not need your pity. I live from day to day and thus far I have survived."

The defiant gleam in her eyes reminded William strongly of Queen Eleanor. He inclined his head, acknowledging her ability and her pride. "But at what cost?" he said. "Your face does not tell a fortunate story just now."

She touched her bruised cheek. "Some men are worthless," she said, "and some are without price." Her voice dropped a notch, becoming husky. "I was hoping when I saw you arrive with the Young King that you were of the second sort. You said when I gave you bandages for your leg that you would not forget the debt owing."

"Nor have I, my lady." He opened his hand towards her. "What I have is yours."

"Then would you give me your protection for as long as I have need?"

Several thoughts flew through William's mind, some noble, some considerably less so. "What kind of protection?" he asked when he was certain of his voice. "Shall I ask the Young Queen to give you a position in her household? Do you need money?"

Rising to her feet, she unclasped the pin holding her cloak together and cast the garment across the stool. Beneath it, she was wearing the tightly laced gown of yellow silk he remembered from years ago with sleeves almost to the floor and a belt stitched with pearls and jet. "They say you are the best knight on the tourney circuit."

William shrugged. "There is always talk on the tourney field," he said. "It's entertaining, but you shouldn't set store by it."

"I don't. I listen and make my own judgements." She swept him a look through her lashes. "Money is always useful. I doubt that the Young Queen would take me into her household—a Poitevan whore with a reputation longer than her sleeves."

"I could send you to my brother in England," William said.

"He is unwed, but he dwells with a mistress and they have an infant son…"

Clara shook her head. "Even if his woman is a saint, she would see me as a rival, and besides, I have no desire to set foot on a ship—ever." She tilted her head to one side. "I could stay with you. There are advantages to not having your servant throw me out."

William had often been propositioned and usually deflected the women with courtesy. Until now he had not been tempted beyond his ability to resist. "I would not delegate such a task to Rhys in this situation, but I do not see what gain there is to you." He stood up, not sure if he was going to see her from the tent or prevent her from leaving.

"Then either you are modest, ignorant, or fishing for compliments." She moved up to him, into the space where he seldom allowed anyone to stand. "What woman would not want the protection of a knight of your prowess? What woman would not desire such a man?" She took his hands and set them at her waist, holding them there, her palms to his knuckles. "If the man desires her, of course," she added in a voice smoky with lust.

"A man in my position cannot afford a mistress," he said, but his hands stayed at her waist, feeling flesh and bone sharpened by an edge of hunger, the delicate ridges of her rib cage, the flat, taut belly.

"I spoke of desiring, not affording," she said. "Think of all the things a mistress can do for you that a servant cannot." She set one arm around his neck and kissed him. It was the kiss of a woman experienced in the seductive arts, her body warm with the southern blood of the troubadours. Her other hand left his at her waist and moved down between them to stroke with spine-tingling skill.

The sensations almost undid him, because no woman had

ever done that to him before, or not with such boldness and knowing. He hissed through his teeth and his hand tightened involuntarily at her waist. She licked his throat and nipped his earlobe. "I can show you ways of pleasuring that will drive you out of your senses," she murmured. Her right hand slipped into his hose, found the leg of his braies and worked upwards. "Jesu!" Her breathing caught on laughter and greed. "The tourney field isn't the only place that you carry a fine straight lance, is it?"

That should have been the moment to stop. Had William been completely sober and his lust not already honed by the performance of the eastern dancing girls, he might have found the strength to give her his pallet for the night and step outside to slumber by the camp fire. But she was dark-eyed, warm, and pliant in his arms, as a young Queen Eleanor of Aquitaine might have been, and her touch was intoxicating. His resistance fell before her onslaught. He set reason aside and let his body take command, although in truth it was she who had the mastery.

Lightly, Clara touched William's naked thigh. "You still bear the scar," she murmured, her lips following the gentle feather of her fingertips.

"I will have it until my dying day," he said, squinting down his body to the dark spread of her hair. "Without your succour that day would have come and gone. I will never forget that kindness."

She gave a breathy chuckle and her lips nipped higher up his thigh. "It was more than kindness," she said. "It was selfishness too, and defiance. Amalric had warned me to leave well alone, so what was I to do except meddle? Even then, sore wounded and mired as you were, I could see your potential." She raised her head and her eyes were those of a night-hunting cat. "Are you going to let me stay?"

William hesitated. A short while ago he had been ensnared by the pure, white heat of lust. That tension was gone now, although what Clara was doing was rapidly rekindling it. Wisdom said he should treat this encounter as no more than a casual meeting. That he should give her funds to help her on her way, and when he left the tourney ground, not look back. Usually he would listen to that inner voice, but something else had stirred in him tonight. Perhaps it was her feline manner, which reminded him of Eleanor; perhaps it was the knowledge that she owned an indelible part of his past and that what she had done for him then deserved more than an embarrassed handful of silver as he rode away.

"I won't demand more of you than you can give," she said, as if reading his doubts.

He dropped his hand to her hair. It was silky under his calloused touch and as cool as cat's fur. "And what if all I can give you is a pittance?" he asked. "What if I say that you will be little less impoverished on your own?"

"Then a pittance will suffice, and I know that you are wrong about the impoverishment." She sat up, straddling him. "You will not regret this, I swear you will not."

It was a long time since he had lain with a woman and his body responded to the position of hers and what she was doing. "Then stay," he heard himself say.

She arched as she sheathed him, and leaned over to kiss his mouth. "How much do you know about courtly love?" she asked against his lips. "Shall I show you how to gain your lady's favour?"

Later, fine-dewed with sweat, William collapsed upon his pallet, gulping for breath. Every fibre of his being felt as if it had been compacted on to the point of an arrow and fired with violence from his loins. A wanton, beatific smile on her face,

Clara watched him through eyes hazy with satisfaction. "You see," she purred.

William nodded, too spent to talk. He did see, and knew that he was a novice in the hands of an expert. He had heard hints concerning the rites of *amour courtois* of which the songs and poetry of the Southern troubadours were the outer circle. He knew the conventions by which a man should strive to be worthy of his lady love and seek no reward but a momentary glance and perhaps a smile. Queen Eleanor had played such games with him and in his turn he had played them gently with Marguerite and her women. But there were inner rings to the circle, where the tokens and the flirting led to the bedchamber, and within that secret red heart, it was still the role of the knight to please his lady and withhold his own pleasure if it be her whim. It was not enough to have control of one's body on the tourney ground. The field of love called for endurance, restraint, and stamina; but there had to be passion too. Clara had taken her pleasure again and again and again, holding him on a fine edge. He could have yielded to temptation, held her down, and surged to his release, but pride and will and a determination to succeed had reined him back.

He gave a weak chuckle and looked at her in the light of the guttering night candle. "I am supposed to lead the Young King's mesnie to victory on the tourney field on the morrow," he said. "How am I to do that when I feel as if all the marrow has been sucked from my bones?"

Clara licked her lips and widened her eyes in mock innocence. "I haven't been anywhere near your bones," she said.

William spluttered. She was incorrigible.

"You will manage." She yawned delicately like a cat. "After all, you are only playing at war. You might have to plan a strategy, you might have to fight hard, but at the end of the day, you can shed your mail, eat a decent meal, and sleep in a feather bed with no greater concern than a favourite horse you might have lost, or when the next tourney is going to be held."

William's mouth tightened. "I have fought in wars," he said defensively. "I know the difference."

"So do I." The look of hazy pleasure left her eyes. She turned over and moved a little away from him, curling on her side, knees drawn up, and fists gathered beneath her chin.

William lay in silence, adjusting himself to her presence. His body was heavy with lassitude, his thoughts made slow and winding by the need for sleep. He eased over on the pallet to set his arm at her waist and kiss her throat beneath her hair. "It is a game, but all games are practice for the business of living...and living itself is also a game with harsh rules."

"But you are a winner," she said. "And I am tired of losing." She turned into his arms and he folded them around her.

The sleep that he courted remained out of reach and as the dawn birdsong began to flute and cool grey light filtered into the tent, William pressed her waist, eased himself from his pallet, quietly dressed, and went outside. Rhys and his squire, Eustace, were building the fire and the former had been into the town to fetch fresh bread. William tore a hunk off a loaf still hot in the centre, and took the cup of wine that Eustace gave him. The youth kept his gaze studiously lowered whilst Rhys bestowed William a knowing look.

"Lady Clara will be travelling with us for a while," William told them. "You should know that I owe her a debt of kindness, and that I expect her to be treated with the same respect you afford Queen Marguerite and her ladies. Nor do I want to find you gossiping about her to the likes of Wigain. Her honour is mine."

"Yes, sir," Eustace mumbled, red to the ears.

An experienced married man, Rhys was less embarrassed.

"I was right to let her wait in your tent last night then?" he asked.

William laughed darkly, and toasted the Welshman. "I don't know about that."

Twelve

SEATED IN THE WINDOW OF THE LODGING HOUSE THAT William had rented, Clara held up the small hand mirror of grozed glass in its silver case and studied her reflection from various angles, inspecting her face and clothing to satisfy herself that all was in order. The town of Pleurs was playing host to a grand tourney and she was here with William and Roger de Gaugi who were fighting on their own behalf, although under the Young King's banner. The latter had remained in Paris, awaiting Marguerite's imminent confinement, but had exhorted his knights to break as many lances on his behalf as they could.

Adorned in a gown of blue silk trimmed with pearls, silver stars stitched on her gauze veil and wound through her plaited hair, Clara had gone to watch the opening bouts of the day's sport. The prowess of William and Roger on the field had bolstered her pride and given her a sense of her own worth as the mistress of the greatest knight on the field. For a time she had followed their activity across the wide tourney ground, watching them win every engagement. Finally, as they ranged out of sight, she had repaired to their dwelling in the town to wait.

Tonight, the great lords who were the patrons of the tourneys would open their houses and throughout the evening the knights and their ladies would drift from one to the other like moths in search of nectar. As two of its most successful and attractive knights, William and Roger were in high demand and would be plied at each lodging with food and wine and rich gifts. Clara enjoyed basking in the reflected glory. William always introduced her as a highborn Poitevan lady, which amused her greatly.

She had been his mistress for three months now—a position she found both satisfactory and frustrating. His manners were impeccable and he treated her with deference and respect. Although a fierce competitor on the tourney field and assertive as a courtier, he was a considerate, restrained lover. When she had shown him wildness, she had sensed his shock, although he had adapted swiftly enough and she still tingled when she thought of a certain night under the stars somewhere in the County of Eu. The shattering of lances on the tourney ground had been as nothing compared to the impact of their pleasure on William's rope-framed camp bed. But for all he gave her, she was greedy for more, and the hungrier she grew, the more reluctant he became. There was a well of reserve in him that she could not win past. On the few occasions she had pushed him in an attempt to wring a response, she had received either courteous platitude or silence. Following her tirades, he would invariably perform like a demon upon the tourney field. Clara had begun to think that the latter was where he exorcised all his anger and frustration, channelling it into clean, physical activity.

Seeing several dusty, weary knights and squires clopping up the road towards their lodgings, Clara surmised that the tourney had ended. In anticipation of William's arrival, she abandoned her grooming, prepared him a bath, and set out meat, bread, fruit, and wine, knowing that he would have the appetite of a bear when he returned. Likely, he would smell like one too, hence the bath.

The water in the tub began to cool and Clara sighed, suspecting that William had lingered to talk with other contestants or else was about the matter of arranging ransom money from those he had taken captive. She had such faith in him it didn't occur to her to think that William himself had been taken for ransom. Looking impatiently out of the window, she saw two knights and a squire approaching the lodging on foot. The squire was carrying a large salver draped with an embroidered cloth. Mystified, suddenly anxious, Clara hastened down to them.

"We are seeking Sir William Marshal, my lady." A dark-haired knight bowed as Clara opened the door. "Is he here?"

She shook her head. "He has not yet returned from the tourney." She glanced towards the cloth. The second knight leaned across the squire to twitch the linen aside and reveal an enormous pike with scales of iridescent silver tabby. It lay upon a bed of herbs and salad leaves, the latter a little wilted. The fish itself still looked fresh though.

"The Countess of Champagne sends this pike to Sir William in honour of his prestige in the tourney," the knight said.

"Is he not still at the field?" Clara looked at them askance.

"No, my lady, he is not."

Clara gnawed her lip. "I cannot help you, except to offer to take the pike and…" She paused and raised her head as Rhys clattered into the yard, William's sweat-caked destrier on a lead rein. Gathering her skirts, she ran to him. "Rhys, where's your lord?"

The Welshman dismounted and unclipped the lead rein. "At the forge, my lady, by the town gate," he said. "His helm took some hard blows and he can't get it off. He sent me to bring his horse back to the stables and to tell you that he will come as soon as he can."

Relief and apprehension coursed through her. If he had taken blows sufficient to crumple his helm, then he could be injured or concussed. Her fear must have shown on her face, for Rhys gave a reassuring grin. "He's sore discomfited," the servant said, "but otherwise unharmed."

Clara shook her head. "I need to see for myself." She turned to the waiting knights and squire with their gift. "Do you want to leave that here?"

The knight who had spoken earlier declined her offer, laughter brimming in his eyes. "No, my lady, my instructions were to present it to him in person and I would not miss the sight of William Marshal with his head on an anvil for anything!"

Hands on hips, brawny features soot-smudged, the blacksmith studied William and sucked a considering breath between his teeth. "There's no rescuing this one from the scrap heap," he announced. "Fact is, I don't even know how I am going to get you out of it with your head intact. I'm neither a chirurgeon nor a midwife."

"Just do your best," William said in a muffled voice. "I don't expect you to be a chirurgeon or a midwife, just a good blacksmith." The tourney field had been full of knights determined to make their mark and the sport had been fast and very aggressive. William hadn't found it difficult to raise his game up to and beyond the new level; indeed he had enjoyed the challenge, but he was paying for it now. The blows he had received had dented his helm so badly that it had become impossible to remove. He could breathe well enough but he couldn't see and there was no way on God's earth that the opening of the helm could accommodate the diameters of his skull.

Muttering to himself the smith set out with hammers, wrenches, and pincers to ease the opening sufficiently for it to clear William's head. The angle at which William had to lay his head on the anvil was distinctly uncomfortable and the muscles in his neck and shoulders were on fire. The smell of sweated iron was metallic and unpleasant. He had often jokingly referred to his helm as a "cooking pot" but it didn't seem quite so amusing now when he was at the mercy of the blacksmith's skill. Twice the smith asked William to try and ease off the helm and twice the attempt failed, the second time almost ripping off William's ears.

"Nearly," panted the smith and told his apprentice to smear goose grease all around the battered rim of the helm. A few more wrenches, some more grunting and swearing, and at the third try, the helm finally yielded to coaxing and brutality. With gritted teeth, a grazed cranium, and very sore ears, a scarlet-faced William was at last able to take a gulp of fresh air. The mangled wreck of his helm did indeed resemble a cooking pot, but one that had been trampled by an ox. The smith was mopping his brow on a grubby square of linen. "Worst I've seen," he declared. He held out his hands which had been steady while he worked, but were now trembling.

William praised his work fulsomely and promised a rich payment in silver. Looking further, he discovered that he had an audience—not just casual bystanders diverted by the spectacle, but two knights and a squire from the retinue of the Countess of Champagne, and Clara, her expression a mingling of consternation and laughter. The squire, who was more than anxious to be rid of the burden which he had now been carrying around for the best part of two hours, stepped up to William and bowed.

"What's this?" Lifting the cloth, William eyed the great gleaming pike. It eyed him back.

"The prize for the most worthy knight in the tourney," said one of the knights, adding drily, "To judge by the remains of your helm, the Countess has made the right decision to bestow the award on you. The wonder is that you are still in a fit state to accept it."

William laughed. "I was beginning to think I'd be wearing that pot for the rest of my life. Certainly I would not have been able to do justice to this magnificent fish." Actually, William wasn't fond of pike, but was too diplomatic to say so, and anyway, it was the symbolism that mattered; he had been deemed deserving of the prize. Besides, once it was cooked and shared around, he need eat no more than a morsel to be polite. "Tell the Countess that I thank her for this gift," he said. "It is generous of her, as is her judgement."

"You could have been killed," Clara said much later. In the small hours of the morning, the street was finally silent, the last carousers having tottered back to their lodgings. The pike had been steamed in a bath of herbs and almond milk, which had imparted a delicate flavour to the flesh, and all that remained were the head and the bones, now confined to the midden bucket.

William watched her lazily from the bed as she removed her belt and gown. Clad in shirt and chausses, his tunic discarded, he was lying on his stomach, his head pillowed on his bent forearms. There were red chaff marks on his throat, evidence of his earlier encounter with the now defunct helm. "There is always 'could have,'" he said. "When I was five years old I was within a few words of being hanged from a gibbet. At Drincourt I had a lucky escape from a thatch gaff." His voice softened. "I could have died of my wounds when my uncle Patrick was murdered, had you not come to my aid. All I have instead is the scar."

Clara smiled, although the expression did not reach her eyes. "We all have scars," she said as she lay down beside him in her chemise.

Taking her hand, he kissed the tips of her fingers. His lips brushed softly over her palm. He grazed his teeth along the inside of her wrist until she shivered, and then kissed his way up to her throat and mounted her.

"Oh William," she whispered and it was as if there was a great hollow inside her, empty and brimming over at the same time. No matter how many times she said his name, or took him into her body, the hollow remained, and grew.

Their lovemaking was wild and sweet, and when they were finished and there was silence, William listened to the liquid notes of a nightingale torrenting the darkness outside the window. "Count Theobald offered me lands if I would agree to go and fight for him," he said after a while.

"What did you answer?" She lay against him, her appetite sated but not satisfied. His arm remained around her and he tenderly stroked her hair. He had fine bedchamber etiquette; he knew the courtesies.

"That his offer was generous and that I was tempted, but that I already had a lord and my loyalty was to him."

"And were you tempted—truly, or were you just being courteous?"

"No, I was attracted by his offer," William admitted. "To have one's own domain is the stuff of dreams to a landless man and Theobald of Blois would be a good lord to serve, but my family is beholden to the house of Anjou. I promised Queen Eleanor that I would do my best for young Henry—and for all his flaws, I love him."

"He may be your King, but you are his master and his mentor in chivalry," Clara said softly. "Perhaps you love him because he is dependent on you in a way that Theobald of Blois will never be. Henry rules you, but in your turn, you rule him."

Her assessment was sufficiently astute to make him shrug uncomfortably.

"His wife is fond of you too," she said, plucking at his chest hair. "The moment she sees you, her face lights up and she makes excuses to touch you."

William laughed and shook his head in denial. "I have known her since she was a child. It is the fondness of familiarity and friendship. I have great affection for her too, but not in the way that a man loves a woman."

Clara was not so sure, but she held her tongue. She thought that William probably wanted to see Marguerite in terms of a child and an old friend, but that the reality was more subtle and therefore dangerous. And she knew enough about the looks that women gave to men to know that William was definitely wrong about the Young Queen's feelings.

"God's bones, how long does it take for a baby to be born?" demanded Henry, collecting a lance and preparing to charge at the quintain. Earlier in the day he had been pacing the rooms of the French royal palace, but the walls had grown too small to contain his agitation and he had repaired outside to the tilting ground.

"Several days for a first one, so I understand," William said. The midwives had already told Henry that, but the information appeared to have gone in one ear and out of the other.

Henry thundered down the tilt and struck the target a resounding blow. "It's been two," he said, trotting back to William. "And weeks before that shut up in confinement with her women and gossips. Christ, I'll be glad when this whole palaver is over."

William levelled his lance and fretted his stallion. "I imagine that the Queen will be glad too." He took his own turn at the quintain, striking the shield with the smooth grace of instinct and long training. He had visited Marguerite on several occasions in the chamber where she had retired to spend the final month of her pregnancy. The room had been pungent with the smell of herbs and unguents; the atmosphere enclosed and anticipatory, as if the room itself were a large womb. Marguerite had appeared content enough on the surface, but he had seen the fear in her wide brown eyes as he took his leave after an evening in her company two days before the birth pangs began. He had carried that image with him ever since. She was trapped; she couldn't take her leave. No one said that she was the daughter of a mother who had died giving birth, but everyone had been thinking it.

The men were leaving the field when a herald came running towards them, waving his arms. "Sire, my lord, the Queen is delivered of a son!" he cried, his face shining with the joy of the news he carried.

Henry shouted a thank you to God and whirled to William, grey eyes fierce with triumph. "Do you hear that, Marshal? A son! I have a son!" He fisted William's arm hard enough to bruise, even through gambeson and tunic.

"That is great news, my lord!" William fisted him back, although without quite as much force. "How is the Queen?" he enquired of the messenger.

"The women say very tired but joyful, sir."

"I must see him!" Henry's expression was incandescent as he spurred for the stables, pulling up in the yard so fast that the horse skidded on its haunches. Flinging from its back, he ran into the palace. William followed at a more sedate pace, a burden lifting from his mind. Marguerite had survived the ordeal and the sight of his young lord's energy and eagerness gave him hope that everything might yet turn out for the best.

"The heir to England and Normandy now has an heir of his own," said Baldwin de Béthune, riding up beside William, his lips parted in a white grin. "That'll change him."

William smiled agreement. He had seen the difference the birth of little Jack had made to his brother...a difference that perhaps he would never know and, through his pleasure, he felt a twinge of regret.

Marguerite gazed at the baby sleeping in her arms. He had been tightly bound in swaddling so that he resembled a little parcelled-up fly in a spider's larder. His eyes were closed and the tiny lashes glittered as if dusted with gold. Delicate blue shadows lay beneath them and his skin had the pale hue of lavender flowers. His breathing was so silent that she could hardly hear it, or feel it confined within the shroud-like layers of swaddling.

"William," she whispered his name to herself and the speaking of it warmed the cold place in her heart. He had been named for his three times great-grandfather, the Norman duke who had conquered England, and for Henry's small brother who had died whilst still an infant and who would have been the "Young King" had he lived. But there was another named William in their lives too, whose presence perhaps mattered more.

She thought of the joy on her husband's face as he entered the birthing chamber, his pride as he held his newborn son, and the way that he had shown the child to all in the room in the same way that he would enthuse over a new piece of harness or jousting equipment. It was the first time in their marriage that he had shown such a spark when it had a direct connection to her. It had made her feel sad and overwhelmed with happiness at the same time. The new Prince had been taken from the room and briefly shown to the other members of their household. She had wanted to ask Henry what William Marshal had thought, but she had been asleep when Henry returned the baby and he had not stayed, but departed to celebrate the birth of his heir with his mesnie. She fancied that if she strained her ears she would hear them in the hall, raising toasts, celebrating her achievement by fêting Henry for all he was worth.

With a soft rustle of movement a midwife parted the half-closed bed curtains. The wet nurse who had been engaged to suckle the baby stood a little behind her. "Is our princeling ready for a feed yet?" The midwife held out her arms for the baby. "He should be by now."

Awkwardly, Marguerite gathered his little body and handed him to the midwife, who cradled him gently across to the wet nurse. The women exchanged glances. "What is it, what's wrong?" Alarmed, Marguerite pulled herself upright on the bolsters and felt the hot trickle of blood between her thighs. "Please…"

"Nothing, madam, calm yourself, nothing is wrong. Your son is just tired after his hard passage into the world. Come now."

A second midwife arrived to tend to her. The blood-soaked cloths between her legs were checked and changed. The woman gave her a bitter-tasting potion to drink and plumped the pillows. Beyond the curtains she heard the rapid whispering of the women like leaves chased before a storm. She knew that something was amiss and struggled to rise from the bed, but exhaustion and loss of blood made her weak and when she set her foot on the floor there was no strength in her limbs and she collapsed. Her women came running and, with cries of consternation, put her back to bed.

"My son," she wept, "where is my son?"

"Hush now, madam, hush now. Do not trouble yourself. He is in good hands." Cool fingers stroked her brow and the soporific they had given her made her lids heavy. She fought sleep, but it came anyway on rolling dark waves. The last she heard was the soothing murmur of her women, soft but treacherous as the sea, and not a single gull-like mew of a newborn infant. As she sank fathoms deep into slumber, forced beneath the waves like a broken ship, her son breathed softly once, twice, and with a gentle shudder in the nurse's arms, died.

❖ ❖ ❖

The younger knights were indulging in a drinking game that involved reciting a poem without forgetting the words and adding a new verse before downing a goblet of wine. William had declined to join in and was discussing tourney tactics with Baldwin and Roger de Gaugi when he glanced up and saw one of Marguerite's midwives talking to Henry's steward and wringing her hands. The steward glanced in Henry's direction and, even from a distance, William could tell from his expression that the news was dire. He watched him clench his fists, straighten his spine, steel himself while the midwife crept back up the stairs, her harbingering complete.

William swallowed his wine in a single fierce gulp and braced his own shoulders, knowing that strength on the tourney field was as nothing compared to the strength he was going to need now. He wondered which one it was, Marguerite or the baby.

Henry banged a dripping goblet on to the board in front of William. "Your turn," he declared, spreading his free arm wide. "Don't spoil the sport…have to do it once, I command it…" His voice slurred at the edges.

"Sire…"

The steward reached them, stooped, and murmured in the Young King's ear. Henry's smile levelled, faded and beneath the tan of a summer spent in the saddle, his complexion was suddenly the colour of ashes. His throat worked. "No," he said.

"My lord King…"

"No!" He would have struck the steward in the face with his clenched fist but William was there first, capturing the descending arm, bearing it down while the ghost-faced servant took a step back.

"He's a stinking liar. It's not true!" Henry wrestled against William's restraining arm. Full of denial and rage the grey eyes blazed into William's and William held on hard, for love, for pity, for the tragic truth ripping through the shield of that denial. A ragged silence had begun to fall; men were staring, lowering cups. William felt Henry's shudder enter his own body as the young man turned from flesh to stone in his arms...and ceased fighting. Stiff as an effigy on a tomb, the Young King pushed William away and, using his entire body as if his individual limbs had fused together, turned to the steward.

"I will see him," he said, his jaw barely moving to enunciate the word and the tendons in his throat like hawsers. "Marshal...Marshal, come with me."

It was the child then, William thought as he followed Henry away from the dais table to the stairs. He thought of the fragile skull he had briefly cradled in his palm, the smallness and vulnerability of the newborn infant.

Men bowed as the Young King passed. The silence had only extended as far as the folk on the dais and a low babble continued in the well of the hall where guests and retainers were still celebrating the birth of their Young King's first child. William made a signal to Baldwin: with a nod, the knight summoned the stewards and began to undertake what was necessary. Messengers would have to be sent in haste to overtake those who had ridden out earlier bearing different, joyful tidings.

Henry halted before his wife's chamber, his breathing hard from the climb up the stairs. His expression remained rigid, but William could see the cracks striating the precarious control. William stood behind him, saying nothing, providing the backbone. The guard on the door stood to attention, his focus blank as if he too were part of this tableau of stone.

"There has to be a mistake," Henry said. He set his hand to the latch and entered the room. The shutters were fastened against the night and candles burned in every sconce. At the end of the chamber, the heavy red hangings closed off the Queen's bed like a sealed box. Her women sat in a huddle, whispering, weeping quietly, clutching their breasts, rocking back and forth in muted grief that would waken neither the sleeping nor the dead.

The senior midwife stood by the cradle, her face pleated with apprehension and sorrow. She dropped in a deep curtsey to Henry and remained with her head bowed. He came to the cradle and gazed down. "Why?" he asked hoarsely.

"It was a difficult birth, sire," the midwife said. "He spent so long entering the world that he had no strength left to live in it."

"Does the Queen know?" William asked.

The woman shook her head. "No, my lord. We took the infant from her to see if he would feed at the nurse's breast and because we were concerned for him. He had scarcely cried since he was born and his colour was poor. I gave the Queen a sleeping potion. She will have peace for a few hours yet."

And then peace no more, William thought pityingly. Now would come the platitudes, about the child having lived long enough to be baptised, about Henry and Marguerite being young and strong and with time enough to begin again. But he wasn't going to be the one to utter them.

Henry gazed down on his dead son for a moment longer, before pivoting abruptly on his heel and striding from the room. William hesitated, glanced towards the closed bed curtains, and then hurried after his lord. Henry had turned aside into one of the garderobes cut into the wall and was retching down the waste shaft, his hands braced on the wooden seat.

William waited, saying nothing, feeling inadequate. There were no words of comfort that would cocoon the rawness of Henry's bleeding grief and lacerated pride. The flood of joy followed by the back-surge of loss was bound to drown all but the strongest swimmer. Slowly Henry straightened and wiped his mouth. His eyes were dull now, quenched of light. "Why does God allow these things to happen?" he asked William in a torn voice. "If he didn't want my son to live, why did he make her quicken with my seed in the first place?"

William shook his head. "You should speak to your chaplain, sire. I have no answers."

"He won't have any either." Henry sat down on the garderobe seat and put his head in his hands. "Christ, I'm drunk. I thought this was a celebration. I thought that in the morning I would…Oh Christ Jesu, Christ have mercy." His body shuddered with dry sobs. "Why does the gold in my hands always trickle through my fingers like common sand and leave me no better than a beggar?" he demanded in an aching, forlorn voice.

William swallowed and felt his own eyes burn. What could he say? That if one spread one's fingers instead of making a fist, one would never hold on to anything. That Henry had the choice between cladding himself in the riches of a king or a beggar's rags. Even now he was mourning for himself, not the piteous swaddled scrap lying cold and pale in the royal cradle. But that didn't make the heartache any less intense. In Henry's case, the opposite.

William cleared the harshness of emotion from his throat. "You should sleep, sire," he said, "and in the morning, do what you must."

Henry swallowed and palmed his hands over his face. "Yes," he said. "You're right. Do what I must."

Clara took one look at William's pouched and reddened eyes, the stubble foresting his jaw, his blank expression and, without a word, fetched wine laced with aqua vitae and pressed him down on the bed. Totally passive, William allowed her to strip his garments, standing when she bade him stand, sitting when she bade him sit. Once he was clad in a fresh shirt and loose-fitting tunic, she laid her hand to his shoulder and placed a kiss at the corner of his mouth.

"Have you eaten?"

He shrugged, unable to remember. The hollow sensation in his gut might be hunger, but could as well be a reaction to the atmosphere at the palace; to being drained by all that he had witnessed and the burdens he had been forced to shoulder. Marguerite distraught and wild-haired in her bed, racked with grief and guilt; her husband drunk, then sober, then drunk again. The wine he had consumed half keeping pace with Henry had soured his gut and caused a dull ache behind his eyes. Babies died unborn or at birth. Children did not survive infancy and childhood. Only the strong and the fortunate grew to maturity…only those blessed by God. Everyone knew that; everyone was prepared until it happened to them.

Clara brought him fresh wheaten bread and a pot of game terrine. When he didn't touch it, she broke the bread herself and put a chunk of the spicy paté on it. "Eat," she commanded.

The strong aroma reached his nose and made his mouth water and his stomach rebel. "I will be sick," he said.

"It doesn't matter. Eat."

William did as she commanded, glad to have someone make a decision for him. She watched him, saying nothing, as William had watched and waited and said nothing, a witness and a beast of burden to the Young King's grief and Marguerite's suffering. The robust flavours of the food awakened his appetite and after the first mouthful, his nausea was subjugated by ravenous hunger, as if he had been starved of life itself and now felt it returning in the tastes and textures exploding on his tongue. He forced himself to eat slowly. Clara replaced the fortified wine with an ordinary jug of Gascony and brought a platter of sweet dried dates and figs to the low bench they were using as a table. Gradually the colours of the world returned and came into sharper focus. He became aware of Clara's quiet stare and the fact that he was wearing more comfortable clothes than his formal court attire, although how he came to be doing so, he could not remember.

"You should sleep," she murmured.

He sighed hard. "Yes, I should, but I don't know if I can." He took her hand and looked down at their linked fingers. "It was bad," he said. "I stood in vigil with Henry last night, as did all the knights of his mesnie." His throat worked. "The coffin was no bigger than a reliquary box. The Queen…" He shook his head. "The Queen has taken it ill. She was sleeping when the child died and she thinks that in some way it is her fault." His mouth twisted as he remembered her pale, tear-tracked face.

"I prayed for her at mass this morning—and for the child and the Young King too," Clara said. "The churches have been tolling a knell the day long." She laid her palm against her own flat stomach. "I grieve that my womb is barren, but sometimes I think that it is a blessing too. It is easier to mourn the children I will never have than see them taken away in the hour of their birth."

William lay down on the bed and she joined him, although it was full daylight. Waiting for him to return, she had kept her own vigil and she was tired, although not with the same exhaustion that William felt. "There is time for them to have other sons," she said.

"That is what her women have been telling her, and what the Bishop of Rouen said to my lord." He closed his eyes, and behind his lids saw Henry's fury at the Bishop's words. Not because they came too soon on the heels of tragedy, but because they were a reminder of a duty that Henry would have sooner forgone. He had little interest in his wife's bed to begin with, and could see no point in mating with her if the result was to be failure. "It makes sense," William said without lifting his lids, "but there's not a lot of that about at the moment. The best I can do for Henry is take him to the next tourney and hope to ride his demons out of him."

"And his wife?"

He pulled Clara into his arms, seeking comfort. "Time, I suppose, and gentle handling, but how much she will have of either, I do not know."

Thirteen

"No, I am certain," Clara said, shaking her head. Her warm complexion was pale as she stood beside William on the wharfside and watched the ships tossing at their mooring ropes like new-caught wild horses. "I will go to the ends of the earth for you, but only if I do not have to cross water."

William could understand her reluctance because he hated sea crossings himself, but her fear went much deeper than his did. Until yesterday when the Young King's court arrived in Wissant to prepare for the crossing, Clara had never seen the sea, and the sight of its grey-green vastness spreading to meet the low clouds on the horizon had terrified her almost out of her wits.

His reassurances about the crossing had fallen on deaf ears, partly because he was being too hearty to compensate for his own fears and partly because Clara didn't want to listen. Nor did she want to see England. From hearsay it was a cold, misty land filled with surly peasants and a dour aristocracy who viewed anyone from Poitou as soft, pampered, and tainted with heresy. That William was English, as were several of the Young King's household, had not allayed her fears. There were always exceptions and much of William's life had been spent away from his native island. She was afraid, too, of meeting his family. On the tourney circuit she was accepted and respected as the mistress of the best knight on the field. But there were no tourneys in England, none of the dazzle and glamour that made for a relaxed acceptance of mistresses, troubadours, and dancing girls. Even the fact that William's older brother had a mistress and a bastard child had not reassured her. She was as adamant about England as she was about the sea.

"I cannot," she repeated with a shudder, her gaze on the milky-green waves slapping against the harbour side.

William made an exasperated sound in his throat, drew her roughly to his side, and hugged her. "I would never put my courser at a hedge too high for him to jump," he said. "I won't push you."

She blinked on tears, her eyes stinging from the cold, salt wind. "Just don't be too hasty to find another mount while you're in England," she said with a tremulous laugh. "One that can jump higher."

William kissed her. "I doubt such a creature exists," he said.

The sailors and porters continued to stow the royal baggage aboard the vessels. Marguerite and her ladies came down to board the *esnecca*, their gowns butterfly-bright against the grey hues of the day. The birth and death of her infant son had changed the Young Queen. Gone was the plump, wide-eyed girl with her spontaneous displays of affection and ready smile. There was a new gravitas to Marguerite these days, and a watchful air, as if she were guarding herself against what the world had to offer by measuring what the payment would be.

She and Henry had separate bedchambers, although in fulfilment of duty they slept together on the days that were not proscribed by the Church. Thus far Marguerite had not conceived again and with Lent upon them, she and Henry were sleeping apart. William could see that beneath her fur-lined cloak she was hugging herself against the cold. He knew that she hated crossing the Narrow Sea, but she always endured the voyage with quiet fortitude.

Henry arrived shortly after his wife, his complexion flushed from the wine he had been drinking to fortify himself for the journey, and his manner ebullient. Sixty years ago the heir to the throne had drowned whilst crossing the Narrow Sea, but Henry considered that the death had paid his family's price, so he was safe. Apart from a prayer before embarkation, he lived in the moment and didn't think about it.

As the oarsmen rowed the ship out of the harbour, William watched Clara's form diminish until it was eventually lost to sight, and then, with a sigh, he turned away to the body of the vessel.

"Three years," Henry said, one hand braced against the mast. "I haven't seen my father in three years." His grimace wasn't caused entirely by the bite of the brisk sea wind. "They say absence makes the heart grow fonder, but I doubt he'll have mellowed any."

"And you have, sire?" William asked.

Henry puffed out his breath. "If I have then he'll see it as a weakness. But then he doesn't think much of Richard and no one could accuse Richard of being mellow. At least it's not for long. Come the tourney season, we'll be back in Normandy." He twitched his shoulders. "It's always damp in England and the spring comes late. In Anjou the trees are in blossom when in London there's still snow on the ground."

"Then you can go skating on Moorgate Pond, my lord."

Henry gave a bark of sour laughter. "And give my father a fit."

"You could take your brother John."

"Yes, and hope that the ice will crack under his feet. He was a brat when he was little and I doubt that time will have improved him. He'll be a spotty, scratch-voiced youth by now." He gave an irritable shake of his shoulders and drew up the hood of his cloak as a sudden rain squall deluged the vessel. "I dare say I'll tolerate him just as long as my father has no more plans for carving him an inheritance out of my territories."

Rain streamed down William's face and dripped off his jaw. His hands were red and aching with the cold. The ship bucked in the freshening wind and lunged through the waves like a half-tamed horse. Clara would have been terrified; his own feelings were a mingling of fear and discomfort. Henry turned towards the canvas deck shelter where the Queen and her ladies had taken refuge from the biting wind and now the lash of the rain. Then he hesitated and looked over his shoulder at William.

"Marguerite thinks that she might be with child again," he said.

"That is good news, sire." William shifted his stance to steady his balance and felt the queasiness of *mal de mer* begin to ripple through his stomach.

"Yes, if it's true. Hopes have been raised before." He continued on his way to the deck shelter, entered within, and dropped the flap.

Sighing, William retired to the well of the vessel where another canvas shelter for the men had been erected.

King Henry the elder rubbed his thigh and scowled. "Marshal, you do not know how fortunate you are." His tone was resentful.

"Sire?" William said attentively. Three years had not been kind to his lord's father. A few months after his tiny grandson's death, he himself had been mortally sick of an infected leg, and his struggle to recovery had left its mark. The red-gold hair had dulled to dusty ginger and the grey-blue eyes were pouched and bloodshot. Then his beloved mistress, Rosamund de Clifford had died of a fever and the King had been distraught. Vestiges of his terrible grief still showed in new seams of care at brow and mouth corner.

King Henry smiled unpleasantly. "My son tells me that you compete in every tourney that comes your way—and some that do not, since you ride far and wide to seek them out."

"Only with my lord's permission, sire, and if he has no need of me."

Henry grunted his disapproval. "The whelp doesn't know what he needs, Messire Marshal. I said that you were fortunate because you have no lasting injuries to show for your frivolous life on the tourney field. I have never jousted, I consider the sport a debauched waste of time and silver, yet I am the one who is kicked so badly by a horse that I am constantly plagued by the wound."

"I am sorry to hear that, sire."

Henry eyed him darkly. "You're polished, William, and shrewd, I'll give you that. I can understand what that perfidious wife of mine saw in you, but, as she knows to her cost, it only takes one slip."

"Sire?" William's nape prickled as he sensed danger.

"You know what I mean," Henry answered, narrow-eyed. "You have risen very smoothly on fortune's wheel thus far, but all that can change in a moment."

Prince John joined them. He had been talking amidst a group of fellow youths but with an unerring nose for conflict had quickened to his father's side. His hair was as black as his mother's must have been when she was young. A rash of adolescent spots flushed his brow and jaw and there was a smudge of dark down on his upper lip. He was of a slighter build than his brothers had been at that age, but William did not make the mistake of thinking John the runt of the litter. He was his father made over again but, in keeping with his colouring, more darkly rendered; and he was Eleanor also, but not her open, generous side.

"You have a great reputation, Marshal," the lad said in a voice abrasive with the change to manhood.

"So your father has been telling me, Lord John," William replied with a bow and a smile.

John responded with a smile of his own, white and vulpine. "Has he? He often speaks of your prowess. A pity that tourneys are banned in England, or I could watch you for myself." He gave his father a teasing, knowing look.

The King ruffled John's hair. "I have enough sons bedazzled by the folly and profligacy of the tourney. I thought you at least had more sense."

"Oh, I wouldn't want to tourney myself," John said with a scornful gesture that echoed his father's tone, "but it might be interesting to lay wagers on the outcome. My brother's kitchen clerk has a pile of winnings the size of a dung heap thanks to Marshal."

The King raised a sardonic eyebrow. "It seems that everyone gets rich except for me. I pay for the horses, the armour, the fine clothes, the food, the minstrels, the petty hangers-on. Do you know how many times your brother's clerks come to me with demands for more funds because he and his mesnie have spent in a month what I have given them to last the year? Even with revenues of his own, he cannot live within his means." Although he was addressing John, his gaze bored accusingly into William. "Indeed," he continued, "I hear that certain knights encourage my son to spend beyond his means."

William said nothing. It was pointless to fuel the confrontation and he was already standing on precarious ground. He had no doubt that someone had been feeding rumours to the King. No man was keen to challenge William on the tourney field where his skills made him supreme, but at court there were many who were prepared to put a knife in his back and clamber over his falling body to advance their ambitions.

"Have a care, Marshal," the King said, his tone ambiguous. "You are not above taking a fall." Still rubbing his leg, Henry moved on. John hesitated, then followed his sire, but he cast a glance over his shoulder and gave William a smile that was as dangerous as his father's words had been.

William breathed out hard, pushing the tension from his body. He felt as if he had just been through a bruising bout on the tourney ground and emerged intact—but by the skin of his teeth; certainly not as the victor. He had thought himself adept at weaving his way through the dark undergrowth of the court, but plainly he was not adept enough. Perhaps it was time to retreat from the field for a while and refurbish his armour.

"William, I love you!" Alais threw her arms around his neck and smacked kisses enthusiastically on either cheek.

"It's nothing," he chuckled. "Call it payment for my board and lodging."

"I wouldn't call a silk wimple and gold hair pins nothing!" Sitting down again, Alais spread her fingers beneath the gossamer blue silk. "It's beautiful."

"So are you."

Alais gave him a severe look, marred by the twitch of a smile and a deepening of pink in her cheeks. "You flatter me."

"Not in the least. My brother doesn't know how fortunate he is."

"You can stop playing the courtier with my woman," growled John Marshal, his humour tinged with annoyance. "Go and find one of your own."

William hesitated. The world of the court made one do that—think long before speaking and then measure every word with caution. "I can't take the praise for the choice of veil," he said. "That was made by…a good friend."

Alais raised an eyebrow. The corresponding mouth corner curved too. "Not a man, I hazard."

William shook his head and smiled. "Her name is Clara," he said, "and she rescued me once."

Alais was determinedly eager to know more; John was amused and smugly prepared to wreak vengeance. "You can't be holier than thou now, can you?" he derided as William told them as little as he could get away with. After all the lectures you gave to me on the matter of mistresses..."

William bit his tongue on the reply that it was different for him and Clara. He did not have an obligation to wed to enhance the Marshal line, and Clara's barren womb meant there would never be offspring. "There are shades of difference," he said diplomatically, "but I agree that I can no longer lecture you from the moral high ground."

"You should have brought her with you."

"I would have done, but she hates crossing water and she is a woman of the troubadour lands. If it rains, she mopes." His smile was forced and the subject was rapidly dropped for other ones. John was troubled about the King's irascibility towards his son's extravagances and what it might mean for his followers.

"He is looking for a scapegoat," John warned. "Everyone knows that you are the Young King's right hand and his favourite. His father's well informed, and not all of it is to your glory."

"Men will say what they want," William answered tersely. "What am I supposed to do? Lose a few bouts at the tourney? Snarl at my lord when he asks me a question? Fart in the hall?" He made a swift motion with his fist. There was a burning sensation in his gut. The anger he was usually so good at damping down flickered like dragon fire.

"You could try being less extravagant and do more to watch your back," John retorted. "I'm the King's Marshal and head of our family, but I would be hard pressed to dress myself like a prince of the realm. What must the King think when he sees a landless knight robed in ermine and purple?"

William folded his arms defensively. "I don't wear ermine and purple."

"Near enough. Look at you now. That's best Flemish twill and at least twice dyed to judge from the depth of colour, and the embroidery won't have been cheap."

William plucked his tunic. "It's Clara's. She's skilled."

"Yes, but how much does a yard of gold thread cost? I grant that your winter cloak's only lined with sheepskin, but it's trimmed with sable."

William drew himself up. "I don't see why you're so bothered about my clothes."

"You don't want to see," John replied with laboured patience. "William, you're a rich man, and your wealth comes from the purse of your master, who cannot keep its strings closed. You know how little store the King sets by outward show. The sight of you clad like a magnate must sour his digestion. At least wear something sober and plain when you're in his presence."

Alais gave a slight shake of her head and laid her hand on her lover's sleeve, warning him that he was pushing too hard.

"I dress myself out of my own coin, not my lord's." William's tone was gritty with anger. "The only gifts of clothes I receive from him are the usual ones at Michaelmas and Christmas. The rest I earn myself on the tourney field."

"I didn't..."

"When I was de Tancarville's knight I had to sell my cloak to make ends meet. I swore that I would never be in that position again, and I've worked at what I do best to keep that oath. Yes, I accept largesse from my lord, but I earn my keep; I'm no squanderer of his coin." William swallowed and made a conscious effort to relax his clenched fists. He knew that when he had time to think at leisure rather than reacting to the moment, he would find much of what John was saying to him made sense.

"Then you should make it clear to the King, for he thinks that the money from his son's coffers is all draining into yours.

His health's been poor and his temper as sour as verjuice since he lost Rosamund de Clifford."

"I will not go justifying my expenditure to ward off petty gossip," William said curtly. "Either the King knows my nature by now or he doesn't. If he hadn't trusted me, he would never have appointed me to the Young King's household in the first place."

"That was Queen Eleanor's doing. He sees you as much her man as you are the Young King's or his—and that's true, isn't it?" John spread his hands. "All I am saying is that you have made enemies as well as friends and you would be foolish not to heed what is being said about you."

William paced to the end of the room and stared at the intricate stitchwork on the wall hanging. "The Young King is only staying with his father until Easter," he said. "In truth I will be glad to return to Normandy and follow the tourneys. At least there I can meet my opponents helm to helm instead of fighting a murk of words."

"You cannot do that for ever," John said.

"No, but it suffices for now." William turned to face his brother's anxiety and censure. "I can look after myself," he said. "I've survived the mêlée of court intrigue thus far."

"You've been lucky," John muttered darkly.

The conversation was curtailed by the arrival of Ancel who had been absent on administrative duties in Wantage. "It's good to see you!" The young man strode up to William and embraced him with vigour. "We keep hearing of your tourney wins across the Narrow Sea, don't we, John?"

Expression pained, John made a non-committal sound. Oblivious, Ancel continued: "Was it true that your helmet got stuck and you had to have a blacksmith prise it off?"

William chuckled. "Yes, that's true. And when he did, I found a squire and two knights belonging to the Count of Champagne waiting to present me with a fresh pike!"

"I wish I could have been there! Is it also true about you and that herald of Philip of Flanders?"

"That depends," William said cautiously.

"That he made up a song on the tourney field with the chorus 'Marshal, give me a horse' and that you jumped on your stallion, knocked some poor competitor off his destrier, and brought the horse to the herald."

"Yes, I'm afraid that's true as well." William rubbed the back of his neck, pretending to be embarrassed.

Ancel looked at William with shining eyes. "Do you think there'd be room for me in the Young King's mesnie?"

John spluttered. William continued to rub the back of his neck. "As it happens, there might be," he said thoughtfully. "One of the Normans has recently come into an inheritance and left the mesnie, so we're a knight short." He looked at Ancel, whose tail would have been wagging his rump off had he been a dog. "Don't hope too hard," he warned. "You'll need to earn your place. It'll be on merit alone and there will be fierce competition. Even if you are my brother, I cannot afford to carry dead weight."

"You haven't seen me fight. I'll earn my place and more." Ancel's complexion was flushed and his breathing swift.

John heaved a sigh and threw up his hands. "I will say no more. There's no point in shouting at the deaf." He turned to Ancel. "I knew you'd go. You've been like a fledged swallow clinging to the eaves for far too long. But don't blame me if you fly too close to the sun and singe your wings."

"Don't worry, I'll look after him." William gave his youngest brother a friendly cuff.

"That doesn't reassure me," John growled.

"I thought you were going to say no more?"

"I'm not. Just don't provoke me. One of us needs the sense he was born with."

"And the other two already have it." William ducked as Ancel responded to the cuff by launching at him and for a moment they indulged in a bout of play-wrestling that left John shaking his head in despair and exasperation. However, despite the provocation, he managed to keep his mouth shut, even when his son ran into the room, stared at his uncles in astonishment, and then joined in with a howl of glee. Alais began laughing. John looked at her, then at the brawl. "You are all mad," he said.

William returned to court by way of Salisbury and Queen Eleanor. Ancel was incandescent with excitement as they rode over the bridge and into the courtyard. William kept a straight face but inside he was chuckling, for Ancel, at six and twenty, was behaving like a green squire in his first year of service. At that age, William had already seen epic battle, had been a hostage, a courtier, and given charge of the military training of the heir to England and Normandy. "Remember to treat the Queen as if she is the most beautiful woman in the world, and you will not go far wrong," William told his brother as they dismounted before the hall of whitewashed stone. He allowed himself a grin as the grooms took the horses away to the stables. "Don't worry, the Queen is indeed one of the most beautiful women in the world. Age may have creased her loveliness, but it hasn't withered it. You won't have to lie."

The brothers entered the great hall and William saw that as well as Eleanor's usher and the watchful guards whose task it was to make sure that the Queen's captivity remained just that, there were other servants whose faces were familiar. A swift enquiry brought forth the detail that, yes, the Young Queen was visiting her mother-by-marriage and she and Eleanor were closeted together in the royal apartments.

William was pleased. "Auspicious," he said. "It is not every day that you get two queens for the price of one." Ancel nervously plucked a lingering dog hair from his best tunic of dark red wool. "There is no need to fuss," William said as he noticed the gesture. "They are both used to King Henry looking like a peasant. You're presentable, and that's enough."

They waited in the hall while the usher sent a servant to inform the women of their arrival. William went among the men he knew, talking to them, picking up the new threads of court gossip. There was nothing about himself and no sign of an atmosphere, he was pleased to note. The act of leaving court to spend time with his family had obviously removed his own particular cooking pot from the fire—for the moment at least. He introduced Ancel to some of the men and then made his way over to Baldwin de Béthune.

"What are you doing here?" he asked. "I thought you'd be with our young lord?"

Baldwin's teeth flashed. "Someone had to escort the Young Queen to Sarum and I volunteered. Like you, I enjoy a change of air and it's no onerous duty to be riding with a lady in the softness of spring."

"No," William agreed, but inwardly recoiled, remembering just such a spring day in Poitou, and the bloody battle that had changed everything.

"And this is Ancel?" Baldwin shook William's brother by the hand. "You can tell that you're both branches of the same tree. The women of the court won't know what has hit them!"

Ancel flushed, prompting Baldwin to laugh. "A shy Marshal will certainly be a change for them," he teased.

William took pity on his brother and diverted the subject. "The Queen is well?" he asked.

"Which one?" Baldwin sobered. "Eleanor is still as spry as a maid half her age, and twice as alluring. That's another reason I agreed to make the journey; she's better company than her husband. But Marguerite…" He hesitated and lowered his voice. "There was no child. It was a false hope."

William's gaze sharpened. "She miscarried?"

"I do not know. All that the Young King said was that she was not with child, and the mood he was in, no one was going to press him for details."

A squire came to escort the brothers to Eleanor and Marguerite. Promising to talk to Baldwin later, William took Ancel by the sleeve and followed the youth to the Queen's chamber. The door was open, suggesting that for the moment at least Eleanor was not confined to her room. The room itself was better furnished than his previous visit, the painted coffers restored to their places, embroideries brightening the walls, and the scented braziers Eleanor so loved gave the room a luxurious warmth that had been lacking before. Her day bed was made up with an embroidered silk coverlet and strewn with bolsters and cushions in all the rich deep shades he remembered from the years in Poitou. Marguerite sat on the edge of the bed, hemming a veil, and Eleanor was playing chess with one of her ladies. The other women attendants were mostly engaged in various pieces of needlecraft, although one was playing a harp and the delicate notes trembled in the air.

As the brothers knelt to the women, William thought that Marguerite looked wan and tired. Her eyes were over-bright and her smile forced. Eleanor was delighted and diverted by the visitors. "If I had known there was another Marshal so close to my prison and a fine chevalier, I would have been much comforted," she said as Ancel bent the knee, his ears as red as embers.

"There is also my brother John, madam," Ancel said, his nervousness drawing the words out of him like an accidental blot of ink on a piece of parchment. "Until recently I dwelt under his roof."

The curve remained on Eleanor's lips but lost some of its pleasure. "John Marshal is my husband's man, although I am sure that he is as worthy as either of his brothers." Her tone was neutral, but not the emotions behind it.

William would have kicked Ancel had he been able to do it without the women seeing. "Ancel is hoping to further his education," he said smoothly. "Until now he has been little exposed to life beyond my brother's manors."

Eleanor's smile softened, although her eyes held a disquieting gleam. "Then, Ancel Marshal, you have a lot to learn," she said. "Listen to William and follow his advice. He knows how to make his way at court." She turned to William. "If you are going to show him the world beyond his small window, make sure that he stays in it." A desolate sheen filled her eyes. "Nothing burdens the soul more than the loss of freedom."

The brothers dined with the women, the meal taken in the privacy of Eleanor's chamber. William noticed that the fare had improved since his last visit too. Although it was Lent, there was pickled salmon and fresh shrimps, good wheaten bread to mop up the salty, piquant sauces, honey tart and almond custard. Ancel was nervous and talked more than he should, but Eleanor was endeared rather than irritated. "He reminds me a little of you when you were in your uncle of Salisbury's service," she teased William, pressing his arm. "You were never as talkative but your ears turned red just like that."

"That was because I was often too innocent for the conversations, madam," William responded with a straight face.

She tapped him lightly in reproof, but her eyes were laughing. "Does your brother sing too?"

William winced. "I would not malign my own flesh and blood, but Ancel has a voice like a rooster at dawn. He does play a hard game of chess though," he said in mitigation. "You are an acknowledged expert, madam, but you would be hard pressed to beat him."

She regarded Ancel with empathy. "I suppose we each have had little else to do of an evening but sharpen such skills. I will enjoy testing his mettle."

Following the meal, Eleanor drew Ancel to sit in the window embrasure where the chessboard stood with its serried ranks of ivory and jet pieces. William grasped the opportunity to talk to Marguerite alone. She had been sitting on a bench close to a brazier, her sewing in her lap, but she had taken few stitches and was plainly uninterested in the project.

"You are well, madam?" he enquired.

She parted her lips to give him the standard reply, then changed her mind and shook her head. "No," she said, looking down. "I am not well at all."

"I am sorry to hear that."

"But not surprised. I know when my maid holds up my hand mirror and I see my reflection that I look like a "walking corpse.""

"No, madam. You look like a creature from the land of faery—half made of shadows, but lovely nonetheless."

She gave a laugh filled with pathos. "Oh, William, your courtesy never fails. I know I look like death warmed up. Did you know that I was with child when we sailed from Wissant?"

"There was a rumour, but I always treat court gossip with caution."

"Then whispers must also have told you that I lost it?"

"I am sorry, madam. It must be a great grief to yourself and my lord."

She compressed her lips and her chin dimpled. "Indeed yes. But Henry…his grief is different to mine. I have scarcely seen him since we have been in England. He…He pretends that nothing has happened, and that I am nothing too. If he looks through me, if he does not see me, then he does not have to acknowledge our failure. I wish…I wish that…" She swallowed and shook her head. Her brown eyes locked on his, beseeching and tear-filled.

William's heart wallowed. "The Young King cares for you," he said and felt the lie burn his tongue.

"Does he?" Her tone was dull. "Then it is probably as much as I care for him. We have our duty, but God alone knows how we will manage to perform it. I heard Yqueboeuf tell Henry that all cats and coneys were dark at night…"

William's face twisted with revulsion. "If I had been within hearing, Yqueboeuf wouldn't have had a mouth left to make his confession," he growled. "What did Henry say?"

Her chin dimpled. "He was very drunk," she said with careful dignity.

William swore under his breath. Reading between the lines, Henry had said and done nothing, perhaps even condoned the remark. Excuses were always made for Henry's behaviour. It was never his fault, but there came a point when the blame had to come home to roost.

Marguerite bit her lip. "If you interfere, you will only make matters worse," she said with dismay. "I should not have told you. For my sake and yours, I beg you say nothing."

William clenched his jaw.

"Please…"

"Very well, madam," he said stiffly, "since that be your wish, but if it happens again and I am by, I won't hold back."

"Thank you." She looked relieved.

He left her side and went to watch the chess game, although what he really wanted to do was go and wash his hands and rid himself of the feeling that he had somehow smirched his honour.

Ancel was holding his own against a fiercely determined Eleanor. Her full lower lip was thrust out and the frown lines between her eyes were heavily demarcated. She made her move and looked up at William. "He's not afraid to risk all," she said, a gleam of approbation in her eyes.

William found a smile, although it was difficult after what Marguerite had just said. "No," he said. "He's not." And thought of the risks facing himself and the dangerous temptation to take them.

Fourteen

LAGNY-SUR-MARNE, CHAMPAGNE, NOVEMBER 1179

THERE WAS A NEW YOUNG KING AND HE WAS FRENCH. The fourteen-year-old son of Louis of France, Philip the God-given, so called because he was born when his father had relinquished all hope of siring an heir, had been crowned at Reims on All Saints' Day and a grand tourney was being held to mark the occasion. All the magnates and lords who had attended the coronation had come to the field with their retinues. Tents and striped pavilions were pitched as far as the eye could see. The weather was cold but clear, the horizon a grainy haze and, as it had been dry recently, the ground was firm for the horses.

William glanced towards the recently risen sun and inhaled deeply. The smell of bread, bacon, and pottage wafted from numerous camp fires and the cookstall booths were doing brisk business as men stoked their bellies for the hard day's fighting to come.

Adjusting his surcoat, Ancel emerged from William's pavilion. The garment was parti-coloured green and yellow with a red lion rampant snarling across the background—William's chosen device. There were several knights kitted out in this barding, their surcoats and shields proclaiming William's blazon. Like William and Ancel they were of English birth and provided for by the Young King from the expenses given to him as his father's representative at young Philip's coronation…expenses that were vanishing faster than water down a piscina with the plug removed.

William admired his brother. "You look a veritable King's Champion," he said.

Ancel flashed him a nervous grin. "Let's hope I perform like one."

"I have no doubts on that score." It was true. Ancel tourneyed throughout the summer at William's side. Nervous and uncertain at first, his skills had blossomed as his confidence had grown. He was never going to dazzle, but he was a competent fighter, always aware of where others were and what they were doing.

Adam Yqueboeuf and Thomas de Coulances were passing and had overheard the brothers' exchange. Yqueboeuf's lips parted in a sneer. "You are the one reckoned to be Lancelot, Marshal, didn't you know?"

William's eyes narrowed. "Meaning?" The antipathy between the men had increased of late, fuelled on William's part by knowledge of what Yqueboeuf had said about Marguerite. Yqueboeuf's hostility stemmed from envy and the higher William rose at court, the more it festered. He would not compare William to King Arthur's best knight unless there was an insult in it somewhere.

"It's obvious, isn't it? You deserve all the accolades that come your way, King's Champion that you are."

The knights went on their way. Out of hearing, de Coulances leaned towards Yqueboeuf and said something that caused both men to laugh and glance over their shoulders.

"Pity they're not opposing us," Ancel said, hands on hips. "I'd enjoy choking them with their own teeth." He gave William a perceptive look. Only last night in Henry's chamber, a troubadour had been retelling Chrétien de Troyes' story of Lancelot, the greatest of King Arthur's knights who had betrayed his lord by sleeping with his wife. "Do you think they are insinuating that you and Queen Marguerite—"

William raised his hand to interrupt his brother in mid-sentence. "Say no more." His features twisted with revulsion. "I will not countenance such filth."

"No, but they might."

"They have no grounds. I am never alone with the Queen. If I talk to her or dance with her at court, I don't linger, and I don't flirt with her either."

"Gossip can destroy even the cleanest reputation," Ancel pointed out.

William made an explosive sound through his pursed lips. "What else am I supposed to do? Everyone, including Marguerite and Henry, knows that I have a mistress and no desire to chase other women."

Ancel shrugged. "It's just wise to take care," he said and then gave a rueful smile. "I know I'm teaching my grandmother to suck eggs."

William looked wry. "And who's to say you're not right? I'll think on the matter and take heed." Slapping Ancel's shoulder, he went to don his armour.

Although William did not dismiss the jealous mutterings of Adam Yqueboeuf and Thomas de Coulances, he set them to the back of his mind. He had more immediate matters to concern him than their petty scheming. Rhys brought William's new stallion round from the horse lines to his tent. Blancart had grown too long in the tooth for the tourneys and Count Philip of Flanders had bought him from William to run him at stud on one of his farms. Blancart's replacement was a Lombardy stallion with a hide of ruby-gold satin and flaxen mane and tail.

Wigain had remarked that his coat resembled the gold bezants brought home by returning crusaders and thus the stallion had come by his name.

"He's been warmed," Rhys said cheerfully. "Put him through his paces myself. Sweet as a nut."

William nodded his thanks, swung into the saddle, and rode to join the English knights who were assembling under his banner ready for the day's sport. He was pleased to note that every man had taken extra care with his appearance. Harry Norreis, William's herald, had plaited his horse's mane with green and yellow ribbons and his bridle jingled with small silver bells. "He looks like a jongleur's beast," William said with an amused shake of his head. "And you look like a travelling player."

"All the better to sing your praises!" As irrepressible as his shock of bright auburn hair, Norreis drew his sword and twirled it in the air like a juggler before revolving it back into the scabbard. Suppressing his laughter, William turned to find a page from Queen Marguerite's household waiting his attention.

"Sir William, the Queen requests that you carry her favour on the field to bring you good fortune," he piped and presented William with a red silk strip to tie around his lance.

William had to accept the gift. To have refused would have caused hurt, insult, and more speculation. Taking it would usually have meant nothing, but with the bad taste of rumour still in his mouth, he wondered if others would misconstrue what they saw. "Tell the Queen that I thank her and I am proud to bear her token." He tied the gaudy flutter of silk to the end of his lance. The page bowed and ran off as the Young King arrived at the head of the two hundred Norman and Angevin knights he had employed for the occasion. The serried ranks of red and gold were a magnificent, throat-catching sight. Henry's surcoat was blood-red silk and two lions snarled across his breast in glittering thread of gold with jet beads for eyes and rock crystal claws. His swordbelt was decorated with enamelled lions, and his horse harness bore more of the lion badges across the brow-band, chest strap, and at each buckle point. William was relieved to see an identical strip of silk to the one just bestowed on him fluttering from the haft of Henry's lance. At least Marguerite had had the good sense to gift her husband similarly. Beyond the knights wearing the red and gold of Anjou were others in disparate hues whom he had attracted to his side at the last moment, and some smaller contingents, like William's, who carried their own flags on the field but were fighting under Henry's banner.

"Ready to take all comers with your doughty Englishmen, Marshal?" Henry teased. There was mockery about the way he said "doughty Englishmen," for the latter were perceived as being less civilised than their Norman and Angevin counterparts—drunken clods with only half a wit to share between all of them. Such prejudices gave the English a gritty, brawling edge when it came to a fight for they were ready with a vengeance to prove their true worth.

"Never more so, sire." William gave Henry an assured smile. In the ranks behind the Young King, his gaze fell upon the partnership of Adam Yqueboeuf and Thomas de Coulances. The latter gestured obscenely at William, who ignored the provocation, knowing that his indifference was more galling than a response. The English, appropriately enough, had a word for men such as Yqueboeuf and Coulances: *nithing*. It was what he called them in private. "The nithings."

Other entourages were riding on to the tourney ground. The Flemish under Philip, Count of Flanders and his brother Matthew of Boulogne, the men of Burgundy following their Duke, the Earl of Huntingdon with his Scots, the French in vast numbers, parading to honour their new Young King. It was a brave and daunting sight and made William's stomach wallow with anticipation while pride tightened his throat. Henry must have felt it too, for there was a sparkle of tears in his eyes as he paused before taking his great helm from his squire and settling it over his arming cap. "There will never be a greater moment than this in all our days of tourneying," he said, his voice raw with emotion. "Never."

A greater moment there might never be, but the fight was hard and bruising and there were so many knights involved that it was often more like a real battle than one played by tourney rules. The noise was deafening and at times there was scarcely room to manoeuvre the destriers. When there was space to charge, men and horses were so strung up that the clashes were thunderous. Lances splintered into myriad shards; knights were thrown; destriers fell—and some horses and men did not rise again. The vine fields over which the companies ranged were trampled and churned. Battle cries and rallying cries rang out. Harry Norreis was as good as his word and bellowed William's name for all to hear at the top of his lungs. "God is with the Marshal!" he roared, twirling his lance, while the bells on his bridle rang and rang.

The field was a wheeling, changing tapestry of movement and at one point William and his troop became separated from Henry by a conroi of Flemings. Cursing, William hacked a path through them and was in time to see his lord's bodyguards, including Yqueboeuf and the de Coulances brothers, haring off in pursuit of some richly caparisoned French knights, whilst Henry, oblivious with battle fire, launched himself into a group of Burgundians with only a handful of knights to back him up. William saw Henry's lance shatter like glass on an opponent's shield, the pieces flying far and wide. His opponent rocked in the saddle but did not fall and his companions closed in on the

Young King, seizing his bridle, attempting to bring him down off his horse.

William spurred into the fray and Norreis's cry rang out. "The Marshal, the Marshal! God is with the Marshal!" Laying about with his sword, William battered his way to Henry's side. The young man had lost his helm and arming cap and his hair stuck up in spiky brown tufts around his flushed face. His arm rose and fell and his teeth were gritted with determination: he was not going to be taken for ransom at such a prestigious tourney with all his peers looking on. However, the Burgundians were loath to relinquish their prize and without control of his horse, Henry was still theirs. William reached out, laid hands to the brow-band of Henry's destrier and pulled. The stallion struggled and plunged. The Burgundians battered at William, but he held on grimly, aided in his endeavour by Ancel who had galloped up on his right. William managed to peel the bridle off the destrier's head, leaving the opposing knights with nothing to grasp. Henry had nothing to grasp either, except a handful of mane, but that was enough and he was able to kick his destrier out of the fray.

"Ware!" Ancel roared, pointing towards a band of Flemish knights who had seen Henry's predicament and were galloping to take advantage. Cursing, William leaned to grab a fallen lance and charged to intercept their leader. Giving Bezant an extra dig in the flank, he ran the lance on to the knight's shield and felt the impact shudder up his arm. The shock flung Bezant back on his haunches, sturdy though he was, and the overstrained length of ash splintered and broke, leaving William clutching a stump. For a terrifying instant William thought that Bezant was going over, but with a tremendous heave, the destrier recovered his legs and William drew his sword, hoping that he had bought Henry time to escape to one of the sanctuary points. Parrying his opponent's determined blows, it was all William could do to avoid being captured himself and it was with a great surge of relief that he heard Harry Norreis shouting the Marshal rallying cry. From some desperate corner of himself, he found the breath to roar an answer. Ancel blocked a blow that would have struck William side on, and Baldwin de Béthune appeared, his surcoat torn and muddy. William renewed his efforts, and his adversary drew off rather than risk being taken for ransom. As the opposition withdrew, William leaned over his saddle bow and gulped breath into his starving lungs. Eyes stinging with sweat, he studied the field through the slits in his helm and was furious to see a blurred cluster of red and gold at one of the respite enclosures.

He spurred Bezant towards them. Arriving at the enclosure, he removed his helm and thrust it at a royal squire. "Good of you to rejoin us, gentlemen," he snarled at the knot of Norman knights, which included Yqueboeuf and de Coulances. "Where were you when your lord was within a gnat's cock of being taken for ransom? A gang of peasant brats has more discipline and control!"

Yqueboeuf strode up to William's destrier, his complexion dusky with exertion and temper. "As far as we knew, you and your mighty band of English lackwits were at our lord's heels. It is not our fault that you were not up to the task."

William flung down from the saddle and seized Yqueboeuf by the throat. "You dare speak thus to me when you lack the competence of a swineherd!"

Yqueboeuf wrenched William's hand away and pushed him, his eyes blazing. "You treat our lord as if he's a babe in need of a wet nurse when he is a skilled fighter in his own right. At least we took some ransoms for our lord's coffers. Your only concern is to promote your own glory. '*The Marshal, the Marshal, God is with the Marshal!*' Hah!" Yqueboeuf spat at William's feet then turned in appeal towards Henry, who had been intently watching the exchange. "Did we do wrong, sire?"

Henry frowned. "No," he said. "It happened in the heat of the moment and as you say, Adam, you took some useful ransoms. I value you both, and I will not have you shame me by quarrelling in public. That too is a slur on my dignity. Let it go. There is still half a day's tourneying left and I want the prize. Clasp hands and set your differences aside."

William swallowed bile. The heat of the wine in his belly had gone from flame to ashes. He was furious, but with himself more than anyone else. He had allowed Yqueboeuf to strike under his guard, which was precisely what his rival had intended. Tightening his jaw, he held out his hand. At least Henry had not asked them to apologise to each other, only to set their differences aside. With bad grace, Yqueboeuf grasped William's hand, gave it a squeeze that deliberately crushed William's fingers together, and then abruptly withdrew.

Satisfied, Henry gave a terse nod and lifted his voice. "Anyone who needs a fresh horse or sustenance, attend to it now. We ride on the moment!"

The enclosure became a surge of knights hastily obeying Henry's bidding. William checked Bezant's legs, but they were sound apart from a minor graze to the left fore. Indeed, William thought, he was probably in a worse case than his mount. Somewhere out on the field was the shattered stump of a lance with Queen Marguerite's ribbon attached to it, but he wasn't about to go and search for it. Collecting a fresh one from his squire and setting his mind to the business in hand, he lined up behind Henry, who had changed his own winded mount for a spirited Spanish roan.

"Stay with me if you can, wet nurse!" Henry shouted, and clapped spurs to his mount's flanks.

Pushing Bezant after his lord, William began to wonder if he was getting too old for this.

The tourney lasted for three days and on the last night, Henry held a feast in his hall for the knights and lords who had fought on his side. There were prizes given out to those deemed the best. Harry Norreis was presented with a silver trumpet in token of being the knight with the loudest voice. William le Gras was given a silver-headed spear for breaking the most lances in the tourney and Thomas de Coulances was awarded a fine silver goblet for being the most drunk. Yqueboeuf too was given a drinking vessel—a gold-rimmed mazer. "It's a loving cup," Henry said with a wave of his hand and a gleam in his eye. "Because your nature overflows with the milk of human kindness." Yqueboeuf thanked Henry with a bow and a forced smile. For William there was a silver-gilt aquamanile in the form of a knight on horseback, and for Ancel a cloak lined with squirrel fur with a clasp of gold and amethysts.

Ancel beamed at William. "What would our brother John say about all this?" he asked.

"That I was leading you down the slippery slope to perdition," William said wryly.

The tourney feast was a masculine affair and no women had been invited (beyond the ubiquitous dancing girls) for which William was thankful. He could not have dealt with the Queen and her ladies this night. Besides, after three days of some of the hardest jousting and feasting he had undertaken in a while, he was tired, his body telling him that he was no longer twenty years old. However, Henry showed every intention of roistering all night, albeit it with a select few. Partway into the feast, he suddenly declared that he had decided that only men named William were allowed to sit at his board, and ordered everyone else to leave. Anyone taking exception was helped on his way by a pair of hefty serjeants.

Ancel chuckled as he fastened his new cloak and, slapping William's shoulder, left the bench. "At least you won't have to suffer Yqueboeuf and the Coulances brothers for the rest of the night, eh?"

William made a face at him. Yqueboeuf glared murder at William as they left the Young King's hall, obviously believing that the jest was William's idea and deliberately aimed at excluding them from Henry's company. William could do nothing about that. He directed a squire to pour wine into his cup and set about getting as drunk as his young lord. Gazing round the hall, he saw that it was far from empty because William was a favourite name amongst all ranks of the nobility. Henry had sent messengers out in search of more Williams to fill the empty benches.

"Now you're one among many the same, Marshal," Henry slurred, giving William a bruising nudge. "But I'm the only Henry."

It was almost dawn when William and the knight William de Preaux hoisted the Young King between them and brought him semi-comatose from the disarray of the feast hall to his lodging chamber. William's feet were unsteady, although he had a harder head for drink than Henry, and de Preaux was staggering too. A squire ran to open the chamber door and William heard the anxious murmur of the Young Queen's maids, and then of Marguerite herself. She was wearing a thick, fur-lined bedrobe. Her hair lay over one shoulder in a heavy brown braid, and as the men tottered into the chamber, her eyes widened and she set one hand to her throat.

"He's all right," William said, "although he won't think so when he wakens." The two knights brought Henry to the bed and laid him face down, turning his head to one side so that he could breathe.

"I am glad that this is the last tourney of the year," she said bitterly. "I do not think that I could bear another one."

"You can't bear anything," Henry slurred, more aware than he appeared. "Least of all a living child."

Marguerite made a small sound in her throat, but it never left her lips which were tightly compressed. William saw the misery in her eyes. "Madam, he is in his cups. He does not know what he is saying."

"He knows exactly what he is saying and it is what he thinks when he is sober. It is what everyone else thinks too." She turned away, her palm pressed over her mouth.

"Madam…" William held out a beseeching hand but she did not see it for her back was to him and facing the dark shadows in the room.

"Go," she said in a trembling voice. "And thank you for seeing my husband to his bed."

William and de Preaux bowed from the room. "I wouldn't change places with either of them for an instant," de Preaux said, shaking his head.

William said nothing. When the Queen had spoken, the cracks in her voice had run through his body. Pity and compassion welled within him. Poor lass, he thought, poor, poor lass, and wished that he had gone back to look for the silk favour she had given him in pride for his chivalry that morning.

Fifteen

LE MANS, ANJOU, AUTUMN 1182

YOU TOOK YOUR SWEET TIME. I DO NOT MIND YOU travelling to tourneys, but you shouldn't linger." Henry's voice was petulant as he received William into his chamber.

William bowed to the Young King. "Sire, the weather was foul and delayed us on the road." He had been attending a tourney at Epernon to which Henry had chosen not to travel. Queen Marguerite looked up from the game of chess she was playing with one of her ladies, her expression warm with greeting, but hers was the only smile in the room. Adam Yqueboeuf and Thomas de Coulances lounged against pillars near Henry's chair and regarded William sourly. Henry was glowering.

"I don't suppose that while you were courting your own fame you heard any news of my beloved brother?"

"Which one, sire? I saw Lord Geoffrey jousting with the Breton team and spent an evening with him and the Count of Flanders. He seemed in good spirits."

"I don't give a whore's slit about Geoffrey's spirits," Henry snarled. "I was speaking of Richard."

"No, sire. If the lord Richard was mentioned, it was in passing. Should I have heard news of him?"

"While you've been breaking lances in sport and hiding from the rain, Richard's been stealing my castles," Henry said, scowling.

"Sire?" William's first feeling was one of weary irritation, but he forced himself through it. This was his path and, for better or worse, he had to tread it.

"He's fortified Clairvaux, which he knows full well is mine, and garrisoned it with his own men." Henry ground his teeth. "Because it's near his borders, he thinks he can take it and do with it as he pleases."

William glanced briefly around. Baldwin de Béthune gave an infinitesimal shake of his head. Peter de Preaux was looking at his fingernails and Roger de Gaugi at the scuffed toes of his boots. "Have you spoken to your father about this, sire?" William asked.

"He won't intervene," Henry spat. "He'll say it's not worth bothering about. He treats me like a child while Richard does as he pleases in Aquitaine and steals whatever he wants from Anjou." He stabbed his chest with his index finger. "I am the eldest, I'm the heir, I'm the one who has been crowned King and yet I have the least standing of all—apart from John and even he's been promised Ireland as soon as he's of age. All my father does is complain like an old miser about how much I cost him." Henry's expression grew pinched and narrow. "He doesn't know the half of what I could cost him if I chose."

William concealed a grimace. Henry was still ploughing the same furrow he had done as a youth of eighteen. Ten years later the bitterness and petulance were much uglier to behold. Lessons had been taught but not learned.

"It's time I paid a visit to my brother-in-law," Henry said softly. "At least he's prepared to see things my way."

He would, William thought. It was in Philip's interest to keep the Angevin family fighting itself.

"Philip doesn't know how fortunate he is," Henry continued. "His father's in the grave and he doesn't have any brothers trying to steal his patrimony. He can do as he pleases."

"Yes, but he has difficult relatives on his borders," William answered.

Henry laughed but wasn't distracted from his purpose. "I've ordered the baggage wains to be readied," he said. "We're leaving on the morrow."

"Sire." William bowed and went to greet Marguerite who indicated that he should take her lady's place at the chessboard. William had not been going to stay, but could not refuse without seeming churlish. She enquired after his success at the tourney and he regaled her with a few incidents to oblige.

"And now my husband travels to the Île-de-France," she said when they had dispensed with the preliminaries. She glanced towards Henry. Yqueboeuf and de Coulances had joined him and the three of them were sniggering together like adolescent youths. Her lips compressed. "I fear that a storm is coming."

"Like the one before when he rebelled against his father?"

Marguerite moved a pawn two spaces. "I do not know. He doesn't talk to me. He never has, but even less now since we—" She broke off and looked down at the chessboard. "He is so eaten up with what he thinks he should have that he doesn't see what he's got. His resentment frightens me—for his sake." She looked at William. "Stop him if you can. You still have his ear. You can still reach him." She laid her hand on his sleeve.

William was not so sure of that. He was no longer the young knight on the white stallion, dazzling Henry's childhood imagination. A charge at the quintain and a clean lift of the ring on to the point of a lance were not enough to secure the Young King's respect and attention these days, and he had little inclination to jump through the hoops of fire that were required. "I'll do what I can," he said, placing a reassuring hand over hers. As he rose from the bench, Adam Yqueboeuf was watching him and Marguerite with calculating eyes. Without taking his gaze from them, he leaned to murmur to de Coulances and a couple of other knights.

Despite the uneasy political situation and the sense of impending danger, William enjoyed the Île-de-France. King Philip was seventeen years old and although there were as many internal politics and power struggles at his court as there were at those of his Angevin relatives, the young man was weathering them well. Like Henry he had a strong sense of his own importance, but it was more focused. He knew what he wanted and had both the steel and the patience in his backbone that augured well for him obtaining it. A streak of ruthlessness too, William noticed, that put him more in mind of Henry's brother Richard, and he also had some of the low cunning of John. Yet he was still a likeable youth, and malleable to a degree. He enjoyed Young Henry's company, the way that one might enjoy a grand feast or the spectacle of a menagerie. It was a diversion from mundane business—a momentary distraction.

Marguerite's mood lightened once she was "home." Although she had been raised at the Angevin court, handed over to Queen Eleanor's household when scarcely out of swaddling, these were still her people and Philip was her half-brother. She rediscovered her smile and when the court came together of an evening she joined the dancing and stayed to watch the entertainments. William took part also, throwing himself into the round of pleasure with an enthusiasm born of a premonition that soon the dance must stop, and when it did, there would be no dancing for a very long time. He kept his martial skills honed by training on the tilting ground with French knights and spent evenings in their company, swapping tall tales until the candles burned low. He and Ancel had kin at the French court. Rotrou, Count of Perche, was their cousin through the

Salisbury side of the family and they spent much time in his company. Taking to Ancel's convivial nature and competence with a blade, Rotrou offered Ancel a place in his own mesnie.

"Will you give me your leave?" Ancel asked William as they dismounted in the stable yard after a day's hunting with the court.

William shrugged. "You are your own man. You have no need to ask me."

"But you gave me the opportunity and you are my brother…"

"And Rotrou is our cousin and Count of Perche. Jesu, take your chance and fly." William thumped Ancel's shoulder. "As matters stand, you are probably better off in Rotrou's household. Go on. Seize your life and your chances in both hands. It's what I did." He braced himself as Ancel engulfed him in an ebullient hug.

"You won't regret this!"

"I will if you don't let me breathe!" William laughed. Shaking his head, he watched Ancel hand his horse to a groom and then hasten off to find the knights of Rotrou's mesnie. The humour remained on William's face but his lips closed and a slight sadness entered his eyes. The age gap between him and Ancel was six years, but just now it felt like a generation. Somewhere he had lost the optimism and vitality that Ancel still carried with him like a pouch of new-minted coins. "I'm getting old," he sighed to Rhys.

The groom looked him up and down and made a rude sound through his pursed lips. "I'll believe it when I see it, sir," he said. "You still run rings round all the youngsters on the tourney field."

William smiled. "That's just experience."

Rhys picked up William's bridle to clean and rubbed his thumb over one of the enamelled green and yellow badges at the brow-band. "A lot to be said for experience, so my wife tells me."

"Does she now?"

"Aye, sir, and she should know. With respect, I'm a few years older than yourself…and I'm not ready to claim my dotage just yet, in bed or out of it."

William looked at his sturdy, dark-eyed groom and felt his spirits lighten. "No, Rhys, you're right," he said. "A man shouldn't claim his dotage until he's well and truly earned it through a baggage roll stuffed with living. I'll do my best not to let you down."

Rhys cocked an eyebrow at him and, with a loud laugh, William gave him two silver pennies. "Buy something for your wife," he said, and went out into the gathering autumn dusk.

"I never see you these days," Clara pouted when he found a moment to visit the hostelry where he had lodged her for the duration of their stay in Paris. "I might as well not be here for all the attention you pay."

William shrugged. "It's not like the tourneys," he said. "I have to attend on the Young King and I have other duties. I thought you would like Paris and the markets. Have you enough silver?"

"It's not money that I want."

William's sigh was not the right response, for she turned her back on him and flounced into the main room. "I suppose you have dined at court too, so you won't want to eat with me."

"Clara…" He looked at the trestle set up in the room, laid with an exquisitely embroidered cloth—her work while she waited for him. There was a bowl of fresh bread, and a platter of stuffed mushrooms—one of his favourite dishes. He noticed that she was wearing her blue gown, the one stitched with seed pearls, and was filled with guilt.

"No," he said, "I didn't dine at court." It wasn't quite true. He had eaten a mountain of cheese wafers whilst playing dice with Henry and several members of his mesnie. Then there had been the dates stuffed with almonds and the small forcemeat pies placed at his elbow during a recitation of the romance of Tristan and Iseult by one of Marguerite's ladies. He removed his cloak and hung it on the wall peg. "I would bring you with me if I could but..."

"But they don't allow whores at court?"

He sat down at the trestle and rubbed his eyes, suddenly realising how tired he was. "Yes, they do permit whores at court, but I would not number you among those women. They belong to any man who has their price, even the courtesans."

She poured wine into his cup, then took her own place at the trestle. "I used to think that I belonged to you, William," she said softly, "but I've come to realise that I don't, and that you will never belong to me."

Made guilty by the tone of her voice and the expression in her eyes, William leaned towards her. "We can go riding together on the morrow," he offered, wondering if he would be able to find the time, but trying to be conciliatory.

She shook her head. "It is too late..." She hesitated. "I have other plans for the morrow."

William laid down his knife and abandoned the pretence that he was going to eat. "Other plans?"

Clara wasn't touching the food either and he could see the tension in her throat. "You warned me when I came to your tent that night that I would be little better than a beggar, but I chose not to hear what you were telling me. I thought it would be enough, or that things would change...but of late I have grown weary of holding out my begging bowl for meagre crumbs."

"I am sorry," William said with contrition. "I know I have been neglectful...Matters are difficult at the moment."

"And will likely not improve." She drew a deep breath and raised her gaze to his. "I have met someone—a vintner from Le

Mans. He's a widower, visiting kin in Paris. He says that he will give me his time as well as his silver if I will marry him."

William stared at her while the words circled his brain but declined to sink in. There was anger, but there was relief too, and not as much surprise as he had expected. Clara was like a cat: self-contained, self-sufficient, but needy for affection. He hadn't been taking the time to give it and someone else had. "You have been busy behind my back," he said.

Clara flushed. "Because that is all I ever see of you—your back. You return to me only when you need sleep or a woman."

Her words stung him, for while they were true in a literal sense, they did not acknowledge the subtleties. "That is not fair," he said reproachfully.

"You are right, it is not," she replied, deliberately misunderstanding him. "Stephen is returning to Le Mans on the morrow and I am going with him."

Stephen. William flinched, for giving the man a name put flesh on his bones. "Have you bedded with him?" His lip curled. "How do you know he won't abandon you in the gutter?"

"All we have done is talk; indeed, we have talked more in a month than you and I have done in the last year. And even if matters do turn sour, I have enough put by to live on…" She faced him with defiance in her eyes, daring him to say that all she possessed had been given to her by him. William declined the challenge, knowing her likely retort that she had earned it on her back was more than he could bear.

"So what is this?" he asked instead, with derision born of hurt. "The last supper?" He gestured at the uneaten food. "Or perhaps the Feast of Fools?"

A tear spilled down her cheek and she swiped at it impatiently.

"Even now…" she said. "Even now I thought there was a chance but…but there isn't, is there?"

A loud banging on the house door prevented William from having to find a reply. They heard the squire open it and then the rumble of voices. With a feeling of relief, William left the table and going to the chamber door, opened it, forestalling the youth's knock.

"Sir, you are summoned to court," Eustace announced, his face expressionless.

"What, at this hour?" William narrowed his eyes. It was late and dark, but he knew the Young King's habit of burning the candles into the small hours. "Did the messenger say what this was about?"

"No, sir."

"Saddle my courser," William told him with a terse nod. As Eustace's footfalls receded down the stairs, William turned back into the room. "I have to go," he said. "We'll talk when I return."

"When is that likely to be?" There was a weary edge to her voice.

"I don't know." He ran a distracted hand through his hair. "Hopefully just a few hours. You'll wait, won't you?"

"For just a few hours, yes."

He kissed her mouth and she kissed him back, and as their lips parted, it felt like farewell.

Sixteen

"SIRE?" WILLIAM STRODE INTO HIS LORD'S CHAMBER, noting that most of the household knights were already present. Clutching a half-full goblet of wine, Henry was sitting upon his bed which had not yet been prepared for slumber. The hangings were tied back and the day cover of grey and cream wolfskins was still in place.

"My father has made me an offer, Marshal," Henry said without preamble, "and I have to decide whether to accept or throw it in his teeth."

William scrambled for his wits. He was tired but knew he would receive no consideration for that. "What does the offer entail, sire?"

Raising his cup, Henry drank the wine to the lees and thrust it out to an attendant to be refilled. "He says that if I will cease making trouble and return to the fold, he will give me seventy pounds a day and stand the expenses for seventy knights for a year."

William nodded and rubbed his brow. "What do the King of France and the Count of Flanders say?"

Henry made a flat gesture with the palm of his hand. "That I should demand my rights in Normandy and take nothing less—but they would, wouldn't they, because it's in their interests to keep my family divided." He took the refilled cup and immediately gulped down the top third. To judge by his flushed cheek and glassy eye, he would soon be too gilded to stand up, let alone make a decision. "But they're right too. It's shameful that Richard and Geoffrey have territories to rule—and ruin in Richard's case—but I have nothing."

"In time, my lord, you will have more than any of your brothers," William pointed out.

"Hah! My father is not yet fifty years old. His father may have died at that age, but his grandsire kept his arse on the throne until he was almost seventy. How old will I be before I have my chance? Perhaps I won't. Perhaps I'll die before the old miser if he hoards his life the way he hoards his power."

"King Philip and the Count of Flanders are right, sire," said Yqueboeuf aggressively. "You should send your father's heralds back with the message that you'll settle for nothing less than the rule of Normandy."

Henry chewed his forefinger. "You think so?"

"I do, sire. It is the only answer you can give." The knight folded his arms and cast a challenge-filled glance towards William, daring him to contradict. Predictably, the de Coulances brothers were nodding too, unconsciously echoing Yqueboeuf's mannerisms. Several others muttered agreement, keen to endorse what looked like the prevailing opinion.

"Baldwin?" Henry turned to Baldwin of Béthune. "What do you say?"

Baldwin scratched his chin. "That you should keep negotiating, sire. I think it unlikely that your father will give you Normandy whatever you do."

Henry scowled. "You do, do you?"

"You asked for my opinion, sire." Baldwin stood his ground. His wide, candid gaze was disarming and belied the fact that he was one of the shrewdest knights in Henry's mesnie.

Henry turned to William. "What should I do? Take my father's offer, or tell him to go to the devil?"

William's brow pleated in a frown. "What Baldwin says is true. Your father will not give you Normandy, or even part of Normandy, but your presence at the French court is causing him great discomfort and aggravation. He is unsure of you. He almost lost his crown last time you rebelled and you were only a youth then. How much more havoc could you wreak now you have come to manhood?"

"You think I could take him on and win?" Henry's eyes gleamed at the prospect.

William shook his head. The notion of father and son facing each other across a battle field curdled his stomach. "Your father won't repeat the mistakes of nine years ago. He will quash anyone he suspects before they can organise and apportion the blame afterwards. But if you do take up arms against him, it is going to cause him a deal of trouble. I would counsel you not go to war with him, but bargain hard for the best settlement you can achieve. If he will not give you Normandy, then you should demand the trappings that would be yours if you were indeed its ruler."

Henry mulled the suggestion. "You're as wily as a merchant, Marshal," he said. "Are you sure you're not born from burgher stock?"

"He certainly likes to keep their company," Yqueboeuf sneered, referring to William's friendship with several of the traders and brokers who serviced the court.

"You can learn a great deal from merchants," William retorted. "You should ask something for the Queen's household too," he added to Henry. "That way King Philip will not feel that his family's dignity has been slighted."

Henry drained his wine. "A good idea." His laugh was hollow. "One way or the other, I will make my father pay."

William would have left then, but Henry was not ready to retire. Like an exhausted child at a celebration he was querulous, excited, on edge, and dangerous. He summoned a scribe and had him pen a letter to his father, setting out the terms by which he would agree to come to peace. William listened to him pile on the demands and inwardly winced, knowing who was going to be blamed. Henry seemed to be enjoying the list he was dictating to the scribe and kept looking to Yqueboeuf and the de Coulances brothers for encouragement.

"Our young lord likes your notion," Baldwin murmured out of the side of his mouth. "Let us hope we won't regret it."

"What else could I do? He's not in a mood to listen except to what he wants to hear. It was better than urging him to war." William dry-washed his face and wished he was a hundred miles away. Henry's musicians arrived, their faces puffy and pale from lack of sleep. Knowing exactly how they felt, William watched them set up in a corner and bring out their instruments—a Spanish lute and an Irish harp. He listened to the bleary plunk and twiddle of notes, and grimaced.

"Speaking of not wanting to hear, you should know that the rumours about you and Marguerite haven't abated," Baldwin muttered grimly. "There are some in the mesnie who would do anything to see you fall. Yqueboeuf talks to the others about how concerned he is for the Young King's reputation, but it's his own rise and your fall that he's courting."

"I do know of the rumours, but thank you," William said quietly and gave Baldwin a bleak smile. "You're a good friend."

Baldwin shook his head and looked troubled. "Yes, but I can't be everywhere at once," he said. "Watch your back."

It was dawn before Henry finally went to bed. The messengers had been despatched to his father at first light, and as the cockerels of the Île-de-France crowed on their dunghills, William made his way back to his lodging house, accompanied by Harry Norreis. William was staggering with tiredness. All he wanted to do was collapse on a thickly stuffed feather mattress and sleep for ever, but there was little chance of that just yet.

"Harry," he said with a jaw-cracking yawn, "next time we are on a tourney field, try not to be so exuberant about shouting my prowess abroad. There are some whom it offends, and while I do not give a cat's tail for their sensibilities, it might be diplomatic for you to hold off for a while."

Harry reddened. "I will do so if you wish it, sir, but those who are offended are naught but cowards and liars whose deeds will never match up to yours." The auburn stubble on his jaw bristled with his indignation.

William found a weary smile. "Your faith commends you," he said. "I am not certain that my deeds will ever match up to theirs though."

Harry blinked and looked at him with the expression if not the wisdom of an owl. "Sir?"

William shook his head. "Go to. Seek your pallet for a few hours if you can. I have no doubt that we'll be called to attend on the Young King the moment he wakes." He slapped Harry on the shoulder and, smiling, watched him shamble off towards his pallet in a corner of the downstairs room. The knight always reminded him of one of the tenacious little terriers that delighted in shoving their heads down fox dens and badger sets and clearing out infestations of rats in barns, often at the risk of being bitten themselves. He wondered how long it would be before one of his detractors referred to Harry as his lap dog.

On heavy legs he mounted the stairs to the bedchamber, set his hand to the latch and shouldered open the door. Although outside a red autumn sun was rising out of the banks of the night, the shutters were still latched and the room was dark and imbued with the lingering smell of snuffed candles. With foreboding but no surprise, William went to the windows, unfastened the boards, and let in the morning. The light from the open window cascaded on to the bed, brightening the colours on the striped coverlet, picking out the lozenges woven into the woollen hangings. It was neatly made and the pillows so plumped and smoothed that not a hint remained that anyone had ever slept there. Clara's travelling chest was gone from its corner, and with it the enamelled box he had given her to hold her combs and brooches. He knew that she must have waited those few hours of his asking, for the brazier was still warm and there was a feel of recent occupancy, but she had not given him the leeway of more time. Why should she? What would they have said anyway? It was over.

William unlatched his belt and dropped it on the floor. With fumbling hands, he stripped to his shirt and braies and, groaning softly, flopped on to the bed. Upon the pillow, a single fine, dark hair pointed up his loss. Pinching it between finger and thumb, he held it up to the light and then scattered it free. He supposed that she was right. He cared, he cared deeply, but not enough to abandon his post at court and chase after her to Le Mans to try and win her back. He turned on his side, drew up his knees, and slept.

Seventeen

THE FRENCH COURT HAD GONE HUNTING IN THE WOODS and pastures to the north of Paris. It was a crisp autumn day, the turning leaves an illuminator's scrollwork of bronze and verdigris against a sky of enamelled blue. Men and women had brought their hawks to fly at game and their dogs to flush the quarry from cover. Henry had a pair of silver greyhounds, fleet and dainty. On his wrist perched a peregrine falcon, its head covered by a close-fitting embroidered hood. Thus far there had been no word from his father, but Henry was not allowing it to spoil the day's sport.

William had never been enthusiastic about hunting. The best practice for war was the tourney field. Hunting might help to develop stamina and ability on horseback, but the skills weren't always of the kind needed to control a destrier in close-in fighting whilst wielding lance and sword. He enjoyed watching the hawks soar and plummet on their prey and he admired the skills of the falconers, but he did not have the same passion for the sport as Henry, Baldwin, and Marguerite. Her excited laughter rang out as she launched her peregrine to climb high above the fields of gleaned stubble. The wind had flushed colour into her cheeks and her brown eyes glowed. She rode her palfrey astride, as Queen Eleanor had been wont to do…and Clara too, her riding boots clipped with stylish silver spurs. Watching Marguerite, William was struck by a poignant sensation of loss. He could go for days on end without thinking about his former lover, but then something would prompt a memory and her ghost would be waiting for him, as once he had found her waiting in his tent.

Shortly after noon, the court stopped beside a stream to enjoy a leisurely picnic, which, besides the hunting, was half the reason for the venture. The hawks were secured to bow perches a little removed from the gathering so that the noise from the company would not disturb them. Cooks and kitchen boys who had been sent on ahead of the hunt laboured over firepits filled with a mixture of charcoal and firewood. There were cauldrons of simmering venison stew to greet the ravenous party, wheaten loaves, salmon baked in pastry, small tarts of chopped chicken and raisins, and apples and brambles stewed in honey. The kennel-keepers and grooms leashed the dogs, tethered the horses to graze, and sat around their own fire. Nearby the huntsmen sorted the morning's kills, neatly tying and bagging.

William took some bread and a bowl of stew and wandered down the stream a way. Usually he would have stayed with the company and sought the banter as a way of banishing unquiet memories, but the loud talk of the hunt was wearisome and suddenly he desired respite.

Shortly he arrived at a grassy bank that was obviously someone's fishing place, for it had been weeded of bramble and nettle and the turf was cropped short. William spread his cloak and sat down to eat. He could still hear the laughter and conversation of the hunting party but it was muted and the distance made it a comfort rather than an irritant. The sun was warm on his back and he was almost content. Having finished the stew he crouched at the side of the stream to rinse his bowl and spoon in the water. When he turned and rose, he found Marguerite and her maid standing behind him. The Queen's pet dog was with her: an exuberant brown and white spaniel with floppy ears and a panting pink tongue. It hurtled past William into the stream where it paddled round in the shallow current with huge delight before emerging and shaking itself vigorously, causing the humans to leap hastily aside. Panting, suddenly intent, the dog put its nose to the ground and set off along the river path. William picked up his cloak and followed; so did Marguerite, her hands gathering her trailing woollen skirts above the moist grass and her gown spotted with water from her dog's coat.

"I haven't spoken to you in a long while," she said, "at least not in the proper way that old friends should talk."

"Madam, there are some at court who would call all ways 'improper,'" William said, his tone filled with warning.

A look of irritation crossed her face. "And we know who they are and what their opinions are worth. I will walk where I will and talk to whom I wish. I am not a child; I am England's future Queen and the sister of the King of France." She jutted her jaw.

"Indeed, madam, but it is dangerous nevertheless."

Her lips pursed with impatience. "Oh William! Stop using your courtier's voice and look at me without your mask."

William blinked at the sharpness of her tone. "If I wear a mask it is the same as the face beneath. How would you have me speak and behave?"

"As if I am your friend and not a stranger to whom you have to be polite." Marguerite took his arm and shook it gently. "Alone or in company, people will see what they want to see, I weary of the lot of them." She breathed out hard and stopped to face him, her gaze steady and forthright and her hand still determinedly on his sleeve. "Do you remember when you played with us in Queen Eleanor's gardens in Poitou? Myself and the Queen's daughters?"

"Hoodman blind, if I recall." William's voice scraped over his larynx.

"You let me catch you. You always swore that you didn't, but I know that you did. You could have evaded us all every time."

He shrugged. "But then I wouldn't have been invited so often into the Queen's garden."

"No." Her smile was wistful. "I always thought that you enjoyed playing with us; it never occurred to me that you were doing it for your own purpose."

"Ambition and pleasure are not always mutually exclusive. Besides, it wasn't so much ambition as a case of being besotted with Queen Eleanor."

"And are you still besotted?"

"Of course I am. She never lets you go." He gave a pained smile. "Clara looked a little like her; she had a similar grace. I suppose that was half of what attracted me in the first place—that and the fact that she saved my life."

"Oh, William." Impulsively, Marguerite took his hand, stood on tiptoe and pressed a kiss to his cheek.

The spaniel suddenly began to growl, and then to bark, its legs stiff, and its ears cocked in the direction of the woods beyond the grass bank. Marguerite's eyes widened with fear. The maid moved swiftly to her side and William dropped the bowl and spoon and drew the long hunting knife at his belt. Nothing moved except the wind-rustled grasses. The breeze was blowing towards them, carrying scents to the dog's sensitive nose.

"Madam, I think you should return to the main party before you are sought," William said, "and it is probably for the best if I follow at a distance."

Her eyes widened. "You think we were being spied on?"

"I am certain of it." He sheathed the knife with deliberate care, forcing control upon himself. It was pointless to go in search of whoever had been watching them. The dog's barking would have alerted them to the danger of being discovered, even as it had alerted William and Marguerite. "Go, madam," he said. "And say nothing. You have nothing to be reproached for, unless comforting a friend's grief is wrong." He bent her an eloquent look to which she responded with a stiff nod. Pale, but resolute, she clapped her hands to the dog and turned back towards the picnic, her maid close by her side. He watched the women from sight then stooped to pick up his bowl and spoon, his expression sombre. He hoped that it would blow over like a storm cloud on a windy day, but acknowledged that he had given the court gossips all the ammunition they needed to cast him down.

Eighteen

RALPH FARCI WAS A DRUNKARD AND A GLUTTON, HENCE his name, which meant "stuffed." He looked as if he had a cushion up his tunic which he frequently wore unbelted to give himself more belly room. Despite his size, he was nimble enough on his feet and had a quick eye and hand—useful for sword fighting, but even more so for dice and games of chance where the rumour was that he cheated. He was in a jovial mood for his hawk had made several kills during the hunt, and his dogs had helped course down a hare. The dinner had been excellent, the wine plentiful, and his favourite court whore had promised him a soft bed for the night. He had lost at dice with the Young King, but that had been deliberate and he wasn't too much out of purse. The pay-off was a place basking in the warmth of the Young King's favour.

Caressing the whore who was sitting in his lap, he nodded genially to Adam Yqueboeuf and Thomas de Coulances as they joined him.

"Fine hunt today," said Yqueboeuf. "Your falcon flew particularly well, I thought."

"She did, didn't she?" Farci pushed the woman off his knee and waved her away. She could easily wait on a discussion about the prowess of his falcon with knights whose approval he sought.

The talk and the wine flowed easily as the men dissected the day's sport and Farci found himself being courted as if he were of great importance, which left him flattered and a little bewildered. Usually he had to do the chasing.

"Of course," Yqueboeuf said, leaning towards Farci and lowering his voice, "there was another kind of hunt in full cry too, and less noble than the one we were engaged in."

Farci frowned at them. "There was?"

Yqueboeuf glanced around and further dropped his voice. "Where do you think the Queen went when we stopped to dine?"

Farci shrugged. "I don't know; for a piss in the bushes. I didn't notice."

"You didn't notice, because for most of the time she wasn't there…and neither was William Marshal."

"Ah." Farci's interest kindled. He had no love for Marshal and was deeply envious of the way the man could eat everything on the table without an ounce of it showing on his hard, athletic frame. The Young King appeared to think that the sun shone out of Marshal's arse, which was another reason to feel antipathy.

"They were trysting in the woods."

Farci looked from Yqueboeuf to de Coulances. "You jest, surely."

Yqueboeuf snapped his fingers at an attendant and demanded a fresh pitcher of wine. "Did you not see the Young Queen returning to the picnic all flustered and flushed as if she'd been well tupped, and then the Marshal strolling back on the same path a few minutes later?"

Farci chewed his underlip. "Now you mention it, the Queen did seem unsettled during the afternoon. She put me in mind of a doe who knows she is being stalked but cannot see the hunter."

"Believe me, she has already been chased and caught and split with a spear," Yqueboeuf said crudely.

"You know this for certain?"

Yqueboeuf nodded and exchanged glances with de Coulances. "There are witnesses."

Farci expanded his chest in indignation. "God's bones, if what you say is true, Marshal and the Young Queen have committed treason!" The attendant returned with a brimming pitcher and Farci immediately helped himself to another goblet of wine.

"It is true," Yqueboeuf said, "but if Thomas or I tried to tell the Young King of our doubts, he would not believe us. He knows that we are hostile to Marshal and he would suspect our motives."

"But you can't let the Young King be cuckolded like this," Farci spluttered. "What if she should get with child?"

Yqueboeuf poured wine for himself and de Coulances. "Indeed, and if someone that the Young King trusted to be more impartial should broach the matter to him, he might be prepared to listen and do something about it."

Farci drank, realised the other two were watching him as intently as a pair of cats at a mousehole, and almost spluttered his mouthful back out. "Me!" he choked. "You want me to tell the Young King that William Marshal has put the horns on him!"

Yqueboeuf leaned forward, his gaze glittering with intent. "For the good of us all, the Marshal must be dragged off his pedestal and shown for the base knave that he is. This shameful state of affairs cannot be allowed to continue."

"But why should the Young King believe me?" Farci asked in bewilderment. "Marshal is his favourite. Henry's not going to take my word over his." He wondered what he was getting into. He didn't like William Marshal, but he didn't want to end up in disgrace for making adverse comments to the Young King about his favourite—unless he could be certain that those comments would topple the knight.

"He would have to if you had others to confirm your story, and he trusts you. There are many knights of the company who will agree with you once the words have been said. The only men who will stand for Marshal are the likes of de Béthune and the de Preaux brothers, and they will be voices in the wilderness. Myself and Thomas will make sure of that." Yqueboeuf folded his arms, making the gesture one of finality. "Henry needs to be told by someone to whom he will listen. Of course, if you would rather not and let us be ruled by an English scab-wit and his friends, that's up to you…"

Farci shook his head and swallowed. "No…no, leave it with me," he said. "I will talk to our lord and see that he knows."

His belly roiling with wine and shock, Henry curtly dismissed the guards and squires outside his wife's apartment. He couldn't believe what he had just been told, but Ralph Farci was a solid, indolent blockhead, without that kind of imagination. It couldn't be true; yet remembering William's courtliness toward Marguerite and the way that her silks were as often tied to William's banner on the tourney field as his own, he was assailed by doubt. A few years ago, Philip of Flanders had executed one of his mesnie for dallying with his wife. It happened, it happened frequently, but Henry had never believed that it would happen to him. He was too sure of his own worth and to have it attacked from this direction was a shock…if, of course, it was true.

Marguerite's maids curtseyed to him as he gestured them out with a swift jerk of his head. The women left with apprehensive looks over their shoulders, especially his wife's favourite maid, Nicolette. He almost bade the woman remain, and then changed his mind. She might know more than he wanted to hear.

Marguerite came to him and he wondered if what he saw on her face was natural anxiety at having her husband burst in on her so late at night, or the more damning traces of guilt and fear. The women had been brushing her hair and it fell in a bright brown skein to her waist. It was her best feature, that and her white, full breasts, tipped by large rosy nipples. She was wearing her bedrobe, and beneath it a chemise of delicate linen. He wondered how often William Marshal had been a party to that sight? How many times had he unfastened the tie of her bedrobe, pulled open the throat lacing of her chemise and availed himself of those white, pillowy breasts? Had he laid her on the bed and mounted her? Had she spread her legs for him and taken his seed? Henry had to swallow a retch.

"Husband?"

Although it was night and the light not good, he thought that she had paled. "You know why I have come," he said harshly.

She shook her head. "No…no, I do not. If you had sent your steward I could have—"

"Could have what?" he interrupted. "Made sure that you weren't going to be caught in the act of whoredom? Made sure that your foolish, purblind husband remained ignorant of what you have been doing behind his back?"

"I…I have been doing nothing," she stammered, and pressed one hand to those white, round breasts. "Of what are you accusing me?"

"Treason in the form of adultery," he snarled. "Do not deny that you and William Marshal are lovers. You have been witnessed at your fornication."

She stared at him. "Whoever told you such a tale is lying." She crossed herself and jutted her chin. "I swear to you on my father's soul that I have not committed the carnal act with William Marshal."

"Then you are forsworn, madam, because you were seen at your tryst this very afternoon. I have witnesses who will swear on the bones of Saint Hilaire that you and Marshal have been conducting an affair beneath my nose."

"That's not true!" she gasped. "You know it isn't. Until recently he had a mistress."

"Having a mistress doesn't render a man faithful," he snarled, "any more than having a husband does the same for a wife. How do I know that he's the only one? Perhaps you have had a string of lovers in your bed!" He seized her by the shoulders and shook her.

"No…no one but you," Marguerite cried, "although I don't know why you should care when you are never in it. I might as well be a nun!"

"Well, that can be swiftly remedied." Henry roughly unfastened the tie of her bedrobe. When she struggled and turned away from his kiss, he grabbed her jaw in his hand and forced her to face him. "You'll not accept Marshal and refuse me," he snarled.

"I haven't lain with William Marshal!" she cried, struggling. "There is nothing between us! I will swear on whatever relics you choose to name that I am telling the truth!"

"Nothing between you?" His voice curled with contempt. "So much of nothing that beneath my nose you creep away to meet him for a tryst in the woods? You must think me stupid indeed."

"It wasn't a tryst. I walked my dog a little way along the bank and I happened upon him—I did not know he had walked that way too." Her voice wobbled on the verge of angry tears.

"You expect me to believe that you hadn't arranged it all with Marshal beforehand?" He dug his fingers into her shoulders.

"You would rather believe your cronies?" she spat with scorn. "Half of them have their swords out for Marshal, you know it. Why would I be foolish enough to agree to a tryst where we were almost certain to be spied upon and discovered? Who was it brought you the tale, Yqueboeuf?"

Henry's complexion darkened. "You were seen embracing him. Do you deny it?"

She lifted her head. "I do. All I did was speak to him as a friend. Whoever has told you that we have fornicated together is lying."

Henry studied his wife. Was she feeding him lies too? Did he believe her, or did he believe Ralph Farci and the five knights who were insisting that his wife and William Marshal had played him false? "Do you know what Philip of Flanders did to his wife's lover?" It was a rhetorical question. Everyone knew that the man had been severely beaten by the household butchers and then hung upside down in a sewer until he suffocated.

"William Marshal is not my lover." She had steadied since the first accusation, although she was as pale as a winding sheet.

"But you love him…"

She dropped her gaze to her hands and rubbed her wedding ring. "Yes," she said. "I love him as a friend or as a sister."

That statement at least was untrue because she would not look him in the face. "You're a lying whore," he said, taking relish in his words. "I am within my rights to beat you within an inch of your life and have Marshal executed for treason."

Her chin trembling, she raised her head and looked at him again. "That is between you and your conscience," she said. "I know what is on mine."

Henry raised his fist, looked at it, then opened his hand and gave her a shove that sent her staggering. Then he turned on his heel and strode from the room. He had always felt antipathy towards his wife. She was neither beautiful nor witty and the steadier attributes of quiet attractiveness and intelligence had small value for him. As far as he was concerned, he was a victim of onerous duty and circumstance. That Marguerite was a victim too, he acknowledged, but gave little consideration to the fact. Perhaps now though, he had a way to be rid of her, if he was prepared to sacrifice his best knight. However, if he ordered Marshal's arrest and execution as he had threatened, the affair would become an open scandal and he would be made a laughing stock, forced to wear his horns in public. Did he really want that? Henry slewed to a halt and stood in the corridor, caught on the tines of a decision.

"Sire?" Rannulf his chamberlain was passing, on his way to bed, and stopped to bow.

"Have you heard the rumours?" Henry demanded of him.

Rannulf raised his thin silver brows. "Rumours, sire?"

"Concerning my wife and William Marshal."

Rannulf shuffled his feet. "A few, sire, but I have paid them the heed that I would pay to a pile of dog turds and avoided them. I know they are untrue."

"Then you know more than me."

Rannulf said nothing, his expression carefully neutral.

"Do you know where Marshal is?"

"No, sire. Do you want me to find him?"

"No," Henry said tersely. "I don't want to see him. Indeed, if he seeks me out, deny him access to my presence. That's an order and you are to pass it down to the guards and squires. He is not welcome."

"Sire," Rannulf said, but looked ill at ease.

"I mean it; I'll not be made to look a fool by any man. It goes without saying that you will keep your silence on the matter."

"No one shall hear anything from my lips, sire."

With a stiff nod, Henry strode on to his chamber. Watching his retreating back, Rannulf pondered for a while on what he should do, and finally went in search of Baldwin de Béthune.

❖ ❖ ❖

William woke to find himself being shaken like a rat in the jaws of a terrier. He squinted at the painful splinters of daylight poking through the shutters. The woman beside him sat up and drew the sheets around her body with a gasp of alarm.

"Jesu, are you set on destroying yourself?" demanded Baldwin de Béthune, his voice gruff with anger. "Get up, for Christ's sake." Bundling up the woman's garments, he thrust them at her. "Out," he snapped.

"It's all right, leave her be," William groaned. He peered through half-closed lids at Baldwin who was simmering like a cauldron with too much steam under the lid.

"That's a fine thing for you to say. Do you know the trouble you're in?"

William pushed his hair out of his eyes. Catching a stench of armpit he grimaced. "No, but I can guess."

"No you can't." Baldwin flicked another look at the woman. With a sigh and a curse at the pain spearing through his wine-abused skull, William reached over the bed, found his pouch, and paid her with a handful of coins. Baldwin eyed her impatiently and tapped his fingers against the buckle of his swordbelt. She wasn't one of the court whores, he knew all of them, but she was handsome and her clothes were of good quality. But then William had taste—Baldwin had to allow him that. The best or nothing…and it had just cost him far more dearly than a handful of Angevin silver pennies.

Knotting her pay in a kerchief, the whore retreated into the bay overhanging the street to don her clothes and braid her hair. William left the bed, washed his face and torso in a shallow brass bowl on the coffer and, drying himself on the coarse linen towel beside it, looked at his friend. "Tell me the worst."

"That is yet to come," Baldwin replied tersely. "Ralph Farci went to Henry last night and told him that you and the

Young Queen were lovers—that you had committed adultery together, and Farci summoned witnesses, including Yqueboeuf and de Coulances, to confirm his accusation."

William froze in mid-wipe. "What?"

"Rannulf the chamberlain came to me and told me to warn you. Henry has taken the news badly…"

William flung the towel towards the bed and dragged a clean shirt off the clothing pole. "I have to speak to him," he said as he dived into the garment. He felt as if someone were determinedly screwing a knife into his left temple. The whore finished her toilet and quietly left the room.

"You can't," Baldwin said. "Henry has given orders that you're not to be admitted to his presence. He doesn't want to speak to you."

William paused in the act of reaching for his tunic. He had known that the situation was serious, but this raised the stakes. "Surely he doesn't believe the rumours? Surely he knows me better than that?"

Baldwin fixed him with a sombre stare. "I do not know how well he knows any of us, or how well we know him. All I can tell you is what Rannulf told me, and that was not a great deal."

Slowly William donned his tunic. His headache and a general feeling of malaise made it hard to think. While he had been seeking oblivion in a flagon of wine and the embraces of a whore, Henry had been finding answers—most of them slanted in the wrong direction by the sounds of it. He concentrated on fastening his belt. "Yesterday, at the hunt, when we stopped to picnic, Marguerite came upon me by the banks of the stream…We talked of times past and she kissed me."

Baldwin's gaze widened with dismay. "Christ on the cross!" he muttered.

William flushed. "It was bestowed out of friendship—foolish

and ill advised, yes, but with no intent to play Henry false. I swear to you on the body of our Lord Jesus Christ that I have never touched Marguerite in the manner of a lover, nor she me. Anyone who says that we have is a base liar." He reached for his cloak. "I need to see Henry."

"I've told you, you can't," Baldwin said in exasperation. "He won't receive you."

"But I need at least to try," William said grimly. He started to the door, and then turned back to Baldwin. "I will understand if you choose to distance yourself."

Baldwin snorted and laid a hand to William's shoulder. "The day that I throw in my lot with toads like Adam Yqueboeuf and the de Coulances brothers is the day I die. If I can help you, I will. I'll send letters to my father. I know he'll aid you."

William didn't like the way Baldwin seemed to think it a foregone conclusion that matters would go badly for him at court, but there was nothing to be done except walk into the lion's den and find out what awaited.

Nineteen

*I*F YOU TAKE MY ADVICE, WHICH I KNOW YOU WON'T,
you'll go nowhere near the Christmas court." Mounting
his horse, Baldwin's father Robert de Béthune cast William a
warning look.

William, who had been lodging with him at Béthune
following a tourney, set his hand to his palfrey's bridle. His
baggage roll lay on the crupper and the pack pony's panniers
were laden with armour and accoutrements. Bezant restlessly
pawed a forehoof on the courtyard floor, eager to be off. "I
have to," he replied. "The Young King is still my lord and one
way or another I must resolve the bad blood between us."

Robert de Béthune gave him one of the sidelong stares that
William was more accustomed to seeing from Baldwin, but said
nothing. The family came out to bid the men Godspeed to the
royal gathering at Caen. Robert's youngest daughter, Matilda,
looked shyly through her lashes at William. Baldwin had hinted
that should William find himself in a bind, their father might see
clear to arranging a marriage, but it was a hint that William had
tactfully ignored. Fond though he was of Baldwin and his family,
he had no intention of settling down with a wife towards whose
relatives he would be eternally beholden for his daily bread.

Robert de Béthune was a taciturn travelling companion,
content to ride in silence through the bare-treed winter

landscape and thus William was able to ponder and take stock of the changes in his life.

The situation with Henry remained awkward and unresolved. Baldwin's fears had been borne out and the Young King had refused to see him, even to the point of having his guards clash crossed spears beneath William's nose. There had been no place for him at the high table or counsel chamber. On a couple of occasions he had managed to slip past the guards, but without satisfaction, for Henry had turned his head aside and refused to acknowledge William's presence. To all intents and purposes, he had become invisible. Marguerite was keeping to her chambers and William dared not send a message to her lest it aggravate the situation.

There was rampant speculation about the rift, the opinion at large being that William's reputation for great deeds and chivalry had eclipsed the Young King's star; that William had risen too high and now must fall. Whispers hinting at an affair between William and the Queen were fed upon with relish, not least because such a deed was high treason and carried the death penalty. Folk watched, awaited the outcome, and were disappointed when all Henry did was ignore William until the latter put an end to the intolerable situation by quitting the court. The bond between them had not been officially severed but there had been no point in remaining. Neither absolved nor dishonoured, William was simply being ignored and he found it difficult. All his life he had been afforded attention, mostly of the positive kind. Now he was an outcast at the hearth where he had dominated for more than ten years, and it hurt.

For a while he had sojourned with Guillaume de Tancarville, who was also out of favour with his royal masters, although for questionable political dealings rather than for taking all the glory at tourneys and stealing the heart of his overlord's wife. Baldwin de Béthune kept William abreast of the situation at court. Farci,

Yqueboeuf, and the de Coulances brothers were lording it over the other knights in the Young King's retinue, especially the English ones who had prospered when William had been in favour. The only good piece of news was that Henry and his father had ended their dispute with a financial agreement that would guarantee Henry a large increase in funds.

William watched a flock of crows take flight from a fallow field and flap ponderously across a smoke-coloured sky. His thoughts drew a deep sigh from him, and Robert de Béthune, who had been dozing in the saddle, squinted a sleepy eye in his direction. "You're brooding up a rare clutch of troubles there," he said. "In my experience the ones that hatch are never those you expect."

William managed a smile. "If I had any sense I'd abandon the nest and build another one far away."

Robert gave a snort of dour amusement. "Aye, roosting with Plantagenets is a hazardous business. If matters go ill for you at court, you know you have a place at Béthune. My daughter is rather taken with you, and I'd be glad to see her married to someone of your fibre."

William laughed acidly. "You do know of what I stand accused?"

Baldwin's father waved a hand in disgust. "Ach, that campaign against you is one of deliberate sabotage; everyone knows that. Your enemies have neither the proof nor the backbone to stand against you, but say something often enough in vulnerable ears and incredulity turns to belief."

"I have a remedy for that," William replied grimly. "I have a right in the King's court to trial by combat. I will challenge my accusers to prove their case against me on the field of battle and let God be the judge."

"That carries its own risks," de Béthune warned.

"I do not fear to be judged."

"No, but they might," the older man said shrewdly. "Knowing your quarry is simple, but flushing it out of the bushes is a different matter." He sighed deeply. "I come to court when I must. I do not think that I could dwell there as a matter of course. My son does, and I admire his fortitude, but I fear for him too." He nodded again at William. "I meant what I said about finding you a place in my family. As a man grows older he needs able deputies. Of course your own family may have a welcome for you…?" He ended the statement as a question to which William responded by shaking his head.

"Probably the kind of welcome that would make hell seem cold by comparison," he said mordantly, imagining John's response should he arrive at Hamstead disgraced and stripped of his position. "*I warned you,*" would be the first, sanctimonious words William would have to parry. "I will bear your offer in mind; you truly do me more honour than I deserve."

King Henry's Christmas court at Caen was a great and lavish gathering. The hall was packed with earls, counts, dukes, bishops, deacons, archdeacons, barons, knights, and their retainers. The room glittered like an open jewel box for everyone was wearing his or her best robes, adorned with every last ring, brooch, and gemstone rifled from the family coffers or bought with credit from the Jews. When William arrived, he immediately stood out, for he was wearing a tunic of a blue as dark as the night sky and chausses of deepest brazilwood red. A single gold ring adorned his left hand and his person was devoid of other embellishment except for his gilded belt. Both the understated nature of his garb and the fact of his presence caused heads to turn and whispers to trail in his wake.

Henry's sons were all attending the gathering, a miracle given the strife between them. Richard ruled Aquitaine with an iron hand and was ruthless to those who opposed him, but he hadn't been able entirely to stamp out the rebels, some of whom had appealed to Henry the Young King for aid, which he had been only too pleased to promise. The brothers had been circling each other warily ever since, a mere fraction from open war. Their father had forced a bridge across the breach between them, but it was a crumbling edifice built on worthless promises and soothing but meaningless murmurs of: "We'll see what can be done." William thought it more likely that it was all going to collapse and plunge everyone into the dark chasm of war.

He made his way unobtrusively closer to the dais. The King sat on a high-backed chair, his red hands clutching the lion's head finials in a way that spoke of assertion and power. At his left hand side Richard was resplendent in a kingfisher-coloured tunic that contrasted with his auburn-gold hair and gave lucent clarity to his eyes. He resembled a young lion, dangerous and fiery. Beside him sat Geoffrey, the King's third son and Count of Brittany, dark-haired and stocky. To their father's right Henry the Young King lounged in his chair, his expression bored and petulant. The candlelight shot his brown hair with tawny lights and slanted across the high cheekbones and strong jaw. He was robed in gold silk, encrusted with gems, and he wore his crown, to emphasise his standing. The knights of his retinue stood close guard, chief amongst them Farci and Yqueboeuf. William was also glad to see Baldwin de Béthune and three of the de Preaux brothers. Henry wasn't entirely surrounded by sycophants and idiots.

"You are mad coming here, you know," Wigain muttered, suddenly appearing at William's side.

"You think so, do you?" William glanced at him. Wigain had long outgrown the simple duties of a kitchen clerk, and was often to be found on more dangerous and delicate missions than sourcing capons for the royal table.

Wigain folded his arms and leaned against a trestle. "I'd back you against anyone on the tourney field. You've the measure and more of every man in this room, but the mêlée of the court is not so clean and honourable." He gave William a penetrating look. "Until recently you've escaped serious injury, but if you fight on now, it'll be to the death, and I'm not sure whose."

William smiled bleakly. "You're not wagering on me to win this time then?"

Wigain gave a sombre shake of his head. "I only bet on certainties."

William pressed the clerk's shoulder. "You're a good friend, Wigain," he said, and meant it. He watched the dais and waited his moment. The court was indeed like a tourney field in many ways and he knew that sooner or later Adam Yqueboeuf and Ralph Farci would quit their posts to pursue their own business. The moment arrived when Farci went to relieve himself, leaving Baldwin de Béthune at Henry's side. Yqueboeuf was watching one of the jesters who was walking on his hands while balancing meat pies on the soles of his feet. Drawing a deep breath, William strode to the dais, mounted it, and bowed head and knee before Young Henry.

Yqueboeuf started to draw his sword but Baldwin warned him back, and de Coulances was similarly stopped by Peter de Preaux. Young Henry ceased slouching in his chair and sat up, a red flush creeping over the stubble on his throat and mantling his face.

"Sire, I ask you the boon of listening to me," William said formally. An upward glance was not promising for it showed him that the Young King was scowling ferociously and looking away. His father, however, was leaning forward and stroking his chin. Geoffrey's expression was neutral, Richard's curious.

Doggedly, William pressed on. "Rumourmongers have been spreading the vicious lie that I have committed treason against you—you know the matter of which I speak, as you know those who have spread these vile stories. Today, before your lord father, in full view of all men who are able to judge right from wrong, I have come to defend myself. I challenge my accusers to come forward and face me on the field of battle." His voice rang along the high table, for he was appealing to be judged by his peers. Although he had not been bid to stand, he rose to his feet and fixed Yqueboeuf, Thomas de Coulances, and the newly returned Ralph Farci with a contemptuous stare. "Let three of their number come forward and I will fight each one, on three successive days. Should I fail on any count, then take me to the gibbet and have me hanged and drawn forthwith. I trust in God to prove my innocence."

Farci's gaze widened, whilst Yqueboeuf's narrowed. Thomas de Coulances shot both of them a look filled with apprehension. The Young King said nothing, although the red flush had now reached his scalp. It was left to his father to wave his hand in a gesture of weary dismissal.

"Marshal, you are souring my digestion with your complaint and I want none of it. This is neither the time nor the place."

"Then if not here before my King and my lord and all my peers, when is the time and place?" William retorted bitterly. "The men who started the rumours against me are present and within listening distance. Why have none of them spoken up to defend their vile whisperings?" He had intended to speak with diplomacy but found it no longer possible. He was known for his implacable good humour but the last few months had worn it threadbare. He raised his right hand and spread it palm facing outwards, towards father and sons, showing the hard, strong span of his fingers. "Take my right hand," he said hoarsely, "the one that has wielded sword and lance in the loyal service of your family for all of my adult life. Cut off a finger and let the man among my accusers who considers himself the best do battle with me. If he can bring me to defeat, then deal with me as you would any traitor. Otherwise let my name be cleared once and for all of these putrid rumours."

The King looked at his own hands and his eldest son at the floor. William stared at them, rage and despair scalding through him. "It is plain to see that a lying tongue will brave all that its owner dare not prove," he said with scathing contempt. "I may be a fool, but I am not blind. You are seeking to be rid of me. Have your desire. There is no point in my remaining if you will not grant me justice in your court. In full hearing of all present, I renounce my service to you. I will seek patronage from men who do not tolerate liars and cowards under their roofs."

At William's words, Young Henry clenched the arms of his chair until his knuckles blenched, but still he made no answer. His father slowly raised his head. "So be it," he said impassively. "You may have a safe conduct as far as Mortagne. All ties are sundered herewith." He waved William away with the indifference he might bestow on a chance-come suppliant he had never met before. Thomas de Coulances eagerly stepped forward to manhandle William from the dais. William thrust him off with an elbow to the midriff that doubled the knight over in a whoof of exhaled breath. His brother and another knight hastened to his aid and William was pummelled and shoved. Yqueboeuf seized William's right arm and rammed it behind his back, intent on dislocating or breaking the limb. Baldwin and Peter de Preaux strode into the fray and sundered Yqueboeuf's grip. A frowning Prince Geoffrey leaned to speak to his father.

The King rose to his feet. "Enough." His harsh voice cut across the babble in the hall. "William Marshal's safe conduct begins here at my feet and you will let him go in my peace."

The knights released William with a final shove that sent him stumbling against one of the trestles. A goblet of wine tipped over and a red stain spread across the napery. William pushed himself upright and straightened his tunic. His heart was hammering against his ribs and a mist blurred his vision. He wanted to lash out, to sweep his hand along the board and see the cups and platters, the loaves and sauce dishes fly in all directions. To use his fists and smash the smug expressions from the faces of the men who thought they had won. It took every iota of his control but he managed to check himself and walk away from the temptation, the sounds of the hall echoing in his ears. The mist across his vision became moisture and seeped over his lids.

The guards stood aside to let him pass and then crossed their spears behind him. There was bile in William's throat. He swallowed and swallowed, but it was no use. In the end, he gave up the struggle and, leaning against the pale grey stone, retched up the wine he had drunk. There was nothing else in his stomach but the hollow sensation of shame and failure and loss.

His gut aching, he straightened up and walked unsteadily towards the stables. Wigain came running after him, clutching the writ of safe conduct, the ink still wet and the sealing wax still warm. "It is a shame, a vile shame!" he said furiously as William signalled Rhys to saddle his horse.

William shook his head. "It is more than that," he replied, then compressed his lips so that he would not say more.

"King Henry is angry with you for making all those demands on our young lord's behalf."

"What demands?" William asked blankly.

"When our lord desired to have Normandy for his own rule and you said that he should milk his father for as much as he could obtain. The King blames you for what he lost from his coffers in order to pacify his son."

"I was trying to avert another war of the kind that almost brought the house of Anjou to its knees last time," William snapped. "I shouldn't have bothered; I should have let them tear each other limb from limb."

Wigain lifted his shoulders. "As far as the King is concerned, you are the one who helps Henry spend beyond his means and waste his time at the tourneys. He thinks that you have grown too great and proud and you need a lesson in humility."

William thought he had control of himself, but something must have shown in his face for Wigain took several steps back and licked his lips. "I am only telling you what I have heard. Do you think I am your enemy too?"

William released his breath on a hard sigh. "No, Wigain, I don't, never that." He took the safe conduct from the clerk and pushed it down between tunic and shirt.

Wigain's dark eyes were robin-bright. "Promise me you will send word if you are going to take part in any tourneys. I'll want to wager on your success."

William eyed him sidelong. "Even now?"

"I never make a bad bet," Wigain said. "That heap of dross surrounding the Young King won't last long. I give them until spring at the most."

William set his foot to the stirrup and swung astride his palfrey. "Is that a wager too?"

Wigain shook his head. "No, my lord," he said. "A certainty."

William did not miss the fact that Wigain had called him "my lord." There was no irony in Wigain's tone, only a troubled respect.

As William turned his mount, Baldwin came striding towards him from the direction of the hall, his expression thunderous. "The whoresons!" he spat. "The bastards! They'll rot in hell for this! I'll see justice done if it kills me."

William shook his head. "Do not jeopardise yourself for me." He drew in the reins as the palfrey caught the tension in the air and pranced. "If you find the opportunity, tell Queen Marguerite that I am sorry and bid her have courage."

"It's not about you and the Queen at all," Baldwin said vehemently. "It's about the petty jealousy of small and cowardly men."

William shrugged. "Then I am free of it now." He leaned down to clasp Baldwin's arm in a soldier's grip. "Tell her."

Baldwin gave a stiff nod. "I will. Where will you go?"

Again William shrugged. "Wherever the wind blows me," he said. "And in a way it will be a relief."

Twenty

The Rhineland, Spring 1183

MARCH SNOW NEVER LASTED LONG, BUT FROM THE DENSITY of flakes whirling from the massed banks of thick, yellow-grey clouds, no one would have believed it. A biting north wind swept William's cloak against his spine. There was no telling the time of day for the sky gave no indication as to the position of the sun but William knew that it must be after noon. He could feel snow seeping through his hood in ice-water tendrils. The flakes were melting to grey slush as they landed on the rutted track. In the trees bracketing the road, a wolf howled and William heard his squire invoking the Holy Virgin to protect their small company from harm. There were terrifying tales of pilgrims being attacked by the packs that prowled the swathes of forest in what had been the heart of the Holy Roman Empire and although sharp swords were a comfort, the fear was sharper still.

William was returning from a pilgrimage to the Cathedral of Saint Peter and Saint Paul in Cologne, where he had visited the shrine of the Three Magi. He had offered up prayers asking for their intercession in the matter of his banishment from the Young King's household. The shrine itself was still being built but its popularity was already widespread. William had been one amongst hundreds, including pilgrims who had already made the journeys to Rome, to Compostela, and even the Holy Sepulchre in Jerusalem. The experience had both humbled and uplifted him. Pride had been taken and pride had been restored.

There was a momentary lull in the wind and the snowflakes became smaller, like drifting hawthorn blossom. "Lights," cried Eustace, jabbing his mittened hand towards a yellow twinkle on the road ahead.

"Praise God." William made the sign of the cross. He wouldn't have relished pitching a tent at the roadside tonight. Moments later a hostel loomed out of the weather, smoke eddying from its louvres and dissipating amid the swirls of snow. With relief, the men rode into the yard and were directed by an attendant to a spacious barn to stable their mounts. As Rhys and Eustace set about tending the palfreys, packhorses, and destrier, William inspected the mounts belonging to the other guests. There were a couple of solid hacks, a handsome grey mule, the usual motley assortment of pack beasts, and a fine, strong palfrey the bitter brown colour of oak gall ink. William stared at the beast as it rested on one hip and champed on the hay in its net. Since horses were a valuable and integral part of his life, he seldom forgot one, and he had long admired this particular animal.

Leaving Eustace and Rhys to finish the stabling, he hastened across the yard towards the torchlit reek of the main tavern, cursing as he stepped in a slushy puddle and liquid ice sprang through the ankle fastening of his right boot. The solid door swung open on a main room with a floor that was almost as thick in straw as the stables, but considerably more trampled and thatched with age. New had been thrown on top of old and the layers piled up to make a thick insulating carpet. Most of the guests were huddled on stools and benches around the central hearth, warming themselves at the fire. William's gaze trawled the assortment of merchants, soldiers, carters, and clerics until he arrived at the owner of the brown palfrey who was hunched over the flames, the beaver lining of his cloak folded over in a deep collar and drawn around his bright red ears. A mug of hot wine occupied his equally reddened hands. He looked round as William's entry swept a gust of icy wind through the room.

"God on the Cross!" swore Rannulf FitzGodfrey, the Young King's chamberlain. Putting down his cup, he sprang to his feet. "At last! Do you know how far I've searched for you? You're more elusive than a blasted unicorn!"

The two men embraced hard with much back slapping. At length, pulling back, Rannulf called to the hosteller for more hot wine, which William accepted with alacrity. "I have been to the shrine of the Magi at Cologne Cathedral," he said. "And before that I was in France and Flanders. You could always have found me there…" He gave Rannulf a keen look and took a seat at one of the benches. The heat glowed out towards him from the hearth bricks. A couple of large earthenware cooking pots stood on them, a savoury steam wafting tantalisingly over their rims. William's stomach rumbled. It seemed an age since his mid-morning meal of bread, mutton pasty, and sour wine, snatched in the saddle.

"Well, I went to France and Flanders," Rannulf said, "but you were always ahead of me, and your reputation with you."

"Oh yes?" William's tone was neutral. "And what reputation would that be?" The door opened again as Eustace and Rhys came in, blowing on their fingers. William made room for them at the fire and pointed to the jug of hot wine sitting on the hearth beside the pottage.

Rannulf said, "Philip of Flanders told me that he had given you money for your journey and offered you a place in his mesnie should you want it. Theobald of Blois and his Countess wished you well. Robert de Béthune said you were like another son to him and he would willingly take you into his family. Not one of them believed the rumours that sent you from the Young King's court."

"It's a pity the Young King could not have done the same," William answered flatly.

Rannulf looked uncomfortable. "He was in a difficult position."

"So was I. Why are you seeking me?"

The Young King's chamberlain rubbed his hands on his knees. "You and I have always been friends," he said, "even in the difficult times."

William nodded. "I bear no grudges towards you." He drank the hot wine, pungent with the flavours of cinnamon and pepper. "I cannot be as forgiving towards certain knights of the household though."

"Then it will gladden you to know that they are no longer members of the Young King's mesnie."

William had to gulp his last mouthful before he choked. Eyes watering, he stared at Rannulf. "What are you saying?"

Rannulf glanced round at their fellow guests and lowered his voice. "The Young King was distressed at the shameful way you were treated at Caen…"

William laughed acrimoniously. "That was not the impression I received. He did nothing to prevent my humiliation. The matter could have been settled long before Caen if he had been willing to listen—but he plainly had his reasons for letting it get so far."

Rannulf cleared his throat and looked discomforted. "He was lied to and badly advised by men he thought were his friends. Farci, Yqueboeuf, and the de Coulances brothers have now been sent forth in disgrace. The reason I am seeking you is that the Young King bids you return to his service as soon as you may. He has great need of your skills."

William drank his wine and for a while said nothing. Rannulf made no mention of an apology from Henry, no admission that he had been wrong. But then, to William's knowledge, Henry had never apologised for anything in his life and would see no reason to begin now. "And if I choose to withhold them?" he finally replied.

The hosteller's wife brought baskets of freshly baked bread to the benches around the fire, checked the pots of pottage, and began doling the thick mixture into wooden bowls.

"There is a great deal you have to know," Rannulf said and gestured to the food. "Eat first. You're going to need your stamina."

Outside the wind howled at the shutters with the same high keening as the wolves in the forest. Satiated with bread and pottage, William and Rannulf moved themselves and a jug of hot wine to a trestle a little away from the fire where there was more privacy. What Rannulf had to say was complicated and convoluted: a squabble here, a misunderstanding there—festering wounds that no amount of money could cleanse and heal. Prince Richard had quarrelled with his father and his brothers. The Young King and his brother Geoffrey had joined the disaffected barons of Aquitaine and had taken up arms against Richard. The money that King Henry had given his heir had gone straight to buy support and mercenaries and the southern Angevin lands were in turmoil. When the exasperated King had set out to separate and deal with his warring sons, he had been turned upon.

"In Limoges, when he came to try and talk to our lord, a crossbowman shot at him from the walls and the arrow passed through his cloak. Two of his heralds were set upon and slain too." Rannulf looked morose and disgusted. "I never thought to see such shame and dishonour in my lifetime."

"Did the Young King order them to it?" William asked with resignation.

"In my heart I pray not, but he has grown hard and bitter

of late. He is angry with his father, but whether he would deliberately shoot at him from the keep walls…" Rannulf spread his hands. "All I can say is that he did not give such an order in my hearing and I hope he did not give it in anyone else's either. Were I to guess at the truth I would say that the arrow-shot was an unfortunate mistake and the ill treatment of the heralds an over-zealous interpretation of an order given by Yqueboeuf."

William winced at the name. Rannulf's expression held a spark of gratification. "Farci showed his true mettle by deserting," he said. "He used the excuse that he had never officially sworn allegiance to our lord. Yqueboeuf tried to prevent him from leaving and during their argument it emerged that there had been a conspiracy against you with Yqueboeuf the instigator. Farci insisted that he had been a dupe. Henry turned on Yqueboeuf and would have cloven him with his sword had not the others stopped him. Needless to say, Yqueboeuf and Farci are no longer in his service; neither are the de Coulances brothers. Henry's lacking a marshal and he wants you to return with all haste."

William drank his wine and listened to the growl of the wind. "The Count of Flanders has gifted me some house rents in Saint-Omer, and offered me more if I will cleave to him. Robert of Béthune wants me to wed his daughter. The Counts of Champagne and Burgundy have made me lucrative propositions. What would you do in my place? Return to a lord who has broken faith with you and shamed your honour before the entire court, or accept the offers of men who respect you and whom you in turn respect?"

Rannulf chose to interpret William's question as a rhetorical one rather than undertake the difficulty of answering it. "What price are you asking Henry for your return?" he said warily.

"You don't put a price on loyalty," William answered. "I

ought to refuse him out of hand, but I cannot do it. It doesn't matter how faithless he is, I made my promise to him…and to his mother the Queen. The rest counts for nothing in the balance." He heaved a deep sigh. "There is no choice for my honour save to return to his service as soon as I may." He held up a forefinger as Rannulf's tired features brightened. "But first I want guarantees, including one from his father." Finishing his wine, he pushed his cup aside. "I want an acknowledgement of my loyalty, not in coin but in letters patent so that they will last for longer than the moment of their speaking."

Marguerite stared at her reflection in the silver-bordered hand mirror that the maid held up for her inspection. She wasn't vain, but today she was pleased with what she saw. Her eyes were bright, her skin was clear, and she was no longer the drawn and distraught creature who had arrived at her brother's court, sent home by her husband in peremptory fashion. Ostensibly Henry had packed her off to Paris to be safe from the growing dissent between him, his father, and brothers, but Marguerite knew that really it was a convenient excuse to be rid of her. Their relationship had soured to the point where even being in each other's company was too great a strain. The rumours about her were constant and Henry had done little to prevent them and, she thought, he probably more than half believed them.

Her half-brother Philip was not yet twenty years old, but mature for his age. Unlike Henry, he weighed all things carefully before he acted. He was prepared to listen to Marguerite's version of the tale—and, knowing his brother-in-law and William Marshal, to draw his own conclusions.

She had her maids dress her in a gown of green silk brocade, its gores embroidered with gold. Her belt was decorated with Syrian bezants that she had once intended as a gift for William

Marshal because of the name of his favourite destrier. She had been going to have them riveted on to a breast strap for the stallion, but that had been before the autumn picnic and its terrible repercussions. Now she arranged the belt with poignant care and thought about lessons hard learned.

A steward arrived to summon her to the dinner table. Since it was still Lent, Marguerite could well guess the fare awaiting her palate. Fish stew if she was fortunate, perhaps enlivened by mussels and oysters. Not eel, she prayed. Her husband's household had always been awash in lampreys and the faintest whiff of them when she was pregnant had been enough to make her violently sick. Even now by association they disgusted her.

Entering the great hall, she accepted the bows and obeisance of her brother's knights and retainers as her due. Philip's court was more organised and formal than the Angevin one. In time it would come to irritate her, but for the moment she found its rituals calming. And then she caught sight of William Marshal and her lights plummeted to her loins. He was seated at the high table with his cousin, Rotrou of Perche, and he was engaged in urbane, smiling conversation as if the past few months had never been. Aware that all eyes, including her brother's, were upon her progress, Marguerite approached the dais as if William Marshal was no more to her than a chance-come guest.

She managed to smile and greet him with the formal warmth expected of the King's sister to a welcome visitor. He responded appropriately with a polite curve of his lips and the bland gaze of a courtier.

"Marshal is returning to the service of your husband," said Philip. "I am sending him with letters of recommendation that all may know the King of France has every faith in his good character." He made the announcement in a raised voice so that all on the dais could hear and take note. When William murmured words of gratitude, Philip gave him a measured look. "I speak as I find. If I thought your honour blemished, I would not be entertaining you at my board; nor would my sister be here."

Marguerite took her place with her brother one side of her and William on the other. Her hand shook as she raised her goblet to her lips and took the first sip of wine.

"I have been to the shrine of the Magi in Cologne, madam," William said conversationally. He launched into a description of his journey complete with small anecdotes and verbal sketches of his encounters along the way. All Marguerite had to do was nod and murmur in the appropriate places. Freed of the encumbrance of having to make conversation, she recovered her composure. Her hands ceased to tremble and she was able to make a passable show of eating the salmon cooked in wine that was the centrepiece of the meal.

"I am glad that you are returning to my husband's service." She tried to match his conversational tone of voice and didn't quite succeed. "He needs you."

"So I am told, madam."

She lowered her voice "As you can see, he has no need of me."

"He must move quickly, madam, and he would not want you to fall into the hands of his father or Richard. You are safer here. Once the dust has settled…"

"Yes," she said, "once the dust has settled…" and then she gave a little shake of her head. "Sometimes you look over your shoulder and see that it was caused by a great fall of rubble across the road and you cannot go back."

He gave her a thoughtful look. "If you have others to bring with you, sometimes you must turn and find a way round," he said.

"Perhaps I do not want to."

William gave a smile. "I didn't say finding a way round would be easy."

She resisted the urge to fold her arms across her body. To

witnesses, this was supposed to be an innocuous conversation. "Do you want to go back?"

"Does the salmon not return against the current?" he replied and she saw pain flicker briefly in his eyes.

Their discussion ended there, for Philip demanded William's attention with a question about tourneys. Perhaps it was fortuitous, perhaps deliberate. She sensed William's relief at diverting from such murky waters and realised that she too was relieved. There was no point in her own turning back for there was nothing to go back for. She and Henry were separated by the stones in the road and neither of them had the inclination to dig a way through.

William had been afforded sleeping space in the great hall, at the end nearer the dais, away from draughts, and granted a modicum of privacy by a heavy curtain. He smiled to himself, thinking of his early years with Guillaume de Tancarville and his often cold and frequently disturbed bed near the door. As he took his blanket from his saddlebag, he checked again that King Philip's letter of recommendation to Henry was tucked down against the worn, scuffed leather—his safe conduct back into the society that had shunned him.

He was spreading the blanket over his pallet when the sound of a throat being cleared on the other side of the curtain made him turn. Parting the hanging, his heart sank as he looked at Marguerite's squire of the chamber. If she had sent an invitation to her apartments, he knew that he would have to be curt and decline it. The youth bowed and held out a pouch of embroidered silk, pulled tight with drawstrings of gold silk cord.

"What's this?" William hesitated to take it from him.

"Queen Marguerite said to tell you that she wishes you Godspeed on the morrow and that she hopes you will accept this as a leaving gift in the spirit it is intended."

William took the pouch from the youth's hand, opened the drawstrings and tipped out a coiled-up braid belt—the one Marguerite had been wearing at table tonight. Gold beads bordered the edges and down the centre were riveted coins of Byzantine gold. It was the kind of token a lady might bestow on her champion on the tourney field…or her lover.

William gave a poignant smile. "Tell your lady that I thank her for the gift. It is gracious of her and I will treasure it always, but perhaps never quite as much as a certain piece of boiled sugar. Can you remember that?"

The youth nodded and William sent him on his way with two silver pennies for his trouble. He was not sure that he would ever wear the belt, but as a memento of the past and a reminder of why he could never let down his guard in the future, it was timely.

No sooner had the attendant departed than Ancel arrived. His brother's gaze fell on the belt that William was rolling up to return to its pouch, and he gave a low whistle. "That'll keep you in wine for longer than a sennight."

William gave a wordless nod. He knew he should be pleased to see his brother, but just now he could do without Ancel's lively presence. Oblivious to atmosphere, his brother unfolded a stool and sat down. He had gained weight. The whipcord leanness of young manhood was setting into maturity, and the living was obviously good in Rotrou's household. The lines on Ancel's face were of fulfilment and William felt a gut-surge of envy.

"I think you are mad for going back to the Young King," Ancel said cheerfully, "especially when you could make a decent living elsewhere."

William closed the drawstrings of the pouch and gave Ancel a warning look. The latter threw up his hands and sighed dramatically. "I'm with the French, you're supporting

Prince Henry, John is with the King, and our brother Henry's with the Archbishop of York, so his prayers should count for something. No one can accuse the Marshals of putting all their eggs in one basket. One of us is bound to emerge covered in glory—although I wouldn't care to wager which one."

William snorted with reluctant humour and his mood lightened. "Neither would I, but I'd settle for contentment above glory."

Ancel eyed him. "If that were so, you'd have retired long since. You chose the wrong word, brother. You should have said you'd settle for achievement above glory."

William blinked. Ancel tended to live life in the shallows, but what he had just said was insightful and shrewd and gave William pause for thought. He had achieved nothing where the Young King was concerned—or nothing of which he was proud.

Ancel rose from the stool. "I was going to invite you to come to Rotrou's pavilion and drink wine all night, but I can see you're not in a carousing mood. I'll not take no for an answer on the morrow though."

William smiled at Ancel and then embraced him hard. "You won't need to," he said.

In his tent outside the walls of Limoges, King Henry studied the letters from King Philip, from the Duke of Burgundy, and the Count of Flanders. Then he raised his head to William. "You have been busy," he said drily.

"My name has been dragged through the mire," William answered. "It is natural that I should wish to have my innocence acknowledged in no uncertain terms." Outside the tent, the April twilight was drawing in and the air was balmy with the scent of spring. A soldier ran past the opened flaps leading a warhorse, the sound of the hooves clumping on the turf.

"I forced your dismissal from my son's service because I was led to believe that you were responsible for his profligate overspending. I realise now that the rumours were overblown, but you do not stint to spend money, and some, although not all, I grant you, comes from my son's coffers, which in turn have to be filled by me. Nor have you displayed wisdom in other areas of your life. Having a henchman bellow aloud your prowess on the tourney field and flirting with my eldest son's wife, no matter that it was indeed only a flirtation, are not the attributes I desire from my son's marshal." He pushed the letters back across the table to William. "Yes, you have been exonerated, and yes, you were the victim of a conspiracy, but you are no washed lamb either. Just so that we understand each other."

"Perfectly, sire," William said, tight-lipped but resolute.

"Good." Henry rubbed the index and middle fingers of his right hand between his brows in a tired gesture. "My son needs you and you're probably one of the few who can help him now. Do this for me, for him, and you'll not go unrewarded, I promise you."

William's stomach leaped at the words. He didn't know whether to feel pleased or insulted. "In what way do you want me to help him, sire? Making him see reason is not always easy, and in the end my loyalty is to him. If he chooses to ride into the fire, I will try to stop him, but if I cannot, then it is my duty to ride in after him."

The King's mouth twitched in a humourless smile. "Coming from someone else, I'd say that statement was grandiose posturing, Marshal, but coming from you, I'll take it as true intent."

"Thank you, sire…just so that we understand each other."

Henry gave a bark of laughter. "Well enough. If you can bring him to his senses without smirching that precious honour of yours, then do so."

"And if I cannot?"

Henry gave him a level look. "Stay with him," he said. "It was a misjudgement to make you leave."

Twenty-one

THE YOUNG KING EMBRACED WILLIAM LIKE A LONG-LOST brother, weeping, declaring remorsefully that he should never have doubted William's integrity. It was as if the weeks and months of black looks and ostracism had been no more to Henry than a passing tantrum—all-encompassing at the time, but completely forgotten now that it was over. His pressing concern was with his campaign against his father and Richard, which was not progressing well and, like a frustrated child, he wanted William to set matters to rights. Of Marguerite he said not a word; it was as if she too had never existed.

William was perturbed to discover that while the Young King had rid himself of Adam Yqueboeuf and his cronies, he had welcomed Geoffrey de Lusignan to his banner. Rannulf had omitted to mention that small detail on the road from Cologne. William had never forgiven the murder of his uncle on that bright spring morning in Poitou, nor the circumstances of his own captivity. To discover that he had to live and fight alongside one of the perpetrators of the crime, and to have to trust him at his back, was almost more than he could swallow.

De Lusignan was entirely pragmatic. "It was my brother who killed your uncle and wounded you," he said. "Perhaps it was ill judged, but all men make mistakes in their lives and pay for them. I do not expect us to be friends, but at least let us have a truce."

William refused to give de Lusignan the kiss of peace or clasp his hand, but managed a stiff nod of acceptance before he walked away from him. Beggars could not be choosers and his young lord was perilously close to being one of the former. However murky his past, there was no doubting Geoffrey de Lusignan's abilities as a fighter and, as he said, he had not struck the blows. Repeating these palliatives to himself, William managed to choke down his disgust.

As usual money was scarce and Henry's mercenaries were complaining vociferously that they had not been paid. Casting around for the coin to keep them employed, Henry had turned to pillaging the Church. When William baulked in horror at the notion of such sacrilege, Henry scoffed at him. "All the silver and gold the Church has amassed does naught but drape their chapels, gawked at by peasants and gloated over by priests."

"It was given to God," William protested, "to the glory of God."

They were seated in Henry's chamber in a fortified house in Martel, which Henry had commandeered. The tents of his mercenaries were spread like a locust cloud over the village and the pastures beyond.

"And God knows that I will repay Him. Have I not taken the Cross in his name?" Henry indicated the bright red strips of silk ostentatiously stitched to the breast of his mantle. He parted his lips in a mocking grin. "Twice taken, in fact." From the open coffer at his feet, he withdrew a cross of gold and gemstones, purloined from the altar of the shrine of Saint Martial. Henry had sworn over the tomb of the saint and in the presence of his father, with whom he had called a truce, to go on holy crusade. But on the day the truce was due to expire, he had plundered the shrine and carried off all the coin and trappings to pay his expenses. Now, short of funds again, he was contemplating more raids on the easily milked churches. Henry tilted the cross this way and that, admiring the way that the sunlight shining through the window reflected off the gold and gemstones and scattered the wall with coloured lozenges.

William swallowed bile. "Surely it would be more profitable to make peace with your father?" he said.

Henry gave a rude snort. "Depends what you mean by profitable. All he'll do is pay my debts and tell me to behave myself in future. Perhaps I really should go on crusade," he mused. "That would whiten the old goat's beard."

"So you have no intention of taking the cross?" William's nape prickled. The flippancy in his young lord's voice frightened him. God was not mocked.

"Of course I'm taking it," Henry said impatiently. "But I can hardly set out now, can I?" His expression turned sly. "Besides, I've no funds, so it's up to the Church to provide them."

William felt like seizing Henry by the scruff and shaking him until his teeth fell out, but he controlled the urge. The Old King had hoped that William could rein in his eldest son's excesses, but for the nonce there was nothing to be done except let Henry run until he was exhausted—and then tackle him again and hope to find a spark of reason. "I should think your father's beard is already white over the treatment of his heralds," William said. "He sends knights to parley with you under a banner of truce and your troops beat and slay them."

Henry looked sulky and tossed the cross back into the chest where it clanged against two candlesticks and a goblet of silver-gilt—the last of the treasure purloined from Saint Martial. "That wasn't my fault. The men were over-zealous. I hanged the perpetrators. What more do you want?"

William shook his head. "Perhaps it saddens me to watch chivalry dying piecemeal."

"It's already dead," Henry retorted. "This is war, Marshal, not a tourney. I told you, I punished those responsible."

William's patience came close to snapping. "I know the difference between war and playing at war, but what your men did shows appalling lack of discipline. You need brutality in soldiers, but you need to be able to contain as well as unleash it. The dog should wag the tail, not the tail the dog."

"Then you lick them into shape, Marshal. That's what you're here for…After all, you don't have a dog and bark yourself." Henry thrust himself up from his chair and went to stand by the hearth, one arm braced against the wall. "I have a desire to pray at the tomb of Saint Amadour. Have the men saddle up."

William's gut tightened and twisted. "Sire, you should not do this," he said hoarsely.

"I will decide what I should and should not do. Does any man dare to question my brother Richard? Am I less than him?" Henry rounded on him, eyes bright with anger. "Do you think that Richard and his mercenaries would hesitate for one moment to take whatever they needed? Jesu, he's been stripping Aquitaine like a butcher fleshing a corpse for the past ten years!"

"But you are not Richard, sire. The barons of Aquitaine hate and fear him, but they do not hate and fear you. If you despoil and strip the wealth from their people and their churches, they will quickly learn to do so. I still say you should not do it."

"I have heard you. Now, order the men, or else stand down as my marshal," Henry said coldly.

William wrestled with his conscience. He wanted to refuse and ride away, but if he stayed, perhaps he could still turn the Young King from his purpose. Besides, he had given his promise to the young man's father that he would ride into the fire with him if necessary. "As you wish, sire," he said, and bowed from the chamber.

The sun was blazing from a sky the colour of the finest blue enamel when Henry the Young King came to Rocamadour and stripped the shrine of Saint Amadour of all its relics, including Durendal, the sword of the hero Roland who had given his life fighting the Saracens at the pass of Roncesvalles. "It is for the crusade," he said, when the monks tried to stop him. They had made a hasty effort to conceal some of the finer pieces, including the sword, but the hiding place was soon discovered and looted.

William looked on, taking no part, but still filled with shame and fear. By allowing Henry's mercenaries to desecrate the shrine, he was condoning the deed of thieving from God and knew the punishment would be dire. "Christ Jesu, forgive me," he muttered, feeling as if the rock walls of the shrine were closing in and crushing him. The gentle, lop-sided smile of a figurine of the Madonna, carved with devotion and rustic joy by a long-forgotten artisan, reproached him as the offerings were stripped from her niche, even down to the small change of half coins and cheap iron rings left by the poorest pilgrims. It was as obscene as rape.

Henry strode through the several chapels, moving with vigorous purpose and enjoyment, the sword of Roncesvalles clutched in his right fist.

"Your sins will catch up with you and take you to hell!" threatened the Abbot, flapping his sleeves like flightless wings. "God will curse you for this!"

Henry wagged his forefinger at the monk and tut-tutted. "You can afford to give generously to poor crusaders." He touched the blood-red cross on the shoulder of his cloak. "I am under oath to visit the Holy Sepulchre in Jerusalem. Surely you would not deny me your donation?"

"You are committing blasphemy!"

Henry gave the priest a tolerant smile. "I'll overlook that you said that." He set his hand to the monk's quivering shoulder. "You have my royal oath that your wealth will be restored to you—I would say five-fold but that smacks of usury and we all know how much the Church is against that, don't we?"

They departed Rocamadour, their saddlebags stuffed with the treasures from the stripped shrine, including several pounds of beeswax for the altar candles and the carcass of a pig that was intended for the monks' dinner. Henry was in a high good mood, laughing aloud to the late spring sky, working his horse to make it prink and dance. "Don't look so grim, Marshal!" he cried, leaning across to belt William on the shoulder. "I've said I'll pay it back and I will. Christ, did you see their faces!"

William said nothing for he was fighting his gorge. The stripping of God's altar and the cowing of a handful of bewildered monks was no great victory but the thin end of the wedge. A knight was sworn to protect the Church, and what they had done was the opposite. He felt dirty and defiled. And when this became common knowledge, Henry's popularity would wane faster than the bloom from a whore's cheek.

At Martel, Henry paid his mercenaries some (but not all) of their arrears. Had he settled in full, there would have been nothing left for his own use. When the men grumbled he told them what he had told the monks—that they would eventually be paid. If they wanted to supplement their incomes, they could always go raiding the lands that were controlled by Richard, or rob one of his father's supply trains.

"That won't ingratiate you with your father," William said darkly.

"Hah, he already thinks me a parricide," Henry replied, pouring wine into his cup, drinking, pouring and drinking again, then looking up as the chamber door opened and Wigain entered the room, a vellum scroll in his hand. The little clerk's sallow complexion had an underlying greyish cast and for once he was not smiling.

"Don't tell me, the pig we sent to the kitchens was going off," Henry laughed, his voice overloud. He looked at the scroll. "What's that?"

Wigain handed the parchment to Henry. "A messenger came from the Archbishop of Canterbury, but chose not to stay, sire. I…we…He said that we've been excommunicated."

There was a horrified silence in the chamber. Henry cursed, set down his wine, checked the seal, and slit it with his eating knife. Unrolling the vellum, he rapidly scanned what was written. Then he gave a shaken laugh and placed the corner of the message into the flame of the nearest candle. "Peace, Wigain. Go and say your prayers tonight. You're still in a state of grace. The good Archbishop and the rest of those crows in Caen have only excommunicated those who would come between myself and my father making peace. They haven't named anyone; it's an empty threat." He held the vellum while it charred into smoke and when the flames came near his pinched fingers, he dropped the final scrap to the floor and ground out the fire with his boot. He looked across at William. "It's a ploy by my father to try and separate me from my supporters. He'll try every trick he knows to bring me to heel, but it won't work. I can't see the Count of Burgundy running in fear, can you?"

"Perhaps it is a sign that the Church is uneasy at what you are doing," William said sombrely. "They don't know about Rocamadour yet, but they will know by now what happened at Saint Martial."

Henry snorted down his nose. "Don't push me on to that treadmill again. My father's behind this, otherwise why involve the Archbishop of Canterbury? What's wrong, Marshal? Scared for your soul?"

"Yes," William admitted curtly and, making his excuses, went to check on his stallion, which had earlier cast a shoe. He knew that they were desperate for money and that the recent raid would only keep them solvent for a short while. Soon they would have to go out and rob another shrine or raid a town and he was not sure that he could continue to do it.

The farrier had seen to Bezant's cast shoe and William had the destrier saddled up. He rode to a nearby field to school the horse, using heels and hands to make him trot out and draw in; to rear and back-kick; to charge flat out: all the tricks of the tourney field. William wished he was back there now. Usually a bout of practice with the stallion would relax William if he felt tense or unsettled, but today his edginess remained. Quitting the field, he went to the village church to pray but even here there was no peace. God would not forgive him for being a party to the robbing of the shrine at Rocamadour. There was going to be a payment; he knew there was. Henry thought that because he was a king's son, he had impunity, but there was no impunity before God. Every ill deed committed on earth was marked for punishment in the afterlife. William stared at the cross shining on the altar until the gold dazzled and his vision made a second, darker image beside the first. When he had lisped his promise to King Stephen in a campaign tent thirty years ago, he had had no inkling that such an oath would lead him into peril for his soul.

It was gone midnight when the Young King retired to bed. His steps were unsteady with drink and his gaze wandered like a guttering candle. Accustomed to seeing Henry in such a state, William set his shoulder beneath his arm and helped him to his chamber. Henry flopped on to the bed and his squire set about removing his boots and loosening his clothes.

"Marshal, stay," Henry said as William made to leave the room and seek his own pallet.

William hesitated, turned, and retraced his steps. Henry looked up at him, glassy-eyed. "Stay with me until I sleep," he said. "I trust no one else."

A pang arrowed through William at the words. What a poisoned chalice trust was, he thought, both for those who poured the wine and those who drank it. Unfolding a stool that was leaning against Henry's coffer, he sat down at the bedside.

Henry's lids wavered as he struggled to lift them. "My father won't let go. He's an old man. He should give me a chance to prove myself. I could rule if he would let me." His hand raised and flopped on the coverlet. "I am going to go on pilgrimage, Marshal," he slurred, "all the way to Jerusalem…I mean it…" His voice tailed off to an incoherent mutter and he began to snore. William drew the coverlet over him as if tending to a child. In a way perhaps he was, for although Henry had grown older, he had not matured and all his life was lived in the superficial glitter of the moment.

"Leave the bed curtains," he said, as the squire made to close them. "And let the candle burn on. I will sleep across the door tonight. Stay within call."

The youth looked surprised, but bowed acknowledgement. Quietly, William unfastened his belt, removed his surcoat, and, dragging a pallet from a pile in the corner, lay across the doorway, his sword close to hand. He felt uneasy, in the same way that his horses would twitch and shiver on the eve of a bad storm. Something was gathering that he was powerless to prevent. He told himself that it was no more than the disquiet caused by their stripping of the shrine at Rocamadour, that it would pass, but the hair continued to tingle at his nape. It was almost a relief when a thunderstorm did roll overhead in the small hours of the morning, for he was able to attribute his edginess to that. He fell asleep as the rumbles rolled away into the distance, leaving behind the steady, soporific sound of falling rain.

It was still raining at dawn and Henry woke to a devilish headache and a roiling gut. He rose late and, with a green face, declined the fresh bread and honey that the others were devouring to break their fast. No one thought much of it then, for several other knights of the mesnie, including Lusignan, had over-imbibed the previous night and were similarly affected. William's own appetite was subdued but still present and he ate the thick heel of a loaf, liberally dipped in the honey dish. Henry turned away, his throat working, and staggered to the slop bowl in his chamber. Moments later, they heard him retching. A few of the knights chuckled and exchanged knowing, sympathetic glances.

Henry chose to remain in Martel that day, playing desultory games of dice and chess, rubbing his forehead, shivering, dashing now and again for the chamberpot. William saw to the patrols and set the knights to practising their lance work. By late afternoon, when William returned to the chamber, Henry was hot with fever and his bowels had turned to liquid. The chuckles had ceased and the knowing glances were now worried.

"It's the vengeance of Saint Amadour," muttered Peter de Preaux, crossing himself.

"It's no such thing," William snapped, although that thought was to the fore of his own mind. "Everyone's suffered from the belly gripes at one time or another. They'll pass."

They didn't. By the next morning the vomiting had ceased, but Henry was still flushed with fever and didn't want to eat; his motions were liquid and bloody; and he was suffering from bouts of severe abdominal pain. No one else had been afflicted and the men lounged uneasily in the hall below the main chamber, mending equipment, sharpening swords, talking in low whispers. There were several squabbles in the mercenary camp and a vicious knife fight that ended in one man losing an ear. Some of the hired men slipped away, but others who were owed more wages than they could afford to lose stayed close to the lodging and watched the doors and windows with hawklike intensity.

The following day there was no improvement and it became plain to everyone, including Henry, that he might die. "Send for my father," he groaned to William. "Tell him that I am mortally sick. Tell him that it's true—that I'm not crying wolf." He was lying in his bed, the curtains drawn back to admit the daylight and the shutters wide to expel the fetid aromas from the chamber. His cheekbones blazed like red stars but otherwise his complexion was waxen, and there was terror in his eyes.

William nodded. "Wigain's already written the letter," he said. "All it wants is your seal. I have summoned the Bishop of Cahors also."

Henry pointed to the casket where his seal was stored. "Take it and be swift about it. I do not know how much time I have. I—" He broke off with a cry as his body was racked by an agonising spasm. William caught and braced him and helped him to the commode. The effluence from the Young King's bowels was pure red, and William could feel the heat of his body burning through the nightshirt.

When it was over, William carried him back to the bed and directed the squires to wipe Henry down with cool cloths. Henry gasped and threw his head back on the bolster, his hair sweat-soaked and plastered to his skull. "Make haste to my father." He seized William's wrist in a febrile grip. "And bring my chaplain to me. I must vouchsafe my soul."

"Sire." William rose and Henry reluctantly released his grip, leaving pale imprints on William's tanned wrists.

"You were right," Henry whispered. "I shouldn't have robbed Saint Amadour's shrine."

William wordlessly shook his head and wondered when the rest of them would be struck down, for although the pillage had been Henry's decision, they were all guilty.

He saw the message sealed and handed it back to Wigain. "Take the grey courser, it's the swiftest," he said.

Wigain looked down at the packet in his hands. "Is he going to die?"

"That is in the hands of God," William replied and as he spoke the words thought that he already knew the answer. He gave Wigain a push. "Make haste. Lord Henry desires to see his father..."

...*before it is too late.* The words hung unspoken between them like an invisible wraith. Wigain gave a swift nod and ran towards the stables, light as a youth on his feet. William watched him, then trod as heavily as a man with lead boots back into the lodging house.

In the grey light of dawn, William was pacing the yard of the house, breathing for a moment air untainted by the stenches of the sick room. Henry had barely slept and the gripes had been unremitting in their severity. Yesterday's glimmer of hope had waned with the moon and not risen with the sun. That Henry was still lucid, despite all, and still had the strength for speech, were testaments to will power and the endurance of a young and well-nourished body, although now he resembled a cadaver, gaunt and sucked dry. They were going to lose him and William was numb.

"Rider!" de Lusignan shouted from the upstairs window where he was keeping watch at Henry's bedside.

William hastened to the gate as Wigain galloped in on a fresh horse, presumably one of King Henry's. He had pushed it hard, for even in the cool dawn air it was sweating, its flanks blowing like bellows and its nostrils flaring red. Wigain flung down from the saddle, panting as if he had run with the horse.

"He's not coming," Wigain gasped. "His advisers told him it was folly and he agreed with them. I tried to tell him how sick our lord was, but he wouldn't risk it being another ruse…He said that one hole in his cloak and two dead heralds were enough and he would rather pray for his son from a distance." Delving in his tunic, Wigain produced a ring threaded on a leather cord. "All he's done is to send him this and say that he forgives him his lies and perfidies. I had to sweat blood even to get him to concede that much." He placed a sapphire ring in William's hand.

William closed his fingers over it and felt the solid pressure of the jewel pressing against his palm. But there wasn't enough of that healing night-blue cold to quench Henry's fever.

"Is he worse?" Wigain asked, as if reading William's thoughts.

William hesitated, then nodded. "He is dying," he said. "I need not tell you to keep it to yourself for the moment. Soon there will come a time when all will have to know, but not yet."

"Not a word." Wigain crossed himself. "God give him peace," he said, his dark eyes bereft of their usual merriment.

"Amen." William crossed himself too, thinking it was more likely that God was punishing Henry by giving him a foretaste of hell. With dragging feet he returned to the Young King's chamber. The room was as crowded as a market place for as well as the knights of the mesnie, the Bishop of Cahors was here with all his retinue and also the Prior of Vigeois.

With soft tread William approached the bed. Henry was propped up against a mass of bolsters and pillows, and looked three times his age: a wizened old man clinging to the threads of life as one by one they were cut from under his clawing fingers. The congregation surrounding the bed parted to make way for William and he gestured people to move back. "Let him breathe," he said curtly.

A choking laugh emerged from the cadaver on the bed. "While I still can, eh?"

"Sire." William knelt on one knee. The sight of Henry's

febrile, dying weakness filled him with pity, compassion, and fear and he had to struggle to keep his expression neutral.

Henry rolled his gaze towards William and licked his fever-cracked lips. "The news must be bad," he croaked. "You always look like that when it is…as if your mind's as blank as your face."

William grimaced. "Is it that obvious?"

"Plain as death…" Henry gave a painful swallow but turned his head from the cup that William was swift to offer him. "Runs straight through…just wet my lips."

William did as Henry asked, then drew up a stool to the bedside. "Your father sends this ring to comfort you and says that he will come as soon as he has received the surrender of Limoges."

Henry fixed his lustreless gaze on the ring William had produced as if he did not know what it was. "He's not coming?" His voice rose and quavered. The anguish in it squeezed William's heart. Silently he shook his head.

Henry stared towards the gathering of knights and clerics who had drawn off a little, but were still close enough to hear and bear witness. "He cannot come to my deathbed. Even now, he'd rather keep his castles than his sons…" His voice was a whisper in his desiccated throat, but he still had sufficient strength to hurl the ring through the gap in the bed curtains. It struck a coffer, bounced off, and landed in the floor rushes, midnight stone shining as if starlit. Henry turned his face to the wall.

William went to pick up the ring, his swift glance warning off the other men. Returning to the bed, he laid his hand to Henry's sweat-soaked shoulder and turned him, then gently took Henry's right hand in his and pushed the ring on to his lord's middle finger. "Sire, you and your father have often quarrelled, but he loves you."

"He doesn't love me," Henry muttered, but his left hand covered his right and he rubbed his thumb over the cold stone.

"Only as much as you do not love him, sire," William replied, "and I know how deep your affection for him runs." An affection that on Henry's part had almost starved for want of attention; fed only on an empty diet of money and vague promises, it had mutated into a creature determined to lash out and inflict harm in its efforts to be noticed. That even on his deathbed he had failed must be the ultimate desolation.

William leaned over the Young King. "It does not matter that your father has not come," he murmured for Henry's ears alone. "You are a king, and if this is to be your final journey, then you must embark on it with dignity and greatness. Make of your leaving such a show that men will pass it down the ages for their sons and grandsons to know. That will be your memorial."

Henry's body quivered with the heat of his fever-tainted blood. Continuing to rub the ring, he gave William a pain-glazed stare. "You are right," he said. "I will show my father the stuff that kings are made of, and when he hears the end I made, he will shred his clothes in grief and my death will be a torment to him for the rest of his days. I will forgive him, because I have to, but he will never forgive himself."

William felt sick at the reply. Even now Henry was scheming vengeance on his father. He feared desperately for the Young King's soul and felt a deep sense of failure. His task had been to mentor Henry, to imbue him with the honour and chivalry that would complement the pragmatic lessons of kingship. It should have been glorious, but instead it had come to this. Squalor and death and poisoned emotions.

Henry turned his attention towards preparing himself for death, arranging the rituals with all the care he had once reserved for the tourney and the court. Instead of layering himself in fine garments, cedar-scented from the clothing chests, he gave his clothes to his servants and retainers, reserving only a linen nightshirt for himself. He gave his jewels away too, except for the sapphire ring from his father, which William was entrusted to deliver to him on Henry's death. He confessed and repented of his sins to the Bishop of Cahors, and then repeated that confession before all the knights of his mesnie. He even seemed to rally for a time as his mind was drawn beyond the suffering of his body by the tragic drama of the rituals being enacted. But the energy expended took its toll on him and he collapsed against the bolsters, struggling for breath.

"Not yet," he gasped, his chest working for air and his mouth opening and closing like a distressed fish. "Make me a bed of ashes on the floor and set a rope around my neck. I would die a true penitent."

Some of the knights baulked at such a show of piety, thinking that it was a step too far, but William ordered them fiercely to do it, for it was as his lord wanted, and it could only help him in the afterlife. As the attendants hastened to make a pallet on the floor and sent down to the midden for some buckets of cold ashes, Henry grabbed William's arm. "My vow to kneel at the Holy Sepulchre in Jerusalem...Marshal, you must fulfil it in my stead." Fresh sweat broke out on his brow as he was consumed by a fierce abdominal spasm. "Holy Jesus, save me..." His grip dug into William's wrist with a desperate strength that was to leave a legacy of oval bruises. "Swear to me...swear to me that for my soul's sake and yours, you will do this thing for me," he entreated.

"I swear." William braced his arm and held firm while Henry rode out the pain. "I will not fail you..."

Henry's grip slowly released and fell to his side. "You have never failed me, Marshal," he panted, eyes squeezed shut. "Take my horses...they will serve you well. My father...he will see you provided for...tell him that I made a good end."

William's throat constricted. "I will do so, sire."

"And my mother…Make sure she hears the news from a friend."

"It shall be done, sire." He willingly shouldered the burdens that Henry was laying on him for they went some distance towards relieving those he was already carrying. Perhaps if he made atonement to God at the Holy Sepulchre he might achieve a measure of forgiveness for the sin of robbing the shrine of Saint Amadour.

Tenderly the knights of the Young King's mesnie lifted their lord from his bed and laid him on the pallet of ashes on the floor. His body was as light as the corpse of a fly sucked dry by a spider. When Geoffrey de Lusignan hesitated to set a rope around his neck, Henry insisted, his command whistling through blue lips. They gave him a cross to clasp between his hands, and then, swords drawn, they stood vigil around him, while the priests prayed for his soul.

While still capable of speech, Henry whispered his desire for his eyes, brain, heart, and entrails to be interred at Grammont Priory, and his corpse to be buried in the church of Notre Dame in Rouen.

"It shall be done, sire," William reassured him, "as you wish…"

"As I wish…" Henry gave a bitter smile. "In the name of God, remember me." He did not speak again. Sunlight poured through the open window, and William watched the doves circling above the red-tiled cote beyond the sweet chestnut trees. The breeze carried the scent of dust and flowers. In the high summer of his life, Henry Plantagenet, son and heir of the King of England, was dying. The pattern of sunlight moved across the floor and brushed the edge of the bed of ashes. It tinted Henry's hair with bronze lights and picked out three grey strands at his brow line. His chest rose and shuddered as he fought for air, but his lungs would not draw properly and there came a moment when they did not draw at all and his soul left him.

For a spun-out moment there was silence. Not only had the Young King left them, but he had taken the hopes, aspirations, and livelihoods of the knights of his mesnie with him. William knelt at Henry's side, his knees in the ashes overflowing the pallet. He checked for breath, for the pulsebeat beneath the skin, and felt only sun-heated stillness. Crossing himself, he rose and stepped back. "God rest his soul," he said. The soft rustle of cloth and clinking of weapons followed his words as the others crossed themselves too. William half expected a cloud to roll across the sun, or the dovecote to come crashing down, but there was no such drama to usher Henry's soul from the world.

The others were looking at him, waiting for direction. William locked his emotion in a watertight part of his mind shut away from everyday thought. "There is much to be done if our lord is to be borne to Rouen," he said, cladding himself in pragmatism. "His father must be told." Stooping to the body, William gently slipped the sapphire ring from Henry's finger. "Where's Wigain? Take this to the King at Limoges. Tell him that William Marshal says that Henry, the Young King, son of the King, has died of the camp fever and that we will bring his body to Limoges on our road to Rouen."

"Sir." It was no easy thing William was asking of the clerk: to bear to a father the news of his son's death, especially when the father had refused to attend the deathbed, but it had to be done, and Wigain had acted the messenger on the first leg of that journey.

Wigain bowed to William, then stooped to lay the palm of his hand on Henry's brow. "Last time I'll see him," he said with a tremor in his voice, and then abruptly left the room.

William clenched his jaw and beckoned one of Henry's squires. "Go to the kitchens and bring a cleaver and the sharpest knives you can find," he commanded. There was bile in his throat and saliva in his mouth. He swallowed hard.

The squire's eyes widened. "A cleaver, sir?"

William nodded. "Our lord must be prepared for his journey."

William leaned against the garden wall, inhaling the scent of roses, lilies, and lavender as he strove to replace the stench of blood and entrails with sweeter aromas. It had been one of the worst ordeals he had ever endured, to stand witness whilst Henry's body was opened by his two huntsmen, their tunics protected by blood-blackened leather aprons. The eyes, brain, and entrails had been removed for burial at Grammont, and the cadaver's interior packed with fistfuls of grey salt crystals, which had rapidly reddened. The body had been wrapped in several layers of winding sheet and sewn into a shroud, then packed in a bull's hide and placed in a lead coffin. After searching through several chests, William had managed to find a good silk cloth with which to cover the coffin, and on top of this was laid Henry's banner, his shield, and sword.

"Sir."

He turned to find Rhys waiting for him, his expression anxious. The groom was holding William's black palfrey. The Young King's horses, gifted to William on the deathbed, had been sold to pay for the expense of the coffin, the pall, and the wages of the cart driver.

William nodded, drew another deep breath, and turned to his mount. In the Young King's honour, every knight of the household wore full mail and the company glittered in the sweltering sunshine like a full fishing net. William pushed his shield to his back and grasped a lance bearing Henry's red and gold banner. The townspeople had emerged from their dwellings to see the cortège on its way and many of the women were wailing, their hair unbound and strewn with ashes. William stiffened his spine and tried to maintain an impassive expression, but it was hard with emotion tightening his throat. He heeled the palfrey to a measured walk and led the column out of Martel. Soft dust rose from beneath the horse's hooves and the cart creaked and swayed beneath its burden.

As they reached the edge of the town, one of Henry's mercenary leaders, a Basque named Sancho, rode out from his camp and blocked the road with his company, refusing to let the cortège pass. Spurring up to William, Sancho seized his palfrey by the bridle. "You go no further, Marshal, until me and my men receive the money that your lord owed to us," he growled into William's face. He had oily curls, eyes as black as olives, and a scar running between his nose and upper lip, causing the latter to curve in an expression caught between a sneer and a smile, both of which were deceptive. William knew him to be as dour and stolid as gouty town burgher.

William raised his right hand to prevent the knights of the mesnie from drawing their weapons. He didn't want the funeral journey marred at the outset by an unseemly brawl if he could help it, and Sancho had sufficient men to make a hard and bloody fight of the proceedings. "And how much would that be?" he asked. It took an effort, but his voice emerged level and reasonable.

Sancho viewed him through narrowed lids. "A hundred marks will suffice. In view of the tragic circumstances, I'll waive the small coin."

William shook his head. "You must know that our master did not have such a sum at his disposal. All you see here is what we have. Are you so governed by money that you would have us strip the pall from the coffin and sell off the lead in which our lord's body is sealed?"

"No, Marshal, you know that I would not," Sancho's tone was regretful but obstinate. "But I seek payment for what is owed. No more, no less. You are in charge of his mesnie. If you will pledge yourself for that sum, then I will let you go on your way."

William could see that short of a pitched battle, there was no other choice and so nodded his acceptance to the Basque, at the same time wondering where on God's earth he was going to find the sum of a hundred marks to honour such a promise. His word was his bond; he had never broken it yet, but Sancho might be waiting a long time.

The mercenary drew off and assembled his troops to ride at the rear of the cortège. William didn't gainsay him; the men would serve to swell the importance of the funeral procession, and he was in no position to argue. Nevertheless his shoulder blades prickled at having Sancho behind him.

King Henry beckoned William to enter the room of the peasant house in Mas not far from Limoges. The King had taken refuge from the summer heat earlier that day and now it served to shelter his grief from the world while he mastered it. The air in the room was stifling and pungent with the aroma of simmering vegetables and garlic.

Henry dismissed all the servants and pointed to the flagon and cups on the rude wooden trestle, indicating that William should pour. "How did it happen?" he demanded. His hands shook as he took the wine from William's hand. "Spare me no details. I need to know."

William told him as if delivering a battle report: tight-lipped but courageous in the face of a disaster, and Henry took it with the same stoicism, although his knuckles whitened on the goblet stem and beneath the red of sunburn his complexion was grey.

"He died with nobility even though the fever and the voiding of his bowels had robbed his dignity," William concluded. "And he asked you to forgive him."

A muscle worked in Henry's cheek. "I'm not sure I can do that..."

William made an involuntary movement and Henry looked at him from faded blue eyes. "For dying," he said. "The rest hardly matters now, does it?"

William forced himself to take a drink of the warm red wine. The sour, tannic taste almost made him gag. "What do you want me to do now, sire?"

With a visible effort, Henry forced himself to mark what William was saying. "You were the head of his mesnie. I charge you with the duty of escorting his body to Rouen and I give you command of the cortège."

"Gladly, sire, but I have promised the mercenary Sancho to surrender myself as his prisoner for a ransom of one hundred marks."

Henry stared at him, red-rimmed eyes incredulous. "You've done what?"

"Your son owed him that money, and pledging myself to redeem it was the only way to prevent a battle around the coffin. But now I am honour bound to find that money before I can do anything else."

Henry's upper lip curled with revulsion. "You are certain that this mercenary was owed such a sum?"

"Yes, sire, unfortunately so."

Henry's throat worked. "My son has cost me more than that in his lifetime, and would that he were still costing me instead of sealed up in a lead coffin." His voice cracked on the last word and his eyes swam with tears. "Go," he said roughly. "I will underwrite the debt…now let me be."

"Sire." William bowed from Henry's presence and went to the chapel tent, there to keep vigil over Henry's remains and prostrate himself before God.

Twenty-two

"JERUSALEM?" JOHN MARSHAL'S MOUTH TURNED DOWN AT the corners. "That is no small undertaking."

"I have debts to God that cannot be paid any other way," William replied. They were sitting outside in the hot summer evening, resting their elbows on a trestle table and drinking wine. Both men had removed their hose and wore only their braies and light summer tunics. "I am doing this for my own soul as well as that of the Young King. I need to find peace; I need to do penance and be cleansed." He glanced towards his nephew, who was playing chase with the steward's lad. Young John, now known by his fond name of Jack, was nine years old and sturdy of limb with grey eyes and bright brown hair. Alais had borne a daughter four months ago and little Sybilla was sleeping in a rush basket on the trestle, her face rosy in slumber.

"It's a dangerous way to go about it," John said. "The grass will grow long in your absence. King Henry may well not vouchsafe you a place in his retinue if and when you return."

"That is up to Henry," William replied. "He is stabling my horses while I am gone and he has given me funds to undertake the task. As matters stand now, he wants me back. Would you have me renege on my vow?"

John gave an impatient shake of his head. "Of course not, but…"

"My body will be no more imperilled than it has been over these last months warring for my lord, and my soul even less so."

"Yes, we heard about what happened at Rocamadour," John said disapprovingly.

William rubbed his palms over his face. "I have my own atonement to make to God for the part I played in stripping the shrine of Saint Amadour. I stood back and let him do it. I let his mercenaries strip the gold from the altar and tear the sword of Roland out of the wall." He shivered. Even now the memory filled him with fear and self-loathing. "At least the sword has been restored to the shrine, even if the other treasures have been scattered far and wide." William looked morosely into his wine.

There was a long silence. John tilted his goblet to his lips and swallowed. Then he wiped his mouth and looked at William. "By all accounts the Young King's funeral was interesting. Twice buried eh?"

A look of distaste crossed William's face. "You heard about that too?" He shook his head. "We brought the cortège to Le Mans and kept vigil overnight at the church of Saint Julian, but when we tried to leave at dawn, the town worthies and the priests refused to allow us on our way. They insisted on burying my lord in their church and there was nothing we could do short of drawing our swords." He pinched the bridge of his nose in a gesture of weary recollection. "The people of Rouen were expecting my lord to rest in their cathedral—it was his dying wish—and they set out to take his body by force of arms. The King had to intervene and command the coffin to be dug up and sent on its way to its resting place." His face twisted at the memory. "All the way along the road we had no money to give the people alms, and yet still they loved him and blamed us and his father that we had nothing for them."

"He was so handsome," Alais said sadly. "And he had the sweetest smile." She checked on her daughter, stroking the downy little cheek with a gentle forefinger.

John made a disparaging sound. "A king needs more than that in his armoury to rule."

"But it will take him a fair distance down the road," William said. "You are right though. It was all glitter and no gold." He traced a ring mark of wine on the trestle. "He was my lord. I am honour bound to fulfil my oath to him."

"Well, I've sworn my own oath to Prince John," his brother announced. "Saving my loyalty to his father, of course."

William gave him a startled look. "Why would you want to do that?"

"He spends more time in England than his brothers do. He's overlooked because he's the youngest, but that doesn't mean he's anybody's fool. The King is ageing and John is his favourite son and the one most like him. You should think about that." His tone was defensive. "He's got time to grow and at least he's got a head on his shoulders, not a vain bucket of feathers. I know what I'm doing."

"At least one of us does," William replied, refusing to be drawn into a needle match on the merits of the King's sons, one of whom was in his grave and the other an untried youth of sixteen who might or might not one day wear a crown.

Twenty-three

NEAR READING, BERKSHIRE, SEPTEMBER 1183

TWELVE-YEAR-OLD ISABELLE DE CLARE GAZED OUT OF THE opening at the back of the covered wain at the unrelenting autumn downpour. She was accustomed to wet days in Ireland, but to her imagination, this deluge seemed harder, colder, and altogether more hostile. Had the weather been reasonable, she could have ridden pillion with one of the grooms. They hadn't let her bring her own mare; they said she would have no need of a mount when eventually they reached London. Today, their intended goal was a night's lodging at Reading Abbey, although it would be dark by the time they arrived, given the lurching pace of the wain through the ruts and puddles. Over-hanging trees dripped on to the top of the wain making heavier sounds around the steady rustle of the rain. The air that blew through the opening was moist and cold. There was a hang-ing that could be drawn across, but that would mean sitting in semi-darkness and Isabelle had slept all she could. Aine, her Irish nurse, and Helwis, her Norman maid, sat in a huddle of furs, the former complaining about a persistent toothache, the latter coddling a heavy cold, her nose a beacon.

Isabelle kept apart from them. Like a cat, she had always preferred her own space. By nature she was pragmatic, accustomed to enduring, but there had been so much to shoulder of late that there was little room in her soul for more. Her upbringing had made her mature beyond her years, but she was still very young. A woman yes, for her fluxes had come regularly now for six months and she was legally of marriageable age, but she had not attained her full growth, and although she would admit it to no one, behind her feline self-containment, she was frightened.

Behind the wain, her escort rode in the deluge; King's knights bearing the lions of England on their shields and dripping red silk banners. Following the death of her brother Gilbert, earlier in the year, she had become an heiress of considerable worth—a marriage prize of such magnitude that King Henry had taken her guardianship in hand and ordered her to be brought to lodge in the Tower of London. She still wept when she thought of Gilbert. He had been three years younger than her, red-haired like their Norman father, but not robust and always succumbing to fluxes and agues, the last one of which he had not survived. She had been devoted to him—as had their mother—and his death had left them both reeling. He was hardly in his grave when King Henry's writ had arrived in Ireland, commanding her mother to bring Isabelle to England and hand her into royal custody. As the sole heir of Richard Strongbow, lord of Striguil, and Aoife, daughter of Dermot McMurrough, High King of Leinster, Isabelle was too great a prize to have at large. Besides, taking her into wardship meant that the Crown could continue to milk her inheritance until she was given in marriage.

Isabelle and her mother had spent a short time at Striguil on its high cliff above the River Wye, but within two months they were parted—Isabelle sent on her way to London and Aoife returning to Ireland. She could still feel her mother's arms tight about her in a final embrace and hear her exhortations that Isabelle be strong for the sake of her father and her ancestry.

"Your father and grandfather never gave in or gave up," Aoife had said. "And you must be like them. Remember who you are, my daughter, and do not let them subdue your spirit."

Isabelle gave a little sniff. She was dangerously close to feeling subdued now: taken from her home, from her friends and family; her only comfort two women, both of them ailing, and the small, sleek hound pup her mother had given her at their parting. The little creature was curled in a heap of blankets sound asleep at the moment. Isabelle had christened her Damask, for her coat bore the silver sheen of Arabian silk.

There was a shout behind them as another troop came splashing up the road. She saw her escort reach to their swords and her stomach swooped. There was always the chance of being abducted or robbed on the road. The country was supposed to be at peace but, as in Ireland, it was a peace fraught with tension and continuous scheming. She sighed with relief when her guards relaxed their hands and exchanged friendly greetings with the newcomers—not a troop, she saw now, but a knight, his squire, and a groom, all heavily cloaked against the rain. The brow-band and breast strap of the knight's horse were adorned with small shield-shaped badges enamelled half green, half yellow, with a snarling red lion in the foreground. Isabelle thought them striking. The knight's shield and banner matched the badges, but having lived in the isolation of Ireland, she had no idea who he was, nor could she see anything of him beneath hood and mantle.

Snippets of conversation drifted to her, disjointed by the rain and the turn of the men's heads as they spoke together. She heard her name mentioned by her guards. "Countess Isabelle of Striguil...bound for London...King's writ."

The knight said something about foul weather for travelling, and her guards replied that they were making a stop at Reading Abbey. "Warmer where you're going though, messire?"

The knight gave a rueful assent and rode on. As he splashed

closer to the back of the wain, she noticed the red cross of a crusader stitched to his cloak. His horse was steaming and his bare hands on the reins gleamed with rain. He wore a gold ring set with a large blue sapphire. His face she could not see for his deep hood and he was swiftly beyond her vision, but as he rode on, she realised that he had spoken to her. One word in acknowledgement, greeting, and farewell: "Demoiselle." His squire and groom squelched past in his wake, together with several laden pack ponies. Isabelle moved back into the deeper confines of the wain. The ends of her heavy blond braids were jewelled with raindrops and her face tingled with cold.

William broke his own journey in Salisbury with a visit to Queen Eleanor, where he knelt to receive her blessing on his pilgrimage. Her touch on his head was light, her voice calm and steady as she wished him Godspeed.

"May you find your peace, and peace for my son," she murmured. "And may God bring you safely home when you have found your road."

"Madam." He rose to his feet at her command and kissed her hand.

She gave him a long, steady look. "You did your best for him, William. He failed you, but you never failed him...and you never failed me. Not once, not for a moment."

She had found the sore spot in his soul and applied the cauterising knife, white-hot with knowing and brutal compassion. "No," he said, "but perhaps I failed myself. It is time to take stock."

She studied him, and then nodded. "Then go and do it," she said, "but do not make a prison for yourself and do not lose the grace you already have."

William thought long and hard about the Young King's mantle. At first he wrapped it in linen and kept it in a waxed leather bag to protect it from the elements, but by the time he had made the crossing to Normandy and revisited the tomb in Rouen, he had changed his mind. If Henry had intended to make a pilgrimage to Jerusalem, then his cloak should be worn for its purpose. William had taken it from its protective coverings and draped it across the Young King's tomb. For a night, it had lain there while William kept vigil, lamps flickering on the red silk cross sewn to the breast above the heart.

In the morning, following confession and mass, William donned the cloak and wore it continuously throughout the long journey, down through Lombardy and Apulia to Brindisi, and across the straits to Durazzo; across Byzantium to Constantinople, and the gruelling ride through Anatolia to the Syrian Gates, then the final journey along the coast to Caesarea before turning inland to Jerusalem. By the time he rode through the David Gate and into the Holy City, he was as lean and hard as whipcord and the Young King's mantle had lost the sheen of royal finery. The red silk cross was frayed, the rich blue dye had faded, bleached in salt wind and hot sunlight, and the hem was uneven where it had come unstitched and William had repaired it himself.

The road had been hard and filled with danger and privation, but each mile travelled towards his goal had seen a gradual lifting of William's burden of guilt and sorrow. The hotter the sun, the fiercer the wind, the harder he was scoured, the better he felt in his soul. Lighting candles, offering the Young King's mantle at the Tomb of Christ in the church of the Holy Sepulchre, he felt as weightless as a husk. He could not have risen had he tried, and so remained on his knees, head bowed, prostrating himself before God and begging His forgiveness until his vision turned to white light and then darkened.

A Templar monk finally stooped over him, helped him to his feet, and, saying little, took him outside to Rhys and Eustace, and then brought them to a hostel on Malquisnet Street where he made William drink sugar-sweetened wine and eat a platter of stuffed dates. Gradually William revived. For the first time in an age, he was aware of the taste of the wine and sweetmeats, and of the hunger still gnawing in his belly. On the road to Jerusalem, food had merely been sustenance to keep him putting one mile behind another, and towards the end it hadn't mattered at all.

The Templar studied him with compassionate dark eyes. His name was Thibaud; he was Norman, originally from the Giffard estates of Longueville and he remembered William from the tourney circuit. "That was in the days before I came to Outremer and took my vows," he said. "You were tourneying with the Young King and there was no one to match you. I can still remember how you seemed to set the field on fire."

William found a smile, although it felt strange to curve his mouth and the muscles quivered. "Yes," he said. "We were good. It's in the past now." He watched the street vendors shouting their wares and inhaled the smell of hot oil from their griddle plates. Malquisnet Street was where all the city cook-stalls and eating hostelries were gathered and it was crowded with hot, footsore pilgrims in search of sustenance. "I doubt I'll tourney again."

The Templar nodded sombrely. "I heard that the Young King was dead," he said. "A pilgrim from Anjou told us two months since. I said prayers for his soul, God rest him." He crossed himself.

So did William. "It was his cloak that I laid upon the tomb of Christ. He charged me to bring it, and to give alms to the poor for the repose of his soul…" A soul imperilled by blasphemy and robbing from Mother Church. He didn't make the remark aloud for there was no point in hauling the story out of the grave again. It was over, finished. He compressed his lips.

Thibaud's gaze was perceptive, but he said nothing, merely asked William how long he was staying and what his plans were now.

"I have pledged myself at the Holy Sepulchre to a year in God's service in expiation of my sins before I turn for home," William said, and turned the sapphire ring on the middle finger of his right hand.

"That is what I did," the knight said, "and then stayed to join the Templar order. There was nothing for me back in Normandy, save a life of tourneying at which I had but small skill, or being someone's hearth knight. God chose me to be His hearth knight instead."

"I have thought about it," William admitted. "My father was a patron of your order and, having seen your castles and travelled with other Templars, I admire your skill and faith and industry…but…"

"But?" Thibaud still smiled but there was a guarded expression in his eyes.

"But I have pledged King Henry that I will return to him and make a report of my journey. Nor am I worthy of taking any holy vows." William ceased to play with the ring and looked directly at the Templar. "I will gladly serve the order while I am here, and help its patronage where I can when I return. That I promise."

The knight inclined his head and looked moderately pleased, although perhaps he had hoped for more. William wondered if Thibaud was hoping to recruit him into the Templars. It was an opportune place to seek out likely candidates—the end of the journey, the holiest place in Christendom.

Later, when William had eaten a full meal of chickpea stew and flat bread, washed down with plain wine, he asked Thibaud to take him to the stalls of the fabric merchants in the covered markets by the David Gate.

"It is usually the women who come here," Thibaud said, looking curious and amused. "The men always head for the sword-sellers, the horse market, and then the tavern."

William half smiled. "All of those in due course, but I have a matter to attend to first."

"Ah, you're buying a gift for your sweetheart?" Thibaud gave a sly grin.

William shook his head. "For myself, for when I die."

The humour fell from the knight's face. "You're buying your own pall?"

Without replying, William paused at a stall and began examining the wares. There were fabulous bolts of gold and red silk, shimmering like fire; blues and greens with an iridescent peacock gleam; Tyrian purple, its price beyond reckoning. Some were woven with patterns of lozenges and fantastical beasts, others had raised designs repeated through the weave. William spent a long time looking. The Syrian merchant spread the cloths for him, emphasising their texture, how fine the weave was. Eventually he selected two pieces of undyed silk with no embellishment, but of a weave so delicate and exquisite, they cost as much as some of the more colourful and elaborate cloths.

"They are my covenant with God," he told the bemused Templar as the merchant wrapped the silks in a square of plain linen to protect them. "I accept that he can claim my life whenever he chooses and that until such time I will endeavour to lead an honourable life and repay the debt owing." He took the wrapped silks from the merchant. They made only a small package, which weighed next to nothing in his hand…but their significance to his life was all-embracing. It was the difference between staying where he was and moving forward.

Twenty-four

RAWING REIN, WILLIAM EYED THE TIMBER HUNTING LODGE standing amid the trees. The court was in residence and the opening in the palisade that divided the forest from the lodge was braided with a host of humanity weaving in both directions. Without the palisade, clustered like fanciful knots of embroidery on a robe, a sporadic overflow of tents and shelters stitched the ground.

William's road to Lyons-la-Forêt had been more than two years in the travelling and he didn't know if it was going to continue past without succour, or lead him back into a world that he had once known as intimately as his armour. There was only one way to find out, and he had never yet held back from a challenge. He nudged his palfrey's flanks and the horse stepped out, a fine beast showing its eastern origins in the arch of its neck, its dished face, and hard blue hooves. He had bought it from the Templars in the week before he sailed from Saint Symeon for home—if home this was. Behind him, Eustace and Rhys rode second and third palfreys and led the packhorses and William's two destriers on leading ropes.

Passing amid the flurry of tents, William approached the gateway of split logs. A pimply young guard stepped forward to demand his business and was immediately drawn aside by a more knowledgeable veteran.

"Messire Marshal." The older man bowed deeply as if addressing a great lord rather than a travel-weary knight with two dusty attendants at his heels. The young guard's eyes widened and flickered from William to the shield athwart the packhorse with its rampant red lion on a background half green, half yellow, and then he too bowed.

William inclined his head. The first barrier was down then. In truth, he did not expect to be thrown out on his ear, but royalty was nothing if not fickle. "Is the King within?" he asked, gesturing towards the main building.

"No, sir. He's out hunting, but should return by dusk. He will be right pleased to see you."

"And I him," William answered with formal courtesy and rode on. Word had already raced ahead. The young guard might not have recognised William until prompted by his fellow and the sight of a shield that not so long ago had been famous across every tourney ground between Normandy and the Limousin, but others were not so ignorant.

"Sir!"

He turned at the call and as he dismounted was effusively embraced by a wiry little clerk with ink-stained fingers and receding curly dark hair. No ceremony here; no bowing. "Wigain!" William returned the hug full measure, feeling a warm rush of affection. "King Henry took you into his employ then?" he asked as he pushed away.

"Yes, sir. There's always room for another clerk in the lord King's household." He gave William a sly look. "I'm not as rich as I used to be since you left the tourney road though."

William chuckled. "Neither am I," he said and began walking his palfrey towards the stable block. "Is the King well?"

Wigain made a face. "Most of the time, although of an early

morning or late at night he sometimes remembers his years and his burdens." He hesitated. "He misses our lord."

William touched his breast where the sapphire ring now hung on a cord with a cross and a token of Saint Christopher. For a moment melancholy engulfed him, but then mercifully receded. It was an ebb tide these days rather than a running one. "So do I," he said, thinking of summers spent in the pleasure of the tourney. Frivolous and fickle and, even while they had seemed endless, trickling through the fingers like grains of sand. The laughter and companionship, and beneath it the darkness and uncertainty. Friendships and betrayals, and that last terrible farewell.

"Did you reach Jerusalem, sir?"

They came to the stables and William gave his palfrey to Eustace and dismissed Rhys who he knew was desperate to go and find his wife who had been taken into the Angevin service as a laundry maid while he was absent on pilgrimage. "Would I be here if I had not?" Taking a travelling satchel from the palfrey's saddle, he slung it at his shoulder and began to walk. "I laid the Young King's cloak at the tomb of Christ, and lit candles for his soul. I am here to tell his father that I have fulfilled his son's dying wish."

"And you will stay?" Wigain looked eager. "The King will welcome you, I know he will...the Queen too."

William checked his stride. "Queen Eleanor is here?"

"Yes, sir, although she returns to England soon."

"Still a prisoner?" William resumed walking.

Wigain looked uncomfortable. "He gives her more freedom now, but he still won't let her out of his sight unless she is closely guarded."

William said nothing, although he wondered if King Henry was ever going to forgive his wife for rebelling against him and wanting more from her life and her marriage than he had been willing to yield.

Reaching the lodge, he took his leave of Wigain and entered alone. News of his arrival had flown before him; the door guards stood aside to let him pass and the usher welcomed him within a long room, lined by benches, its walls decorated with brightly painted shields and the skulls of boar and deer. William stood for a moment, allowing his eyes to adjust to the gloom after the spring brightness of the courtyard.

"Messire Marshal."

William turned to face a striking fair-haired youth whose voice had but recently broken to judge from the way it strained between the first and second word. The lad bowed. "I am to take you to the Queen. She bid me say that you are most welcome."

William nodded gravely in response and followed the youth. Eleanor still had an eye to a likely young man, he thought with amusement. Her apartments lay behind the main lodging and as her good-looking page led him through the door, the scented heat of the room reached out to William like a warm hand. Eleanor always complained that the northern climate was too chill for her thin southern blood and braziers burned in every corner of the room. The perfume of cinnamon and frankincense was sensual and familiar and overran his mind with a smoke of memories.

"William!" Eleanor hastened towards him, one hand extended in greeting, the other holding the embroidered hem of her crimson wool gown above the floor rushes.

"Madam." Kneeling, he kissed her hand.

"Oh, it is good to see you!" Eleanor's voice still travelled down his spine. Even at two and sixty and her husband's prisoner, she had retained the ability to bring men to their knees, either broken or adoring.

"And you, madam, are a pleasing sight for travel-weary eyes," William responded gallantly. "Of all the fair women I saw between here and Jerusalem, there were none to match the Queen of England."

She laughed and, removing her hand from his possession, gestured him to his feet. "Ever the flatterer. Raoul, wine for Sir William." A swift snap of her fingers sent the page hurrying to his duty.

"Madam, it is the truth. You will only ever receive truth from me."

Eleanor looked pleased. "Then I must believe you, for even my beloved husband says that William Marshal does not know how to tell a lie."

William took the cup from the page. The wine was the same hue as Eleanor's gown and he studied it suspiciously.

"It's all right to drink," she assured him. "It is mine and for my use only. I refuse to touch the vinegar that my husband forces everyone else to swallow."

William responded with a genuine grin. "Then in that case, madam, to your health," he toasted her, and took a swallow. The taste was like her voice, rich, smooth, disturbing, and until this moment he hadn't realised how much he had missed it.

Eleanor turned from him and resumed her chair behind a broad tapestry frame that was long enough for two of her women to work upon also. "Jerusalem," she said and indicated that he should sit on a foldstool facing her. "Tell me."

William drank his wine in which there were no lees, and by and by accepted a second cup and told her what she wanted to know, but kept many things to himself. It was her son's dying vow that he had borne on his own shoulders to the Holy Sepulchre and seen fulfilled; she was entitled to know about that, and about the colour and taste of the land that she had once seen during her first marriage when she was the young Queen of France. He gave her too a small ampoule of rock crystal, containing waters from the river Jordan. But on other matters, such as the pall cloths he had purchased, he was reticent and Eleanor did not press him.

"You are changed, William," Eleanor said softly, "but perhaps that is not surprising."

He shrugged. "I shed my old life in Jerusalem, madam."

"No more jousts and tourneys?" Her voice was teasing, but not the concentration of her stare.

"No," he said. He had drunk his second cup to the dregs and was beginning to feel light-headed. He needed food and rest. It was not wise to have a wine-wild tongue in Queen Eleanor's presence.

"Then what else will you do?"

He smiled. "Find a good woman and settle down."

Eleanor narrowed her eyes at him, then gave her throaty laugh. "Well, that will be a quest and a half, but I can hardly see you carving out that role for yourself, whether you are changed or not. You're a courtier, William, a knight, a soldier, a commander. The day you settle down is the day that you are buried. I still know you better than you know yourself."

"Likely you do, madam," he said graciously. "But of late I have thought of quiet days and nights with a wife at my side and sons at my feet."

Eleanor pursed her lips and picked up her needle. "That shows you how much you know of marriage," she said, and her amusement was now tinged with asperity, "...and that you must have ridden around with your eyes closed for the last twenty years." She gave him a shrewd look. "I do not know how well informed your travels have been, but Marguerite is no longer at Philip's court. She wed King Bela of Hungary last year."

The thought of Marguerite sent a pang of emotion through William like sudden pressure on a healing wound. "I hope that she finds happiness in the match," he said, realising that he would probably never see her again.

"Oh yes," Eleanor said acerbically, "there is always hope." His face must have given something away, for her expression softened slightly. "It was a good match," she said, "better than either of mine have been."

William was spared from answering as a knock on the chamber door heralded his summons to the presence of the King, who had returned from his hunting trip. As he rose to leave and bent over Eleanor's hand in farewell, she said, "Be careful what you wish for, William, for you might receive it."

"I hope so, madam," he said with a rueful smile.

Eleanor watched him bow from the room, still graceful as a cat despite his travel-tiredness.

"I am a good woman," offered her youngest maid, Gersendis, hopefully.

Eleanor gave her a pitying look. "Not William Marshal's sort of good," she said as she resumed her sewing. Now and then her eyes went to the small ampoule he had given her and she thought about what he had said, and even more about the spaces between his words.

William was shocked to see how much King Henry had aged in the three years since they had parted company at his son's tomb in Rouen. Henry's eyes were bloodshot, as if with too much wine or not enough sleep. His complexion was wind-blown and ruddy from hard exercise, but he looked neither healthy nor robust. Prince John, now nineteen years old, had accompanied him on the hunt. He possessed his mother's high cheekbones and fine hazel eyes. An attempt at growing a beard had edged his strong chin and petulant upper lip with a minimal dark grizzle.

"Hah!" Henry clasped William's arm in a hard grip and raised him to his feet. "You've returned to me then?"

"It was my duty…and my loyalty, sire."

"Loyalty," Henry repeated the word as if he didn't know

whether to choke on it or roar with laughter. "You always have the right words, Marshal, I'll grant you that." He turned to his half-smiling youngest son. "Loyalty is as valuable as gold," he said. "Especially loyalty like the Marshal's. Remember it well."

"It can be bought with gold too," John said, "or bought off." He looked at William. "What's your price, Marshal?"

William hesitated, tempted to tell John that it was more than a too-clever stripling like him could afford, but prudence curbed his tongue. He reminded himself that his elder brother was one of the Prince's men. "That is between myself and your father, Lord John," he replied, "should he wish to retain my services. What I did for your brother, I did for love, not gain."

"But you will gain by it, won't you!" the youth said with bright malice in his eyes.

"John, enough, stop teasing." Henry raised an indulgent hand towards his youngest son. "Come, Marshal, share wine and tell me about the pilgrimage."

It was very late when William returned to his tent, staggering through the cool spring evening, his way lit by stars and the soft flare of cooking fires. Time and again he was stopped by men who wanted to greet his return and welcome him home. He found the smiles, the right words to say; he managed brief conversations. He had had a long apprenticeship in the art and even when less than sober could still hold himself together to play the game. But it was wearisome and he felt a powerful sense of relief as he finally reached his pavilion. His fingers, usually so swift and dextrous, fumbled at the flap ties and Eustace had to undo them for him.

"Never drink the King's wine, especially after the Queen's," he told the squire. "They don't agree with each other."

"Like their owners," Eustace said. "Have you eaten?"

William snorted at the first remark and waved away the

second. "Less than I've drunk but more than enough if my gut's the judge. All I need now is sleep."

Eustace saw him inside the tent and loosely retied the flaps. By a lantern's dim glow, William lay down on his pallet, grateful to find that the squire had stuffed it with plenty of fresh straw. But although he was exhausted, sleep was slow in coming and his brain, like his abused stomach, continued to churn and swirl upon its contents. Henry had wanted to know about his pilgrimage, but in different substance to the Queen. Not for him the colours and texture of the journey, but the stark facts succinctly given like a battle report. The only images he demanded in detail were those of the laying of his dead son's cloak at Christ's tomb and the lighting of a candle for the young man's departed soul. William had given him what he required, as he had given Eleanor, but at cost to himself and with Prince John looking on and absorbing every word and nuance with the greedy eyes of a predator. At least it was over now, he thought, trying to recover his mental balance as the tent whirled around him. At least now that it was told, it could be put in a chest with the silk palls—always there, always a reminder, but not for daily inspection.

When William had done with his tale, Henry had asked him to stay, speaking of grants and riches that could be his for the taking of an oath of fealty while John looked on with a knowing smirk. "I have an heiress in wardship," Henry had said, "and I have been looking for a suitable administrator for her lands. She is of marriageable age. You can be her warden or her husband as you please."

William closed his eyes and pressed the heels of his hands against his lids until stars came. Her name was Heloise of Kendal and she held substantial estates in the north of England. Henry had given him other wardships too, but they were insignificant when compared to the main one. He had also granted him a piece of land abutting Heloise's domains, to do with as he chose, although his homage for the land would be owed to Prince John who held it of his father. William had accepted the grant, had drunk a toast of the King's musty household wine, and sworn his fealty. He had a new lord, a new cloak to put on, but whether it would fit him well was another matter.

Twenty-five

WILLIAM HAD NEVER HAD A WARDSHIP BEFORE, ALTHOUGH he had trained several squires and mentored plenty of young knights. The youth who stood before him now was his responsibility in every sense of the word. Jean D'Earley's parents were dead and his guardian, the Archdeacon of Wells, was recently deceased. At fourteen Jean was still too young to administer his lands by himself. Not too young though to be wearing a sword at his left hip and the long sheath of a hunting dagger at his right, William noticed, concealing a smile. The sword was far too cumbersome for the youth's light frame and from the somewhat outmoded style of the hilt was a family heirloom, probably passed down several generations. William recognised the pride, the challenge, and the uncertainty.

"Jean," he said pleasantly and extended his hand. The youth gave him a wary look out of slate-blue eyes half hidden by a fringe of night-black hair, and after a moment responded. His wrist bones were long and narrow, speaking of recent rapid growth. His damp hand revealed his apprehension, but the strength of the grip showed that he was determined not to be overwhelmed. "I assume you have been told that while the Crown will administer your lands, you yourself are to be trained in my household until you reach your majority."

"Sir," the boy said and compressed his lips.

"And you do not know whether to be resentful or pleased."

The lad looked startled but said nothing—not that William had expected him to. "Let me see your sword."

His charge drew the weapon and handed it over hilt-first, anxiety entering his expression. William examined the blade thoroughly, noting how the edge was keen and bright and how it had been oiled and looked after. "You care for this yourself?" he asked as he tested the balance.

"Yes, sir." The youth reddened.

William handed it back to him. "Good," he said. "Cleaning weapons is the first duty a squire learns, and you're already competent. How much training in weapon play have you had?"

The youth's flush deepened. "Only a little, sir."

Probably next to nothing, William thought. His father had died when he was eight, and the Archdeacon had been an elderly priest. Buried here, all the training the youth had likely received was some basic spear and shield work and the rudiments of swordplay. Likely, the same applied to courtly skills. The only thing polished was that great sword, which was entirely unsuitable. Nevertheless, the lad clearly possessed ability, and was a hard worker if the shine on that steel was any indication.

"That doesn't matter. As my squire, you'll learn."

"Your squire?" The slate-blue eyes widened in surprise.

"What else did you think I was going to do with you? You're old enough to start full training and you won't get that here, even it is your home. By the time you come of age, you'll have all the skills you need and more."

The boy looked at him, the surprise fading to be replaced by something more measured and thoughtful. William realised with amusement and a strange quirk in his gut that while he had been assessing the lad, he too had been under thorough scrutiny. "You have something to say?"

"Is it true that you were tutor in arms to the sons of King Henry?"

William inclined his head gravely. "It is."

"And a great tourney champion?" A gleam entered Jean's gaze.

"I was once." *Were. Was.* With the boy's young eyes upon him and those answers defining his past, William felt a surge of melancholy. The last tourney he had attended had been near Saint-Pierre-sur-Dives before his pilgrimage and although he had taken the prize, the gloss had tarnished. The boy had obviously been given a résumé of his new guardian's past achievements. Whether he had been given the scandal alongside them, William was not about to ask. "I'll teach you sword- and lance-play," William said, "but don't expect to attend any tourneys, and don't believe half the tales you hear."

"But if half are untrue, that still leaves half that are," Jean pointed out, shedding some of his awe to reveal a glimpse of the personality beneath. Reminded of Ancel, William smiled.

"Yes, and you'll have a laborious task sifting wheat from chaff, but that's part of the training too. Do your best for me, and I'll do mine for you."

"Yes, sir."

"You won't be alone in your duties. My nephew will be joining my household as a squire too. He's about your age and you'll share duties between you. We're fetching him on the morrow."

Jean nodded, his expression a mingling of apprehension and eagerness. William gestured to the long scabbard at the lad's hip. "Go and take that off," he said, "and put it somewhere safe. Let's start you off with something lighter and less precious to you."

As the youth departed, William tried not to think of the one he had trained in the past who was sealed in a tomb in Rouen. Let sleeping princes lie. Jean D'Earley had a future, and so—he hoped—did he.

"Your son looks more like you than you do yourself," William said to his brother as they watched Jack draw back his arm and hurl the spear towards a straw target. Jean D'Earley and some other boys were watching and waiting their turn. A lithe little girl with dark braids hovered on their periphery.

The men were seated on a bench outside the hall, enjoying the sun and catching up on the years apart before William collected his second squire and rode north to inspect his other, more lucrative wardship.

"People are always saying that," said John Marshal. "It is good of you to take him on, but I still do not know if I am doing the right thing."

William looked at him. "Because of me, or because of him?"

John snorted. "Because of his mother. She dotes on him and Sybilla." His gaze flickered to the girl who was practising dance steps around the group of boys. "There will be a vale of tears when he goes." He folded his arms. "Oh, she knows she has to let go and that it is the best for all concerned. She puts a brave face on it, but it will be hard. Of course, she'll still have Sybilla, but when the girl reaches betrothal age she'll go to be raised by her in-laws. I can't settle a great dowry on her, but she's pretty and related to the earls of Salisbury, so that counts for something."

It was Jean's turn to throw the spear and William watched the lad take aim and hurl. He winced, for the technique was execrable, but there was potential. His niece patted Jean on the arm in consolation.

"I suppose in a way it is a boon that Alais is with child again," John said, his expression wry. "It will take her mind off losing our son."

"You are not losing him…"

"He will leave a boy and return a man, or I hope he will. It is a rite of passage and she cannot follow. The new infant will keep her busy."

William gave his brother a sharp glance. "I would congratu-
late you, but you do not seem overjoyed at the thought of
another child."

John twitched his shoulders. "It came as a surprise, I admit.
We have been careful, but plainly not careful enough...John
and Sybilla are proof of that. I think it happened after our
mother's funeral. That was a difficult time and we sought more
comfort in each other than we had done in a long while."

William looked sombre. "I was in the Holy Land when she
died," he said. "I lit candles for her at the Holy Sepulchre, even
though I didn't know then. God rest her soul." Feeling a wave
of guilt and sorrow he crossed himself. Since young manhood
he had not visited his mother as often as he should, and now
it was too late.

"No, you manage to avoid family funerals," John said a
trifle snidely.

"It's not intentional," William growled.

John must have sensed that he had stepped close to the mark
for he swiftly changed the subject, although it too was a probe
at William's personal life. "What of this heiress you're set to
wed?" he asked. "Do you know anything about her?"

William eyed his brother obliquely. "Who said anything
about wedding her? She's only my ward at the moment."

"The King intends her for you."

William folded his arms. "Yes, he does."

"But you're not going to."

"I have yet to decide, and that depends on the lady herself,"
William replied and would not be drawn by further searching
from his brother. He had originally been of a mind to marry
Heloise of Kendal whatever the circumstances, but on the
sea crossing from Normandy to England Queen Eleanor had
chosen to give the cauldron a quick stir, murmuring to him that
he had accepted far too low a reward for his services.

"You can do better for yourself, William," she had said, laying her hand on his sleeve. "My husband can give you much more than the meagre portion he has doled out to you thus far."

"It is enough, madam," William had answered, made uncomfortable by her knowing gaze.

She had nodded shrewdly. "Perhaps it is for now, but will it be enough in the future when you realise how much more you could have had? Think on it. There are more heiresses in my husband's gift than Heloise of Kendal."

He had been thinking ever since, his mind plodding like an ox on a treadmill. He had been offered more than he had ever had in his life. Lands to administer, the rents and produce of which would keep him solvent and allow him an entourage; a young wife, the chance of heirs; his own hearth instead of warming himself at the fires of others. Yet Eleanor said he should risk asking for more. Whether out of a genuine concern for him or a desire to make mischief he was not certain, although, knowing the Queen, it was probably a mixture of the two.

With an effort he broke the traces and shook himself free. "I'll go to London and fetch my new charge," he said to his brother. "And then I'll govern the lands entrusted to me and bide my time. There is no need to rush into any decision."

Twenty-six

THEY WERE FEEDING THE LIONS. ISABELLE DE CLARE WINCED at the distant sound of roaring. She had gone to watch once, but the sight of the great beasts tearing apart the carcass of a horse had not been one she was desperate to repeat. Damask, her small silver hound, would shiver if Isabelle took her any-where near the lion pit, but sometimes Isabelle would go with-out the bitch to watch the great golden beasts prowl the walls of their confinement. After all, she told herself, they were a rare sight and when she left the Tower she would probably never see their like again—if she left the Tower, she amended gloomily.

It was three years since she had entered this place and dwelling within its confines like a pawn shut up in an ivory chess casket was immensely frustrating. Her childhood homes had been the windswept shores of Ireland and South Wales, with occasional forays into the Marches, to her family's great keep of Striguil, hugging the cliffs above the River Wye. Now it was difficult to remember any of them. The faces of her family were growing hazy in her mind too, as if successive layers of mist were being drawn across their images. If she tried she could still picture her mother's blond braids, but then her own were the same and a constant prompt. Her brother and father had travelled deeper into the fog and at times were almost wholly obscured.

The roars echoed and although they were far from the lions' quarters, Damask squatted nervously on the grass to urinate, her ears trembling back in the direction of the sound.

"I do not blame her," said Heloise of Kendal, joining Isabelle on her morning walk with the dog. "The lions make me want to do that too."

Isabelle smiled at her companion, glad of the company. Like her, Heloise was an heiress, although her lands were nowhere near as great and she had only been here for a few months rather than the three years of Isabelle's residence. She was a dumpy pigeon of a girl with mead-brown eyes and a freckled complexion. Whereas Isabelle spoke French with the soft lilt of her Irish birthplace, Heloise's accent was strong and forthright and held the distinct influence of the north.

"The justiciar has had orders about me," Heloise announced as the girls crossed the sward. The late spring weather had chosen a day to pout and rain clouds threatened in the distance. A cool wind blustered their cloaks and tugged at their veils, exposing Isabelle's heavy wheat-gold braids and Heloise's glossy dark ones.

"You're not leaving?" Isabelle's gaze widened in dismay. Although Heloise had not been at the Tower for long; she had already made an indelible impression on Isabelle's lonely existence and she could not bear to think of losing her friend so soon.

Heloise shrugged. "I'll probably have to. Lord Ranulf said that he'd received letters from the King releasing me into the hands of a warden."

"Did he say who?"

Heloise wrinkled her nose. "William Marshal," she said, and sniffed. "He's not of the north."

Isabelle shook her head. She had not heard of the man either, but, like Heloise, her upbringing had been away from the hub of all court affairs and the important men she knew about were those of Leinster, Striguil, and Longueville.

"Probably some Norman with planks for wits," Heloise added. "Lord Ranulf didn't say much, but I could tell he wasn't impressed."

"What will you do?"

"What choice do I have?" Heloise folded her arms inside her cloak. "I suppose if I don't like him I can always dose his wine with hemlock or cause him to fall in a bog on the moors. The peat pools swallow sheep and cattle whole, so I don't see why they shouldn't swallow a man without trace."

If Heloise had hoped to elicit a horrified response from her friend, she was disappointed. Coming from Ireland, Isabelle knew all about bogs that conveniently swallowed troublesome folk. Her own mother had not been above muttering such sentiments on occasion—especially about Normans. She wished this unknown William Marshal to perdition for taking away her new-found friend. "When's he coming?" she asked.

Heloise shrugged. "Lord Ranulf didn't say. You know what he's like. Getting anything out of him is like trying to prise a limpet off a rock. Soon I hope. I want to go home."

It started to rain and Damask turned tail and streaked back the way she had come, her coat as sleek as watered silver. Sated by their meat, the lions' roaring had settled to an occasional desultory rumble.

"I wonder who the King will set over my lands." Isabelle shivered as she made to follow her dog. The drops struck her face like tears. She wanted to go home too, but that would never happen until she had a warden set over her, and God alone knew how fit for the purpose that man would be. He might buy the office with no more intention than to milk her lands dry, and she would be powerless. A pawn removed from her casket and knocked sideways on the chessboard. Her hands had tightened into fists as she walked and she could feel the tension seeping up the back of her neck and throbbing at her temples.

"Not worth worrying about until it happens," Heloise said cheerfully. "Nothing you can do about it…except bide your time if he proves unworthy."

"And what if it doesn't happen?" Isabelle choked. "What if I am kept here until I rot?"

"Oh, you won't!" Heloise said, reaching out. "Here now, don't cry."

Isabelle twitched away from her. "I'm not crying," she snapped.

Heloise looked hurt, but took the hint and didn't persist.

Through the sudden slant of the rain, Isabelle watched a man dismount from a fine black palfrey and hand the reins to one of his squires. She thought how unfair it was that an unknown knight could come and go at will while she was incarcerated like a felon.

William could tell that Ranulf de Glanville, England's justiciar and King Henry's senior administrator, was displeased at the royal command to release Heloise of Kendal into William's keeping, but then Ranulf always had an eye to heiresses for the aggrandisement of his own family and his opinion of William was somewhat jaundiced. A tourney circuit wastrel and suspected adulterer, with a fast sword and a smooth tongue. William knew exactly what Ranulf thought.

"You are to be congratulated on your good fortune," de Glanville said insincerely, although his lips did stretch to a wintry smile. "Not only the lady Heloise, but the lordship of Cartmel too, I understand."

"I am aware of the King's generosity," William replied evenly. "I would like to see the girl and make arrangements for her to leave."

The justiciar raised his thin, silver eyebrows. "You are in haste…my lord." The last two words were added delicately and could have been taken as either compliment or insult. William allowed both nuances to bounce off him.

"Naturally I am. I have lands to discover and govern and they are at the other end of England. Since Heloise of Kendal is now my ward, I desire to meet her and give her a day's grace to pack her baggage."

De Glanville's nod was grudging. "I'll have her summoned." He beckoned to an attendant. "I assume you intend to wed the girl?"

William made a non-committal sound, thinking that everyone was suddenly very concerned about his marital status. "I have heard that you have another heiress lodged in your keeping," he said thoughtfully.

"I have several heiresses. They come and go as the King sees fit to grant them to wardens and husbands," de Glanville said coldly. "And I doubt he will see fit to grant you more than he has already given."

William answered the rebuff with a smile. He had heard that the daughter of Richard Strongbow was lodged in the Tower and everyone knew that she was one of the greatest marriage prizes in the kingdom. Only the heiress of Châteauroux on the French border had any claim to greater tracts of land. A man who gained such property would not be just a simple baron, but a magnate. He had been wondering for several days if Queen Eleanor was *that* ambitious for him and also how ambitious he was for himself. He had glimpsed Strongbow's daughter fleetingly on the day he had set out for Jerusalem—a thin girl in the early stages of turning into a woman, with wide blue eyes and ropes of rain-jewelled fair hair.

The attendant returned, escorting two young women: a willowy blonde and a buxom younger girl with a freckled complexion and bright brown eyes. Ranulf de Glanville's own complexion darkened until it almost matched the madder-red of his woollen tunic.

"As I understood," he said curtly, "I sent for the lady Heloise alone."

The attendant stared like an owl caught in daylight and began to stutter an apology. Overriding him, the plump girl took a swift pace forward and said, "I asked Isabelle to accompany me. Have I done wrong?"

The justiciar compressed his lips. "Had I wanted both of you, I would have sent for both of you." He gestured to the discomforted attendant. "Escort Lady Isabelle back to her chamber."

William rose and bowed to the girls. "They may both remain as far as I am concerned," he said easily. "A flower gladdens the eye, but two flowers doubly so."

"This is not the court of the Young King," de Glanville snapped. "Your speeches are inappropriate...my lord, as is Lady Isabelle's presence."

"But surely the lady is your guest, not your prisoner." William perused Isabelle de Clare more closely. The wan, slender waif of his brief glimpse three years ago was developing into a beauty. No wonder de Glanville had turned puce at her exposure to William. She returned his regard calmly from eyes flecked with different tones of blue like a summer sea, and then she lowered her gaze towards her neatly clasped hands. Her complexion was pale but pink warmth had seeped into her cheeks.

"Lady Isabelle is the King's ward, and it is my duty to protect her and do as I see fit for her wellbeing," de Glanville replied testily and waved his hand at the attendant. "I would hope that your manners are as fine as your speech."

"My manners are better than most," William said pointedly and inclined his head to Isabelle de Clare. "Another time perhaps, my lady."

"My lord," she murmured and turned with the servant, but not before she had cast a look filled with resentment and anger at Ranulf de Glanville. Not meek then, William thought with amusement, but too mannerly to cause a scene, and perhaps still not experienced enough to exert her authority. Dragging himself back to the matter in hand, he addressed Heloise of Kendal, who was almost as red in the face as the justiciar.

"You have been told I am to be your warden?" He gestured her to sit on the bench and bade a squire give her wine.

"Yes, my lord," she replied, plumping her ample haunches on the cushions. "I didn't mean to cause trouble."

"You haven't," William said "even if my lord Glanville would dispute the fact." He gave the justiciar a ribbing glance. "It is a good thing he is not the Queen's keeper for he would know the meaning of trouble then."

De Glanville loudly cleared his throat but otherwise did not rise to the bait, his expression one of controlled irritation.

"So," William said to Heloise, "how long do you need to be ready to ride home? Will the morrow be too soon?"

He watched her eyes brighten. "Oh no, my lord," she said. "I would go now if it were possible." And then cast a swift glance at de Glanville and put her hand to her mouth.

William grinned. "I still have matters of my own baggage to attend to, or I'd oblige. As it is, we'll set out at first light. I take it you can ride?"

Heloise wrinkled her nose. "Like a sack of flour, my lord, but it suffices." Her tone suggested that even if she couldn't ride she'd teach herself in a day just to be out of the Tower.

Chuckling, William decided that he was going to enjoy being her warden.

Isabelle watched Heloise lumber like an overgrown puppy round the chamber they shared. The lid of her travelling coffer was thrown back and she was tossing items of baggage to a maid for packing. Half these items had to be rescued off the floor for Heloise was terminally untidy. A wrinkled leg of hose came to light from its hiding place under the bed, stiff at the toes and in need of darning.

"I wondered where that had gone," Heloise said, giving it an experimental sniff and then making a face.

Isabelle shook her head, torn between laughter and disgust. Her own portion of the chamber exuded an orderly tranquillity. "Well," she said, "tell me what happened. Does he have planks for wits? Are you going to push him into a bog?"

Heloise rolled the hose into a cylinder and stuffed it down the side of the chest. "I don't think so. Even if he doesn't know Latin or ciphering, he's just as sharp as Sir Ranulf. It'll be hard running rings round him." Heloise gave a mischievous giggle. "I might try though. He's not like Sir Ranulf to purse his lips as if he's an old woman. He likes to laugh."

"You learned a lot about him in a short time," Isabelle said peevishly.

Heloise rolled her eyes. "I did, but not from him. He jests and makes easy conversation, but it's all on the surface. I spoke to Lord Ranulf's steward and he said that William Marshal used to be the Young King's tutor and that he's recently returned from a pilgrimage to the Holy Sepulchre. He also said that he's never been defeated in a tourney and that Queen Eleanor dotes on him."

Isabelle sat down on her bed and stroked her hound's silky silver ears. She felt green with jealousy and hated herself for it.

Heloise paused in gathering up her belongings. "I'm sorry," she said, suddenly contrite. "You don't want to hear me say things like that, do you? I wouldn't in your place."

Isabelle swallowed her envy and forced a smile. "Don't be so foolish. If I'm out of sorts it's because I wish I was going with you. Take your good fortune and squeeze every drop from it; that's a command."

Predictably Heloise rushed over to engulf Isabelle in a tearful bear hug. "I'll have a scribe write to you with news," she said. "And I'll visit you if I can...but who knows, you might have left here by then."

"Who knows," Isabelle repeated bravely, thinking that even if she did, it wouldn't be with an unbeaten tourney champion with a courtier's burnish and an easy, smiling manner.

In the morning, Heloise left soon after dawn to begin her journey home to Kendal. Standing on the sward, Damask in her arms, Isabelle watched William Marshal boost Heloise into the saddle of a placid brown mare. Heloise said something to him that made him laugh as she gathered the reins and adjusted her seat. He fed the mare a piece of purple carrot off the palm of his hand and rubbed her nose. Gilded in pale sunshine, his garments immaculate, he might have stepped straight from a stained-glass window or the pages of a psalter. He slapped the mare's neck and turning to his own black palfrey swung into the saddle as lightly as a youth. Heloise waved to Isabelle and with much kicking of her heels and flapping of her reins, managed, at last, to turn her mare. William Marshal looked across the sward to Isabelle, saluted her, and heeled the palfrey about. Biting her lip, Isabelle watched the party ride away. Then she turned and putting Damask down, walked her beneath the great, imprisoning walls. The lions were silent today and Isabelle's eyes were so dry that they burned.

Twenty-seven

WILLIAM CAME TO KENDAL IN FULL SUMMER, THE SKY deep blue with high feathers of cloud and the curlews calling over moor and pasture. A place of empty spaces, richer in sheep than in people, and those sheep providing a fine income from their fleeces. It was a landscape of lowering hills, lakes, and meres, fields divided by dry stone walls that had stood time out of mind. A beautiful, wind-cleaned world, and one so different to any William had encountered before that it overwhelmed him almost as much as the Holy Land had done. Here there was no harshness of sun, no desiccating heat, but there was the same sense of majesty, a brooding quality and the hint of a desolate harshness that was only a rainstorm away.

He explored his new responsibilities thoroughly, from the great lake of Windermere to the wide flat sands of Morecambe Bay. He visited the castles and priories and the forests, still populated by boar and wolf, creatures that had been hunted to the verge of extinction in the more populated south. Soaking up this new, strange landscape, he was exhilarated. After the tense and dangerous life he had led in the Young King's entourage, his arduous pilgrimage and spiritual scouring, it was a relief to have naught but mundane administrative duties to attend to, and time to enter into a firmer peace with God.

Heloise accompanied him everywhere, for as her warden he was responsible for her safety and security. She dined with him most nights, and he enjoyed her company for she made him laugh and she was incorrigible. But he decided that he was not about to make her his wife, whatever King Henry had intended. She was an entertaining distraction, and her wellbeing and that of her lands was his responsibility, but she was not his future. At the back of William's mind, Queen Eleanor's words continued to haunt him and he often thought about Isabelle de Clare…and wondered.

They heard the news in the autumn that the King's son Geoffrey had been killed in a tourney in Paris, trampled under the hooves of his stallion. William said prayers for his soul and kept vigil in memory of the little boy he remembered watching practise on the tilt ground at Argentan, and of the uneasy young man who had tried to play both sides in the disputes between his father and brothers and often fallen between two stools. He left a small daughter, Constance, and an unborn child growing in his wife's womb. William thought of the life's grace afforded himself; he had survived the tourneys, the bitter internal warring of the Angevin royal house, and a pilgrimage to Jerusalem. He had the conviction that God had reserved him for a purpose, and although it was not William's place to question, he did not believe that it was to wed Heloise of Kendal and dwell here in obscurity.

For almost two years, William tarried in the north. The leaves of his second autumn as lord of Kendal changed the trees from green to fire-red and gold, and as the weather grew cold he topped the linen layers of summer with woollen tunics and heavy, fur-lined cloaks. The roars of rutting stags echoed through the woods and smoky mist drenched forest, moor, and pasture. News came that Jerusalem had fallen into Saracen hands and a rallying cry rippled through Christendom, calling for a new crusade. King Henry pledged to go, so did Philip of France, and Prince Richard also, but for the moment, they were travelling no further than words. William felt a pang of guilt, wondering if he should have remained in the Holy Land and pledged his sword to the Templars...but had he done so, he would now be a rotting corpse on the field of Hattin where the Saracen commander Saladin had led his troops to overwhelming victory. To assuage his feelings of guilt and restlessness, William began plans to found a priory on his lands at Cartmel and spent much time, thought, and prayer upon the creation of the establishment.

The business of administering the lands for which he had fallen responsible was largely a matter of common sense and putting capable men in positions that suited them. He enjoyed the tasks but they did not stretch him and he began to feel like a man with insufficient food on his plate to make a satisfying meal. It helped that he had the squires to train. They were lively, likeable lads, although it didn't prevent them from being fiercely competitive with each other. His nephew was the sturdier of the two and better at wrestling and hand-fighting. Jean D'Earley was lighter on his feet and excellent at swordplay. He was a good rider too, although Jack, with his more robust build, was going to have the edge as a jouster.

Just before winter, William's brother visited him on his way to Lancaster on business for Prince John. Alais had borne another daughter but the child had died at little more than a month old.

"Alais has taken it very hard," John said morosely. "She says that it is God's judgement on us for our sin of fornication outside wedlock and I cannot reason with her. She spends all her time shut away, weeping."

"The Young Queen was like that for many months after she

and Henry lost their son," William said. "It is a wound that only time will close."

John's mouth turned down at the corners. "She refuses to lie with me lest she conceive again. She says that she will no longer be my whore...Jesu God, when she said that word..." He rubbed one hand over his face then looked at William, his gaze heavy with weariness. "Ach, I know why she spoke as she did. It's not just the death of the child."

William said nothing and waited, letting the moment ripen. He had suspected that there was more to it than grief for the death of a baby. When he had visited John and Alais at Hamstead before coming north, he had noticed small signs of strain between them. Looks, silent reproach, anxiety.

John sighed deeply. "Soon after our mother died, Adam de Port offered me his daughter Aline in marriage, and I said I would seriously consider the proposal."

"Ah," William said. That explained a great deal.

"The girl's not yet of marriageable age, but soon will be. Her father has influence at court and the girl's dowry is rich. I'd be an idiot not to accept the offer. I know our mother would have approved."

"And Alais?"

John made an impatient sound. "I cannot marry her, she knows that—it's been understood from the start. I've always respected her; never have I treated her like a whore, but she won't see sense. She says that our child dying and the offer of marriage are holy signs that we shouldn't cohabit...and nothing will convince her otherwise."

William shook his head. "I am sorry," he said, thinking of John and Alais a few years ago, and the envy he had felt for the aura of warmth and contentment surrounding them. Now that envy had become pity. "Perhaps given time..." He knew he was mouthing platitudes.

"Perhaps," John agreed, but his expression was that of a soldier who had fought to a standstill and didn't have the strength to go on. "What of yourself? Have you made a decision about your ward?" John's glance flickered towards Heloise, who was playing at knucklebones with the squires.

William watched her too. Her hair was escaping its net and there was a smut of dirt on her cheek from some escapade or other. He loved her dearly but in the way that he would love a puppy; in the way he had once loved a princess named Marguerite. It was unbearable. "I doubt I'll be inviting you to our wedding," he said quietly.

"But surely even if she doesn't suit, her lands do," John said.

Since his brother was on the cusp of taking a bride for her dowry with no consideration for compatibility of character, William didn't think it tactful to argue that particular point. "Yes," he said, "and they are mine to administer as I see fit, whether I marry her or not."

"They'd be more secure if you were to wed her."

"Indeed, but I'd not be free to look further afield."

"Ah," John's eyes narrowed astutely. "A taste isn't enough. You're ambitious for more."

William tugged his ear lobe. John had hit close to the truth of his dilemma. Should he take what Henry had freely given, or hold out for what the Queen said was his due? "I cannot see me living out my years in this place," he said after a moment, and was surprised to hear the note of impatience in his own voice.

John folded his arms. "Just make sure that you don't overreach yourself," he said darkly. "A handful of crumbs is better than no loaf at all—as you should well know by now."

William took the royal writ the scribe had just finished reading to him and stared at it. The neat lines of brown-black writing were incomprehensible to him. William's attempts at understanding and mastering the skill of literacy had left him with little more than ink-stained fingers and a deep frustration. No matter how many times his tutor had tried to beat the meaning of the symbols into his skull, his brain had stubbornly refused to make sense of them. He had long since accepted that what came naturally to some men was a mystery to others. Faced with besieging a castle, or getting the best out of a company of serjeants, William knew exactly what to do…and that was why he had received this summons. His stomach wallowed queasily, but outwardly his expression remained mild.

Harry Norreis was looking at him as expectantly as a hound waiting for a titbit. "You're going to answer it, aren't you?" he asked eagerly.

"No," William said flatly. "I'm going to sit on my arse and do nothing."

The comment was met with a look of horrified astonishment. William folded the parchment in four and grinned. "Of course I'm answering it, you dolt. Do you think I'd do anything else?" He glanced down at the letter which he had memorised as the scribe read it to him. It was a summons to join the King as soon as he could. King Philip of France had seized Henry's fortress of Châteauroux. War was brewing up faster than summer lightning and Henry needed experienced, stalwart men to stand in the storm. "The King wants me to bring as many knights and experienced men as I can." William clasped his shoulder. "You can start by passing on the news and mustering the men. I'll need to talk to those here and send out fast riders to the rest. I want to be ready to leave by the morrow dawn."

Heloise looked at William, her puppyish manner now decidedly hangdog. "I knew you would not stay," she said with a drooping lower lip.

It was late at night and they were sitting in his private

chamber, supposedly playing chess, but neither of them had taken a turn in a while. William's mind was far away, already with the King, and Heloise's had been glued to the thought of his imminent departure.

William toyed with a stubby ivory pawn, turning it between his fingers. "I cannot," he said. "The King has need of me."

"And it is what you have been waiting for."

William looked across the board at her and adjusted the focus of his thoughts. "Yes," he said.

"What of your duties in the north?"

"I have able deputies to leave in my stead."

Her eyes filled with accusation. "So all you have been doing is marking time and milking the cow."

He looked at her steadily until she dropped her gaze. "I have been doing both of those, but I am sorry if you believe that has been my entire purpose." William leaned back in his curved chair and folded his arms. "When I take on a task I do my best and I don't renege," he said softly. "You will not suffer under my wardship, I swear to you."

"I suppose you are thinking it a godsend that you did not marry me," she said in a small voice.

William smiled. "I am thinking that it is a privilege to have you for my ward." He took her hand in his. There were gold rings on two of her fingers, but carelessly worn, the claw setting on the one with a stone was damaged. She had been biting her nails again and there were grazes on her knuckles where one of the hound pups had chewed her hand. He lifted it to his lips and kissed it in the fashion of the court, and then he turned it over and kissed her palm and folded her fingers over the kiss. He had done it a hundred times before with different women, sometimes in flattery, occasionally as a prelude to more intimate embraces, and sometimes, like this, in a spirit of affection, compassion, and regret.

"You do not need to humour me," she said with wounded dignity.

"I am not. I may dress words in courtly language, but you have my honesty."

Heloise studied her hand, still folded over the courtesy of his kiss. "What of Denise de Châteauroux? Will she have your honesty too?"

William frowned. Henry's plea for aid had arrived with a bribe. Only let William come to his aid, bringing as many knights as he could muster, and Henry would give him the fortress of Châteauroux to hold by right of marriage to its young heiress, Denise, lady of Berry. He shrugged. "In the end she may have nothing of me at all." Stretching, he rose from the chessboard, abandoning all pretence at playing the game.

Heloise toyed with her braid, winding it around her forefinger. "I do not understand," she said in a puzzled voice.

"Châteauroux is in the hands of the French King. Henry has promised me something for which I will have to fight tooth and claw to regain. He is never generous unless forced to be."

"Can you do it?"

"It remains to be seen how hard the King of France wants to hold on to it and how deep the distrust between Prince Richard and his father has etched." He rumpled his hands through his hair and sighed. "God forbid that I should ever raise sons the like of Henry's."

Heloise eyed him curiously. He was usually smilingly reticent about the royal masters who played their tunes from a distance and expected lesser mortals to dance to them. "You dislike them?"

"No," William said, "but I am glad that they are not mine. They will tear their father and each other to pieces in their seeking after power. If Richard has to trample over his father's body to take what he sees as his due, then he will do so, and

John will follow the direction of best advantage to himself. My young lord was the same. He wanted power to wield, and in the end his wanting and his discontent were the end of him—God rest his soul." He crossed himself.

"And yet you still desire Châteauroux for yourself?"

"I am not certain that I do," he said thoughtfully, "but I am hoping that the King is open to negotiation."

Heloise eyed him. "Then what do you want?"

"My bed for the moment," he said with a finality in his tone that told her the questions had gone far enough.

"What about our game?" She indicated the chessboard.

"I concede," he said. "There's no shame in yielding to beauty."

Heloise gave a small, forlorn smile. The shield of the courtier was firmly back in place and there would be no more getting round it tonight—or perhaps ever again. For a moment she hesitated, and then she ran to him, threw her arms around his waist, pressed her head to his chest, and hugged him fiercely. "Don't forget me," she said.

"As if I could." His tone was wry, but his arms came around her and he returned her hug full measure.

Twenty-eight

WILLIAM AND BALDWIN DE BÉTHUNE HAD BILLETED themselves in a wine merchant's house in Châtillon. Arriving back from the counsel chamber, William left his squires to tend the horses and slumped on a bench in the main room, feeling drained to the marrow. At times like this, a quiet life in England's North Country began to look very attractive. A summer of optimism was rapidly turning into a difficult autumn. Henry and Philip of France had been meeting and negotiating in sporadic fashion since July, but each time the outcome was the same. No agreement, escalating skirmishes, then a truce and another meeting more barren than the last. At first, Henry had had the upper hand, but matters had begun to curdle faster than three-day-old milk on a hot morning.

"At least the wine's good," Baldwin muttered as he handed a cup to William and sat down beside him. "You won't find grape-treaders' toe-parings in the lees." The habit of making light remarks was ingrained and meant nothing for his mood was grim. "If I find out who started the rumour that Henry intends to pass over Richard and leave his crown to John, I'll have his guts for girth straps."

"You'd have to go to the French side to do that," William said. "Philip will do his utmost to drive a wedge between Henry and Richard—and it won't be hard, given their characters." William accepted a cup from the squire. The scene between father and son had been ugly. They both had wills of iron and each thought himself the better ruler, one by dint of grit and long experience, the other bursting with ambition and fierce military talent. Younger than the King, older than Richard, William could see both sides of the frequent arguments between them, but tried to avoid becoming embroiled.

"Do you think he really would give England to John over Richard's head?"

"I think that he would like to and I know that John eggs him on in all kinds of subtle ways to slight Richard…but if it comes to the sticking point, he won't do it, not after the way he fought for his own right to rule when he was a young man." William took several swallows of wine. "The situation is still dangerous. Richard doesn't have the patience for such games—as we've just seen." He grimaced at the memory of Richard storming out of the counsel with his father, saying that he would be damned in hell before he saw John take the throne. John had said nothing; he hadn't needed to: his smirk had spoken volumes.

"Supposing Henry does disinherit Richard in favour of John?" Baldwin said sombrely. "What sort of king will John make? He was a disaster when his father sent him to Ireland."

William shook his head. "He was too young to tackle Ireland, and his father should never have given him the responsibility. The King was ready for command at sixteen years old—we've heard the tales until they've worn grooves in our ears, but men don't mature at the same rate—especially not the sons of great men. Our young lord was eight and twenty, but still a feckless lad when we buried him…God rest his soul." William crossed himself, so did Baldwin. "John has the ability and the wits," William added after a pause. "He's as sharp as a needle, but too often he uses that sharpness to stab and wound, instead of sewing a good seam. He's jealous and covetous too, especially of Richard."

"If my brother were Richard, I would be jealous," Baldwin replied. "He's got the looks, the prowess, and a knack of making men want to follow him to the ends of the earth. John will never command that kind of loyalty."

"No," William agreed bleakly. When he had entered Queen Eleanor's service, John had been an engaging imp with a ready smile. But Eleanor had not loved her last-born child; Henry had doted on him; between them, his parents had twisted him awry.

The men drank in morose silence while the sky bruised into dusk. "Have you approached the King about making good on his promise to you of Châteauroux?" Baldwin asked at length.

William shook his head. "Not yet."

Baldwin eyed him thoughtfully. "Do you want her?"

"It's a fine prize, but it's going to be a hard fight to gain it, and will the King be willing to give it up when it comes to the point?" William turned his cup contemplatively between his hands. "Also it's a long way from England."

Baldwin snorted. "Says the man who has spent more than half of his life wandering the tourney roads through France and Flanders, and taken a pilgrim's cross to Jerusalem."

William smiled gravely. "Indeed, but perhaps when I am not warming my hands at the hellish fires of the court, I would prefer to be in England."

"Then ask him for an English heiress instead."

"That's what I intend to—when I find an opportune moment. His mood's too chancy just now. Anyone who asks for anything is likely to receive the sharp edge of his tongue."

"Had you any particular heiress in mind?"

William set his cup on the scrubbed wooden board. "Isabelle de Clare."

Baldwin pursed his lips assessingly and nodded. "The estates are not as valuable as Berry."

William shrugged. "Almost, and they're not on the French border."

"Welsh and Irish though," Baldwin smiled.

"That is a challenge, not a difficulty," William answered and returned Baldwin's smile, albeit that the curve of his lips was dour. "As matters stand, it's not as if I am about to become a bridegroom soon, is it?"

In the morning the counsel resumed and William watched the situation between Henry and his eldest surviving son deteriorate as each man made demands untenable to the other. King Philip, who had instigated the dispute between father and son by declaring that he would retreat from the territory he had occupied if Henry would confirm Richard as his heir and see him married to his betrothed of twenty years, Alys, Philip's half-sister, looked on like a spectator at a lion fight. Red in the face, fists clenched, Henry glared at the King of France and at Richard, whose own complexion was hectic.

"I will not be backed into a corner by your petty scheming," he snarled at Philip. "I will designate my heir at a time of my choosing, not yours."

Philip spread his hands. "It seems a fair enough compromise to me. Confirm your eldest son as your heir, see him wed to his bride in honour of your promise. He asks nothing that a reasonable father would not grant to his eldest son."

"No, *you* ask!" Henry snarled, stabbing a short, nail-chewed forefinger at Philip. "It's your intent to drive a wedge between me and my sons."

"I do not need a wedge when you have a much larger one of your own," Philip said. "Do not blame me for your troubles when they are all of your own making." He extended his open palm towards Richard. "Confirm Richard as your heir; set his wedding day to my sister. That is all you have to do."

Standing on guard at Henry's side, William could see the King's body shuddering with the force of his rage. Beside his father, John sat with the inscrutability of a cat, although William suspected that inside his mouth he was grinning from ear to ear. "I have to do nothing. You will not force me to it," Henry said in a constricted voice. "All you will do is beget yourself a war that will cost you dear."

Richard unfolded his long body and stood up. His grey eyes glittered like chips of polished serpentine as he turned towards his father. "No," he said, "it will cost *you* dear. Why should I keep faith with you when you refuse to acknowledge my rights? Are you so eaten up with bitterness and your contrary will that you would leave your kingdom to a fool boy who's proven he can neither rule men nor fight his way out of a flour sack?" He gestured contemptuously at his youngest brother. "You think he's worthy? God's death, everything he touches curdles and turns sour."

John's tawny gaze narrowed.

"It is not John who is curdling my gut," Henry said. "Sit down."

William's right hand crawled involuntarily towards the hilt of his sword. Richard's eyes flickered as he caught William's intention and his own hand went to his gilded swordbelt. But instead of drawing his blade, he unbuckled the belt and slowly removed both it and the attached scabbard. Turning his back on his father and brother, he slowly approached the King of France and just as slowly knelt before him, laying the scabbard at his feet. "I hereby give you my homage for my lands of Normandy and Aquitaine," he declared in a voice that rang around the hall, "and I swear you my fealty saving only that which I owe to my father the King." The last words were loud and bitter. "And I beseech your aid should I be deprived of my rights as his heir."

Henry leaped to his feet and had to be restrained by the Archbishop of Canterbury. "You purblind fool!" Henry raged. "Can't you see that you're being manipulated!"

Richard looked at his father, his own control deadly. "No," he said in a voice husky with tension. "I have chosen freedom from manipulation. Look to the plank of wood in your own eye before you remove the mote of sawdust from mine!" Turning on his heel, summoning his retainers, he took up his swordbelt and strode from the hall.

Philip of France rose and also turned to leave. "War is upon you," he said to Henry, "and of your own causing. If I ever envied you, then today I have been cured. You know where to seek if you come to your senses and desire not to see your heartlands burn beneath the wrath of your son. He has given me his fealty and I am honour bound to help him."

Henry flung from the meeting in a blind rage, taking the opposite direction to Richard and Philip. When the Archbishop tried to remonstrate with him, he snatched the crozier out of the old man's hand and hurled it like a spear. "By Christ I wish that my seed was barren when I see what it has brought forth!" he choked as William retrieved the crozier and pressed it back into the Archbishop's hand. "They want war, I will give them war! I...Jesu!" Henry doubled over with a choking cry, his hands folded against his midriff.

The Earl of Chester hastened to support him, as did the Archbishop of Rouen. William sent an attendant running to fetch Henry's physician. Filled with anxiety, his retainers bore him back to his chamber and laid him on the bed. Henry's brow was beaded with droplets of pain. His body shook with rigors and he groaned through his clenched teeth.

"You see what Richard has done to him?" John said with a curl of his lip. "You see what his betrayal has wrought?"

"Come now," said Ranulf of Chester, "the King has suffered these bouts before. You cannot lay all the blame at the lord Richard's feet."

"I can and I do," John said icily.

William quietly absented himself from the group and went in search of Richard. He found him drinking wine in his chamber with his knights and in savage mood. William noted with alarm that his attendants were packing the baggage chests.

"If you have come to plead my father's case, Marshal, you can save your breath," Richard growled. "If my father wishes to speak to me, let him come himself, and with different words on his lips."

"My lord, you should know that he is ailing," William said.

Richard snorted down his nose. "He always ails when he cannot get his own way. You know as well as I do the spell that John works on him and that he has always loved me the least of his sons."

William looked at the choler flushing Richard's pale complexion. Men who had known his grandsire, Geoffrey le Bel of Anjou, said there was a strong resemblance. The latter had been goldenly handsome, volatile, and possessed of an acerbic intelligence. William could often see Eleanor in Richard too. There was the same determination to be the centre of attention. "I do not believe that he will deny you your rightful inheritance, my lord," he said diplomatically.

"Has he told you outright that he will not?"

"No, my lord. Nor will he do so to any man, yourself included, while he is backed into a corner."

Richard tightened his lips. "In what way is he ailing?" he asked suspiciously.

"A gripe of the belly. His physician is with him now."

"Hah! I warrant it's a surfeit of his own bile." Richard pierced William with a bright grey stare. "Why do you stay with him, Marshal?"

"Because I gave him my oath when I returned from pilgrimage, and once given, only death can revoke it."

"Yours or his?"

William said nothing and Richard's expression became pitying. "I commend your loyalty," he said, "but you were a fool to give it to him when you could have given it elsewhere—and for more than empty promises."

William bit the inside of his lip, determined not to respond to Richard's words. If you could avoid it, you never showed your opponent that he had hit home. "I owe him my fealty. I am a simple man, and I live by simple tenets."

"You're not simple, Marshal. You've more layers than a blade of pattern-hammered steel."

"No, lord Richard. I am plain, unadorned iron, and true."

"Sharp too…" With a smile and a shake of his head, Richard poured the lees of his cup into the floor rushes. "Tell my father that I am leaving, and that unless he agrees to my terms—which are not unreasonable—we will be at war, and he will not win."

"My lord, please, will you not wait and reconsider?"

Richard looked hard at William. "No," he said. "Let my father do the reconsidering."

Rain slammed against the shutters as a full-blown autumn storm hurled the last of the leaves from the trees. Outside the sky was a scudding mass of ash-grey and charcoal clouds. Inside Henry's chamber the beeswax candles fluttered in the draughts from ill-fitting shutters and braziers had been kindled to heat the room. Bundled up in a fur-lined cloak, Henry sat on his bed, a cup of hot wine between his hands. His stomach gripes had abated somewhat, but one of his attendants had told William that there had been blood in the King's motions. "So, Richard has gone with the King of France," Henry said to the men gathered in his chamber. "My sons destroy me and they destroy themselves. What am I to do?"

Aware that there were men of higher rank in the room, William hesitated, but when no one spoke, he stepped into the silence. "Sire, you should send after him and ask him to return. There is much that still needs to be said, and better in words than on the edge of a sword."

Henry raised yellowed eyes and William saw in them both hope and despair. "And if he doesn't turn back?"

"Then at least you will have tried."

Henry flicked a weary hand at William. "Then go; see what you can do. Take Bertrand de Verdun and bid my son return to me."

"Sire." William bowed from the room.

He had his fastest courser saddled up and he and de Verdun rode hard in Richard's wake. But Richard had been riding hard too. William and de Verdun arrived in Amboise at midday only to find that Richard had spent the previous night there and ridden out at first light.

"You'll not catch him," Richard's steward said. "My lord is long gone and deliberately so. There is no point in you riding on."

"I'll be the judge of that," William said, but he was dismayed. Their horses were spent and with Richard and his mesnie having passed through Amboise so recently, fresh mounts were unlikely to be found.

The steward folded his arms and shrugged. "The lord Richard spent the night with his clerics and scribes. Over two hundred letters have been sent out to his supporters bidding them come to his aid. Soon there will be war in earnest. You are too late…" He gave them a pitying look. "Lord Richard was eager to dictate the letters and there was no hesitation in him. I am sorry."

William smoothed his hand over his mount's sweat-caked neck. "So am I," he said grimly.

Twenty-nine

THE WAR BEGAN AND LASTED THROUGHOUT THE WINTER and early spring, with skirmishes up and down the border. Several of King Henry's castles fell into the hands of Richard and Philip. Negotiations came to nothing and the antagonism and bitterness increased on both sides. Henry's health continued to deteriorate until he could barely ride his horse. His stocky frame diminished and wrinkled until he resembled a half-empty sack, and all the former energy and vigour was concentrated into one small, sharp flame, fed only by a determination not to let Richard win. Like a wounded fox heading for a bolt hole, Henry turned for Le Mans, the place of his birth, and prepared to defend it against his son and the King of France.

It was late evening and much of the royal household had retired for the night, but not the King, who seldom slept more than a few hours at a time, even in sickness. Seated on his bed, robed only in his nightshirt and a light mantle, he ordered William to take out a reconnaissance party at dawn and see if he could find the French army and discover King Philip's intentions. "I need to know how far away he is," he said.

"Sire." William bowed. There were a few others in the room with him, including the marshal of Henry's household, Robert de Souville, and Hubert Walter, who was representing

England's justiciar, Ranulf de Glanville. There was also Henry's bastard son, Geoffrey, who had been at his side throughout. Like his father he was short and sandy-haired, belligerent too, and fiercely protective of his parent in a way totally lacking in the legitimate sons. The lord John was not present, having a prior engagement with his current mistress, who had been taking up a great deal of his time of late.

"Wait, Marshal," Henry said as William prepared to leave.

William turned. "Sire?"

The pouches beneath Henry's eyes could have held at least a dozen silver pennies each and the tremor in his hands sent ripples through the wine in his cup. "I want to talk to you about your wardship of Heloise of Kendal."

The words sent a jolt through William, but he managed to look no more than politely concerned. "Sire?"

"I take it you do not intend to marry the girl yourself, or you would have done so when first you became her warden."

"Sire, I…"

Henry waved him silent. "I may be ill, but I have been robbed of neither wits nor hearing. I promised that if you came to me I would consider you for the position of lord of Châteauroux, but from what I hear, you would rather wed a different heiress—Isabelle de Clare?"

William cleared his throat. "Yes, sire…that is so."

"Then take her and I will bestow the right to Denise de Berry on Baldwin of Béthune. Heloise of Kendal's wardship can go to Gilbert FitzReinfred. I've been looking for something likely to settle on him." He looked to Hubert Walter. "Make note of my promise and convey it to my lord Glanville. William Marshal is to have Isabelle of Striguil in marriage and governance of all the lands that come with the lady's hand."

Hubert Walter bowed and murmured that it would be done. His family might have been cherishing hopes of a match between

Isabelle de Clare and Hubert's brother Theobald but he was too consummate a politician to bat an eyelid in front of Henry.

Swallowing, William rallied the wits that Henry's offer had scattered to the four winds. He went to Henry, knelt at his feet and, with bowed head, proffered his sword. "You will always have my loyalty, sire."

Henry gave a bleak smile. "Then let us hope that my life is as enduring as your fidelity, for both our sakes."

William led a small scouting party out of Le Mans as the first cockerels crowed the dawn. A thick mist was rising from the River Huisne and visibility was so poor that William was reminded of a deep English autumn rather than spring in Anjou. He and his men were all lightly clad and the morning chill penetrated through their cloaks and tunics and seeped into their flesh. Their horses moved stiffly at first, but their pace gradually eased as they warmed up. Clopping through the suburbs and across the wooden bridge over the river, William tried to concentrate on the task in hand, but his mind kept returning to the promise Henry had made to him. Isabelle de Clare. At one fell swoop, her lands would make of him a magnate, a lord of the highest rank. The girl was lovely too. It would be no hardship to beget children on her to follow in his line. He had to remind himself sternly to keep a rein on his hopes. For him to claim his heiress, Henry had to live long enough to uphold his word, and retain his authority, both of which hung in the balance. It was glittering all, or ragged nothing...and probably what Henry was counting upon.

They rode through pasture and meadow. Willow branches dripped with moisture and the smell of new, green spring clung in sap-heavy tendrils amid banks and hedges. As they left the immediate vicinity of the river, the mist became patchy and started to clear. By William's order the knights rode in silence, their bit chains muffled with strips of cloth. Their brief was to locate the French army, assess its intentions and report to the King. Robert de Souville, marshal of the royal household, rode at the rear, looking nervously around as if he expected to be pounced upon at any moment. In contrast, Geoffrey de Brûlon, a young knight of Henry's mesnie, trotted confidently at the front and William could almost see him spoiling for a fight. One to egg on, one to hold back, he thought with a pained smile, remembering himself at Drincourt. And then there was Gilbert FitzReinfred, nephew to Walter de Coutances, Archbishop of Rouen. He was a likely enough young man, nothing distinguished about him, but as steady and true as a good hound.

"Heloise is a rare jewel," William commented with quiet emphasis to FitzReinfred as they rode. "Make sure you treat her as such, or you will be answering to me."

"Yes, sir," FitzReinfred replied, reddening. His light blue eyes were bright with intelligence. "I have every intention of being a good husband."

William nodded curtly, man to man. "Then there is nothing more to say, except to wish you joy of each other." He had been speaking in a low murmur, but now other sounds impinged on his awareness and, raising his hand, he drew rein. Through drifting grey swags, they saw a dozen knights dismounted by the edge of the trees on the other side of the hill. They were lightly armed and were eating hunks of bread and drinking from leather costrels. One of their number emerged from the wood further down, lacing his hose to his braies and jiggling his crotch. Adjustments completed, he took his horse from the man who had been holding it and swung into the saddle. Within moments his companions had followed suit. The spare bread was stowed in saddlebags, the costrels slung over the pommels, shields and lances were picked up, and the party turned away from the woods and trotted in a northerly direction. The last man in line paused and looked round before riding after his companions. The mist closed in again and when it cleared there was nothing but a few breadcrumbs scattered on the ground and crushed grass springing back from the imprint of the horses' hooves to show they had been there at all.

"Scouts from the French army," William murmured, skirting the tracks and drawing rein.

Robert de Souville licked his lips and tightened his grip on his spear haft. "We should tell the King." He started to turn his horse.

"No." William shook his head. "What is there to tell at the moment? We think we saw what might have been some scouts from Philip's army? Where are they bound now? How close are they to their master?"

De Souville reddened and mumbled something into his beard. "You remain here," William commanded. "Myself and Geoffrey will follow them at a distance and discover their purpose. On no account are you to return to the King until we know more."

Leaving de Souville with the other knights, William and de Brûlon followed the direction the French had taken. The hoofprints led them through fields grey with deep dew, the land rising in a gentle undulation. Soon the men heard more sounds: voices; the rattle of weapons; the thud of hooves on moist turf. William signalled to Geoffrey and they dismounted. Leaving their horses tethered to an elder tree, they crept stealthily to the top of the hill, the dew soaking icily through their boots and hose. On the summit, crouching low to avoid being seen by a stray glance, they peered down.

"Jesu," muttered Geoffrey, crossing himself. "There are thousands of them."

"The entire host," William agreed. Scouting parties flanked the French knights and footsoldiers and from where they hid, he and Geoffrey could have picked off the outriders if they had

had crossbows to hand. Swiftly William retreated from their position. It only needed one of the scouts to ride to the top of the slope and the game would be up. Mounting their horses, he and Geoffrey hastened back to their companions. Geoffrey was hot to attack the outriders and do some damage, but William swiftly disabused him of the notion.

"Yes," he said, "we could make a charge and take a few of them, but that would be like thrusting a stick into a nest of hornets and expecting not to be chased by the entire colony. Our horses would never stand the chase and they need their wind for speeding this news to King Henry in Le Mans. Don't worry. You are going to have time aplenty for valorous deeds very soon!"

Henry received the news of the approach of the French army with a tight mouth and no surprise. He was ailing again, with pains in his chest and shortness of breath, but he refused to rest and ordered that the fords across the river be staked and the bridge across the Huisne destroyed, emerging to view the work himself from the back of his favourite grey hack. Prince John came with him, and watched the men hammering the stakes into the sluggish flow of the river, his gaze intent.

Even as the work was being carried out, the outriders of the French army started arriving on the opposite bank and pitched their tents amongst the woods.

"Just out of bowshot range, sire," William murmured, measuring the distance with narrowed eyes. "They know what they're about."

Henry rotated his jaw as if chewing on gristle. "If the French try and march on the town, I'll fire it. Let them have a taste of hell on their way to it."

"Will the French come, my lord?" asked Jean D'Earley in a strained voice.

William looked at the youth. His two squires had stayed up late, polishing armour, checking buckles and straps, making sure that all the equipment was in order. Not that William expected any defects, but there had been no point in sending the youths to bed when it was obvious they wouldn't sleep. Indeed, William suspected that the only inhabitants of Le Mans to have slept at all last night were the babies and the senile, too young or too old to know that a French army was massing across the river.

"I would say so." William stretched, testing his muscles, knowing that today he would probably have to fight. Going to his scabbard, he drew his sword from its sheath and examined the edges. "Sharp as a harridan's tongue, Jean, good work," he said. "The time for negotiating is long past. Philip of France and Count Richard desire to see King Henry on his knees. It's our job to thwart that desire, hmmm?" He included both squires in his glance.

"Yes, my lord." Jean's throat worked up and down. Jack nodded stiffly. William had no intention of letting either of the youngsters join the fray. They would have to be blooded sometime, but preferably not in what was likely to be bitter, acrimonious fighting with the added complication of fire. "Help me arm up," he said and pointed towards his gambeson.

His nephew's eyes widened. "You are going to mass in your mail?"

"If the French are going to attack, then it will be soon and they won't wait while we dress to meet them," William answered. "Let others do as they will, but I would rather be ready." He thrust his arms into the gambeson sleeves and pushed his head through the neck opening. "Your great-uncle Patrick was ambushed and slain when riding escort without his armour. Had he been wearing it, the chances are that he would have lived."

King Henry eyed William in disapproval when he came to church in his hauberk. One or two others, including Prince John, had thought to do so, but had been shamed into removing their mail at the church door. If William harboured a fear of being unarmed in the face of threat because of his uncle's demise, then Henry was uneasy to see armed men in a church following the infamous murder of Thomas Becket. Invited to remove his mail, William declined. Scowling, Henry would not stand near him for the mass and was abrupt with him when it had finished, keeping his back turned as he waited for the groom to bring his palfrey round.

As Henry placed his foot in the stirrup, a panting serjeant ran up crying that the French were massing to attack. "They've found a fording place with their lances, sire!" the soldier gasped.

Henry cursed, swung into the saddle, and spurred his palfrey. William mounted up and hastened after him. Behind him there was a mad scramble as men sought to don their armour and collect their weapons. By the time they reached the Huisne, a handful of French knights had succeeded in crossing, more were splashing in their wake, and there had already been several clashes with King Henry's Angevin defenders. Henry regarded the French advance with dismay. "There shouldn't be a ford!" His chest rose and fell unevenly and his breath rattled in his throat. "There shouldn't be one!"

But there was and nothing to be done. William signalled for his helm and a wide-eyed Jean D'Earley helped him don it. Two Angevin knights galloped to meet the foremost Frenchmen at full tilt. One shattered his lance to the hilt on a French shield and brought both of them down. The second encounter left the knights still in the saddle and swords were drawn. "Go, sire!" William gestured vigorously to Henry. "You are unarmed and in no state to fight!"

Henry stared across the Huisne at the oncoming French troops. Sailing amid the banners of France were those belonging to his son and supposed heir, Richard, Count of Poitou, the silks brightening with the advent of sunrise. Henry bared his teeth. "He wants Le Mans?" he snarled. "I will give him Le Mans and let him see how he likes it!" Rounding his horse, he galloped back into the city with an escort of serjeants and knights, leaving William and a contingent of hastily assembled men to hold off the French for as long as they could.

Baldwin de Béthune joined William before the town gate and gave him a fierce grin before donning his helm. "I hope your sword's sharp," he said. "By the look of what's upon us, it's going to be blunt by the day's end."

Inside his helm, William returned the grin, which was really more a baring of teeth. There was no hope of holding the town against the French now they had found such an easy crossing point. The best they could do was keep them at bay long enough for Henry and his troops to make an orderly retreat.

The fight, like the fight for Drincourt when he was a young knight, was one of hard battle in cramped spaces, of sudden sallies that gained ground, followed by forced withdrawal. The churned turf was littered with broken shields and lances; with pieces of abandoned equipment and corpses of horses and men. As William pivoted to strike at an opponent, his stallion came down on the sharp edge of an iron point and jinked hard sideways, blood welling from the gash. Cursing, William managed to disarm his opponent, forced him from his sound destrier and mounting it himself sent his injured horse back through the lines. The new destrier, a dappled Spanish stallion, was fresh and headstrong, and for a while he had to fight it as well as the French. His sword arm was white hot with effort, his shield arm was numb, and his vision a blur. He and Baldwin were doing no more than holding the French and their own smaller contingent was rapidly tiring.

"Christ, he's fired the town!" Baldwin suddenly panted.

William lifted his head. He had been too preoccupied with gulping air to feed his starving lungs to notice the difference in quality, but now Baldwin had spoken, he became aware of the stench of burning that went way beyond the normal aroma of cooking fires.

"He said he would, rather than give it to the French…" He lashed out with his sword, buffeted someone with his shield, and plunged the destrier at a footsoldier. Baldwin struck several blows with his mace and bought them a few seconds of respite. There was a sudden flurry of reinforcement, but it was only a temporary relief caused by the King's bodyguard as Henry himself arrived at the embattled gate. His lips had a bluish tinge and his face wore such an expression of grief and rage that William had to look away. What met his smarting eyes through the slits in his helm was the sight of the French and Poitevan soldiers rallying for another charge, the footsoldiers massing to cross, and the gathering pall of smoke along the city walls.

"The defence of the other gates is too weak, they're going to fall," Henry said hoarsely. "We have to withdraw. I'll not let that hellspawn son of mine and his French catamite take me while there's a breath left in my body." He gave a jerky nod. "Pull the men back, Marshal. We'll regroup at Fresnay."

"Sire." William rallied the men from the gate and followed Henry through the burning city towards the Fresnay road. Fanned by a stiff breeze, the flames were spreading fast, consuming thatch and wooden roof shingles, eating through beams, licking through straw, and bedding in outhouses and stables, filling the air with a grey fog alive with red sparks that stung like hornets when they alighted on flesh.

They rode past a merchant's house, several-storeyed with

wooden shingles; it was burning fiercely, the fire having spread from the warehouse next door. A woman was striving to rescue her possessions from the flames. William stared at her and felt his heart kick in his chest. Her face and waistline were softer and plumper, but there was no mistaking the way she held herself. "Clara?" Gesturing peremptorily to his squires to help, William dismounted and hastened to her aid, snatching a quilt from her arms. The underside was on fire and as the smoke filtered through the slits in his helm he began to cough. Jean hastened to help him unlace the helm and William dragged it off, red in the face and choking. "Fetch me my pot helm," he gagged at the squire. "I can't wear this." He stamped on the quilt to put out the fire and felt dismay and shame as he gazed upon the singed embroidery beneath his boots. Somehow, the sight of the charred bedcover was more distressing than the sight of the house burning in its entirety.

Jean came running back from the packhorse with William's lighter helm which had an open face and a nasal guard. Clara had retreated to sit on a painted coffer in her garden and watch her home burn.

"You have to leave, the French are coming." William strode to her, grabbed her arm, and hauled her to her feet. "They'll be on us at any moment." He turned to cough into his sleeve.

She shook him off. "They can't be any worse than Henry of Anjou!" she spat and gestured towards the house. "It's not the French who have fired the town! Stephen said this would happen."

"And where's Stephen now?" William snarled. "You must get out!"

"Don't worry." She gave him a look from the old days, gleaming with mockery and challenge. "I've always chosen men who can take care of me. We took the wine out of the city two days ago, and put our money in a safe place. He's gone to fetch the horses from the stables. I…" Her face lit up and, gathering her skirts, she pushed William aside and ran towards a barrel-bodied merchant and a servant who were hastening towards them on horseback, with a palfrey and two packhorses following on lead reins. William watched the man dismount and kiss Clara before boosting her into the palfrey's saddle. With the servant he set about securing the painted chest and the more portable belongings to the packhorses, his actions rapid and efficient. Clara nudged her mount over to William and looked down at him. Numerous fine lines webbed her eye corners, she had a double chin, but her gaze was still as dark and bright as his memory of her. "I know you would have saved me," she said in a gentler tone, "and I thank you, but as you can see, I did not need it."

"No." He glanced towards the man to whom he had lost her—a nondescript, broad town burgher with a paunch at his belt and unprepossessing features. William was both reassured and unnerved. "Godspeed you," he said. "Make haste."

"And you," she said with a half-smile that held remembrance and farewell. For a moment their eyes locked, and then she was reining away and her man was fastening the last strap on the packhorse and leaping to his saddle, nimble despite his bulk. He nodded stiffly to William and without further ado clapped spurs to his mount's flanks. He, Clara, and the servant faded rapidly into the smoke like a dream and William turned back to his horse, feeling saddened, yet perversely lighter of spirit.

William de Mandeville, Earl of Essex, rode up with his troops and confirmed to Henry that Le Mans was lost. "The French are pouring into the town through the gates, with the Count of Poitou at their head." His breath tore in his throat. "Sire, you have to leave…"

Henry jerked as if struck at the mention of his eldest son and William flinched with him. He knew that, of all things, Henry

dreaded being brought face to face with Richard and humiliated. What pride he had was bleeding, battered, and dying, but
to have the final blows delivered by one's own son, in malice,
was not a coup de grace but ignominious murder. "Go, sire,"
William said. "I will hold them off."

Henry looked at him, nodded once, and, without speaking,
spurred away. William leaped to horse, ordered his squires
to ride hard with Essex's troops, and with a handful of other
knights, took up his position as the King's rearguard.

At first their way was clogged by people fleeing the town,
their possessions in sacks and hand carts, across the backs of pack
ponies or piled in ox wains, women weeping, children screaming.
William had curses heaped on him by wailing refugees as he
pushed his way through. He ignored them. Nothing mattered
but seeing Henry to safety. He saw no sign of Clara and assumed
that she and her merchant had taken another road, for which he
was glad. He would not have wanted to pass her.

Once clear of the suburbs and the fleeing people, they set
their horses to a canter. The King clung grimly to his saddle, his
face ashen-yellow, but when Baldwin of Béthune enquired if
they should slow the pace, he shook his head and insisted instead
that they should increase it. De Souville's horse was lame and
the knight was struggling to keep up. Turning in the saddle to
look over his shoulder and check de Souville's progress, William
saw a Poitevan knight hurtling towards the fleeing party, lance
couched. De Souville raised his shield and tried to rein his horse
out of the way, but the knight turned with him and rammed him
from the saddle. As de Souville struck the ground, more Poitevans
galloped up, dust flurrying from beneath their horses' hooves. The
foremost was riding a powerful dun destrier with flaxen mane
and tail. Although the rider carried no shield, William recognised
Richard immediately and his blood ran cold. Levelling his lance,
he pricked his stallion forward to bar the road.

Richard reined back so hard that his horse reared. "Don't be a fool!" he roared across the ground between himself and William. "Stand aside!"

William fretted his destrier and prepared to charge. "My lord, you will turn back if you value your life!"

Richard laughed with contemptuous rage. "You would not dare," he sneered and slapped the reins down on his stallion's neck. Without hesitation, William spurred his mount. Richard's eyes widened; he tried to draw aside, but William changed the angle of his lance and thrust with his full might. It was a clean blow and it killed on the instant. Abandoning his lance in situ, William snarled, "Let the devil take you, my lord," and, wheeling about, galloped off up the road.

A shaken Richard extricated himself from the saddle of his dead horse and pulled back the knights who would have continued the chase. "No," he said brusquely, "let them go. They're on the run and we'll catch them soon enough…and then we'll have a reckoning."

Thirty

$\mathscr{I}$T WAS QUIET IN THE VILLAGE OF COULAINE OUTSIDE
Chinon. William squinted into the sky, seeking the sky-
lark that was flinging its song to heaven and finally located the
dark pinpoint of sound high in the blue. The throaty warble
continued for a moment then ceased as the bird plummeted
to earth and was lost to sight amid the grasses of the spring
meadow where several mares and colts were grazing.

William had brought his troop out this way with the excuse
of inspecting the stock of a local lord who bred destriers, but
the truth of the matter was that he needed a respite from
watching King Henry deteriorate, his pain so acute that even
the strongest potions and soporifics afforded him no ease.
And with his deterioration, came the failure of William's
hopes of advancement. William knew he had probably ruined
his own future by killing Richard's stallion under him, but
since the alternatives had been either to kill Richard himself
or court dishonour and let him past, William's choice had
been simple.

The horse-breeder reclaimed William's attention by
enquiring after the King and expressing his concern that the
French would overrun Chinon. "I have spent a lifetime on
these animals," he said, gesturing to the grazing mares and

foals. "I would rather die than see them thieved by Poitevan and French gutter sweepings."

"A truce has been agreed; they will not come to Chinon," William replied more confidently than he felt. The way that Richard had been hounding his father, he would not put anything past him. A week ago, King Henry had met with Richard and Philip outside Fresnay. Watching Henry's distressing struggle to face his enemies with dignity, William had felt sick with pity and rage. Before the meeting, Henry had taken refuge in a Templar church and so great had been his pain that he had had to hold on to the wall to stay upright. William had sent a message to Philip and Richard that Henry was indisposed and unable to attend the counsel. Richard had refused to accept the reply and loudly proclaimed that his father was feigning illness in order to wriggle out of the talks and that if he did not come, then more fire and sword would follow. Henry had dragged himself from the church and forced himself across a horse. Teeth clenched in agony, he had ridden to the meeting place, gasping to William that if God granted him time enough, he would have Philip and Richard pay for what they were doing to him. On seeing Henry's condition, Philip had realised how ill he truly was and had offered him a cloak to sit upon whilst negotiations were conducted, but Henry had refused, preferring to remain on his horse, which at least gave him some small touch of dignity as the humiliating terms for peace were dictated to him. Richard had shown no pity for his father, neither by look nor by gesture. William could not decide if it was a deliberate ploy by Richard to further hurt his father, a defence against being hurt himself, or just blank indifference. Whatever it was, the mask had not cracked throughout the negotiations.

Henry had returned to Chinon and taken to his bed. Abhorring the stenches of the sick room, Prince John had been conspicuous by his absence; but Henry's bastard son Geoffrey had spent much time at his father's side, wiping his brow and comforting his rages.

"I have heard rumours that the King is sick unto death." The trader looked intently at William. "You are close to him, so men say. Is it true?"

"It is true that he is heartsick over the behaviour of his eldest son," William replied, skirting the issue, "and his health is not robust, but he has a will that is as strong as sword steel and it is far from broken." His tone did not encourage more questions and he addressed himself to the purchase of a mare and foal and a promising two-year-old colt. He would not think about where he was going to settle the horses in the months to come. For now, he arranged to keep them with the breeder, saying with a wry smile that his decision to do so was a sign of his confidence that the French and Poitevans would not pillage the region. In truth, William did not know what was going to happen and was as much a straw in the wind as any member of the King's entourage.

As he rode slowly back towards Chinon, he was joined by another company riding in that direction and headed by Roger Malacheal, keeper of the King's seal. Malacheal was returning from Tours where he had been on business for Henry. King Philip had undertaken to give Henry the names of the men who had turned against him and Malacheal had been to collect that list. He greeted William sombrely, his expression one of utter weariness. William knew better than to enquire directly of his business, but a general question brought a shake of Malacheal's head and a further downturn of the mouth. "Worse than you know," was all he would say.

When they arrived in Chinon, Malacheal went directly to Henry's chamber, and William accompanied him. The King had not risen from his bed, although he was dressed and sitting upon it, attended by physicians and clerks to whom, even in his weakened state, he had been dictating letters. His bastard son

Geoffrey clung jealously to his side and watched everyone like a suspicious guard dog.

Malacheal approached the bed, bent his knee, and bowed his head. Henry gestured him to his feet and held out a quivering right hand. "You have the list of traitors?"

"Sire…" Malacheal hesitated.

"Let me see," Henry said hoarsely.

Giving in to the inevitable, Malacheal handed over the scroll. Henry broke the seal and unrolled the parchment. His eyesight was failing and he had to hold the document at arm's length to read it. Even then he could not see the names and returned the document to Malacheal with a frustrated shake of his head. "You read it," he said.

Malacheal took it as if it had been painted with poison. Moistening his lips, he scanned the list. "My lord, so Jesus Christ help me, the first name on the list is that of your son, Lord John."

Henry whispered the name. He repeated it several times, becoming louder on each occasion, and the shake of his head increased in vigour. "I will not believe this," he rasped. "John would not do that to me. Bring him to me now."

Men exchanged glances. "I will go and find him, sire," William said.

He met Geoffrey's gaze where the young man stood behind his father and saw the negation in it.

William strode from the room and through the palace to the stables where the grooms informed him that John had left that morning, soon after his own departure to visit the horse-breeder. The prince had taken his bodyguard, his servants, and two laden packhorses and as yet he had not returned. Tight-lipped, William combed the town. The brothels and drinking houses had no word of him, nor the cloth merchant, goldsmith, or the man who dealt in rare gemstones, of which John was fond, and William returned to the palace empty-handed. The King was awaiting the news like a prisoner on the morning of execution, looking for a reprieve but knowing in his heart that none would come.

William stood straight and tall to deliver the blow and no matter what he felt inside, did not let the pity show on his face. "Sire, your son left at dawn this morning. He is no longer in the city."

Henry looked at William, then at the knights and officials surrounding his bed. His focus slipped and turned inwards as if he had closed a door on the world. "You have said enough," he muttered. "Draw the curtains and leave me, all of you." He gestured weakly towards the hangings surrounding his bed.

It became clear that King Henry was not going to recover from his illness. The news of John's desertion had destroyed his will to fight death. He refused all sustenance. The low fever that had been plaguing him for several weeks worsened and soared beyond anything the physicians could do to help him. Henry lost his wits and even when his eyes were open, he did not see the people surrounding him; nor could he respond to what they said.

On the third evening of Henry's deteriorating condition, Baldwin and William were taking a brief respite in a wine shop not far from the palace. Wigain had accompanied them, and Walter Map, and many of the knights of the chamber were sequestered around the scrubbed benches and trestles. Geoffrey, Henry's bastard son, was among their company and more drunk than William had ever seen him.

"I saw more men leaving today," Baldwin announced, hunching over his cup. "The hired soldiers know that there is nothing left for them here. Either they're going home to their farms or riding to join the unholy trinity of Richard, Philip, and John."

A girl came to refill their wine pitcher. Wigain's pinch of her bottom was half-hearted. "You should ride for England and claim your bride while you still can," he told William morosely.

William shook his head. "How long do you think I would keep her if I did? The lord Richard is not well disposed in my direction, is he?" He tipped wine into his cup. "At least I have some rents in Saint-Omer and a standing offer from Philip of Flanders."

"Not the same as an earldom though, is it?"

William smiled without humour. "Beggars can't be choosers."

At the other table Geoffrey FitzRoy raised his voice in angry protest. "I may have been trained in Holy Orders, but I'm not taking vows. Even if Richard does become King, he'll not make me."

Walter Map tilted his head in Geoffrey's direction. "He wants to be a prince," he remarked. "He was hoping his father would give him lands and titles and set him up in his own little kingdom, but when Henry dies, Richard and John won't wear it. Whether he likes it or not, 'brother Geoffrey' is going to become 'Brother Geoffrey.'" He smirked at his own pun. No one else did.

"And what of 'brother John?'" Wigain asked. "What's to stop him from testing his backside on the throne?"

"If John had wanted the crown, he'd have stayed with his father," William said, "not gone running to Richard. I am not saying that he does not desire the crown, but since he is Richard's heir and Richard has sworn to go on crusade, he has time to bide while he chooses his path."

"The slippery one to hell," Wigain muttered.

"Very likely," William answered, emptying more wine into his cup. He wasn't so much drowning his sorrows as toasting farewell to an almost glittering future. As he started to drink, Jean D'Earley shouldered his way through the press of soldiers and courtiers. William immediately set the cup back on the trestle, for the squire's features were grim.

"You need to come quickly, sir," he said.

William climbed the stairs to King Henry's chamber, the wine roiling in his gut and filling the back of his throat with a sour taste. There were no guards on the door, save for his nephew and another white-faced squire who was swallowing convulsively. William strode through the door, noting immediately that the walls to either side of the entrance had been denuded of their hangings and the pole above the doorway was bereft of its embroidered curtain. The chamber was bare, as if it had been stripped ready for a move. The King's clothing and storage coffers were still in place and a fire was charring to ash in the grate, but all the smaller boxes and chests were gone, including the fine enamelled ones that contained the royal jewels. The sideboard was bare of the cups, plates, and flagons that should have adorned it and the bedcovers and hangings had gone, leaving the bare wood and the curtain poles. On the bed itself the king lay naked with not so much as a sheet to shroud him.

William went swiftly to him and stopped as if he had been struck. "Christ Jesu have mercy on his soul," he muttered before his throat closed with pity and horror.

The body was sprawled like a child's doll abandoned in mid-play and the King's pallid flesh was stained with the blood that had gushed from his nose and mouth in his final paroxysm. The grey eyes stared, dull as dry stones. Behind him, William heard someone retching into the floor rushes.

Gilbert FitzReinfred silently handed William his cloak and William spread the garment over Henry's body and gently closed the staring eyes. Geoffrey came to the bedside, wiping his mouth. "I should have stayed with him." Tears streamed down his face. "God forgive me, I should have stayed." White and shaking, he knelt by the corpse.

"We all should," William said grimly. He laid his hand to

the young man's shoulder and gave it a brief squeeze. Anger simmered within him. Turning, he barked swift commands to several of the knights and with hands on swords they strode from the stripped and desecrated room. He had no doubt that the thieves were long gone, but if they could be caught, he'd see them strung up higher than the man in the moon.

The King's body was carefully washed and tended. His coffers had all been robbed and there was no robe in which to fittingly clad the corpse. Geoffrey, who was the same size as his father, donated his best one—of costly dark red wool.

Henry was borne to the chapel and following high mass William and the knights of the household kept guard around the body in full mail, their swords drawn. All of them were suffering pangs of guilt brought on by the knowledge that while they had been drinking in a hostel, the King had been enduring his death throes as his chamber and body were robbed of possessions and dignity. It was the latter that most affected William. No one should die like that and it froze his marrow to think on it.

In the morning the body was placed on a bier and the knights took it in turns to carry it on their shoulders as they set out from Chinon to Henry's designated resting place at the Abbey of Fontevrault. There were no alms to distribute to the poor, for Henry's strongboxes were all empty and his seneschal denied all knowledge of the money. The crowd that had gathered in the hope of receiving silver as the funeral cortège made its journey were disappointed and had to be dispersed with a niggardly handful of coin distributed from the pouches of the knights who had remained to see the King to his grave.

At Fontevrault the Abbess and the nuns emerged in procession to lead Henry's bier into the church, their voices raised in sweet plainchant. William measured his steps to the altar and to the trestle that waited before it to receive the bier. His shoulders were burning with the weight of bearing the King's body, but his heart felt as if it were carrying the greatest burden of all. He had borne the Young King to his tomb; now he was doing the same for the father, and once again his own future was in turmoil. Dry-eyed, numb, William helped the other knights to ease the bier down on to the trestle. Resisting the urge to rub his shoulder, he bowed to the Abbess and left the body in her care. His eyes were gritty with fatigue as he returned to the open air, cooling now as afternoon shadows crossed the grass and mellowed the stone—a sight that Henry would never feel and see again.

"Sir?"

He turned to face his squire, Jean, who was standing quietly in the background. He hoped the lad wasn't going to bedevil him with questions that he was in no case to answer.

"Jack's arranged stabling for the horses and we've stowed your baggage in the guest house."

William nodded absently for he would have expected the squires to have done so as a matter of course. "And?" he said a trifle irritably.

Jean flushed. "I thought you might want to bathe and eat. I persuaded one of the lay sisters to fill a tub and I begged some food from the kitchens."

William was immediately contrite. From somewhere he found the semblance of a smile. "You're both fine squires," he said and clapped Jean on the shoulder by way of apology.

The tub was a large oval affair, used for the scrubbing of laundry as well as the occasional bathing of guests. William would have liked nothing more than to wallow in the steaming water until it grew cold, but that would have been selfish, and his squires deserved a reward for their labours, so he gave them the use of the water once he had finished and indicated that he would dry and dress himself. There was some jesting in the guest house about William's fastidiousness and more than one knight declared that washing the goodness out of one's body wasn't wise. There was nothing wrong with the smell of good, honest sweat.

"I know some ladies who would dispute that with you," William retorted as he pushed a comb through his damp hair.

"Not nuns though," grinned Maurice de Craon, a florid knight with a full black beard. "Who else are you likely to meet here? The Count of Poitou, when he arrives, won't care what you smell like."

"Hah, don't be too sure of that!" someone else shouted.

DeCraon waved the declaration aside with a swipe of his ham-sized fist. "Rumours and gossip!" he growled. "Richard's no sodomite."

The word hung in an uncomfortable silence. Men busied themselves with other tasks amidst a lot of throat-clearing and harrumphing.

"You shouldn't have said that," William murmured to de Craon.

The knight spread his hands in bewilderment. "Why in God's name not? I was defending the Count of Poitou's reputation!"

William set the comb aside. "But also calling attention to the whispers. True or not, the tales will grow with each telling. What began as a grain of sand will eventually become a mountain…as I know from experience."

De Craon snorted and blustered, but soon grew quiet and wandered off, a thoughtful look on his face like an ox with cud to chew.

With a pensive sigh, William straightened the creased folds of his plum-coloured tunic and sat down to the food his squires had brought. The other knights came and joined him to discuss their predicament. As supporters of the old King were they going to be disgraced and exiled? What price were they going to have to pay to keep their lands? Most expected that they could buy Richard's favour for a fee, especially as he needed the money for his imminent crusade. Their assessment of William's situation was less optimistic, but William shrugged it off with the comment that what would be would be. "I haven't starved yet," he said, thinking that there was always a first time.

Richard arrived early the next morning. Unlike his sick, exhausted father who had jounced along like a half-empty sack of cabbages as he fled from his eldest son's harassment towards his deathbed, Richard looked every inch the warrior king. He rode a Spanish grey and his tunic was of crimson silk, thickly embroidered with snarling lions in thread of gold. His swordbelt was gilded, so were his shoes, and his cloak was edged with braid that shone with gold filaments. A little to one side and behind rode his brother John, his colour high and his expression defensive, and with him, Richard's chaplain and chancellor, William Longchamp. The look the latter cast towards William seethed with malice and disdain. William returned the stare with antipathy for there was no love lost between himself and Longchamp.

A hollow feeling in the pit of his stomach, William bowed head and knee in submission to England's new King. The remaining knights of Henry's mesnie did the same, sending each other sidelong glances. Staring at the ground, William waited. He knew it was foolish, but he half expected to feel the bite of a sword across the back of his neck. However, the touch when it came was to his shoulder, and of a hard, firm hand. William could remember the days when that hand had not been big enough to fold around the grip of an adult sword; he could remember parrying the attacks of the juvenile blade.

It had been easy then, but he suspected that nothing was ever going to be easy again.

Richard commanded the men to rise, his voice strong but neutral. "Some grudges I harbour," he said, "but not against men who are loyal." He squeezed William's shoulder before he stepped back and moved on. Exhaling a shaky breath, William rose to his feet and straightened his tunic. Prince John was looking at him, his pale tawny gaze a replica of his mother's. He raised a sardonic eyebrow and corresponding mouth corner and followed his brother towards the church where their father lay in state. William lowered his gaze for he could not be certain of concealing his anger. If Richard had hounded his father during the failing King's last days, then John's desertion had hastened the death and made it into one of despair, lacking all comfort and peace.

The lords and knights followed the royal brothers into the church. John side-stepped softly in the shadows like a cat, but Richard strode forward to the bier; the only sign of his disquiet was the way in which his left hand clutched the grip of his sword.

He stood a long time looking down at his father's body, his expression contained and devoid of emotion. After a while he moved up to Henry's uncovered face and gazed upon it, saying not a word to the gathered knights and retainers. John emerged from the shadows, but would not approach the bier. It was said that a corpse would bleed when in the presence of its murderer and William wondered if either brother feared a sudden gush from their father's body. He wished that they could have seen Henry in his death chamber at Chinon. They deserved to do so, but whether it would have provoked any feelings of pity or remorse was another matter. William suspected that Richard, at least, had no notion of the meaning of the word where his father was concerned. John might have, but although the latter sometimes showed his thoughts on his face, the inner workings of his mind were a mystery. Nor did William want to delve into them, because he suspected that he would find things lurking in their darkness that had grown beyond redemption.

Finally Richard turned from his scrutiny of Henry's face and between the dead father and the living son there was not an iota of difference in the rigidity of the expression. Richard's gaze fell upon William. "Marshal, a word." Gesturing everyone else to remain where they were, he drew William outside. "Ride with me," he commanded. Rather than wait whilst William had his palfrey saddled, he gave him Longchamp's chestnut—a move which caused the latter to glare daggers at William. Longchamp harboured jealous suspicion of anyone who he thought might challenge his own influence with Richard and he considered William not only a rival but an enemy. William returned Longchamp's glower with the indifference that he knew would gall Richard's chancellor to the bone.

Richard rode straight-backed and with a natural, supple grace, one hand at the reins, the other down by his side. William adjusted the stirrup leathers, which had been strapped to suit Longchamp's much shorter legs, and brought the chestnut alongside Richard's stallion. They rode away from the abbey in silence, the hooves making a hollow thud on the dry ground and raising a powder of pale dust. Over Chinon the sky was hazy and suggestive of thunder. William could feel the first hint of pressure building within his skull. He pondered breaking the silence between him and Richard and decided against it. Let the new King set the tone, and if Richard was waiting for contrition or apology, he would wait for ever.

Finally, Richard looked across at William. "You tried to kill me," he said. His voice had a hoarse catch, but William thought it more a matter of being rusty from too much bellowing on the battlefield than because of strong emotion.

William drew himself up. "No, my lord, I did not. I am still strong enough to direct a lance at a target and be certain of hitting it. If I had wanted to kill you, I would have driven my point through your body with ease, as I did to your horse. I will not apologise for the act. I was defending your father and given the choice again, I would do the same."

"I thought that you were going to spit me on your lance." Richard gave William a look that in itself was as piercing as a steel point.

"I almost did, sire, but I decided that skewering your horse would be just as effective as skewering you."

Richard gave a reluctant laugh. "And it was." He glanced sidelong at William. "It took great courage and a steady hand."

William shrugged. "I've served a long apprenticeship," he said.

"And if I said that I had work for you and that I wanted your oath of loyalty now that my father is dead, would you give it?"

William studied the brooding sky and took his time to reply. There might only be one answer but let Richard wait to hear it. Besides, he had to summon his courage for what came next. "Before he died, your father gave Isabelle of Striguil to me in marriage."

Richard drew hard on the reins, causing his mount to start and sidle. "He didn't give you anything," he snapped. "I have my spies; I know what he said. He only promised you, and a promise is so much dross until it is fulfilled. You know that."

William struggled to read Richard's expression, but the new King was adept at hiding what he chose not to show.

"I will do more than promise," Richard said in a grating voice. "This very day you will set out for England bearing messages. You can marry the girl at the same time. Take Isabelle de Clare, take her lands and plough them both with my blessing."

It was hard for William to draw breath. "Thank you, my lord," he managed, the words heartfelt and unembellished.

Richard waited, as if expecting more, but when none came,

he nodded curtly. "You stood by my father when lesser men deserted. You risked your life for his and jeopardised your own future security. I desire to harness that steadfastness for myself. As you say, you have served your apprenticeship. I have just given you your share of reward and punishment. *Given*," he emphasised, his voice hardening. "I have done more than promise. You received nothing but empty words from my father and my brother."

"I started with nothing, my lord, not even a promise. I—"

"But high expectations," Richard interrupted sharply. "If not, you'd be stuck in England at your brother's hearth, with a fat-arsed slattern in your lap, instead of riding at my side with a rich heiress within your grasp. You have always made the best of what's been offered and you cannot deny that I have offered you the most."

"I do not, my lord, but it will not make me any more loyal."

Richard gave a brusque laugh. "You're a good sparring partner, Marshal. I dare say I could best you now, but I'm not willing to take the risk." He reined his horse about and turned back towards the abbey. "Mark me: I'm going to make you work harder than you have ever done in your life."

"Thank you, my lord," William said again, a slow smile breaking across his face.

Thirty-one

"MADAM, FORGIVE ME IF I DO NOT KNEEL," WILLIAM SAID to the Queen. "It is not through lack of respect, but because I am incapable of doing so."

"What have you done?" A snap of Eleanor's fingers brought an attendant hastening forward with a chair. Her tawny eyes, which had been aglow with welcome a moment since, were filled with concern.

He made a face. "The ship's deck collapsed when we were boarding at Dieppe. I'm one of the fortunate ones; there were shattered limbs aplenty and one poor soul impaled through the ribs on a stake." Grimacing with pain, William eased himself down in the chair. "I managed to grab a strut and save myself, but my left leg is almost beyond bearing weight."

"Have you had a physician look at it?"

William's smile was wry. "He said I should rest it." He presented her with the letters that Richard had given him.

Eleanor signalled the same attendant to bring wine. "Well, you can do that while you give me your news, can you not? Gersendis, a cushion for Messire Marshal's back."

William looked chagrined. "I am about to go and claim a young bride and yet here I am easing myself into a chair like an old man," he groaned.

Her lips twitched. "I doubt the parts that matter have lost their sap, William," she remarked. When he looked at her askance, she gave a mischievous laugh. "Your spirit, William, the strength of your will." She sat down opposite him in a swirl of silk skirts and rested the letters in her lap. "A young bride." She nodded sagely. "Not Heloise of Kendal, I suspect?"

Eleanor more than suspected, William thought. Even though Henry had kept her under house arrest, she had her spies and her ways and means of getting to know everything that she wanted. He had no doubt that part of Richard's willingness to give him Isabelle de Clare was down to the Queen's interces-sion on his behalf. "No, madam, not Heloise of Kendal. She is to be wed to Gilbert FitzReinfred." He grinned. "She will lead him over the hills and back again, but I do not think they will be displeased with each other. He is kindly disposed towards women and knows that I will still be watching out for her from a distance. I am fond of her…" he admitted.

"But with the prestige she brings you, you will be fonder of Isabelle de Clare," Eleanor said shrewdly.

"I hope to make a good match, madam." He gave a pensive shrug. "I may not look a bargain at the moment, but rest and polish will rectify some of the damage. I met her at the Tower of London last time I was in England. My lord Glanville was not best pleased."

Eleanor frowned. "My lord Glanville is sworn to go on crusade with Richard," she said. "He will not have custody of the heiresses in the Tower for much longer."

William noted that the new rule was beginning to flex its muscles and he could see that some personal circumstances were not going to change for the better. He found it hard to imagine the dignified, urban Ranulf Glanville taking the road to Jerusalem via what was likely to be some hard and bloody fighting. "I have to thank you for my good fortune, madam," he said, his words partly born of his thoughts. "I could also see why the justiciar might want to hide the lady Isabelle from prying eyes."

Eleanor's expression softened. "I do believe that you are smitten," she teased.

William chuckled. "That would not be difficult, madam. The girl is eighteen years old and beautiful. What she will think of a grizzled old warhorse like me is another matter."

Eleanor laughed. "Either you are shamelessly angling for praise or you do not see yourself as women do." She reached a beringed hand to touch the side of his face. "You wear more years than when I first took you into my service, but you were still a boy then, and time has wrought experience, not lines. Isabelle de Clare will have no cause to complain of this match."

"I pray not." He had his doubts and dreaded the thought that Isabelle might look upon him as a surrogate father, or that despite her lands and her beauty she might prove to be feather-brained and giggly. If he were to rule the vast estates of Striguil, he needed a solid bedrock of domestic and marital harmony. Knowing that he was striving after the rarely attainable made him feel determined and on edge.

"I trust you still have your singing voice?" Eleanor enquired.

He gave her a puzzled look. "I do not know, madam. It has been so long since there has been anything to sing about, and I have been too busy."

"If you are to take a bride, I suggest you find it again." Eleanor's smile wavered. "Neither of my husbands could sing. Who knows what might have been different if either of them had bothered to learn?" She let out a shaky breath and looked down at her hands. "You may think it strange," she said, "but even after what has happened, I mourn for Henry. There was a time when it was very sweet between us. Even all the bitterness that came afterwards cannot alter those memories. And he gave me children." Her lips curved with bleak humour. "He said that they were all mine except for John, but he was wrong. Even John belongs to me." Eleanor glanced around the chamber which was bright with hangings and banners and painted coffers. A pile of books stood on a chest, the top one open revealing an illumination of a man and woman playing chess in a garden. "When he took away my freedom I swore that I would outlive him. On my knees I prayed to God to give me the strength to live through each day that I was caged. He didn't trust me. Every minute of every day I was watched, if not by his guards then by his spies." She sighed and made a weary gesture. "God rest his soul and God rest mine. William, if you are going to love your wife, and have her love you, then take some advice from one who has lived with it and without it and knows its price and its value."

"Madam?"

"Isabelle de Clare is an heiress. Remember that the lands you rule are hers and that she might desire to have a say in what you do with them. Take her with you when you can. Use her as your captain and your deputy when you cannot, and never give her cause to resent you, because she will have the raising of your sons and daughters."

William's colour deepened at the mention of sons and daughters. "I will do my best," he said.

"You may think me an interfering old woman, but I have had your interests at heart ever since I took you into my service." She instructed a maid to bring over an enamelled jewel casket and, taking it from the girl, presented it to William. "This is my wedding gift to your bride."

William thanked her. It was weighty, but it seemed impolite to ask what it contained. Eleanor smiled at him. "Open it," she said. "It holds the gauds that women enjoy and men do not always think to give them."

William raised the latch and looked upon a magnificent cloak brooch fashioned of gold set at intervals with dark blue sapphires. There was a smaller one, suited to fastening the neck of a gown, and a wimple band of silk brocade stitched with peridots and pearls. "It is a queenly gift," he said with the spark of a smile.

Eleanor acknowledged his jest with a smile of her own. "Trust me, your bride will think it so, and if you can add to it, then so much the better. A little generosity will be more than repaid, providing you don't substitute gems for affection."

William strove not to grin. Most noble households possessed at least one elderly female relative who would spend her time gossiping by the fire, keeping an eye on the young women of the bower and meting out advice to all and sundry. Eleanor suddenly reminded him of such women, but he knew that it was more than his life was worth to say so. "I will make sure that my wife has plenty of both," he said blandly, receiving in consequence a sharp look from Eleanor.

"See that you do," she said in a peremptory tone. "You have already been given your wedding gift from me. You are an earl in all but name. All I ask in return is that you prove yourself worthy of my faith."

"I will not fail you, madam," he replied and would have risen to kneel, save that whilst he was sitting his leg had stiffened and bending it was nigh on impossible.

She arrested his struggle with a raised hand. "No," she said. "You will have plenty of opportunity in the days to come to kneel at the feet of women." Humour lit in her eyes. "Go to your bride and your lands," she said, "and remember my advice. And give this to her from me." Again she touched his face and her lips brushed the corner of his mouth in a tender salute compounded of mischief, affection, and abiding friendship. "I trust you to give it the correct interpretation," she said.

When William had gone, Eleanor sat down to open and read her letters, a smile curling her mouth corners. William had just bitten off a very large mouthful, but she did not believe that it was more than he could chew. Indeed, in the months to come she fully intended to heap his trestle with further courses and hope that he lived up to his squirehood title of "Gasteviande" or "Guzzleguts." But first let him have a moment's respite to enjoy his new status as lord of vast lands and husband to a young wife. "Let her lead him a merry dance," she said softly, and half wished that she could change places with Isabelle de Clare.

Thirty-two

THE NEWS OF OLD KING HENRY'S DEATH HAD THROWN everyone at the Tower of London into turmoil, even the keeper of the menagerie, who had been stamping about growling like one of his lions. On the few occasions that Isabelle had seen Ranulf Glanville, he had looked grey and preoccupied. She had attended several masses to honour the old King's soul and all the talk in the great hall was of what Richard would do when he arrived in England. Men feared for positions they had held for a lifetime. Glanville was particularly concerned, for he had little rapport with Queen Eleanor who was currently responsible for governing the country. Isabelle tried not to think of what was going to happen to herself. King Henry had been content to milk her lands and keep her walled up in the Tower. She knew that the Count of Poitou, now the King of England, had sworn to go on crusade and liberate Jerusalem from the infidel, and to do that he would need money—a lot of money, and that meant selling heiresses, shrievalties, positions, and titles to the highest bidder. He might decide to continue milking the lands of Striguil or he might sell that privilege elsewhere. He might even give her to his younger brother, John, although there was another heiress first in line for that honour. Havise of Gloucester didn't seem to know whether to preen or be terrified at the notion of wedding Richard's brother, currently the heir to the throne.

In the meantime, all of Isabelle's needs were met by the Crown, who paid for them out of the revenues that came from her lands. She never saw any of that revenue personally. She had almost forgotten what a silver penny and a tally stick looked like. Her mother had been at pains to have her educated to fit her position as a wealthy heiress and that meant more than smiling sweetly and sewing a fine seam. Being the daughter of a Norman warlord and granddaughter of Irish royalty, Isabelle knew her pedigree, knew what it was worth, and also knew that it wasn't worth a damn whilst her wings were clipped and there was no one to fight her cause.

Of late she had been kept under closer guard than usual. Her walks around the grounds of the Tower had been curtailed and she was confined to a small area of sward in front of her lodgings. She was watched at all times—even when she was sitting over the privy there was a maid within earshot. She would have laughed had the scrutiny not made her so irritated and anxious. What did they think an abductor was going to do? Clamber up the waste shaft and ravish her in the latrine?

Arms folded, Isabelle paced to the window of her chamber, but there was little to see but sky through the narrow slit cut into the stone. It was a fine summer's day; she could tell that by the expanse of pale woad-blue. A day to ride out and enjoy the surge of a sleek Spanish palfrey beneath her, to watch Damask nose hither and yon among the bracken for small game, and to feel hot life surging in her veins.

It surprised her that she could still recall the intensity of that kind of pang for it came from her life in Ireland. There the colours and the memories were dappled green and grey, mossy and soft as light summer rain: the smell of turf fires, the harps of the bards in the dark winter halls, and the long summer nights of May and June. She had a recollection of her father swinging her up in his arms and of his beard tickling against her neck while she squealed. His hair had been deep madder-red, and his voice husky with laughter.

Isabelle blinked to clear her eyes and turned from the window. It was in the past, long gone. Even if she returned it would never be the same, for then she had been a small child running in her smock, and now by her very status she was not allowed to run anywhere.

In her basket near the door, Damask whined and thumped her tail on her cushion. Isabelle sighed and summoned her maids, who were de Glanville's creatures and would do as he bid them. Her own women had long since been dismissed. Walking her dog on a limited course was the nearest she could come to any kind of freedom these days. Queen Eleanor might have released prisoners throughout the land as a boon to mark the start of the new reign, but that generosity did not apply to heiresses in royal care.

When her serving woman opened the door, Isabelle was startled to see guards standing either side of it, and shocked when they would not permit her to leave.

"Lord Ranulf's orders," one said, refusing to meet her widening gaze.

"What?" Isabelle's throat tightened in panic. "He has no authority to confine me. I demand that you let me pass."

He shuffled his feet. "My lady, I cannot. It is more than my life is worth."

She felt hollow and sick. "And what is my own life worth? I demand to see the justiciar."

The other guard cleared his throat. "That is not possible at the moment, my lady."

"It is for your own good, my lady," said his companion.

Isabelle scorched him with a look that he would not answer. "Whoever is benefiting from this, it is not me," she said in a low voice. Then she indicated Damask. "If my dog squats in the rushes they will stink and be foul underfoot. At least find someone to walk her."

The guards exchanged glances but didn't reply and she knew they were waiting for her to do the predictable thing: turn back and slam the door against them in a female tantrum. Stemming that urge, she drew herself up. The sound of footsteps mounting the tower stairs caused the men to turn and present their spears. Isabelle remained where she was as de Glanville's nephew, Theobald Walter, arrived. Panting from his climb, he waved his hand and bade the soldiers lower their weapons. Isabelle's heart began to pound as she met Walter's impassive gaze. She knew that de Glanville harboured designs of conferring her on him. He was a handsome man in his late prime, with fair curls cropped sternly short. Isabelle had met him several times and liked him, but that did not mean she desired to be his wife.

He bowed to her with impeccable manners: de Glanville's nephew was a polished courtier. "Lady Isabelle, you have a visitor. Since he cannot climb the stairs, I have come to fetch you to him."

His words were so unexpected that she could only stare at him while she struggled to find her manners. "Who?" she managed to say, smoothing her hands nervously over her gown. Whoever it was must be important, otherwise an ordinary attendant would have borne the summons. Surely not the new King or his brother Prince John? Why could he not climb stairs? Her mind raced through the various older men who might have reason to visit the Tower, but could think of none who would make a point of summoning her.

Theobald Walter's mouth tightened. "William Marshal has come with letters from King Richard and the Queen," he said a trifle curtly. "No doubt he will explain to you why he is here."

William Marshal. The name was more familiar to her than their single brief meeting three years ago warranted. Heloise had sent her occasional letters from Kendal about her doings in the north and the disposition of her warden. It had become clear that he was not about to exercise the right he had been given to take Heloise in marriage—and that Heloise was relieved to be forgoing the honour. "He would have asked too much of me," she had written.

Her maids in tow, Isabelle followed Theobald Walter down to the lower chamber. Her heart was pounding but there was no time to compose herself. The door was already open and she was ushered straight into the presence of William Marshal. He was leaning against a trestle table, but he pushed himself upright as she entered the room. Vaguely she took in the detail that he had two squires with him, a couple of knights, and a clerk. Feeling acute apprehension, she met his composed dark stare.

"If I were you, Marshal, I would be quick about the matter," said Theobald Walter with a meaningful look. "My uncle does not like to be crossed, and even if his days are numbered, they are not yet over."

The calm stare left Isabelle and fixed instead on Theobald Walter.

"Is that by way of threat or just friendly advice?" said Marshal.

Walter shrugged, his gaze equally unruffled. "You do not know me well, my lord, or you would not ask such a question. It is not my way to threaten, and I have no quarrel with you. My uncle's ambition brought me to court and, as you know, a man has to make the best of the opportunities he is given, but I am not a fool to go against the will of a king." An acerbic smile curved his lips. "And especially not the will of a queen. I do not believe that my uncle Ranulf will go against it either, but it would still be wise not to linger." He nodded in salutation, went to the door, and on the threshold turned. "I hope you will remember my goodwill in times to come. I wish you both well."

Isabelle looked at William, feeling shaky. If Theobald Walter was wishing them well, then it could only be for one reason.

"My lady," he said. "Will you be seated?" He indicated one of the benches at the side of the room.

Isabelle knew that if she sat down she would probably not be able to stand again. His assumption that she needed to be seated made her feel contrary. "Thank you, messire," she said, "I would rather stand and face you."

"Then perhaps we should both sit. It would certainly be more comfortable for me." He limped heavily to the bench. "An accident when boarding the ship to England," he said with a wave of his hand. "I may be an old warhorse, but I'm usually sound of wind and limb." He eased himself carefully down and she saw his eyes tighten with pain.

Since it would have been ungracious to continue standing, Isabelle reluctantly followed suit, glad that the full skirts of her gown prevented him from seeing how much her legs were trembling. She forced herself to meet his eyes. Fine lines were etched at their corners as if he smiled a lot, or spent time narrowing his gaze against the weather. Their hue was that of a stormy winter sea.

"My lady, I do not know if you remember me. My visit to the Tower was brief then, and we met for a few minutes only."

Isabelle touched her throat. "Yes, I remember it. You came for Heloise and I thought that you were going to marry her."

He opened his hand. "I thought so too, but matters changed."

He had a pleasant voice, neither high nor deep, but well modulated and without any particular accent—unlike her own which bore the cadences of her Irish childhood.

"Heloise wrote to me and said that you were not of a mind to wed her."

"Did she?" He raised an eyebrow but didn't look particularly disturbed. "I know that she wrote to you: she told me herself; but I never asked what she had the scribe write. It seemed to me that she was entitled to a little privacy."

Isabelle eyed him, uncertain whether to approve or feel slighted. Giving a little privacy sounded suspiciously like placating a potentially fractious child with a sweetmeat, yet having lived with none of late, such a gesture would feel like consideration beyond price. "Are you going to ask me what she wrote?" she asked.

"Since it was from her to you—no." He rubbed his jaw thoughtfully. "I dare say if I had married her, we would have tolerated each other's failings—either that or driven each other mad and settled for different households once our heirs were begotten. I'm still fond of her and I hope she remembers me with a smile too." He studied Isabelle. "In truth, for more than two years my mind has been set on a greater prize."

Isabelle stiffened. "Heloise's northern lands must pale in comparison to the estates that come through me," she said.

"I was offered Denise de Châteauroux instead of the lady Heloise, but I refused because I knew what I wanted...and, truth to tell, had wanted since I laid eyes on you."

Her face grew hot. He was a courtier; such words came easily to him. Any landless knight would desire her for the lands and prestige she brought, irrespective of her person. "And if Heloise had been the lady of Striguil?" she asked.

He spread his hands and she noticed that his fingernails were clean and that he wore more rings than a soldier, but fewer than a court fop. "Then we would have learned to live with each other. I may have a few romantic bones in my body, but not enough to overthrow reason...However, one always hopes for the best of both worlds."

"And what of me?" Isabelle asked. "What choice do I have?"

"How pragmatic are your own bones, my lady? You have no choice in the matter of your marriage, even if the Church plays lip service to the fact that you do. Your lands and yourself have been entrusted into my keeping. You can make the best of your bed or shroud yourself in martyrdom."

Isabelle returned his stare and then lowered her lids. Anything was better than remaining here and, as he said, she had no choice in the matter. "I do not know you," she murmured, "nor you me." She wondered if her parents had ever spoken thus. Her mother too had been a prize. She had seldom spoken of her marriage to Richard Strongbow, and on the rare occasions she had made mention of it, she had done so with a tight mouth and sad eyes. Isabelle didn't want to look like that.

"That's a remedy I have no cure for except time, my lady. I swear to you that I will treat you with all the honour and deference due to your rank, if you will do the same for me as your husband."

Isabelle tried to steady her panic by breathing slowly. She felt sick and the palms of her hands were cold. Slowly she raised her head. "I do not know how pragmatic my own bones are," she said, "but I will try."

He was careful to exhale without making a sound, but she saw the long movement of his chest and realised that he too was under considerable strain, although he was better at concealing it. "Thank you," he said and, pushing to his feet, reached out his hand to her. She saw the beads of sweat on his brow and the way he held himself. She didn't want to place her hand in his for then he would know how frightened she was, and her mother had said that one should never show fear in the face of challenge. Soon it would be more than just the joining of hands; soon they would be sharing the bed of which he had just spoken. Not that she knew much concerning that aspect of marriage. Her usually forthright mother had been singularly uncommunicative on the matter. Heloise had been a fount of information, but Isabelle was unsure how much of the detail was the result of an over-active imagination. Thinking swiftly, she laid her hand to his sleeve instead, in the manner of the court, and saw his eyelids tighten, but whether in amusement or displeasure was hard to tell.

"I have a boat waiting. If you are ready, we can go now."

"Now? This instant?" Isabelle shot him a questioning look. "What about my household and my baggage?"

"How great a household do you have?"

Isabelle pursed her lips and then said decisively, "Two ladies, a chaplain, and a scribe—although in truth they are all in my lord Glanville's employ not mine."

He nodded. "Do you wish to keep them?"

She shook her head. "Not if I can have the choosing of others."

"It is for you to say and order your own household as you desire."

Isabelle felt a stirring in her solar plexus as if some part of her that had gone to sleep in chains was now awakening and discovering that its fetters had vanished. "Then I will have new maids," she said. "There's a chaplain, Walter, who has been kind to me. I would reward him with an offer of service. My baggage will fit in one coffer."

"Then let it be forwarded and I will ask Theobald Walter to arrange for your clerk to come to our new lodgings if he desires employment."

She frowned. "Is such haste necessary? Am I truly in danger?"

"Not you, my lady, no," William said, "but I would be happier to be away from this place and among friends. If you have no objection to leaving immediately, then I would like us to be on our way."

It was a command couched as a polite and deferential request. Isabelle noted it and wondered what would happen if she baulked and said that she wanted to supervise her own packing and that she was going nowhere with him. Not that she had any intention of cutting off her nose to spite her face. She would give anything to go beyond these imprisoning walls. She was the key to his wealth and status, but he was her key to freedom. "No," she said, lifting her chin. "I have no objection."

William handed Isabelle down into the boat. The weedy smell of the river was strong in her nostrils and the water lapped against the sides of the vessel in small green tongues that occasionally burst in a white saliva of spray. He had lent her his cloak, for although it was a bright summer's day, the wind off the river was stiff. She seated herself on one of the benches along the boat's sides and watched him gingerly do the same. Behind them, the Tower was a great, limewashed bulwark and it was the sight of the massive walls rather than the breeze off the water that made her shiver and hug the double woollen folds of the cloak around her body.

"Cold?" he asked solicitously.

Isabelle stroked Damask who had curled at her feet, and shook her head. "Some walls protect, and some imprison," she said. "I was little more than a child when I came here, but it has never been my home the way that Striguil and Leinster are."

William nodded. "There are always places of the heart," he said absently, his own gaze upon the great walls of the Tower as the boatman and his crewman pulled away upstream. Isabelle looked over her shoulder once and then fixed her gaze on the gulls and cormorants wheeling above the water. She wondered where his places of the heart were, but it was too soon to ask him such a question. She could sense his tension, and see it in the way he kept his hand on his sword hilt. It was only as they continued upstream with nothing more untoward happening than a bare-legged pair of urchins on the riverbank casting stones at the boat that he breathed out and relaxed. She risked a glance at him from beneath her lashes. Now they were in the full light of day, she could see the shadows under his eyes and the gaunt hollows beneath his cheekbones. She had seen that look before—on her mother's face in the days following the death of her brother and her own forced departure from Striguil. It came from the strain of bearing up, of shouldering burdens of grief and care and still managing to go on. Ranulf de Glanville had looked like that too in recent days.

"Where are we going?" she asked.

"To the lodging of Richard FitzReinier."

"Ah," she said. The name meant nothing to her. De Glanville had not seen fit to keep her abreast of goings on outside the Tower and she had had to rely on her quick ears and Walter the clerk for what small snippets of news came her way.

William leaned back against the side of the boat. "He's a merchant and city dignitary," he said. "When I was in the retinue of the Young King, he used to provide us with goods. We would tell Richard what we needed and he would obtain it—anything from a box of pepper to a warhorse. I've known him for a long time. He has a house on Cheapside close to the cathedral and he has offered us his hospitality while we are in London." He looked wry. "I am afraid that I have been in too much haste to make good provision for a wife and her household, but Richard has come to my rescue and assures me that he has everything in hand." He leaned forward. "I am sorry there has been no time for a proper courtship. To be blunt, if I am to be secure then the marriage needs to take place immediately."

Isabelle realised this, but to hear him say so still made her stomach lurch. "How soon is immediately?" she asked, trying to sound practical.

"Today, if you can bear it. I will give you what time I can to compose yourself."

Which was no time at all, Isabelle thought. A piece of water-logged wood bobbed away from them on the opaque green water. Isabelle eyed it and thought that she could drift aimlessly like that—let fate take her where it would—or she could be a passenger in a boat with this man and steer a true course. "I can bear it." She raised her eyes to his. The look he returned was unsettling. She had received stares like that from other men, but she had never been alone with them at the time and had never liked any of them enough to dare to make a tryst.

As they travelled upriver, she gazed at the landscape that had been so close but never seen: the jetties and wharfsides; the bustling dock at Billingsgate where a fishing vessel was unloading a bulging net of salmon. The churches and dwellings with their gardens running down to the waterside. She tried to hold herself on the surface of the moment and not panic. William Marshal pointed out landmarks and spoke with easy humour. He left her space to respond but did not let the silences drag out and put no pressure on her to reply. She supposed that such skill was part of being an accomplished courtier. Their boat passed under the arches of London Bridge and for an instant the world was dark and strongly scented with weed. The water churned beneath the keel of the boat and she felt moist spray on her face.

"It is best on a full tide," he said with a smile. "But you need to be prepared to be soaked, and you need to enjoy danger."

Isabelle considered. "I am Richard Strongbow's daughter," she said. "I think I would like to do this at high tide."

He laughed and looked at her again and she knew that flying through the arches of London Bridge at high tide could not match the fear and exhilaration that were running through her just now.

Richard FitzReinier's fine timber house stood on the west corner of Cheapside, the hub of London's commercial wheel. The outer walls were plastered and painted blue, which immediately set it apart from its neighbours, and it was roofed with wooden shingles. In the height of luxury and refinement, the windows were glazèd, revealing that its owner was wealthy beyond the norm. There were stables and barns and other outbuildings so that the site almost had the aspect of a castle bailey.

FitzReinier himself emerged to greet them: a tall man of slender bones and a small, taut paunch that spoke of the good living bought by success. He was clad in a striped tunic of blue and gold silk and rings gleamed on every finger. An ostentatious cross set with red stones hung at his throat. On first glance, a stranger would have thought him the knight and William the merchant.

"Countess," FitzReinier said and flourished her an elaborate bow. "Welcome to my house. It is a privilege indeed."

Isabelle inclined her head and from somewhere found an appropriate response.

"You will be wanting to prepare yourself for your wedding, my lady," he added and indicated the fair woman who had belatedly followed him from the house. She was plump and breathless from hurrying. "I will leave you in the capable hands of Madam FitzReinier."

The woman curtseyed deeply to Isabelle, then rose and indicated the stairs down which she had just hastened. "If you wish, my lady, we have prepared a bath and fresh raiment." Her cheeks were red. A collar of pearls at her throat sat just a little too snugly against her ample flesh.

Isabelle looked at William, who formally kissed her hand. "Go with Madam FitzReinier," he said. "I've to prepare myself too, but I'll join you shortly."

Isabelle suppressed the urge to cling to William, knowing that it was born of suddenly being thrust into so much change. Holding herself erect, she followed the merchant's wife up the timber stairs to the large chamber on the first floor of the main building. Here, she almost gasped at the opulence of the room, which was grander than anything she had ever seen. Every inch of wall was bright with embroidered hangings, the benches bore matching silk cushions, and the coffers were all painted with hunting and biblical scenes. Several maids chattered as they busied themselves around a large bathtub wafting tendrils of scented steam. Towels were warming on a stand before a brazier and the hangings of the day bed were drawn back to show the coverlet strewn with a colourful array of garments. A bemused Isabelle was pressed down on to one of the benches and a cup of spice-infused wine put in her hand.

Madam FitzReinier declared it a great honour to be entertaining the Countess of Striguil and that she and her husband were delighted to be of service. Isabelle could see that the woman's pleasure was genuine, but had no doubt that she also had an eye to the profit. To be of service now was to ensure a long-term favourable relationship with the wealth of Striguil. Isabelle sipped the wine. It was like red silk on her tongue with just the right pungency imparted by the spices. It was delicious and she said so to her hostess.

Madam FitzReinier smiled. "Lord William has asked my husband for several barrels. I can give you the recipe for the spices. Mostly nutmeg and ginger. Here, you should eat something with it. It's very potent." The last word, although spoken innocently enough, had certain connotations. One of the maids giggled and Isabelle blushed. With a throaty laugh, Madam FitzReinier presented Isabelle with a platter of toasted bread, cut into small strips and spread with a tasty venison terrine. Although nervous, Isabelle still found the appetite to eat several. The other women joined in with relish and Damask devoured several as if she were a wolf and not a small, sleek greyhound.

Fortified by food and wine, Isabelle allowed the women to disrobe her and stepped into the bathtub. A heady floral scent perfumed the steam and she exclaimed in pleasure.

"Attar of roses," said Madam FitzReinier, showing her a tiny glass vial. "My husband imports it from the Venetians, who obtain it from Arabia."

She didn't need to say how expensive it was: Isabelle could guess; but she made note of it all the same. As the women pummelled and scrubbed her, Isabelle asked her hostess about her future husband. Forewarned, after all, was forearmed. "I have heard many things about his reputation," she said. "Most is high praise, but there are some rumours too…"

Madam FitzReinier gave a shrug. "Men are men and even the best of them far from saints, but if you are referring to his supposed affair with the Young Queen, then you can take my word that it was all falsehood, invented by his enemies to destroy his reputation. It was friendship they shared, not lust of the body."

Isabelle bit her lip and wished she hadn't spoken her doubts aloud. Ranulf de Glanville had been scathing of the rumours too—but in the opposite direction, for he had chosen to believe them and he had little to say about William Marshal that was positive. "I know so little," she said, but more to herself than her hostess, and there was an edge of frustration to her tone.

Madam FitzReinier fetched a warmed towel from beside the brazier and brought it to the tub. "But you can learn. Besides, you're young and pretty and such keys will open most doors. If you're clever up here"—she tapped her head—"you can make sure they stay open."

Isabelle looked at Madam FitzReinier in surprise. No one had ever told her before that she was pretty and she had never seen her image in a gazing glass. In her childhood, if people talked of beauty, it was always with reference to her formidable mother, Aoife, Countess of Hibernia. She knew that golden hair was prized, and she had an abundance of that, but fair tresses alone did not a beauty make. There had often been remarks that she resembled her father, but since all she remembered of him was a beard and thick red freckles, that didn't help her much.

The women assisted her from the tub and vigorously dried her until her skin tingled and glowed. The precious rose oil was dabbed sparingly at her wrists and throat, and the clothes that had been laid on the bed were brought forth for her inspection.

"I am not certain how well they will fit," said Madam FitzReinier apologetically. "Lord William left us very little time to organise the purchase and he had to tell us your size from memory."

Isabelle blinked. "He only saw me fleetingly three years ago."

The older woman chuckled. "Well, you must have left a lasting impression on him, for he knew what he wanted. No," she amended, "he knew what he thought you would like."

Isabelle shook her head in bemusement. In her experience thus far, the only men who thought they knew a woman's wishes were either effeminate or smooth-tongued troubadours. She could not envisage any of the dour knights of her father's entourage or de Glanville's being concerned with the kind of garments a woman might like—unless of course their preference was for a delightful package that was titillating to unwrap. The latter thought made her blush, and then laugh. When Madam FitzReinier looked at her askance, Isabelle shook her head and raised her arms so that the women could dress her in the undershift of finest linen chansil with a silk ribbon tie. There were hose of pale silk with garters of delicate braid. Isabelle shivered to feel such luxury whispering against her skin. Although she was an heiress, precious few funds for clothing had come her way while she was in de Glanville's care. She had grown accustomed to make do and mend. Now, she began to wonder if her husband to be was a spendthrift. De Glanville had spoken grimly of the profligate household of the Young King and how William Marshal had been one of the main instigators of the squandering of wealth. But the fabric felt glorious to wear and it was a pleasure to be indulged after so much privation.

The undergown was of ivory silk with tight-fitting sleeves and the overgown of deep pink silk trimmed with pearls. The women braided her thick blond hair with ribbons that matched the gown and pinned a light veil to the crown of her head. Then they brought a jewel casket, brimming with rings and brooches, and Isabelle could only gasp.

"You have a man there who values you," said Madam FitzReinier with a smile. "And who also knows the value of show." She presented Isabelle with a mirror. Banded in ivory, the disc of tinned glass startled Isabelle with a reflection that actually looked not unlike her mother, save that the eyes were wider and bluer and the lips fuller. There were no lines of control and disillusion either, only smooth features waiting to have their life story mapped.

"See, you are indeed lovely," said Madam FitzReinier. "It will not take much to ensnare your husband. He's halfway to besotted already."

"He is?" Isabelle eyed her hostess with interest and blushed at the intimacy of the words "your husband."

"Trust me, my dear, I know men. Yours doesn't give away a great deal, but I've seen the way he looks at you."

Isabelle gave a rueful laugh. "He's probably seeing Striguil, Ireland, and my estates in Normandy," she said.

Madam FitzReinier laughed too. "Undoubtedly so, but he would have to be blind not to notice the other assets that go with it."

In another chamber, William too was bathing—with some difficulty given his injured leg, but determined not to be defeated. A bath was as much a feature of the ritual of marriage as it was in the preparation for knighthood: a cleansing preliminary to a rite of passage.

"There has been little time to organise a feast, but I have done my best," FitzReinier said. "I spoke to your Welsh groom and had the cooks prepare dishes of leeks and lava bread to honour the bride." He wrapped his hands around his belt in a self-congratulatory gesture. "I even managed to find an Irish bard to sing at the feast."

"I cannot thank you enough," William said. "I know how much store women set by such things and even for myself I want my wedding day to be more than just a few words muttered in a dark corner. It should be a great celebration, and you are playing your part to the hilt."

FitzReinier smiled. "It is always auspicious when business and pleasure combine."

William nodded and clenched a yawn between his teeth. The hot water was filling him with lassitude.

"If I were you, I'd ask an apothecary for a potion to liven you up," FitzReinier advised with a grin. "You're not going to get much sleep with a new bride in your bed and you already look as if you've been ground through the mill."

William pulled himself up in the tub and sluiced his face in the cold water jug standing next to it. "That's because I have," he admitted. "I don't remember what sleep feels like and a feather mattress will seem like a ridiculous luxury. I won't be able to close my eyes unless I bed down in a stable with my horse."

"Hah, and I know what your bride would say about that."

William looked wry. "Then you know more than me. If I were a girl of her age faced with a husband twice my years—and damaged goods at that—I'd probably be wishing him further away than a stable."

"You underestimate yourself and your bride."

"I don't," William answered. "We'll both do our duty, but that's the facade. What goes on behind it may be entirely different."

FitzReinier conceded the point with a shrug. "But you have made a fine start. Even if she is not looking forward to being bedded, you have shown her that you are no ogre. Whatever her misgivings, this has to be a better life than the one she had cooped up in the Tower."

"I hope she thinks so." William fell pensively silent as he attended to his ablutions, but at length he looked up at the merchant. "I can do nothing until Richard arrives in England for his coronation. I've borrowed the manor at Stoke from Roger D'Abernon—it's far enough from London to be secluded, but not too far to travel when the King lands."

FitzReinier lifted his brows in surprise. "I thought you would be taking yourself off on progress to the lady's lands?"

William shook his head. "I considered it, but I can't travel any distance until my leg has healed and as I said I need to be close to the court. The lands have been in stewardship for so long that they can wait a little longer and there are others who can go in my stead. I need to recuperate and sleep—and spend some time alone with my wife. Once Richard arrives in England there will be precious little time for leisure and dalliance."

His squires helped him from the bath and he dressed in the fine garments that FitzReinier had obtained for him. The brazilwood red of his tunic was of a deeper but toning hue with the gown that Isabelle would be wearing. His belt, which he hesitated over and then buckled on, was the one Marguerite had given him, stitched with gold bezants. After all, he reasoned, it was a gift from a friend and he knew the truth of the matter. He combed his hair and refused the use of a gazing glass, not sure that he wanted to see what Isabelle would see. Swallowing his apprehension, he presented his squire Jean with a bridal chaplet of twined fresh flowers: roses pink and white and clove-scented gillyflowers, interspersed with tendrils of ivy. "Go to the women's chamber and bid my lady wear this to celebrate our wedding day," he told the youth. "And tell her that I am ready to go to church, if it please her."

Isabelle regarded William Marshal's squire. She had paid him little heed before, but now she focused on him as he stood in the doorway, bearing a bridal chaplet on a silk cushion as he delivered his message in a voice tight with nervousness.

She felt nervous too, but because she was concentrating on her role it was not as bad as it might have been. The youth was an inner member of the Marshal household and as such she would come to know him well and sometimes have to rely on him. "Thank your lord," she murmured, taking the chaplet from the cushion. "He has been naught but thoughtful of my welfare and I appreciate his concern. Tell him that I am almost ready."

"My lady." His colour bright, the squire bowed and retired.

Madam FitzReinier smiled. "Not a little smitten," she said. "And I do not blame him."

The women arranged the chaplet over Isabelle's veil and once again showed her the result in the mirror. Isabelle swallowed. You are Countess of Striguil, she silently told the wide-eyed girl looking at her from beneath flower-shrouded brows. You are his prestige, and he is your freedom. You need each other; all will be well.

Her head high, she went down to meet William and found him waiting for her at the foot of the stairs. His dark red tunic complemented the colour of her gown and was girded with a beautiful and unusual belt made of metallic braid, stitched with gold coins.

"My lady," he said and limped forward to take her hands in his and kiss them. "Are you ready to go to church?"

Ready to give herself and her lands into his keeping? What if she said no, ran back upstairs and slammed and bolted the door? For a moment she imagined doing just that and in her mind's eye saw the mailed men breaking into the chamber with axes and seizing her by force. She blinked away the vision and stiffened her spine. "Yes," she said, "I am ready."

Isabelle lay in bed beside her new husband and, breathing shallowly, listened to the sounds wafting up from the torchlit courtyard and garth of FitzReinier's house. The wedding guests were still celebrating with gusto and the strident throb of tabor and wail of bagpipe had replaced the liquid notes of the Irish harp that had played throughout the courses of the feast. She hadn't been able to do full justice to the food, which had saddened her, since it had been prepared in her honour. The playing of the Irish bard had misted her eyes with tears and brought a lump to her throat, robbing her of speech and certainly the ability to swallow food.

Now she had to hope that her husband's consideration would extend as far as the bedchamber. She knew a little about the act of procreation, none of it particularly reassuring. The detail that she would bleed was worrying, for surely if there was blood, there would be pain…but if there was no blood she would be disgraced. Not that he would repudiate her. Her lands were too valuable.

"You need not be afraid of me," William said suddenly, as if he had stepped into her mind and seen her thoughts.

"I am not, my lord," she replied valiantly, her words given the lie by the tremor in her voice.

He smiled. "Well then, if not of me, then of what is expected of us both this night."

She clasped her hands. "I…I know my duty."

He snorted. "I dare say that you do—as I know mine, but there is no reason why duty and pleasure should be separate things."

"Yes, my lord," she agreed apprehensively.

He made a sound, through his teeth, whether of humour or exasperation, she wasn't sure. "We have been thrown together have we not, without any time for adjustment. I have no doubt that consummating this marriage tonight will be awkward at best and probably a painful disaster for both, given your virginity and my injured leg. I've waited long enough for a few days to make no difference."

Isabelle continued to stare. "But what about the blood on the sheet? There has to be proof."

"There will be blood." Leaving the bed, he limped to his folded clothing and took the knife from his belt sheath. Isabelle's eyes widened further, but then she steadied herself. He wasn't going to hurt her, for without her he had nothing.

Raising his arm, tensing his eyelids, he made a swift, shallow cut in his left armpit. "Less noticeable there," he said, going to the bed and taking blood on his fingers, smearing the centre of the sheet. "There doesn't need to be a great deal. The better the lover, the less there is—or so I'm told," he added with a smile. "Never having deflowered a virgin before, I can only speak from hearsay. We only need FitzReinier and his household to bear witness. It's not as if the entire court is looking on." He wiped the knife and returned it to its sheath. Pressing his fingers to his side, he went to the shutters and released the catch. The revellers had spilled into the garden. People sat on stools or stood in groups talking and laughing under the influence of the free-flowing wine. Candle lanterns made pools of light among the orchard trees and night-flying insects flurried around the glow. It was strange not to be amongst the crowd.

"Tomorrow we'll set out for Stoke," he said over his shoulder. "I need to be rested before the King's coronation. Once he arrives, I suspect that I'm not going to know my head from my heels." He smiled and held out his good arm towards her. "I also need some time to know my wife...and she me."

Isabelle came to his invitation and took his hand. His grip was hard and warm and dry. Her own was moist with heightened tension. "Has the bleeding stopped?" she asked in a concerned voice.

"It stings, but yes, it's stopped." He gave a sudden chuckle. "I warrant that Adam had considerably more pain having a rib cut out for his Eve."

Thirty-three

*I*N THE MORNING, THE SACRIFICIAL CUT THAT WILLIAM HAD made mattered not a whit, for Isabelle had begun her monthly courses during the night and the sheet beneath her was puddled in blood. Her fluxes had always been regular but on this occasion were several days early—probably caused, Madam FitzReinier opined, by the shock of the sudden change in her life. Isabelle was chagrined and afraid that William would be angered, or revolted. However, he treated the happening with equanimity, remarking that it was God's will and nature's way, but had he known what was going to happen, he would not have bothered to take a knife to himself. Isabelle was still mortified, but Madam FitzReinier, who was helping her to pack her belongings for the morning's journey to Stoke, was pragmatic and cheerful.

"He's an experienced man, no foolish youngster," she said. "It'll have happened to him times before, considering the years he had a mistress."

Isabelle's eyes widened at this new information. "A mistress?"

Madam FitzReinier clucked her tongue. "A woman of Poitou, a tourney follower. No one knew much about her and they both seemed to prefer it that way. He never brought her to court, but she always had the best lodgings in the town. She bore no children, so I assume that he was well accustomed to the times of her flux."

Isabelle digested the information thoughtfully. There was so much she did not know about her new husband—and that perhaps she was never going to find out. And yet it had shaped him as surely as her own shorter past had shaped her. "What happened to her?"

"They came to a parting of the ways. From what I heard, she left him and settled down with a vintner from Le Mans."

"Oh." Isabelle bit her lip. "Has he had other mistresses?"

Madam FitzReinier looked round from the coffer, a half-smile on her lips. "I dare say he has bedded women here and there along his route, but apart from that one time, he has kept no woman at his side. Your way is clear."

"If I can find the path," Isabelle said doubtfully.

Madam FitzReinier's smile widened. "Oh, I don't think you need worry, my dear," she said. "For even if you do not, then it is bound to find you."

The journey to Stoke took a full day and it was late in the dusk when they arrived. Bats swooped against a dark lavender sky and the first stars glimmered like new-kindled lanterns. Isabelle was bone weary, her thigh muscles were screaming, and she was suffering strong cramps from her flux. Once she had enjoyed long rides in the open air, but her time in the Tower had dulled her stamina and her muscles were no longer toned and accustomed to the activity. However, she endured without protest. She would not have her husband see her as a whining milksop. He too must be in some discomfort from his injured leg but he had not complained.

William had sent outriders ahead to Stoke and they arrived to a torchlit welcome with grooms waiting to take their horses and stewards to lead them into the hall. Bowls of warm water were brought to wash their hands, faces, and feet. A fine meal of stuffed mushrooms and trout baked with almonds was set before them, together with dishes of green herbs and preserved fruits. Isabelle had not realised how hungry she was until she began to eat. Despite her aching body and her cramping loins, she still had a healthy appetite.

She and William shared a trencher and a cup, served unobtrusively by his squires. As yesterday, the bard was on hand to provide soft music to accompany their dining, but this time there were no wedding guests, just a handful of retainers and the chaplains and clerks that William had picked up in London. The great retinue required of their status had yet to accrue.

"When I was your age," William said, "people said that I was always either eating or sleeping and that, except in those occupations, I would amount to nothing."

"Then they were obviously wrong, my lord," Isabelle replied tactfully.

He chuckled. "No, they were right about the eating and sleeping, and I intend to do as much of that while I can. As to what I amount to…I've heard a variety of opinions and come to the conclusion that few of them matter save the one I have of myself."

"And is mine one of the few, my lord?" she asked, emboldened by the strong wine in the cup they were sharing.

He nodded gravely. "Assuredly so, since it is by your hand in marriage that I have my reward. Queen Eleanor told me that I should consult you in all things and remember that what I have is yours."

"I wager that hers is another of the few," Isabelle said, touching the gold and sapphire brooch at the throat of her gown—one of Eleanor's wedding gifts.

"Yes," he said quietly. "I have more time and respect for Queen Eleanor than for most men of my acquaintance…but her advice only confirmed my own thoughts on the matter of our marriage. I need you too much to ride roughshod over your wishes."

Isabelle sipped again from the cup. Of course he needed her, for without her he had nothing—or at least not until she had produced an heir of their mingled blood. If she could make herself indispensable to him, then her opinions would stand on their own merits, rather than him humouring her out of diplomacy.

During the following week, he was as good as his word and spent a deal of time rising at a leisurely hour, enjoying the pleasures of the table, and being as indolent as the largest sleepy male lion at the Tower. Although Isabelle enjoyed her slumber, William seemed to have an infinite capacity that far outstripped hers. Had she not heard the tales of his deeds, some of them legendary, she would indeed have believed in the original sobriquets of "Guzzleguts" and "Slugabed." During the few hours when he was not eating or asleep, he was content to stroll in Stoke's well-stocked garden, inhale the perfume of the flowers, listen to the bard sing Irish songs, and to sing songs of his own. He had a fine voice. He played chess with her and merels, and laughed when she matched him. He wove her tales of the tourneys and his early life, but he seldom touched on serious matters, indeed seemed to be deliberately avoiding them, and Isabelle began to wonder what kind of man she had married and whether de Glanville's sour tales of William Marshal's frivolous nature were in fact true.

Gradually, however, as the days passed and his strained leg healed, he became less lethargic. Isabelle woke one morning to find his side of the bed empty. He was not in the chamber and his clothes were gone from the top of the coffer. "Out riding, my lady," said the maid when Isabelle made enquiries as she washed and dressed. She noted that there was no blood on last night's flux cloth, which meant that her husband could now bed her without incurring God's displeasure. She wondered how she was going to impart such news without seeming immodest. Perhaps he would ask her, or just make assumptions based on the passage of time?

In the hall, a scattering of crumbs and drips of honey on the napery at the high table bore testament to breakfast devoured. There was no sign of the squires. Isabelle broke her own fast in haste and, with the maid in tow, went outside. The day promised to be hot, but it was still sufficiently early for the air to be fresh and scented with dew. Hearing masculine voices loud with camaraderie, she followed the sound until she came to the paddock beyond the stables, and then she stopped.

Her husband was putting his destrier through its paces. Watching man and horse execute a series of intricate manoeuvres, Isabelle was astounded, for the performance seemed to her nothing short of magical. The lightest touch of heel, a command from the hands, and the horse pivoted, changed lead legs, stopped, backed, caracoled. William and his mount moved as one. Isabelle knew that he was a good horseman, but until now she had not realised the true level of his skill. He was obviously teaching his squires various aspects of horsemanship, for the youths were mounted. Following the demonstration, he began to break down some of the simpler moves so that they could try them for themselves. Isabelle gazed, enthralled. As William performed a turn, he saw her watching and, with a word to the squires, reined about and trotted over.

"You are awake early this morning, my lord," she said, with a smile.

He shook his head. "No, for once I am not abed late."

"How is your leg?"

He rubbed his hand along his thigh. "Improving. It still twinges, but that might just be old age setting in." The latter was spoken with a self-deprecating grin. "It's a fine day—do you want to ride out and picnic in the forest?"

"I would like that." She shaded her eyes on the palm of her hand. "I had not realised how skilled a horseman you were."

William inclined his head. "It's a while since I've practised," he said. "I've grown a little rusty since my tourney days." He slapped the destrier's golden hide. "Fortunately Bezant hasn't forgotten, and it'll be a while before my squires are ready to challenge us." He winked at Jean and Jack.

Isabelle returned to the keep to don a gown more suitable for riding. William exchanged his destrier for his black palfrey, his saddle pack laden with a rushwork basket and two costrels of wine. The squires accompanied them, but rode well back out of earshot. By the way the youths sat their mounts, heads up, spines proud, Isabelle could tell that they were pretending to be serious knights on a sortie and it made her smile. She wondered if she should lift her chin and try to look like an imperious noble lady, but since there was no one to see, save her husband and squires, it seemed a little foolish.

"I am sorry if I have been poor company for you thus far," William said as they rode along the side of a field and entered broad, sun-dappled woodland. "If I were your age I would not be thankful to be buried in the middle of nowhere with a husband who spends most of his life asleep."

"It is true that you do sleep a lot," she said with a judicious wrinkle of her nose, "but my mother always said that sleep was good for healing, and I think you have been in much need of that."

"More than you know," he said softly.

She gave him a swift glance but he was staring ahead along the path. "I think I do know," she ventured. "Oh, not the details," she added quickly as he looked surprised, "but the very reason that you do not speak of them suggests that they are too sore to touch. You talk of light things and matters that you think will entertain a young wife...and they do, but I cannot be your consort without knowing more."

There was a long hesitation, filled with the clop of hooves, the creak of harness, and the voices of the squires arguing a jousting point. Then he sighed. "If I have not bared my life to you, it is because I did not want to burden you with its weight until I knew how much you were capable of carrying."

"How will you know unless you try me?" she asked. "How will *I* know?"

His smile was bleak. "Perhaps I was trying to break you in gently."

"Like one of your horses?"

Genuine humour lit in his eyes. "If so, I don't seem to be doing very well, do I?" He looked thoughtful for a moment, and then he shook his head and laughed. "When I was a very young knight, I was given a horse that would not tolerate one of these bridles." He indicated his mount's harness. "I had to fashion one especially for him, and even then I only rode him by his tolerance, not my mastery. His name was Blancart and he was unsurpassed." He gave her a considering look. "Whatever you want to know, ask it of me and I will do my best to answer...and if I don't then you will know that it is ground I choose to tread with no one at all."

Isabelle gnawed her lower lip. "Is that to be my new bridle?"

"No, let it be the yoke that joins us from now on."

Isabelle frowned at him, wondering how far he was humouring her. His expression was difficult to read, but learn to read it she must. "Ah," she said, "like a team of oxen then."

"Just so," he answered seriously. "But hopefully not as ponderous nor as dumb." Their eyes met and held, and suddenly she saw the humour deepening the creases at the corners of his and she giggled.

They rode along the banks of the River Mole, which twisted

through the woodlands and pastures belonging to the demesne, and finally halted to rest their mounts and eat their food where a fringe of willows dropped over the brows of the bank. An otter plopped and swam downstream away from them. On the far bank, two swans and a clutch of half a dozen cygnets preened on a large, untidy nest of dead reeds. Fish made lazy rings out in mid-stream.

"What happened to your destrier?" she asked as the squires hobbled the horses to graze and William tied strings to the wine costrels and dropped them into the lazily flowing water to keep cool. "The one that wouldn't tolerate a bridle."

"He eventually retired to grass with a herd of Flemish mares belonging to the Count of Flanders." William sat down beside her. "There are several young stallions on the tourney circuit that claim him as their sire. My brother John has a couple of brood mares that are of his getting too."

"You have said little about your brother," she murmured.

With a slight shrug he investigated the contents of the basket and produced a roasted fowl wrapped in a linen cloth, a small loaf, and some raisin tarts. "That is because there is little to say. We are of the same blood and we will watch each other's backs, but we are not close. You'll meet him soon enough because he'll come to court when King Richard arrives. He holds the official position of the King's Marshal and he's been Prince John's seneschal for two years now. And he'll want to see his son." He glanced over his shoulder at his squires who had sat down beside the horses to eat their food.

Isabelle glanced also. "His mother will want to see him too, I warrant."

"Yes." William said. He hesitated. "The boy's not his heir, but his bastard, and there's a daughter too. Alais has been John's mistress for a long time." He divided the chicken neatly into portions with his hunting knife, wiping the blade on the linen and his hands on the grass. "Alais is no whore," he added emphatically, "and I am fond of her."

Isabelle took note of the warning in his tone. "The Irish and the Welsh are more flexible about such matters. You will not find me disparaging or judging a woman I have not met," she reassured him, using a napkin to lift one of the chicken pieces. Damask immediately came to claim her share. She hesitated. "Madam FitzReinier said that you had a mistress for a long time...but that your ways parted."

For a moment Isabelle thought that she had crossed the line on to ground that he would not share, but then he set the chicken aside, rested his hands on his knees, and sighed. "Her name was Clara and she once saved my life. We rode the tourney circuit together when I was a young knight, but she grew weary of the amount of time I had to spend at court, time I couldn't give to her, and yes, we parted."

"You had no children?"

"She was barren—which was both a blessing and a pity."

Isabelle gnawed her lip. "Irish or Welsh, I do not think I have the generosity to share you with a mistress."

"Isabelle—"

"I will give you children," she said with sudden ferocity. "Strong sons and daughters with the blood of the High Kings of Ireland and Earls of Pembroke in their veins. Heirs for Striguil and Leinster and Longueville. I will go whither you go, even into the thick of the fight...I will..." Feeling foolish, not understanding the storm she had unleashed upon herself, she made a small sound and turned away.

He gripped her arm and pulled her back to face him. "Yes," he said. "You will give me sons and daughters, and yes, you will accompany me even into the thick of the fight. If you are with child by then, so much the better. If ever I hear complaint from you, I will remind you of this day and what you said."

He drew her into his body and kissed her, and Isabelle, who had not been kissed by any man except within the bounds of affection and courtesy, was ravished. The first pressure of his mouth was hard and forced her lips apart, but as she prepared to fight in panic, it changed, becoming a silken thing of subtle strength that turned the marrow in her bones to liquid fire. Clinging to him, she answered him fiercely, and when the kiss broke for want of air, they stared at each other, breathing hard.

"You will not need to remind me," she gasped. "Every step of the way I will match you." The words emerged almost as a challenge. She did not understand the wildness, except that it was somehow connected with a dull ache low in her pelvis somewhat akin to the cramps of her flux. The feel of him breathing just as rapidly as she was, the look in his eyes, exacerbated the sensation.

"You don't know where you're going yet," he said in a harsh voice.

She lifted her chin. "Neither do you…"

His arm tightened around her body and he drew her in close. "Don't wager on it, because you'd lose." His words were a hot whisper against her earlobe and made her shiver. "I know exactly where…"

A loud noise of crunching bones distracted him from the end of his sentence and Isabelle from the drug of lust. Tired of waiting for her share, Damask had helped herself to the roasted fowl that had been lying on Isabelle's napkin and, clutching it between her front paws, was engaged in chewing her way down the drumstick. Beyond her, the two squires were pretending to be very busy with their own meal, but Jean's ears were the hue of beetroot and Jack was studying a cloud of fungus on the branch of a tree as if it were the most fascinating thing he had ever seen.

William cleared his throat and dropped his hand. Blushing

furiously, Isabelle smoothed out her gown. She risked a glance at her husband through her lashes and saw the humour sparkling through the frustration. He gave a reluctant chuckle. "You're right," he said. "I don't know where I'm going, only where I want to go. I suppose we could tie up the dog with the rest of our dinner and tell the squires to go for a walk, but there's a fine feather bed in our chamber at the manor…if you are…"

Isabelle looked down. "I no longer have my flux," she murmured.

He nodded and rescued the rest of the chicken. "Eat," he said, handing her another portion and taking one for himself, a playful gleam in his eyes. "We'll need our strength."

The rest of their ride passed in a haze for Isabelle composed of lust, anxiety, and the fact that she had too much to think about. His brother; his mistress. The things he had and hadn't said, and her own words which had come from a suppressed part of her that she had not even realised existed…and now the consequences, which brought her back to the beginning. She wondered what he would do on their return. Take her by the hand and lead her past all their attendants and retainers to the bedchamber? Or perhaps she should take him! Her face was already hot, but the latter notion made it burn. William said little on the ride back, but the looks he sent her made her shiver to the bone.

When they arrived, however, their intentions were thwarted by the sight of several mules being led away to the stables. "Visitors, my lord," said Rhys as he came to take their horses. "Monks from Bradenstoke. There's also a messenger from the Queen."

William groaned softly. "It's beginning already," he said. "Mark me, by the end of our stay, this place will be as busy as a castle." He lifted Isabelle from her mare and she slid down his body. For a moment they stood within each other's breath, pressed together. He shook his head. "My own fault. I should have tied the dog and sent my squires for a wander." He glanced into the stables at the mules and palfrey. "There isn't even an empty stall."

Isabelle reddened and glanced quickly at Rhys who was looking into the middle distance, lips pursed as if he were about to whistle. "I had better go and change my gown if we have guests," she said and stepped away from intoxication.

William watched her hurry across the yard, admiring the fluid movement of her young, lithe body. He had either been hard or half-hard since sitting down by the stream. Having to concentrate on other matters when most of his mind was currently south of his belt was going to be difficult. At first the waiting had been easy enough. Indeed, her flux had been of benefit for it had given him the time he needed to recoup his energies, both physical and mental. To rest and sleep and recover. He hadn't bargained for her intensity and forthright sense of possession, but then he supposed that her father's personality had hardly been shrinking and the Irish were known for their turbulent spirit. But he suspected that, like himself, she was pragmatic and a workhorse too. She wouldn't shirk what had to be done, yet there was a gentleness about her—a vulnerable core that resonated in a deeper part of himself that had not been touched since the days when Clara had ridden at his side.

Brother Daniel was the leader of half a dozen monks from the priory at Bradenstoke, a cheerful, vigorous man in his thirties, the dark hair around his tonsure beginning to thread with the silver of wisdom and experience. William desired to found an Augustinian monastery on his northern lands at Cartmel, which were his own and no part of Isabelle's portion.

Although the charter had yet to be written and witnessed, he wanted the monks of Bradenstoke to form the nucleus of Cartmel's community and required them to be established as soon as possible. The six monks who had arrived at Stoke were the first volunteers and their visit was by way of gaining William's approval. Although he had yet to be formally endorsed, Daniel's position as Prior of the new foundation was a foregone conclusion.

William spoke of the charter he intended for the priory and which he would have confirmed as soon as he returned to court. "It is to the honour of God," he said. "And in payment of the debt I owe Him for granting me His mercy and showing me His great favour." He took a drink from his goblet. The wine was from a barrel that they had brought from FitzReinier's house in London and silken as it slipped over the tongue. He was aware of Isabelle listening at his side. She was wearing her pink silk dress, but her hair and throat were modestly covered by a plain linen wimple in deference to the monks and she had been demurely silent, although William knew that she was paying close attention. He cleared his throat. "The foundation is also for the souls of myself and my wife and any heirs we may have…" He darted her a swift glance and she responded with the faintest curve of her lips and a slight pinkening of her cheeks, "and for the souls of King Henry, King Richard…and my lord, Henry the Young King." He spoke the last words in a voice filled with poignant sadness. "He has much troubled my thoughts and I would have peace of mind for myself as well as for him."

"Prayers shall be said every day, my lord," Daniel replied gravely. William nodded, feeling relieved. Although the charter had yet to be ratified, it was good to know that by the time it was, these men would have laid the spiritual stones and be at work. He needed to pay his debts to the past and to God so that he could go forward on a clear road.

Having spoken with the monks, he had then to deal with the Queen's messenger, a slender, young cleric named Michael who, it emerged, was Wigain's cousin. William was not surprised. Trades often ran in families and there was a definite resemblance in the jaunty air and slight build. The letter was written in the Queen's elegant hand, but since William could not read, he handed it to her messenger to do so.

Michael licked his lips and reddened slightly. His voice was not that of a herald, for it was pitched high and flat. However, he was fast and assured. The first item to emerge after the salutation, which was to both William and Isabelle, was that the Queen was recommending Michael to them as a skilled clerk and lawyer, fluent in Latin, French, and English, of whom they could make valuable use. His discretion was assured.

"You come highly recommended, Master Michael," William said drily. "What can I do but take you on? A position is yours if you desire it."

"Thank you, my lord. Shall I have someone else read this lest you think I am spinning a tale?"

William laughed at that. "I wouldn't put it past Wigain if he were japing, but since you have come to me in earnest and it would be easy to check, I'll believe your integrity. Pray continue."

The remainder of the letter contained the wish that William and Isabelle were finding marriage agreeable, and then the meat of the matter—the detail that Richard would be arriving in London, winds permitting, by the beginning of August, with the coronation planned for the third of September in Westminster Abbey. The language grew more circumspect, but hinted at further advancement for William and his family and praised his loyalty. William thanked the clerk when he had finished, had him repeat the message so that he could commit it to memory, and then sent him to find food, drink, and a bed.

Thoughtfully, William cupped his chin. While he might be unable to read, he could read between the lines. So could Isabelle.

"You were given Striguil for more reasons than a mere reward for loyalty. You were given Striguil to raise you up and give you authority," she said.

He twitched his shoulders. "The Queen remembers those who have served her well. Now that she is in a position to bestow favours, she is generous."

"Indeed, but she is also sharp. When Richard goes on crusade, there will need to be loyal and willing men to shoulder the responsibility for keeping his domain intact. You would not have been raised to the dignity of an earl without a stronger motive than reward."

"I am not an earl," William said, his tone distracted as he was caught off guard. If Queen Eleanor was sharp, then his new wife was not far behind her.

"In all but name you are, and you are promised more. It is obvious that you are being fitted for a high position when Richard rides to war."

He gave her a wry look. "So it seems."

"And you are not pleased?"

He took her hands in his. "I know I can do whatever is appointed to me. I have never shrunk from challenge; indeed I enjoy it." He studied her face and her enquiring expression. "But there is a part of me too that craves tranquillity. I came to Stoke not only to recover from the storms of the past year, but to garner serenity for the future because there will be more dark weather to come, mark me." Still holding her hands, he rose to his feet and pulled her with him. "Come to bed," he said. "Be my harbour; give me shelter."

While Isabelle could still think, she came to the conclusion that she was the one needing shelter as she was caught on hot riptides of sensation that dragged her out to sea and threatened to drown her. She had thought she had known what to expect but the reality was at once more brutal and more tender than anything she had imagined. The heat of his lips at her throat, at her mouth corner, then on her mouth; lover's words breathed upon and into her body until she was turbulent with them and gasping. The request of tongue and intricate delicacy of fingertips that cajoled her to respond. She was teased and coaxed until sensation swelled like a full moontide under the stars and surged shorewards in a mingling of purpose and abandonment.

Isabelle tossed her head on the bolster, her long fair hair unbound like a siren's and webbing her pale body. The July heat had built up in the timbered upper storey of the hall during the day and the shutters were open to admit snatches of cooler air. The sky through the aperture was a deep marine-blue. Sweat ran in delicate trickles down the declivity of her breasts and made her flanks shine as if she had just stepped from the sea. And he shone too, as wet as herself, his hair tangling and dripping at his brows and his eyes as dark as a river at night, running to the sea, swift and hard.

When he entered her there was pain, and she let it out on a single breath, indrawn hard and exhaled on a soft cry that welcomed the intrusion too. He held himself above her, suddenly still, his own breathing ragged and shallow. She touched his ribs, exploring each ridged contour and the breadth of his chest, then followed the breastbone down to the hollow of his diaphragm, and grew accustomed to the feel of him within her. She felt too stretched and full to move, and yet beyond the strange discomfort the sea song whispered of pleasure and of deep, muscular tides that waited the turn.

He spoke her name softly and took his weight on his left arm so that he could cup and stroke her face with his hand.

She turned her head and kissed his fingers. She would have asked him if this was it, had he found safe harbour and shelter, for she knew no different, but he lowered his head and sealed her lips with his own, pre-empting her question. His right hand moved to cup her breast, and his hips gently surged and retreated with the rhythm of the kiss and the motion of his thumb across her nipple. Isabelle wanted to gasp at the intensity of the feeling, but she couldn't because he would not relinquish the kiss. She clung to him and arched her body. The pain arrowed through her loins, but so did the pleasure, until her eyes widened and her voice mewed in her throat. Still he would not let her go and the relentless, gentle friction brought her to a precipice and held her there, trembling, desperate. And then she was tumbling fearfully, blissfully over the edge, and as her climax rippled through her loins he finally broke the kiss, buried his face against her throat, thrust hard, twice, and shuddered in her arms like a ship wrecking in a storm.

Stillness descended by degrees as harsh breathing softened and thundering heartbeat slowed. As Isabelle returned to herself she became aware of mingled twinges of pain and pleasure, like strings on a musician's lyre next to each other and softly plucked. There was the capacity for renewal of both. He raised up and, still within her, gazed down into her face.

"Jesu," he croaked. "That was a close-run race." He dipped his head to kiss and nuzzle her. "I haven't felt like this since I was a green youth…"

Warm gratification flooded Isabelle at his words. "So it was like your first time?" she teased shyly.

He laughed and it was strange to feel that mirth inside her. "Oh, nothing like it—for you at least, I hope. Lads of seventeen summers might have a great capacity for the sport and wander around with their pricks permanently to attention, but consideration and experience are sadly lacking…but tonight it was good to be reminded of that desperation." He eased from her body and, rolling to his side, pulled her against him. The faint breeze drawing from the window cooled the sweat on their bodies.

"I do not suppose that a man's first time is like a woman's," she murmured as he gently stroked the valley of her spine.

"No," he said and lifted his head to look at her with anxiety in his expression. "I know there must have been pain, but I hope you gained at least some pleasure."

Isabelle smiled and touched his face. "A little," she agreed mischievously. "Madam FitzReinier said to me that for a woman to conceive, she needs to enjoy the act of mating," she said, "otherwise her seed will not descend and mix with her husband's."

He gave an amused grunt. "Yes, I've heard that before. It's what the Saracens say. At Queen Eleanor's court in Poitou, when I was a young man, it was widely known. I'm not sure that the men were entirely convinced. The women liked the notion of being pleasured, but some of them were doubtful about being turned into mothers."

"And did you make any of them mothers?" she asked lightly.

He chuckled. "If I say that no woman grew a big belly because of me, you might infer that either I am an unskilled lover or not potent enough to sire a child." His hand slipped over the curve of her buttocks, drawing her against his groin. "I hope tonight I have proven that neither is true. No, when I was a young knight, I lay with women who knew how to protect themselves, and Clara was barren. Since we parted I've mostly slept alone. I suffered some troubled times at court and decided that taking a woman to bed would cause more trouble than the deed was worth. In the end it became a habit."

"Weren't you ever tempted to break it?" Isabelle murmured

sleepily. Lassitude was creeping through her limbs. She pressed closer to him in a snuggling movement.

"Not until now," he answered.

She recognised the courtliness of the response, but also something deeper, and lifted her head off his chest to look at him. His expression was relaxed, his eyes heavy with tiredness and satiation…and peace.

"Not until I found a safe harbour."

Thirty-four

I SPENT MUCH OF MY CHILDHOOD HERE," WILLIAM TOLD Isabelle. They were preparing to celebrate the marriage of Prince John to Havise, heiress of Gloucester. "My father was the seneschal and I and my brothers used to drop pebbles on each other from that window up there." He pointed through the open flaps of their tent towards an aperture high in the tower. "That was our chamber. It had red hangings on the walls and we all slept in one bed like a tumble of hound pups." His voice was nostalgic. "King Henry took Marlborough from my father soon after he came to the throne. I haven't set foot here since I was ten years old, and it feels strange." Very strange indeed, especially to think that Prince John would be spending his wedding night in William's former boyhood chamber, while William and his entourage slept in tents in the bailey with the rest of the court, Marlborough's keep being reserved for the royal entourages. Richard was back in England, the preparations for his crowning were well in hand, and he was making his way to London via some of his southerly holdings. On the morrow, the tents would be taken down and the court would progress to Windsor.

"But at least your family is to have Marlborough again," Isabelle said pragmatically. "Your brother has been entrusted it by the King. You can visit that chamber whenever you want."

William made a non-committal sound and took his sword-belt from Jean, saying that he could buckle it on himself. He had given Jack leave to go and spend time with his father who was camped in another part of the bailey. Father and son had awkward matters to discuss, given that John Marshal had also joined the ranks of the married, having recently wed the thirteen-year-old daughter of Sussex landholder Adam de Port. "It would not be the same," he said. "You can never go back." He latched the belt and tugged his tunic straight. "Ready to gild the lily?" he asked, holding out his arm to his wife.

She laid her hand upon his sleeve to show that she was. She was wearing her pink silk wedding gown. Although she had other fine dresses now, it was still her favourite. All that she had done was to embellish the sleeves with added embroidery of gold and pearls. "You are not comfortable here," she said. "You've been looking at the keep and circling like a dog that scents something amiss."

William rubbed the back of his neck. He was rapidly discovering how perceptive of his inner moods Isabelle was. A smile and a genial comment might fool the world at large but not his bride of six weeks. She would question him or touch him or give him a look and he would feel as if she had peeled away his skin and left him exposed to the air. "You are right," he admitted, "I do feel like a dog that scents something wrong, but were you to ask me what, I would have to say I do not know—unless it be the presence in one place of de Glanville, Longchamp, and Prince John. That's enough to raise the hackles of any hound!"

Isabelle looked thoughtful. "I was never fond of de Glanville, although he did nothing to harm me…"

"Beyond shearing the revenue of your estates to the bone while he could and paying himself from the proceeds," William said acidly. "Nor were you the only one. Wigain told me that he's guilty of embezzling more than fifteen thousand marks which should have gone into the exchequer."

Isabelle silently mouthed the amount, her eyes widening.

"Wigain does tend to elaborate, but usually about his love life and the size of his equipment. He's reliable when it comes to gossip. Being in Richard's household he's in a position to hear all kind of things." He shrugged. "De Glanville sets my teeth on edge, I admit, but he's no threat. He's pledged to accompany the King on his crusade and his time of influence is over. But Longchamp…" His lip curled. "He is a fine fiscal administrator and loyal to the King, and if that were all, I would embrace him, but he craves power and has so high a sense of his own worth that he views everyone else as if they are maggots crawling at his feet."

Isabelle could feel William's irritation in the rigidity of his forearm. Unlike her husband, she had had no exposure to Richard's chancellor until she had met the royal entourage when it convened at Winchester after Richard's landing from Normandy. Like William, Longchamp came from a family with higher ambitions than rank, and such a background automatically bred envy when royal favouritism was shown. She had been prepared to take Longchamp as she found him…and she found him just as William said. It made no matter that she was a great heiress: Longchamp's look had cut her down, telling her without words that he had little time but plenty of scorn for young women whatever their status. "And yet you must come to terms with him," she said. "What else can you do?"

William snorted with bleak amusement. "Do you really want to know?"

She gave a small laugh and pinched him.

As they stepped from the tent into the public domain, he said, "Supping with the devil is one alternative, but I don't know if my spoon is long enough, and the devil may well not want to sup with me."

Isabelle looked at him askance. "I do not suppose you're going to explain that remark, otherwise you wouldn't have spoken in riddles and put that closed look on your face."

"My face isn't closed."

"Yes it is," she said with amused resignation. "The more innocent and open you look, the deeper your thoughts go."

"I will tell you later."

"And I will hold you to it," she said, giving him fair warning, and then smiled and dipped a curtsey as they were joined by the Earl of Essex and his Countess, who had also emerged from their pavilion to go to mass and witness the wedding of the King's brother.

Isabelle sipped the wine. The taste was agreeable, but she wanted to keep a clear head. William said that the wine at old King Henry's court had been like drinking mud, and that in consequence it was rare to see a drunkard there unless he had access to his own supply. Richard was plainly more discerning, as was Prince John, and in consequence many folk were already in their cups. William was too experienced a hand to be one of them, for which Isabelle was glad. Wine made men swift to laugh and far too swift to take offence and draw steel. She had noticed that Prince John was not drinking much either, but then he was a bridegroom, and he had his duty to perform. His new wife, Havise of Gloucester, sat quietly beside him, her eyes downcast and her expression so determinedly blank that Isabelle could tell she was dreading the ordeal. One didn't need to school happiness from one's face but fear and antipathy were different matters. At least Prince John was said to be an experienced lover. Rumours of mistresses among the court women were probably true, and he had caused a scandal by bedding his own cousin, the daughter of Earl Hamelin de Warenne, and getting her with child.

Currently he was glancing laconically around Marlborough's great hall, fixing on this man and that in assessment. He caught her watching him and for a moment, trapped in his tawny stare, she felt like one of the live lambs with which the keepers at the tower had occasionally fed the lions. But then he dazzled her a smile, inclined his head, and his gaze moved on. Isabelle took a swift drink of wine to steady herself and choked. William bent round solicitously to ask if she was all right and she managed a weak reply. Suddenly she was very glad that she was not Havise of Gloucester.

The main courses of the feast were cleared away, leaving fruit, nuts, and subtleties on the trestles, and the musicians struck up a lively carole dance. Bride and groom rose to tread the first measure. John was light on his feet and kept easy time to the beat of the tabor. Havise was less sure of herself and several times tripped on her gown and missed steps. The dowager Queen joined the floor with Richard and others who were sober enough to dance, had an aptitude, or wished to honour the couple. As newlyweds themselves, William and Isabelle left the trestle to take part. Since the carole was progressive, Isabelle found herself having to be very nimble on her feet to avoid crushed toes, and had to turn her head from gusts of wine-laden breath. More than one lord thought she should be pleased to be congratulated on her recent marriage by a whiskery kiss and she had to tread a path between diplomacy and self-preservation. She partnered King Richard, who was flushed with drink but still in command of his faculties and a graceful dancer. Although he smiled at her, she knew he was looking through her and that any woman could have stood before him and he would not have known the difference. John, however, was well aware of her presence as he took Richard's place. His hand touched her waist, his hazel eyes flirted, and such was the charisma of his body that her spine tingled. "William Marshal is a fortunate man," he said, glinting her a smile. "He's been landing on his feet all the years that I've known him, and he's done it again."

"My lord?" Isabelle said and prepared to move on.

"I could have had you, and he could have had Havise." There was malice in the curl of the handsome mouth.

"Then I am a most fortunate woman, for I might have had you," Isabelle replied, smiling too.

John's laughter followed her to her next partner. What a foolish thing to say, she chastised herself. She was going to have to be more circumspect.

"Sister…" The next man bowed to her as she pressed her palm to his and with a start she realised that she was partnering her husband's eldest brother. Another John, another man to be handled carefully. He had come to Winchester to bow to Richard, but his allegiance was to the Prince. He and William had embraced with smiles, but there had been an underlying friction and Isabelle was still trying to unravel the bond between them. She suspected that John Marshal was envious of William but trying not to be; that he was an ambitious man who hoped to profit from his position in Prince John's retinue. He had recently been promised the shrievalty of York and had been at pains to insist that the appointment was by his own merits and not at William's behest. Whether men believed him or not was another matter and, she suspected, a sore point.

"Brother," she responded as they pressed palms together and turned. He was only two years older than William, but the difference seemed more like ten for William looked young for his age, with only a few silver hairs amid the brown and skin still tight to his bones. There were deep vertical furrows between John Marshal's brows and where William's mouth curved up at the corners, John's curved down. A small paunch filled out his good wool tunic, whereas, despite his capacious appetite, William still had the lean flanks of a hound. "You must be pleased to be named seneschal of Marlborough," she said.

He gave her a wintry smile. "Indeed I am, since it was an office my father held many years ago and he was unfairly deprived of it."

Isabelle noted the tone. William's brother clearly felt that Marlborough was no more than his due.

Later she danced with John Marshal's wife in a carole involving the sexes dancing in two rings, men to the left, women to the right. Aline de Port was a little over thirteen years old, a pale, slender creature, her breasts scarcely budding against the tight lacing of her silk gown and her hips as narrow as a child's. William had told Isabelle that his brother had not bedded her. Although the girl had had her first flux, she was still physically immature and were she to quicken now, she would likely die and the child with her. Isabelle suppressed a shiver at the thought. She was a fully developed woman, robust and healthy, but she felt trepidation when she thought of giving birth—an ordeal that seemed ever more probable with each day that her flux continued overdue.

The dance ended on a flourish, with the participants almost running the steps and Isabelle took a moment away to recover her breath. Aline joined her, declaring that she was thirsty and gulping down a brimming cup of wine. Thin tendrils of mouse-fair hair had escaped net and wimple to curl around her flushed face. Sipping from her own goblet, Isabelle asked her sister-in-law how she was finding the married state.

Aline shrugged. "I like the court," she said in a high, almost transparent voice. "And I like my fine gowns." It was her third cup of wine and she was swaying on her feet. "I didn't want to marry him but my mother said that because he's so much older than me, he'll die after a few years and then I can pay a fine and wed whom I choose."

Isabelle almost choked. When she had been told she was to marry William, it had been the first thought that had run through her head. But she was older than Aline and William was younger than John, and in the six weeks since her marriage, she had thanked God every day for her own situation.

"I have my own chamber," Aline babbled on, "and he has his. I know he has women there sometimes, but it doesn't bother me. While he's making the beast with two backs with them, he isn't making it with me."

"No," said Isabelle faintly, unsure how else to respond.

"He's got a proper mistress. I know all about her. She won't make the beast with two backs with him either. She says that it's a sin outside of marriage and that's the reason why their baby died. But he still visits her and pays for her keep. It's good of him to make provision...he's a good man..." Her voice faltered and wisped away like a fine trail of smoke. From being flushed she had begun to turn a delicate shade of green. Isabelle hastily escorted her from the keep and held her while she vomited up the wine that she had drunk to the detriment of both stomach and tongue.

With soothing voice and gentle guidance Isabelle returned Aline to her tent on the sward. The girl's maids came hastening to attend to her, but Isabelle sat with her awhile, feeling sorry for her and also a little irritated. And because she was irritated, she felt guilty too. There but for the grace of God went all brides...and many bridegrooms too.

"Poor lass," William said later in their tent when she told him about her encounter with Aline. He dismissed his squires and sat down on his campstool to remove his boots. "But her circumstances could be worse. My brother indulges her and he hasn't bedded her—which he is within his rights to do, young as she is. He brought her with him to court, which he didn't have to do."

"Her family would object strongly if he didn't," Isabelle said sharply. "Her presence hasn't stopped him from entertaining whores in his chamber."

William reached for her and drew her into his lap. "I don't condone what he does, but perhaps he seeks more than release of the body."

"He won't find that with a whore," she sniffed.

"Mayhap a semblance if she knows her trade and has some touch of compassion. Certainly he won't find it with that child-wife of his, and he can't turn to Alais. That road is strewn with too many thorns." He unfastened her veil and drew out the golden pins securing the jewelled net. "Your hair," he said as her braids tumbled down, heavy as rope, glossy as silk. "I love your hair. I want daughters with your hair…" He buried his face in its softness.

She closed her eyes, her heart full, her loins liquid. The words were in her mouth that he might soon be getting that wish, when the tent opening flapped back and the evening breeze ruffled the interior, guttering the candles. His complexion as red as fire, Jean stepped inside. He avoided looking at Isabelle as she sprang from William's lap, her tresses wild and the neck opening of her gown unfastened.

"My lord, I…" was as far as he got for hard on his heels came Prince John, who, as far as everyone knew, should have been enjoying his wedding night. William's brother John followed him into the tent, his expression one of discomfort and unease. Isabelle curtseyed. William rose slowly to his feet and in his own time made his obeisance to the Prince.

The latter gave a mocking smile. "I am sorry to disturb your privacy, Marshal. You at least seem to be enjoying your bride." He inclined his head to Isabelle, his gaze frankly admiring her state of dishabille. "Had I thought about it properly, I would have pushed Richard to give me the de Clare lands instead."

William gestured his squire to bring more stools. "A good thing for me that you did not," he replied. "To what do I owe the honour of this visit? It must be important if it brings you from your marriage bed."

"Conspiracy is infinitely more interesting than futtering, don't you think?" John said and taking the foldstool from the wide-eyed squire, opened it out and straddled it. "You can go," he said.

Jean looked to William, who curtly nodded his head.

The Prince flicked his gaze to Isabelle. "My lady stays," William said coldly. "She is mine to me and the de Clare lands are hers."

John shrugged. "As you wish, but remember that women's tongues need a firm bridle."

"I trust my wife as I trust the Queen your lady mother—with my life and my honour," William answered impassively. "The tongues that have done me the most damage throughout my life have been those of other men." He rose to his feet, took Isabelle's hand and made her sit in his chair. She gave him a quick look through her lashes compounded of pride and trepidation. Gathering her hair in her hands she swiftly tied it back with one of the ribbons from her loosened braid, but made no effort to don wimple or veil, thus saying without words that this was her and William's private domain and that she would do as she pleased within it.

"Supping with the devil," William mouthed at her in such a way that she was the only one to see. Her gaze widened briefly before she lowered it to her lap and clasped her hands.

"As you wish," Prince John said, although he was plainly not overjoyed.

"What can I do for you, my lord?" William asked. "If this is about my wife's Irish lands, then I'll be glad to have the matter resolved." He sat on the rope-framed bed and folded his arms. As lord of Ireland, the Prince had rewarded his followers with fiefs in Leinster that were rightly under Isabelle's jurisdiction, and was proving loath to return that authority to her estate.

"No," the Prince said curtly, "we can deal with that issue later. That isn't why I've come, and you know it."

William shrugged. "It did strike me as strange that you would abscond your marriage bed to discuss Ireland," he replied.

The Prince looked annoyed and William's brother stepped into the breach. "What my lord has to say is of great concern to us both," he said. "You would do well to listen."

William spread his hands. "You have my attention."

For a moment the Prince looked as if he might leave, but he restrained himself, his irritation revealed in the choleric flare of his nostrils. "While my brother is on crusade, he intends to leave his lands in the hands of justiciars fit for the purpose."

That much was obvious and William said nothing, merely rubbed his chin and waited.

"Some of those men are as good as appointed. Others will buy their way in. Richard has virtually every office in England up for sale." John flicked William a keen glance. "William Longchamp will play a leading role. Richard's made him Bishop of Ely and that means Longchamp's fingers will be in the fiscal pie. It's always the tradition that Ely watches the coffers."

William nodded, still wary, but more interested now. "I heard from the Queen that the senior justiciars were likely to be the Earl of Essex and the Bishop of Durham," he said.

"And if either of them should fail, then who do you think will step into the breach?" Prince John rose to his feet, paced the tent, and turned. "Longchamp will take advantage in any way he can."

So will you, William thought, eyeing his royal visitor impassively.

The Prince sighed. "I can see you are hostile, Marshal, and I can understand that. You think ill of me because of my father, but I had to make some difficult decisions. If I chose differently to you, that does not mean that you are right and I am wrong."

"No, my lord," William said stiffly, knowing that he would never forgive John for abandoning his father on his deathbed. Whatever his reasons, none could be strong enough—not even fear for his own life. The Bible said that love was as strong as death, but that applied to honour too.

The Prince's gaze hardened. "How would you feel if you were subject to the tyranny of William Longchamp? Which of us would you choose then?"

"My choice is Richard."

"Who will be gone years at best. I'm not asking you to compromise yourself, just to think. My bride has vouchsafed me lands throughout the south-west of England. Your brother has lands there too as well as being granted custody of Marlborough and the shrievalty of York. With your Giffard manors and the estates of Striguil, you can either add your strength to mine, or oppose me—should we come to trouble...I am making contingency plans, no more than that."

There was always more than that with John, William thought cynically, and yet the Prince did have a point. Once Richard was gone, even if his lands remained stable and well governed, there were bound to be power struggles and every man would have to decide who were his allies and who were not.

"The shrievalty of Gloucester is for sale at a cost of fifty marks," John said softly. "That means the control of Gloucester Castle and the Forest of Dean. You are in great favour with my brother. He'll sell it to you willingly."

"And if I do this and then choose to oppose you?"

John shrugged. "Then you would be mad. My brother is

keen to promote the Marshal family, but Longchamp is not. We may not always see eye to eye, but it makes sense for us to do so now." He rose to his feet and went to the tent flap. "Think on what I have said. My mother would tell you it's good advice."

'Perhaps I should consult her then."

John gave an arid smile. "Do so. She will doubtless warn you against me, but she is no lover of William Longchamp either. She has no time for men who do not see the sunrise in her face. I bid you goodnight. I have my duty, as you have your pleasure." He lifted a sardonic eyebrow in farewell to Isabelle.

There was a short silence after he had gone. John Marshal cleared his throat and pushed his hands through his greying hair. "He's right. We should look to our own interests. You should ask Richard to give you Gloucester. He won't deny you. Fifty marks is no great sum." His tone was brittle and edgy, like a man on the eve of a battle campaign, and it filled William with unease.

"But a price to be paid." He looked at Isabelle. "What do you think?"

John Marshal blinked, plainly surprised that William should consult his wife.

Isabelle chewed her lip. "I think it would be a good thing to offer for Gloucester," she said after a moment. "The more powerful you become, the more choices you have. Prince John is the King's only adult heir and your overlord for your Irish lands. You need to tread a careful path, neither leaning too far towards him, but not rejecting his overtures either. The men with the best sense of balance are going to be the ones who remain intact."

John Marshal stared at her with a dropped jaw. William's expression was one of pride and admiration. "I agree," he said. "I have given my oath to King Richard and I will hold by it until death, but I must protect myself as well." He looked at his brother. "As Isabelle says, we must tread carefully. I will not condone any attempt by the Prince to take the crown whilst his brother is gone, but the more land and influence we have as a family, the better protected we are." He poured himself a cup of wine and swilled his mouth as if to rid himself of the taste of his words.

John Marshal shrugged. "I will do what I must," he said. "You protect me from Richard if it becomes necessary, and I will do what I can to smooth your path with John…and hope that none of it comes to pass."

William nodded. "Pray God," he said.

When his brother had left, William sighed and rubbed his palms over his face. "Jesu, I begin to think I should have stayed in Kendal."

Isabelle came to him. Picking up his wine from the coffer, she took a drink herself. "No," she said. "You would never have warmed your hands at such a small fire. You know that." She handed him the cup. "You said to me at Stoke that you were preparing for the storms ahead. This is the first squall and it may well blow over. Whatever happens, you should take Gloucester."

William drank, set the cup aside, and lay down on the bed, his arms pillowed behind his head. Isabelle leaned over him, unbound her hair again, and let it tumble around them, scented like a distant rose garden.

Thirty-five

DRAWING REIN, WILLIAM SUCKED CRYSTALLINE AIR THROUGH his teeth and gazed at the massive walls rising out of the frozen winter haze. Ermine snow puffed the ground, bordering the rough grey silk of the River Wye. Deeper snowfall was threatening in the yellowing clouds and the light was fast spiralling away from midday towards dusk.

"Striguil," he said on a billow of dragon's breath. "Thank God." He curled his mittened fists around the bridle and wondered how stiff his knees would be by the time he attained the keep.

"Cold enough to freeze the tits off a witch and the cock off a warlock," said his knight Alan de Saint Georges.

William's lips twitched. "Let us hope for their sakes there are not many of them around here then, hmmm?"

Roger D'Abernon spat over the side of his saddle. "William Longchamp would certainly be cockless if he ventured away from his hearth—spawn of hell."

William said nothing. He had been attending on King Richard for the past four months, himself and his brother given prominent positions at the royal counsel table. Isabelle had spoken of storms and there had been plenty of those to weather. Richard was opinionated and volatile. At times, with so many offices for sale, government had been more like a session of beast trading at London's Smithfield Fair. Factions were rife, and although everyone smiled at everyone else, or at least strove to be civil, the knives were out and awaiting an unguarded moment. In spite of the dangers and tribulations, William was enjoying his new responsibilities. As a household knight, he had had limited authority, much of it grounded in his military prowess. Now his opinions were sought and weighed in full counsel rather than on an informal basis. His brother's too, although John was less adept at playing courtly politics and put on the defensive by Richard's chancellor Longchamp who seemed to take a particular pleasure in baiting him. William's eyes narrowed in response to his thoughts. Longchamp's contempt for the Marshals was thinly disguised beneath a veneer of strained courtesy. However much William mistrusted him, Prince John had been right. Longchamp would bear watching—especially now.

Wrapped in a fur-lined cloak, Isabelle was waiting in the bailey to greet him and William's heart swelled with pleasure to see her. Her cheeks and lips were flushed with cold. Showing below her veil, her gold braids were lustrous and as heavy as ripe corn, and through the opening in her cloak, her body showed a glimpse of fruitfulness too, just beginning to round.

The groom led William's horse away to the stables and in the purple dusk, as the first stars of snow began to fall, William embraced his wife with tender hunger. She kissed him, oblivious of the audience of knights and retainers. "I was counting down the days to Christmas and beginning to wonder if you would arrive in time," she said.

William laughed with wryness and pleasure. "I was counting down the days too. I've missed you hard." His look grew concerned. "How have you been faring? You look beautiful."

Isabelle pressed her hand lightly over her womb. "I am beginning to look as if I have done nothing but sit by the fire and eat bread pudding," she answered ruefully, "but I am well. The sickness stopped soon after I arrived at Striguil."

William nodded and felt relieved. Isabelle had wanted to remain at court with him, but she had been unwell in the early months of her pregnancy and as the court was constantly on the move, she had had little opportunity for rest. While Queen Eleanor was sympathetic to Isabelle's condition, she had not wanted a puking pregnant woman attending on her. William had to stay with Richard and he had deemed it best for Isabelle to go to Striguil. She was its Countess; she could take fealty of her vassals, make treaties with her neighbours, see to the interests of the earldom, and at the same time rest in one place.

"The child has quickened," she told him as she led him towards the hall. "Not that you can feel with the palm of your hand as yet, but I have felt him stirring within my womb."

"Him?" William said with a smile.

Isabelle nodded with calm serenity. "It will be a son," she said.

William gazed at the keep as they approached it. The entrance was via a timber stair that led up to a decorated entrance with a guardroom to the left and a door to an undercroft beneath. The castle had been built by the Norman warlord William FitzOsbern in the years immediately following the Norman Conquest and although some work had been done to keep it strong, William thought that there was room for expansion and improvement. The great hall itself was a large rectangle set above the storeroom, with a fire burning in a large central hearth. Benches occupied niches created by decorative blind arches cut into the walls. Banners and hangings draped the white plasterwork, and an array of painted shields, alternating round and kite-shaped, English and Norman. A doorway at the end of the hall gave on to an external stair while an internal stair led to the private quarters set into the roof space and it was to this that Isabelle drew William.

The room above could hardly be called a solar, although there were a couple of squints looking out on to the river side of the keep. The space was divided into two rooms by a heavy woollen curtain—an antechamber for attendants and an inner sanctum where the lord and lady could enjoy a modicum of privacy. The latter was cosy with the heat of several charcoal braziers and there was a large bed, lined with straw and piled with two thick feather mattresses. Isabelle's painted marriage coffer stood beside it and another large wooden chest for William's gear. A cradle of polished cherry wood nestled in a corner. William went to look at it, tried to imagine it filled with a baby, and felt his stomach wallow with anticipation and fear. Not wanting to show the latter to Isabelle, he busied himself removing his cloak and hood. His squires had followed them upstairs with items of baggage and Isabelle's ladies waited unobtrusively in the background. William dismissed them all. Later he would take proper stock of Striguil and attend to outstanding business. Later he would have time for others, but just now he was feeling rather selfish.

William laid his hand on Isabelle's softly rounded belly and kissed her throat beneath her loose, fair hair. Her pulse thundered in time with his heartbeat and her breath was as short as his as they slowly returned from the pleasure of rediscovering each other's bodies. He laughed softly. "I have gone for years without the comfort of a woman in my bed," he told her, "but now, after two months away from you, I feel like a green boy with his first woman."

"You said that before, at Stoke," Isabelle said huskily.

"Well, it's true. It is what you do to me."

"You didn't feel like a green boy to me."

"But too hasty…"

"Not for me. You have been two months away from me

also." She stroked his face. "We have all the winter's night before us, and a double feather mattress and warm furs…there is time for leisure as well as haste."

Her words, her light, deliberate touch, brought weakness and warmth to William's limbs and he wrapped her in his arms and kissed her again. Isabelle responded fervently, then pulled away and laughed as William's stomach rumbled as loudly as distant thunder.

"Shame on me," she said, "for putting my own desires before the needs of a starving man!"

"That would depend on what I was starving for the most," William interrupted with a lazy smile, "but I wouldn't refuse food now, especially if I've to spend the night in leisure and haste. Besides," he added, sobering and reaching for the furred robe lying half on the bed, half on the floor, "there are things I have to tell you, and it'll be easier whilst eating than making love." Rising, he went to a low trestle table where food and drink had been set out. A leek and almond pottage had been keeping hot under a small brazier of coals and there was wheaten bread freshly baked, soft and fresh. Whatever refinements the sturdy, dour Striguil was lacking, Isabelle's cook was not one of them. William had known he was hungry, but hadn't realised the extent of the hollow feeling in his stomach until he sat down and began to eat. Isabelle joined him, and if William had had any lingering doubts about the state of her health, it was dissipated by the sight of her tucking into the food almost as heartily as himself. He hoped that what he was about to tell her would not destroy her appetite.

"So," Isabelle said as she broke another morsel of bread and dipped it in her rapidly vanishing pottage, "what do you have to tell me that is better suited to soup than coupling?"

William snorted at her words. "I am not sure that it is suited to either activity." He let his own spoon rest. "The Earl of

Essex is dead, God rest his soul." He crossed himself. "Of a quartan fever in Normandy."

Isabelle crossed herself too, her expression filling with distress for the man she had known and liked, and then, with the dismay of a deeper realisation. "He was to be the joint justiciar," she said.

"Richard has appointed William Longchamp in his place." William made a face. "The choice was not unexpected, but it's still a blow. The only consolation is that four sub-justiciars have been appointed to regulate those who might be tempted to abuse their power with Richard gone."

"Then I hope such men are our allies." Isabelle set her bowl aside. She fixed William with a sombre gaze.

William smiled diffidently. "Well, one is at least," he said, "because Richard has appointed me to a position. We are answerable only to him and the Queen."

Isabelle's eyes widened. "That is excellent news!" Her expression brightened. "Who are the others?"

He told her, leaning forward and taking her hands, and she was pleased to hear the names. William Briwerre, Geoffrey FitzPeter, and Roger FitzReinfrey were men of similar ilk to her husband, raised through the ranks and of trusted mettle. Longchamp was trusted mettle too and of humble background, but in his case he had sought to eradicate that stigma by behaving as if he had been born royal. "Of course," William added with a grimace, "as well as Longchamp, we'll have to keep an eye on the ambitions of Prince John and there is bound to be friction between the two of them. You saw the posturing before you left court."

"But you can do it," she said with conviction. "You have the strength."

"I suppose I'll find that out, won't I?"

Isabelle narrowed her eyes and decided that his tone bespoke assurance rather than uncertainty. He had changed in the months they had been apart. It was as if a sword had been taken from the armoury and honed on a grindstone until its edge was blue and keen.

He drained his wine and refused her offer of more. "I'm summoned to attend the King in Normandy before Eastertide," he said, glancing at her belly. "It's going to be hard leaving you behind."

"Then bring me with you," Isabelle said.

He started to shake his head but she pre-empted him. "It was right that I came to Striguil in October. I was greensick and, besides, it was necessary for one of us to take fealty of the vassals, but I am well now; I want to come with you."

William opened his mouth, but again she stole his words. "I could take homage of the Longueville vassals in Normandy. Let them now see their lady and the store she sets by the father of their future heir."

He considered the point and had to agree. Her presence in Normandy would certainly advance his position with the Norman vassals who were hers by right of blood.

"Not only that," she said, "but I can rest at Longueville while you are in service to the King and you can escape to me there whenever you can."

William gave an admiring laugh and shook his head. "My love, you should have been sitting in the counsel chamber in my stead. I'm certain that you would have run rings around William Longchamp."

Isabelle gave a shudder. "To the contrary, my sickness would have continued. He reminds me of a black hairy blowfly."

The analogy made William grin with appreciation, although he wasn't really amused. With his heavy black hair growing wild around his tonsure, his long black beard and bright black eyes, Longchamp did indeed resemble a corpse fly—annoying and dangerous and giving no respite to his victims. The only hope was in swatting him when he was too bloated to avoid the blow. "His downfall will come," he said. "I have no doubt of that, but we have to be careful that ours doesn't precede his. It is like the tourney. You have to be able to control your lance and your horse without thinking and then you have to know when to launch yourself into the fray and when to hold something back." He pushed his cup and bowl aside and went to unlatch the shutters and peer out through the squint on a world of whirling whiteness.

Isabelle joined him and stood on tiptoe to peer over his shoulder. "A good thing you arrived when you did," she said. "Otherwise you'd have had to turn back for Gloucester. It looks as if we're going to be snowed in for a while."

"I'm sure we can find things to do," William said, setting his arm around her thickening waist.

Thirty-six

LONGUEVILLE, NORMANDY, APRIL 1190

WILLIAM CLATTERED INTO THE COURTYARD AT Longueville at a gallop, flung down from his sweating courser while still reining the beast back, and strode into the keep. There was something so close to frenzy in his gait that the servants eyed him askance. Ignoring them, he ran up the twisting stairs, almost losing his footing but refusing to slow. His chest was pounding, his breath roaring as he reached the level, strode down the passage, and came to the bedchamber. Setting his shoulder to the door, he burst inside.

Several pairs of female eyes turned in surprise and shock at his precipitous entry. His wife, whom he had expected to see in bed, was kneeling Madonna-like on the floor, bathing a tiny pink skinned rabbit in a shallow bronze basin. The rabbit was squeaking. Isabelle's hair hung free to her waist and she was dressed in her chemise and a loose bedrobe. Her dark blue gaze had widened in alarm, but seeing William, she smiled. She raised the rabbit from the bowl, wrapped it gently in the towel that a maid was holding out, and crossed the room to him.

"I told you it would be a son," she said. "He has been christened William to follow in your name." She placed the bundle in his arms and took a moment to issue orders to her ladies with a few hand gestures and murmured words.

William gazed down into the baby's face. He had been attending on Richard when a messenger from Longueville had arrived on a lathered horse to tell him that his wife was safely delivered of a son. Richard had given him brief leave to return home and see his heir—although the way he felt just now, permission or not, he would have left anyway. He had tried to outride his demons on the way here, but no matter how relentless his pace, they had kept up with him. Now, for a moment, they receded as he gazed into the pink, wizened face of his newborn son and marvelled anew at the wonder of God's creation. Even unformed and without definition, he could recognise Isabelle in the feathery pale brows and the little cleft on the chin. A small arm wriggled free of the towel and waved with determination but no purpose. William captured the miniature hand in his and was himself captured. He swallowed a constriction in his throat and looked at Isabelle. There were tears in her eyes too, and a tremulous smile on her lips. He drew her to his free side and kissed her. "This is the greatest gift you could have given me," he said hoarsely.

She gave a wobbly laugh. "Better than Striguil, Leinster, and Longueville?"

"Better than all those," he said. "You do not know…" He swallowed again and forced control on himself. "How are you faring? Should you not still be abed?" Looking at her more closely, he noticed the shadows beneath her eyes.

Isabelle threw a defiant look at one of the midwives who was nodding agreement with William's remark. "I am sore and tired," she admitted, "but women of less degree have to bear their children and begin work again the next day. If I had stayed a moment longer abed, I would have set with boredom."

The baby's squeaks had subsided to soft murmurs and William saw that his son was on the edge of sleep, one little hand still curled around his wide tanned thumb. Isabelle took the baby gently from her husband, bore him to the cradle, and laid him on the soft fleece lining. He gave a few sleepy, protesting cries, but as she set the cradle rocking with the gentle rhythm of a moored craft on a summer river, he drowsed off to sleep.

William watched entranced. "I think adult beds should have rockers too," he said. While he had been occupied with his wife and child, Isabelle's women had been preparing a bathtub. His squires had arrived and were duly brought to view their lord's new heir. Jack was indifferent, Jean regarded the infant with an expression compounded of fear and fascination.

"It's all right," William grinned. "I won't hold it against you if you don't think he is the most beautiful thing you have ever seen—although my wife might. As long as you pledge him your loyalty, I'm content."

"He's so small," Jean said in a wondering voice.

"He was quite big enough," Isabelle answered with mock severity. "Don't leave your lord standing there in his sweat. There is a bath prepared and food to hand."

A tad sheepishly, the squires went to attend William, taking his sword and spurs, and handing the clothing he discarded to the maids for laundering. William dismissed them with a wave of his hand. "We've ridden hard," he said. "Put away my weapons and then take your own food. You can have the bathwater when I'm done, if you want."

Isabelle had seated herself on a cushioned bench running parallel to the foot of their bed and was watching him thoughtfully. William ducked his head under the water and sluiced his hair, but there came a point where he had to raise his head and look at her. It was ridiculous when he thought about it. At court he could dissemble with the best and the skill came to him as naturally as breathing. But Isabelle could see straight through to his core and was not content to let him conceal things.

"You might as well tell me what nest of serpents you are sitting on," she said. "I will find out sooner or later. Why should I have the double ordeal of worrying about what it is that you won't say?"

William pressed water from his eyes and faced her with a sigh. "I hope that you have a wet nurse at the ready lest what I tell you curdle your milk."

Isabelle raised an eyebrow. "That bad?"

"There have been more riots in England against the Jews…"

Her face filled with dismay. "I thought that King Richard put a stop to it after the massacre at his coronation." She shivered at the memory. An attempt by the London Jews to present Richard with a gift had been misunderstood. Blows had been struck and a frightening anti-Semitic riot had ensued. Richard had been furious with the mob and had issued strict orders for the protection of his Jewish communities for they were a vital source of wealth and revenue to the Crown.

"Richard thought so too," William said grimly. He rested his arms on the edge of the tub and took the wine that Jean had poured for him. "But the moment he sailed from England, the riots started again. First in Lynn, then in Norwich and Stamford and Lincoln." He drank deeply from his cup. "The Lincoln riots were quelled sharply enough because the sheriff and the Bishop knew what they were about and took the Jews into their protection in the castle but in York it was a different story." He glanced towards his squires, but they were busy eating and talking to Isabelle's maids.

"York?" Isabelle's brows twitched together, and then comprehension dawned. "Your brother…" She raised one hand to her lips.

He lowered his voice. "…couldn't organise a drinking session in a tavern but managed very easily to mishandle a mob into massacring every last Jew in the damned city."

Her eyes grew huge. "No," she said against the pressure of her fingers.

William finished the wine, his expression harsh.

"How did it happen?"

"You do not want to know."

"Tell me!" she demanded. "I have a strong stomach."

"So do I, but not for this, especially here in my private sanctuary with my wife and newborn son. Suffice to say that the mob attacked the Jews who then took refuge in a tower of the castle. My brother was summoned to quell the riot." William shook his head, his expression filled with revulsion. "Instead, he lost control. His own soldiers joined the besiegers and when the Jews realised there was no succour to hand they took their own lives...men, women, children...babies."

Isabelle swallowed saliva, her stomach suddenly queasy. Even if the Jews were infidels and sinners, the image of a despairing mother sealing off her baby's nose and mouth, or a man slitting his own wife's throat, was shocking. Pushing her maid to one side she rose to her feet and stumbled to the window arch where she drew deep, slow breaths until the nausea subsided. Her womb twinged with the aftercramps of childbirth and she felt the slow trickle of blood between her legs. In the cradle, the baby snuffled in his sleep and Isabelle felt the pressure of tears behind her eyes.

"I should not have told you," William said remorsefully as he left the tub.

"Yes you should." Her voice wobbled. "It's not something you can hide under the bed like a ball of fluff, is it?" She returned to her bench, her legs weak and trembling. To steady herself, she set her mind to practical matters. "So what is the consequence of this?" she asked. "What has Richard said?"

William tucked a towel around his waist and used another to dry his face and chest. "Richard exploded like a cauldron over a hot fire with the lid too tight," he replied. "Not only has he been disobeyed the moment he turned his back, he's lost all that revenue from the Jews. My fool of a brother is summoned to attend on him and explain how he managed to handle events so badly." He inhaled deeply. "And William Longchamp has been sent to England with a mandate to restore order."

Worse and worse, Isabelle thought.

"You know what he'll do." William flung a towel into the corner laundry heap. "He'll strip my brother of the office of sheriff, and John will have no one to blame but himself. Longchamp's bringing his own brother with him, so who do you think is going to take over the position of sheriff of York?"

"Jesu!" Isabelle breathed. "Is there nothing to be done?"

"For the moment, no. Longchamp has the King's mandate and, having seen the rage Richard was in when he heard about York and the other cities, I doubt that he'll relent and reinstate my brother. I can try to rectify the damage with diplomacy, but Richard is in no mood to listen at the moment." He rumpled his hands through his damp hair. "Christ, it's a mess."

'Does your brother have a reason to hate the Jews? Is he in debt to them?"

"Not as far as I know, but then what do I know of John? I wouldn't have thought him capable of such idiocy, but he is." William went to look at his sleeping son. "My father used to say that someone ought to explode a barrel of pitch under John to ignite his wits, but it looks as if they've been scattered to the four winds instead." He sighed at Isabelle. "I suppose that mutual support is an obligation of brotherhood, but John sometimes makes it very hard indeed. We could have done without Longchamp sticking his finger in the pie at York."

"You can say nothing to me that I have not already said to myself," John Marshal told William and Isabelle. He had arrived at Longueville en route to join Richard and face the royal ire. Since William was preparing to return to the court, the Marshal brothers would at least arrive together and united. In the circumstances, William thought it fortuitous and the best he could do, but he wasn't prepared to forgive his brother's crass stupidity easily.

"How much do you care to wager?" William growled. They were sitting in William's chamber, the great bed made up with its day covers and the hangings secured back. "If Richard does not string you up by your thumbs, you will be fortunate. How did you let it happen? God's bones, the sheriff of Lincoln managed to save his Jews from the mob!"

"Well, I'm not Gerard de Camville and my wife's no Nicolaa de la Haye," John snapped. The whites of his eyes were veined with red and there were deep pouches of sleeplessness beneath them.

William raised an eyebrow. Nicolaa de la Haye was a formidable woman of similar years to themselves, brisk, forthright, and personable. But what concern wives were in this instance was not immediately clear to William.

"I thought it would burn itself out if I let them have their way a little." John gave William a belligerent look from beneath his brows. "You didn't feel the hatred blistering off the mob. Rather they should turn it on the Jews than a Christian sheriff."

Jesu," William said through his teeth and suppressed the urge to strike his brother in the mouth. "What sort of a commander of men are you? What sort of a cowa—" He clamped his mouth on the rest of the word, but John knew full well what he had been going to say and colour rose up his throat and into his face.

"You weren't there," John snarled. "Let he who is without sin cast the first stone. It's a setback. I'm still castellan of Marlborough. You still have Gloucester."

William's jaw was aching with the strain of holding back the words. Suddenly he felt very weary, as if he had been sparring all day and gained neither advantage nor improvement in skill—a waste. "I suppose that Longchamp has installed his brother as the new sheriff of York?"

"It won't last," John said moodily. He too looked as if he had fought all day for nothing beyond a deadening of the soul. "I may have had my punishment for mishandling the York riots, but Longchamp's arrogance will be his downfall."

"As your incompetence might be ours," William said irritably.

"And of course you're infallible...the flawless knight, the perfect courtier, the greatest that's ever lived outside a minstrel's lay," John snarled. "Only you know what deeds lie on the other side of that coin!"

William recoiled from the accusation as if from a striking snake. The baby woke in his cradle and began to wail with fretful hunger. John jumped at the sound and then huddled into himself as if protecting a wound. Going to the cradle, Isabelle lifted her son in her arms. Retiring a little from the men, her back turned to her brother-in-law for modesty, she put him to suck. John studied mother and child with bitter eyes. "My wife miscarried of a son during the riots at York," he said.

William stared at his brother. "Jesu, John." He couldn't keep the revulsion from his expression or his voice. "I thought you weren't going to bed her yet?"

John flushed. "She'd begun her fluxes," he said defensively, and rubbed his hands together as if washing them. "She took me to task over one of the Marlborough whores I'd had in my bed and I said that she'd not like the alternative."

William's nostrils flared. "You raped her?"

John shook his head in vigorous negation. "Why do you think the worst of me? No, I didn't rape her! She was willing to do her duty—insistent, in fact, for it was she who came to me. I was drunk and I hurt her, but it wasn't rape. I wish it hadn't happened but sometimes things unravel despite the best of intentions. I didn't touch her again, but once was enough. At least she didn't die."

Isabelle looked over her shoulder, her underlip caught in her teeth. "Oh, John," she said softly with appalled dismay and compassion.

"You wouldn't want to walk a mile in my shoes just now," he said wearily and stood up. "I'll wait for you in the courtyard."

"God's bones," William cursed as the door closed behind John. He released the tension of the moment in a long shudder and crossing the chamber began jerkily to gird on his sword. Isabelle finished feeding the baby, handed him to the nurse, and hastened to her husband. William adjusted the weight of the blade at his hip and took her in his arms, resting his chin on the top of her head. "I lost my temper," he said. "I should not have done that."

"Better than letting the anger fester within you," she replied. "You had to say those things to him for both your sakes."

He was silent for a moment, then he sighed. "He is right though. There is a reverse side to the coin of my honour."

She tightened her grip on his arms. "Then that makes you a whole man, and I count your honour untarnished."

William regarded her with a deep swelling of affection. She was half his age, yet she had a feminine wisdom that outstripped his own paltry efforts at sagacity. "Ah, Isabelle," he said softly, and kissed her with gratitude and tenderness before going out to find his brother.

Thirty-seven

LONDON, CHRISTMAS 1190

*I*SABELLE WATCHED HER SON CRAWL ACROSS THE FLOOR OF Madam FitzReinier's solar towards the coloured ball she had just rolled for him. Occasionally his coordination failed and he shuffled backwards or had to pause to decide which limb to move next, but he was determined.

"Men are so delightful at this age," declared Madam FitzReinier. "What a pity they have to grow up."

Isabelle laughed. "There's some truth in that," she agreed, "although I shall enjoy watching him develop. I wonder if he'll look like William."

"Likely so," said Madam FitzReinier. "He has the same good nature."

"Oh, you haven't seen him yet when he's tired and hungry," Isabelle said.

"The babe or your husband?" the dame jested.

Isabelle giggled. "No, they're not at all the same. My son will scream and fret. William just grows quiet and sombre." The mirth left her expression. "These are difficult times," she said softly as she watched the infant stretch small fat fingers for the ball that was just beyond his reach. He gave a squeal of impatience, tried harder, and went backwards instead.

"And worse to come before they get better," Madam

FitzReinier predicted gloomily. "Between the ambitions of the Bishop of Ely and Prince John, we'll be ground like grain between two millstones."

Isabelle sighed agreement. York had only been the beginning of Longchamp's bid for power. Two months after that, while she and William were still in Normandy, he had attempted Gloucester Castle and only the arrival of the Bishop of Winchester with a substantial escort of soldiers had forced him to back down. Longchamp had stripped his fellow justiciar, the Bishop of Durham, of his powers and ridden like a roughshod conqueror throughout England, his power bolstered by a large band of mercenaries. Richard, overwintering in Sicily, had done little to curb his chancellor's excesses. Perhaps Longchamp's ability to squeeze funds out of every last corner and crevice mattered more to Richard than the complaints coming from those who were being squeezed.

A commotion in the yard heralded the return of the men from their visit to the wharves where FitzReinier had been eager to show off his new barge to William. It had been an excuse as well for the men to stretch their legs and leave the women to their own gossip. The baby finally reached his ball, grasped it in his chubby hand, sat up, and threw it down again, his lower lip thrust out in concentration. Deed accomplished, he squealed at his own cleverness and looked round at his mother in search of praise. But Isabelle wasn't paying attention to her son, she was listening to the voices of the men as they mounted the outer stairs to the solar. Worryingly, they were not filled with the pleasure and bonhomie she would have expected from their outing, but were muted and anxious. When they entered the room, their expressions were bleak.

The baby abandoned his ball and stretched his arms towards his father, demanding to be picked up. William did so, but the gesture was instinctive, without conscious thought.

"What is it?" asked Isabelle. "What's happened now?"

FitzReinier advanced to the brazier to warm his hands. "I am a loyal man," he said, "and I bow the knee to my King, but I begin to wonder if he will have a kingdom to return to. One of my men came to me at the warehouse with grave news." "One of my men" was a euphemism for "spy," of which FitzReinier had as efficient a network as any magnate or prelate in the land. "Longchamp claims to have a letter from Richard designating his nephew Arthur of Brittany as his heir should he die whilst on crusade and entrusting Longchamp as regent."

"But Arthur of Brittany is still a child in smocks," Isabelle said. "How can Richard choose a baby above his adult brother?"

"Whim, spleen, misrepresentation," FitzReinier said curtly. "And Longchamp is not above forging documents, as Hugh of Durham could tell you. Longchamp owns a copy of Richard's seal and he doesn't always use it for legitimate purposes."

"Does Prince John know about this?" Isabelle looked anxiously at her husband. This could well be disastrous for them. As a royal sub-justiciar, William was supposed to support Longchamp, but it was already proving difficult. To defend the haughty Bishop as regent would be beyond swallowing. Yet refusing to do so was treason.

"He must do by now," William said. "The same messengers will have gone to him. He'll be putting his castellans on alert and stocking his castles to defy Longchamp even as we speak. God knows what's to be done."

Isabelle thought about Madam FitzReinier's comment that they would be caught like a grain between two millstones. There had to be a way of pegging Longchamp's ambition while still keeping Prince John sweet. "Perhaps a woman's touch is what is needed," she said after a moment.

"Meaning?" William asked.

"The Queen," Isabelle said. "She has no love for William

Longchamp and Richard will listen to her. He trusts her advice and she may be able to sway his opinion. She won't want to see her family dominions ruled by a pederast priest on behalf of a three-year-old. If the sub-justiciars send their letters to her, rather than straight to Richard, she may be able to intervene and make him more disposed to listen."

William looked at her, and the frown between his brows lessened. "That's a sound notion, my love—a woman's touch indeed."

Isabelle flushed at his praise. The tense atmosphere that had entered the room with the men eased a little. An attendant brought two silver-gilt platters heaped with pastry wafers and gingerbread, and flagons of hot, sweet wine. William gave one of the wafers to Will to maul with his new teeth and set him back down on the floor.

Between them, they drafted a letter to Queen Eleanor. William summoned his scribes and had them write fair copies to the other justiciars, whose approval and additions would be sought before the message was sent. Another letter went to William's brother John who was attending on Prince John. "For what good it will do," William said as he pressed his seal into the soft red wax. "My brother is the Prince's man first and he won't have the strength or inclination to rein him back."

FitzReinier cleared his throat. "If you had to decide between the Prince and Longchamp, what choice would you make?"

"The right one, I hope," William said, his gaze on his infant son.

William had known Walter of Coutances, Archbishop of Rouen, for most of his adult life, although their acquaintance had only deepened over the last few years. Walter, like William, was of English birth, a stocky red-faced Cornishman with a fluffy white tonsure and benign mien masking a will of iron. His nephew was married to Heloise of Kendal and he and William were natural allies. The Archbishop had set out on crusade with the King, but had turned back at Cyprus with a slew of royal orders including a remit to aid in the governing of England that gave him authority over Longchamp.

Sitting in council with him and the other sub-justiciars at Westminster, William digested the letters that de Coutances had just read out. "So this means," William said slowly, "that if Longchamp ignores our advice and guidance and stirs up trouble, we have the authority to override him and depose him from office?"

"That is indeed the case, my lord," replied the Archbishop with a dry smile. "My brief and yours"—here he included all the sub-justiciars in his glance—"is to steer a path between the rocks of the various factions and keep the ship intact for the King's return. Providing my lord Longchamp consults with us and is governed by our advice, he is to be allowed to conduct his business as he sees fit—as long as he is within the law. These letters are not to be shown to him or used unless it becomes necessary. Should the chancellor come to hear of them in a premature way, it is possible that he might seek to take countermeasures. Do I make myself clear?"

"Eminently, my lord," said Geoffrey FitzPeter. "I speak for us all when I say that no one will breathe a word of this, but I do not think we will have to keep these letters secret for long."

"That remains to be seen," said de Coutances. He flicked a warning glance around his fellow justiciars. "We need to act swiftly if it does, but not in the haste of men desiring to precipitate a quarrel. We must stay within the law."

His words were met with muted murmurs of assent.

"We are only grateful and relieved that the King has sent you to us," said Geoffrey FitzPeter. "God knows we would have been struggling without you."

De Coutances's smile was dry. "Your thanks should go to Queen Eleanor," he said. "It was her word above all others that persuaded the King he had to act." His small, shrewd eyes fixed knowingly on William. "It was a good thing that your messages reached her on the road."

William returned the smile. "Yes," he said, "it was."

De Coutances shuffled the parchments on the trestle before him and neatened them together. "I have more news for you to digest, and celebrate," he said and, folding his hands on top of the parchments, proceeded to tell them.

Following the council, William had his barge rowed upriver to his manor at Caversham where Isabelle was awaiting him, together with a modicum of peace and quiet—if the bustle of a large baronial household could be called peace and quiet. There were letters to be dictated, messengers to send on their way, supplicants and vassals to see, household officers and knights of the mesnie to consult. However, they could wait a few hours. First, he needed to refresh himself and talk matters over with his wife.

Clad only in shirt and braies, he lay on their bed in the solar chamber, his head pillowed in her lap against the swell of her belly. She had conceived again in January, was just entering her sixth month of pregnancy, and was as stately as the swans gliding on the river beyond the manor house. Glittering motes of dust hung in the sunlight crossing the foot of the bed. Their son was tumbling on the floor with an infant of a similar age belonging to one of the knights and watched over by a vigilant nurse. He had given Isabelle the news concerning the success of her letters to Queen Eleanor and had taken pleasure and pride in the gleam of satisfaction it brought to her eyes. "I know men who don't give a fig for the opinions of their wives, but they are the poorer for such blindness," he said.

"Ah, but if you disagreed with my opinion, you wouldn't follow it," she answered with a knowing smile. "You'd tell me to mind my distaff and you would go your own way."

"I'd tell you no such thing," William said indignantly, "even if I did go my own way…but that's not going to happen. We both want the best for Striguil and our children. Don't you want to hear the rest of de Coutances's news?"

She gave his hair a tug, not enough to hurt, but sufficient as a warning. In truth, he had the right of it when he said that they both wanted the best for their lands and their offspring. And he did seek her opinions and include her in every aspect of their rule. No one was in any doubt that she was the Countess of Striguil. On the documents to which he set his seal, he never styled himself an earl and still used the small oval seal of his knighthood. It amused—even exasperated—her sometimes that he took only what was his by right and refused the extra trappings that he could have possessed without anyone cavilling, least of all her. "Tell me, what news?"

"By now King Richard will be a married man. Eleanor was on the road bringing Berengaria, daughter of King Sancho of Navarre, to Cyprus for their wedding."

Isabelle's mouth opened to ask a question and remained like that for several moments. "Jesu!" she said at last. "Why? Were there any plans before he left?"

"Not that I know of, although his mother might have had them, and Richard himself keeps his inner thoughts and schemes well hidden. I suppose there are reasons to do with Aquitaine and Poitou that made sense to take a Navarrese bride. I do not think he was ever going to marry Alys of France. Richard has ever looked to the south rather than the north."

Isabelle resumed stroking his hair. "So it is likely that the King will soon beget an heir," she said thoughtfully.

"Certainly if God is good. It didn't take us long." William spoke with conviction and hoped that the rumours concerning the King's predilections were like most court gossip: untrue.

"What will that do to Prince John? He's already on edge because of what Richard said about making his nephew his heir."

"I think that issue has been resolved of its own accord in John's favour. No English baron is going to swear for a French-backed Breton brat of three years old above a man of four and twenty with Henry Plantagenet and Eleanor of Aquitaine for parents." He rubbed his jaw. "Of course, Richard's heir would be a different matter...I suppose it would depend how much John's ambition eats him up. I know full well that he envies Richard his possessions and he craves power and adulation. You've seen what he is like for yourself. But how far he would go..." He shook his head. "Only John knows that."

"Does he? I think perhaps he doesn't." Isabelle shivered. John's charisma was powerful and she was not immune to it, but she had an intuitive awareness of the dark twists in his soul. He wasn't to be trusted, and in his turn he trusted no one and sought to strike before being struck. Quickly she pressed her palms over William's eyes while she composed her expression. "I am troubling you with John when you have Longchamp to deal with," she said lightly.

William snorted. "In truth I don't want to talk about either of them." Abruptly, as if shutting off his thoughts in movement, he sat up and turned and placed his hand upon her belly. "Richard," he said. "We'll call the new little one Richard—or Richenda if it's a girl."

"For the King?" Isabelle raised her brow.

He looked wry. "It won't do any harm for Richard to think so, but I had your father in mind. I knew him somewhat, and I liked him—although not as much as I love his daughter."

"Flatterer," she laughed. "Small wonder you rose so high at court."

"But I never lie because lies will always find you out." He captured one of her hands and kissed it.

Isabelle was facing the door, and the sleepy laughter froze on her face as her husband's brother suddenly barged into the room, shoving two clerks and a steward out of his way. Alerted by his wife's gasp, William hastily turned and then stared. His brother's clothing was dusty from the road and he was wearing his hauberk. The expression on his face precipitated William off the bed and sent him reaching for his tunic.

"Longchamp is besieging Lincoln," John said before William could ask what he was doing here. "De Camville has ridden straight to the Prince for aid and left his wife defending the castle against the bastard. The whoreson's got footsoldiers, knights, serjeants, and a company of two score underminers. You can't sit on your arse any more, brother, he has to be stopped." He bared his teeth. "Prince John has seized Nottingham and Tickhill in retaliation, and if Longchamp does not retreat from Lincoln, he will visit him with a rod of iron. You're a justiciar, what are you going to do?" Hectic colour blazed across his cheekbones.

William listened to the joyful squeals of his infant son; he felt the silent wideness of Isabelle's stare. "Keep my wits about me," he replied more calmly than he felt. "Contrary to what you think, myself and the other justiciars have not been sitting on our arses. Neither William Longchamp nor John will be permitted to start a civil war, I promise you that."

"How will you stop them?" John demanded. "The Prince is recruiting mercenaries from his Glamorgan lands and men are flocking to his banner because they are sick of Longchamp's rapacious ways."

William waved his brother to a chair. "Sit," he commanded. "A few moments on your own backside won't make any difference to the outcome, and I can't talk to you while you're snarling like a baited bear."

Still glowering, John threw himself into the chair, which creaked with the violence of his action. For the first time he acknowledged his sister-in-law, giving her a slightly shame-faced nod of the head. Isabelle returned the gesture graciously. Aware of the way his glance lingered on her exposed fair plaits and the fecund swell of her belly, she quietly veiled her hair and arranged her gown so that her pregnancy was less obvious. She was not in the least embarrassed, for this was her private chamber where she could dress with as little formality as she chose, but she could sense John's discomfort; given the circumstances of his own marriage, this warm domestic scene must be like salt in a raw wound.

"I'll fight under my lord's banner if it comes to the crux, and with pride." Challenge gleamed in John's eyes. "My oath is to him. I'm his seneschal and his vassal. You're his vassal too for Cartmel and the Leinster lands, brother. You might want to think about that."

"I do, constantly," William answered. "But I am also the King's justiciar. I have duties and loyalties that lie beyond my personal desires and possessions."

"Well, you're going to have to decide one way or the other," John said. "If you have any sense, you'll join the Prince."

William felt Isabelle's involuntary twitch of movement beside him and he responded with a swift, surreptitious lift of his forefinger. "I will gladly speak with Lord John," he said, "but I won't be joining his battle lines. When I ride out of here, it will be to Walter of Coutances and the other justiciars. You might believe that we don't know our brains from our buttocks, but I promise you that we do."

John started to sneer but William silenced him with a raised hand. "Take my word for it…and you can pass that message to the Prince. The Archbishop of Rouen will repeat my stance when he speaks with him."

John jerked to his feet. "I hope you know what you are doing," he said curtly.

"And I you," William retorted, then pushed one hand through his hair in an exasperated gesture. "Jesu, I don't want to quarrel with you. For what it's worth, should it come to the crux and, God forbid, Richard die on this crusade, I will support John as the next King of England—but only in those circumstances, no other."

His brother nodded stiffly. "I don't want to quarrel with you either. I'll hold you to your word though."

"You won't need to. It's given, that's enough."

The brothers embraced in a stilted fashion. Declining to remain to eat, John accepted travel rations for himself and his men and rode out of Caversham, his son accompanying him for several miles so that the pair could have at least some time together.

Awaiting Jack's return, William made his own preparations to leave. "I have a suspicion that today really was the still before the storm," he said to Isabelle.

She set her arms around his neck and kissed him. "But you and the other justiciars can hold the country steady," she said, "especially with Walter of Coutances at the helm."

"I pray so," William said grimly. "The alternative does not bear thinking about."

Thirty-eight

RICHARD MARSHAL'S ENTRY INTO THE WORLD WAS A protracted struggle. Although he was positioned head down, the angle was difficult and he was a large baby. Labouring to deliver him, Isabelle realised that they both might die. She wasn't ready to leave the world yet, but God's will frequently took small notice of human desires. Battling anger, fear, and self-pity, she squeezed her prayer beads in her fists and trapped a cry behind gritted teeth as another pang tightened her womb. A midwife wiped Isabelle's brow and murmured words of encouragement and exhorted her to direct her prayers to the wooden figurine of Saint Margaret, patron saint of labouring mothers. The image stood on a prie-dieu surrounded by lit candles. Twice they had burned down to the stub and been renewed.

As the contraction eased, Isabelle panted with relief. She wanted William here for her own reassurance, but was glad in a way too that he was absent, dealing with affairs related to chancellor Longchamp. She hadn't seen her husband for half of the month that she had retired to her confinement in the solar chamber at Caversham, and only then in fleeting moments when he came to her between engagements to replenish himself. Perhaps she was never going to see him again; perhaps this was her death chamber. Unable to bear the dark, warm stuffiness of the room and the metallic stench of mortality, she spoke peremptorily to the women. "Open the shutters, I need to see the daylight."

"But my lady, the cold air will be bad for you and the child. You will take a chill," protested one of her maids.

"Open them!" Isabelle repeated. "I order you. If you do not, I will rise from this bed even as I am and do it myself!"

Lips pressed together, the maid unfastened the latches and pulled back the shutters to reveal arches of blustery grey daylight. Isabelle drew a lungful of cold, moist air. The next contraction gathered and tightened in her loins and as she bore down, she sensed a change in the pressure against her pelvic floor.

The wind had been behind William and his mesnie all the way from London, roaring in their ears, assisting the speed of their journey. Hoods pulled up and mantles fastened against the chill flurries of rain, they rode into Caversham shortly after noon.

William's eyes were gritty with tiredness, but as always his spirits had lifted as he approached the manor which had fast become one of his favourites. It was close to London and to Wiltshire, convenient as a stopping point on his way to the ports of the Narrow Sea, yet despite being near the hub of activity, it was a tranquil haven too—somewhere he could relax his vigilance and let the weight slide from his shoulders.

As he dismounted from his blowing courser and tossed the reins to his groom, he noticed that despite the inclement weather, the shutters and casements were open at the upstairs chamber windows. While he was frowning over the detail, an agonised cry flew down to him from the aperture and froze him to the marrow.

He took the outer timber stairs to the hall two at a time, bursting in on the room like a Viking through a monastery door. Servants and retainers stared at him in shock as he strode towards the stairs leading off from the dais. Plainly having been told of his arrival, a flushed midwife was hastening down them to bar his way.

"The Countess Isabelle," he said tersely, "she is all right? I heard a cry…"

The woman bobbed a curtsey. "Yes, my lord. The Countess is in travail and the labour has been hard, but there is hope…"

William blenched as her words filled him with fear. "What do you mean 'there is hope'?" he snarled.

She trembled beneath his anger, but bravely held her ground. "The child is large and the head was in a difficult position, but the babe has turned of his own accord and my lady has good wide hips. With God's help and if my lady's strength holds up, all will yet be well."

William shuddered. He had arrived in expectation of shedding his burdens, but instead he had to brace himself and shoulder new ones. The feeling of impotence was terrifying. There was nothing he could do for Isabelle, neither protect her nor take away her pain. The realisation of the potential cost had not really hit him before. When Will was born he had arrived home after the ordeal was over and to the sight of Isabelle tired but smiling with triumph. Perhaps she had cried out before, but he hadn't been there to hear it.

"My lord, I should go back to attend to the Countess," the midwife said, turning on the stair.

He swallowed and gestured. As she opened the door, another muffled scream attacked him. He had heard similar sounds before—in the aftermath of battle when wounded men bit down on rags and wedges of wood while their broken bones were set. Turning abruptly, he moved away from the stairs. His knights were arriving in the hall: stowing their baggage in their favourite corners; greeting wives and children, sweethearts and friends. Feeling a tug at the tunic at the back of his knee and turning, William found his son looking up at him out of wide dark eyes. "Horse," the toddler said, waving his favourite wooden toy at his father and smiling with two neat rows of milk teeth.

William stooped and swung the child up in his arms. "Yes, horse," he repeated, his throat tight. The nursemaid was close behind her charge, but he waved her away and bore the infant to a bench against the side of the room. The warm weight of him was a poignant comfort. William was also distracted by how much Will had changed and grown while he had been absent about the business of running England and trying to prevent a prince and a bishop from foundering the country. The baby limbs were still buttery and plump, but there were hints, like buds on a spring branch, of developing sinew and muscle. The toddler chattered to him, words pouring out, some meaningless, others making perfect sense and almost, but not quite, sentences. To hear him, to respond to him and receive response in turn, sent a throat-tightening pang through William.

In a pause between the babble, William thought he heard a sound from the room above and his shoulders tensed. A glance at the nurse, who was still hovering nearby, revealed that he had not imagined it, for her own glance had darted towards the stairs. Nausea churned his belly. He thought he was inured to anything that life could throw at him, but against the thought of Isabelle's suffering he was defenceless. The sound came again, louder, filled with effort...then silence. William's straining ears caught the faintest thread of a baby's wail and it was the final goad that pitched him over the edge and destroyed the iron self-control that had carried him through a hundred tourneys unscathed, brought him to the Holy Land and back, and seen him rise to become co-justiciar of England. Thrusting his son into the nurse's arms, he strode to the stairs, galloped up them, and hurtled into the chamber above the hall. Ignoring the dismayed gasps and cries of the women in the anteroom, he flurried aside the dividing curtain and strode into the bedchamber. Isabelle was half sitting, half lying on their bed, her shift pushed up exposing her belly, blood smearing her inner thighs and pooling the bedstraw beneath her. Her hair, sweat-darkened at her scalp, frizzed around her face, which was tear-streaked and shadowed with pain and exhaustion. If he had seen her as a beautiful Madonna at Striguil when Will was born, now he was witness to the reality of childbirth, every bit as bloody and merciless as a long day on the field of battle, with survival just as uncertain. She gasped his name, her eyes widening. On the far side of the bed, a woman was jiggling a towel-wrapped bundle in her arms and trying to shush the increasing strength and indignation of its wails.

The senior midwife drew herself up and addressed him as if he were a serf. "You should not be here," she admonished. "It is not seemly…my lord." She tried to turn him around, but William remained rooted to the spot.

"Seemly or not, I am here," he answered the woman without removing his gaze from his wife. "Isabelle…" His throat worked.

Through her pain and exhaustion she found the ghost of a smile. "William, you great ox," she croaked. "Take our second son and go and present him to the knights and his brother. We have an heir for the Longueville lands."

Hearing how hoarse and dry her voice was, he didn't want to think how much she had screamed in the hours up to the birth. A frowning midwife brought a drink to Isabelle and drew the coverlet over her thighs and the collapsed mound of her belly. The woman holding the baby came to William and placed the screaming bundle in his arms. He winced. "He certainly has lungs loud enough to command an army," he said.

"I suppose his entry into the world was no less difficult for him than it was for me," Isabelle replied, adding quickly as she saw her husband's expression: "We may both have been mauled by the ordeal, but we're alive. Go." She made a shooing motion. "Let the midwives finish their work and allow me to rest awhile and we'll talk." A spark glimmered through her bruised exhaustion. "You've returned, so you must have news about Longchamp?"

It was her question more than anything else that reassured William about Isabelle. As she said, the birth had mauled her, but not enough to quench her inquisitive mind. The baby was all right too. Unlike Marguerite's child, who had barely had the strength to draw breath, this particular scrap of humanity was bawling like a young bull. "Yes," he said and finally found his smile. "And you'll enjoy hearing it when you're ready."

It was the next morning before William settled down to telling Isabelle what had happened. The midwives had insisted that she was left in peace to eat, drink, and sleep and William had bedded down in the main hall with his men rather than disturb her again. Armed now with a breakfast of bread, cheese, and cider, he sat on the edge of their bed. The baby, having guzzled like a toper at Isabelle's breast, was sleeping against her arm, a look of concentration on his little face. It was almost as if every aspect of his tiny existence had to be met with full dedication. Changing his swaddling was not going to be an enviable task.

"Longchamp," William said as he broke bread and handed her a piece, "has been banished from England...but the manner of his going took even the most hardbitten of us by surprise." He grinned broadly. "You know that he's been as slippery as an eel—avoiding our demands that he face us and answer the accusations against him? When we finally brought him to bay at the Tower of London and he found he couldn't wriggle off the hook, he gave his own brothers as hostages and promised to yield us his castles and authority. He swore also not to leave

England until those castles had been taken into the possession of our castellans." William paused for effect.

"Obviously he broke his promise," Isabelle said.

William nodded. "He handed over the keys of the Tower and was escorted to Dover, which he'd been allowed to keep under his jurisdiction. He was still under oath not to leave England because he hadn't handed over his other castles to the justiciars' officials, but he decided to try and escape to Normandy anyway. He sent his servants to find a boat and disguised himself as a woman in a green dress and hood."

Isabelle almost choked on her bread. "No!" The image of William Longchamp, Bishop of Ely and King Richard's chancellor, robed in feminine apparel was a boggling image to conjure.

"It gets better!" William laughed, thoroughly enjoying himself at Longchamp's expense. "Whilst 'my lady' was waiting by the shore for his servants to return, a fisherman mistook him for one of the town whores touting for custom and received the shock of his life when he groped between his 'sweetheart's' legs. So did Longchamp, I hazard."

Isabelle gave a yelp of laughter and then wished she hadn't as her tender muscles cramped. "Jesu, Jesu!" she gasped, pressing her hand across her belly.

"Christ knows, that fisherman must have been desperate or short-sighted!" William guffawed. "He was beaten off by Longchamp's servants, but then some women tried to speak to him and when he couldn't answer their questions because he spoke no English, they pulled off his hood and the game was up." William knuckled his eyes and strove for sobriety, but after relating such a farce it was difficult. "They turned on him then, spitting on him and stoning him with shingle from the beach. He was rescued by a couple of serjeants in the town, but locked in a cellar since they couldn't trust him not to escape. He's been released and sent on his way now that his castles are in our hands, but he has been made a complete laughing stock and of his own doing. It is no more than he justly deserves, but I cannot help feeling sorry for him."

Isabelle didn't feel compassion for the odious William Longchamp; only relief that he was no longer an imminent threat. "And what about Prince John?" she asked. "I suppose he is like a dog with two tails now?"

William cut a chunk of cheese. "Yes," he said wryly. "The Prince is indeed delighted with the way matters have turned in his favour. He has been acknowledged Richard's heir and the chief thorn in his side has been ridiculed and thrown out of England. Not that he has a free rein. We'll be watching him. Richard is still the King, and John ignores that at his peril." He twitched his shoulders. "Still, at least for now there is peace." He finished his cider and wiped his mouth. "There's good news for my brother too. He's been appointed sheriff of Sussex to replace the loss of his position at York."

"Is that a good thing?" Isabelle asked. She settled herself more comfortably against the feather bolsters and stifled a yawn.

"Better for him than York was. It's closer to his heartlands and the office better suits his talents. He's pleased, and I'm pleased for him."

She knew that it was the closest he would come to saying that his brother's capabilities were limited. "So am I." She couldn't prevent the next yawn. Her eyelids were beginning to feel like lead weights.

Immediately contrite, he leaned forward to kiss her and rose to his feet. "I've tired you out," he said. "I'll return later."

She gave him a sleepy smile. "Not too much later," she said. "I need to sleep, but I'd rather talk, and I know you'll have to leave soon."

"Not for a few days at least," he said. "I'm in safe harbour and a captain doesn't put out to chancy seas again without repairing his ship."

Thirty-nine

QUEEN ELEANOR BIT HER LIP IN AGITATION AND, HUGGING her ermine-lined cloak around her body, moved to warm her hands at one of several braziers heating the room. The weather had turned bitterly cold and even at midday, hoar frost rimed doors and lintels. Water butts and horse troughs were solid ice and the outside air was like a knife in the lungs. Many of the barons and magnates were gathered in the great Rufus Hall, but the Queen had retired to her apartments early, bringing only a select few guests with her, William and Isabelle among them.

"Another crusader ship has put in to port without news of Richard," Eleanor muttered to William as he joined her at the brazier. "I am beginning to worry for him."

"There is still time yet, madam," William said.

Her reproachful look told him that she judged him guilty of mouthing platitudes. "There should have been word or sight by now. We know he sailed from Acre in October and that his galley came safely into Brindisi, but we have heard nothing since. How long did it take you to travel back from Jerusalem, William?"

He twitched his shoulders. "Less than two months, but that is not a time carved in stone for all men."

"Richard would not dally. He knows the trouble that Philip

of France will cause in his absence and he also knows that there are matters in England to resolve." She shivered and washed her hands together. "Yesterday my youngest son told me that I should prepare myself to hear that Richard is dead…but I won't. I refuse to do that." She swallowed, the tendons in her throat taut with strain. "He is the child of my heart. I would know if he were dead. John would usurp his place in an instant. I know that he's stuffing his castles to the rafters. I know that word has gone out to his castellans to prepare for him to become a king…" Her eyes narrowed. "I have given my full consent to John being Richard's heir, but that is all—his heir, and until I know for certain that Richard is dead, I will not countenance any attempt by John to take the crown." She studied William. "We have been friends through thick and thin."

"Yes, madam," William said gently. "And I have known your sons since they were infants and children."

She smiled bleakly. "And watched them grow into men and squander the promise…"

He gave a wordless shrug that was open to interpretation.

"I have relied on you in the past, and you know how much you owe me." Her tawny glance flickered to Isabelle who was talking to Walter of Coutances. "Your lands, your wife."

William drew himself up. "My loyalty is not dependent on gifts and largesse," he said stiffly.

Eleanor quickly laid her hand on his sleeve. "Of course not. I never meant to imply that it was and I am sorry if I have offended you. Worry makes my tongue clumsy. Even though your brother is John's man and you are John's vassal for your Leinster lands, I do not doubt your fidelity…and I truly mean that…It is just that it would comfort an old woman to hear you say that come hell or high water you will stand up for Richard." Her fingers gripped. Looking down at them he saw how the shanks of her rings were loose on her bones and how her skin was mottled. If Richard was dead, he thought, it would kill her, but while she yet believed he lived, the fire in her was like a hot coal.

He gave her a knowing look. "Not that old, madam," he said, "but I would not deny you comfort. You have my word. Come hell or high water, I will stand up for Richard while he lives—as I stood for King Henry your husband and for the Young King your son." Before all the company he placed his hands in hers and knelt to her like a vassal to a feudal lord.

Eleanor's eyes grew moist. She stooped, kissed William on either cheek, then lightly on the mouth and raised him to his feet. "The point is made and taken," she said. "You are right. I am not, after all, that old."

A frozen silver-blue dusk was falling over the city as William and Isabelle returned to their riverside lodging, both in pensive mood following the gathering in the Queen's chamber. If news of Richard did not come soon, there were going to be changes and shifts in the power at court. They had to be prepared to acknowledge Prince John as King, but it would not be an easy transition.

"My lord, my lady, you have a visitor," his usher said as he bowed William and Isabelle into the main room. William raised his brow. There was never a time when he didn't have visitors, but for his usher to mention the detail, it had to be personal. And then his gaze lit on his brother's former mistress and her daughter who were warming themselves by the hearth. They had but recently arrived, for they still wore their cloaks and their faces were red from the cold. Alais was talking animatedly to a man sitting beside her, and he was smiling and paying her close attention. Seeing William enter, she laid her hand lightly on the man's sleeve, then, leaving him, hurried over, drawing her daughter with her.

"Alais," William said with genuine pleasure, kissing her on

either cheek, and then Sybilla, who was slender as a young deer with glossy dark braids and wide eyes of clear grey-green. "Holy Mother, you've grown up!"

"Almost ten years old," Alais said with a smile that was affectionate and a little sad. "She'll be a woman all too soon."

"Mama!" Sybilla wrinkled her nose.

Alais dipped a curtsey to Isabelle, who greeted her as William had done with kisses on the cheek, but there was a certain reserve between the women. Owing to the ambivalent circumstances of her position in the Marshal family, Alais was awkward with Isabelle. Being more familiar with Aline, John Marshal's young wife, Isabelle's attitude towards Alais was cool and restrained.

"What brings you to London?" William asked once he had brought Alais and Sybilla to the private chamber and seen them furnished with hot wine and a platter of date pastries.

"My son brings me," said Alais with a smiling glance towards William's squires. "I did not think you would mind me paying a visit, and I have a gift for him to celebrate the season. I'm also here to visit the markets. As you say, Sybilla is growing and she needs to be clothed." She flushed and lowered her voice. "John has sent us money and bid us use it as we require."

"You do know that if you lack for anything you can come to me," William said quietly.

Alais accepted the offer with a dignified tilt of her head. "I know that, and thank you, but you are already doing enough in raising my son to knighthood, and truly, there is nothing we need. John is generous...perhaps more generous than I deserve."

"Or perhaps not generous enough. Do not set yourself at naught," William said, and received a poignant, grateful smile in response. "Have you seen him of late?"

She studied her hands. "He came to Hamstead after Michaelmas with money for us...I think he regards us as part of his accounting much of the time, and I think he has regrets—as I do. But you cannot dwell in the past, can you?" She raised her chin bravely. "He's at Marlborough for the Christmas season with his wife—and caught up in matters concerning Prince John, so I understand." She gave William a curious look. "There have been rumours about King Richard…that he is missing."

William felt Isabelle stiffen at his side. "Rumours are all they are," Isabelle said with a bland smile. "He is expected any day and the Queen has every confidence in his return."

"Of course…I didn't mean to imply otherwise," Alais said, reddening. "It's just that I overheard the talk in the cloth market."

"There is always talk in the cloth market, most of it not worth a wisp of latrine hay," Isabelle said. Although she had not intended it, her words made Alais appear like a foolish chattering housewife. William tactfully eased the awkward moment by leaving Alais and Sybilla alone with his nephew who was the reason for their visit, and returned with Isabelle to the noisy hall to give them some private moments.

"Who was that knight talking to you?" Isabelle nudged William. They were lying in bed, the curtains drawn closed, secluding them from the other sleepers in the room. They had recently made muffled, surreptitious love and she had been drifting into slumber when the memory caught her and pulled her back to the shore of consciousness.

"A lot of knights talked to me tonight," he mumbled.

"The one with the dark curly hair. He was sitting at the fire with Alais and Sybilla and he was with them when we arrived back from the palace."

"Guillaume de Colleville. His second cousin Thomas is in my retinue." He yawned and turned over, dragging the bedclothes with him. Isabelle promptly dragged her portion back.

"Is he in search of a position?"

"No, he has lands in his own right," William replied in a sleep-blurred voice. "Just claiming a night's hospitality on his way to other business."

"Does he have a wife?"

"Not that I know of...and probably sleeps the better for it," he growled.

Isabelle took the hint and fell silent. She curled herself against William's spine. The warmth of the bed and the heat from his body gradually lulled her back into drowsiness but she had plenty of food for thought.

Forty

"HE'S ALIVE, HE'S BEEN FOUND!"

On her knees, Isabelle looked up from the chest of cloth she had been sorting through as William strode into the room waving a piece of parchment bearing Queen Eleanor's seal. "Who?" she asked, her tone vague for her mind was still half occupied with mental tallies of how many bolts of linen they had and how many they were going to need for summer garments.

"King Richard! He's been found, praise God!" There was relief and agitation in William's tone as he swept his youngest son into his arms and swung him round, making him squeal. "What is not so good is that he's in the dungeon of Emperor Henry of Germany who has no cause to love him."

"He's what?" Isabelle stared at him.

"He was captured crossing the lands of Leopold of Austria, who's no friend to Richard and sold him on to the Emperor."

"But surely his captors' souls will be imperilled if they interfere with a crusader?" Isabelle rose to her feet and stifled a sneeze caused by fabric filaments.

"Silver buys absolution," William said with distaste. "Even if the Emperor doesn't love Richard, he has an affinity for money. I warrant that he'll allow Richard to go for a consideration."

Isabelle looked disgusted.

"At least we know that he's alive." William set his son down on the floor and went to the clothing chest next to the one his wife had been sorting through. He threw back the lid, stared at the contents, and absently massaged his thigh over the area of the lance scar from his youth.

"What is it?" Isabelle knew there was more. "Tell me."

He sighed out hard. "The Queen has summoned the justiciars to a meeting to discuss the issue. Prince John already knew about Richard through his spies. He's gone to King Philip and done him homage for England and all of Richard's lands over the Narrow Sea."

"Holy Mary!" Isabelle gazed at William with foreboding while gooseflesh rose on her arms. Richard alive but helpless, John on the rampage for the crown. It was a disastrous brew even before it was stirred.

William dragged his winter court robe from the coffer and a pair of thick woollen braies. "We'll have to alert all the shoreline castles and keep a watch on John's vassals—and find a fast way of releasing Richard from prison, which is going to involve a lot of silver that we don't have. The council will have to make some swift decisions." Going to another coffer he removed his baggage roll and wrapped tunic, braies, a pair of fine court shoes, and a clean shirt inside it, fastened the ties, and lifted his fur-lined cloak off the peg in the wall. "I'll be home with news as soon as I can. If we ride now, we can be in Oxford before nightfall." He turned back to her, embraced her hard and swiftly, kissed his two sons, and blew out of the room.

Isabelle leaned against the coffer, her lips tingling from the pressure of his. After a moment she went to pick up Richard. Carrying him at her hip, ushering little Will before her, she took her sons down to the courtyard to watch their father and his mesnie ride out into the raw February afternoon, gold and green silks snapping against a leaden sky.

Rain lashed against the shutters of Eleanor's chamber at Oxford Castle, the drops striking so hard that they sounded like stones. Outside it was full night and black as hell. The Queen shivered and huddled into her fur-lined mantle. Her right hand clutched a water-stained parchment. The ink had run and smeared, but the words were still legible to those who could read, and those who could not had been apprised of the contents. A messenger from John had been intercepted on his way to Windsor and from the details Eleanor had just read out, it was obvious that the Prince and the King of France were assembling a fleet at Wissant and hiring mercenaries hand over fist, ready to invade England. It was also plain that the messenger captured had only been one of several and that all of John's castellans would be receiving letters from the Prince that would put their keeps on a war footing.

"We should call out the fyrd along the south coast," William said. "If we are vigilant, we can prevent the enemy from landing."

Eleanor's jaw jutted as she agreed. There was fire and anger in her eyes. Over seventy years old she might be, but still a lioness. "I will have every baron in the land swear allegiance to Richard. Let all faithful castellans look to their defences and prepare to deal with invaders and rebels."

"It shall be done, madam." De Coutances bowed acknowledgement. "I will draft the notices tonight. The Abbots of Boxley and Robertsbridge will go immediately to Germany and open negotiations for the King's release."

"Good." Eleanor's agitation showed in the way she kneaded the thick fabric of her mantle between her fingers. She glanced irritably towards the shutters. "This accursed rain," she snapped. "I've never grown used to it."

"Other difficulties I can do my best to allay, madam," said de Coutances with bleak humour, "but all I can offer to do about the weather is pray."

Eleanor gave a hollow laugh. "I think we have more important things to ask God," she said. "My husband kept me prisoner for sixteen years in Salisbury. I know how it corrodes the spirit." Her face took on a stubborn cast. "I will have my older son returned, and I will have my younger one put in his place—and it is not Richard's, nor will be while Richard draws breath."

William exchanged glances with the other justiciars. Richard and John had never been renowned for their brotherly love and where John at least was concerned, fratricide was probably well within his lexicon of capabilities. The Queen must know it too, but from the way she was holding herself, the men judged it wise to keep their own counsel.

John Marshal gazed over the battlements at the Welsh mercenaries pitching camp in Marlborough's bailey and swallowed hard. A March wind roared around his ears and his cloak kept trying to take off like a huge bird of prey. Wales being a traditional enemy as well as a fruitful place to recruit mercenaries, he was made uneasy at the sight of so many of them so close to the keep and armed with their innocuous-looking but deadly longbows. However, he could hardly refuse to house them when his royal master was standing next to him, a sour smile on his lips and his amber eyes narrowed against the bite of the wind.

The Prince had crept into England by crossing the Narrow Sea during the night in an unlit fishing boat and beaching in a bay where the only witnesses, a pair of fishermen, were now feeding the denizens of the sea floor. Of course others would be aware of his presence here now, but he had stolen a march on the justiciars and by coming around behind them had succeeded in buying troops that otherwise he would have had difficulty obtaining.

"I'm glad to see the keep is well stocked," the Prince said.

"Yes, sire," John Marshal replied, thinking that he would have to find the wherewithal to restock it unless the Prince moved on very soon with his locust army of Welsh. He had ordered his wife to stay in her chamber—not that there was much chance of her emerging of her own accord. Unlike his brother's Countess, she didn't have that kind of backbone.

The Prince paced along the wall walk to the next merlon and leaned against it. "Richard's dead," he said. "My mother refuses to believe it because he's always been her favourite, but she's old and deluded."

"It is not true that he's in prison in Germany?"

The Prince snorted. "That's a tale concocted by Walter de Coutances and the justiciars because they want to keep their power. Richard may have arrived in Germany, but he'll never leave. You are my sworn vassal and you've been my man for what, ten years now?"

"Ten years this midsummer," John confirmed.

"Your loyalty will be rewarded." The Prince tugged a ring off his finger and presented it to his castellan. "Wear this. Send it if you have need."

"Sire." John felt a flush of importance and pride. If John were made King, he wondered what those rewards might be. Greater than William's perhaps? At his darkest core nested a secret hope that William might find his fortunes reversed and have to eat humble pie for a change.

"Where will I find you, sire?"

The Prince gave a sardonic grin. "Worried that I'm going to eat you out of supplies or take a notion to that boney little wife of yours?"

John coloured. He hated the Prince's cruel sense of humour, but was not of the nature to fence with him or let it roll off his back. All he could do was grit his teeth and wait for it to run its course.

"These men are bound for my keeps at Wallingford and Windsor and the lady Aline has nothing with which to tempt me. Your brother's wife, though…" The Prince's grin broadened. "Not that I'm foolish enough to try." He raised his hand to blow eloquently on his fingertips. "Let him handle her. There are plenty of sweet apples in the orchard without resorting to that one." He glanced sidelong at his castellan. "Don't look so purse-mouthed or I'll begin to think that self-righteousness is a Marshal trait."

John Marshal stared at his feet, enduring, unable to force a smile. He heard the Prince give an elaborate sigh. On the sward below the tower, one of the canvasses caught a gust of wind and flapped across the grass like a huge wounded bird, several bare-legged mercenaries in pursuit. "Speaking of Marshal traits," the Prince said thoughtfully, "how likely is. it that your brother could be persuaded to bolster my cause…if you were to have a word with him?"

John made a face. William's lands and confirmed military ability made his support a very attractive proposition to the Prince, but John Marshal had no intention of giving William a chance to usurp his own position at the Prince's side. "He won't listen to me," he said brusquely. "He's always gone his own way. If he is anyone's man, he is your mother's…" He didn't need to add that Eleanor would be the last person in England to give up hope on her eldest son's life and that William would sustain her to the end of that belief.

The younger man's mouth tightened. "We'll see about that," he said and moved along the wall walk to the tower stairs.

"Christ's bones, you've heard nothing from Germany. Face up to the fact. Richard is dead!" Prince John snarled at the justiciars who had convened in Westminster's Great Hall to hear what he had to say. They were still in a state of agitation over the fact that he had managed to sneak around behind them, recruit mercenaries, and bolster not only Wallingford and Windsor, but Tickhill, Nottingham, and Marlborough.

"Sire, whose word do we have—save your own, which is scarcely unbiased—that King Richard is dead?" asked Walter de Coutances, his voice one of frozen courtesy. "We need more proof than hearsay."

"God's blood, it's no more than hearsay that he's alive!" John snapped. "When are you all going to wake up? I demand that you hand over the realm to me and order all men to swear allegiance."

"You are the dreamer, John," said Eleanor, who had so far listened in silence to her youngest son's diatribe. Her expression was one of weary contempt. "Your brother lives. We have proof and more will come. You are commanded to disband your troops on both sides of the Narrow Sea and help us seek a way to free Richard from prison."

"Why, when I have an inheritance to win from those who will not accept the truth?" John glared at them all. "If you will not give me what is mine by right, then by God, I will take it by fire and sword."

Eleanor raised one eyebrow. "You haven't had much success this far," she said scornfully. "Three days ago my Kentish fyrd caught two shiploads of your Flemish mercenaries trying to land. I understand that a handful of survivors are in fetters. The remainder are fish food. The country holds for Richard, and so do the barons."

"Not all of them," John's eyes glittered dangerously. He flicked a glance towards William, who returned it impassively.

"The men who matter," his mother retorted.

John stared at his mother and the justiciars, at the hovering clerks and squires and attendants, their expressions studiously blank. "Is that your last word?"

"Of course not," Eleanor said, her voice still level and calm. "I am willing to talk for as long as you wish…my son."

John had gone beyond flushed and was now as pale as a winding sheet. "I am done with talking, Mother. From now on, I'll let my sword speak for me. Richard is dead; let him rot in hell." He turned on his heel and strode from the room.

Pale and shaking, Eleanor finally relaxed and sat down on a cushioned bench. "Do you believe I am deluded?" she asked the men seated around the trestle.

"No, madam, and I do not believe that your son believes it either," William said. "But perhaps he hopes that others do. If a lie is spoken often enough and with sufficient conviction, it can appear more convincing than the truth—as I have had cause to know." Rising to his feet, he brought her a cup of hot wine from the jug that had been warming by the hearth and knelt like a squire to present it. She accepted it with a wan half-smile.

"We must make the truth shout louder," William said. "And if talking is over and done, and it must be with swords, then so be it."

Eleanor looked at him. "Your brother holds Marlborough. Will he yield it to us if you were to speak with him?"

William rubbed his neck. "I can try," he said doubtfully.

"Do so," she said. The wine and a moment to compose herself had done their work and her voice was firm again, even if her hand still trembled on the cup. "If we are to lay siege to Windsor, we will need men and supplies. William, you are well placed in the Marches to recruit them. My son may have stripped Glamorgan, but you have access to Gwent and the Striguil lands."

"Madam." William inclined his head.

The justiciars set about discussing the tactics and logistics of a campaign against the Prince and William made a mental note to send one of the squires to the shieldmaker to find out if his new one was ready yet. He was going to need it.

Forty-one

"SIT DOWN BEFORE YOU FALL DOWN," ISABELLE commanded her husband who had newly returned from the siege at Windsor. He was swaying with weariness and the cloak he had tossed towards the coffer had missed its destination by several feet. Jean picked it up and completed the action. Isabelle pressed William on to the bench beside the bathtub. She ran her eyes over him but could see no sign of wounds. He was thin though, and she didn't like the grey shadows beneath his eyes. "You have been pushing yourself too hard," she scolded. He had sent a herald ahead to warn her of his arrival so at least she had had attendants prepare a hot tub in their chamber and hastily assemble a meal of barley and onion pottage with cold capon and bread. Outside, night had overtaken a thick lavender dusk; their sons were asleep in their cot, watched over by a nurse.

He leaned his head back against the wall, his hair flat and greasy from his helmet liner. She noticed a narrow healing scab that ran from outer cheekbone to eye corner. "Quite likely," he replied, "but there was need." He rubbed his palms over his face in a rasp of beard stubble, then gave her a red-eyed look. "Just knowing that Gaversham was within reach kept me putting one foot in front of another. Prince John has been persuaded to yield Windsor to his mother—on the condition that it be returned to him if Richard remains in prison. There's a truce until All Saints' Day and the Prince's mercenaries have been dispersed—thank Christ."

She brought him wine and watched him drink as if his throat were on fire. "We heard there had been fighting over Kingston way," she said as she knelt to remove his spurs and boots. He was pungent, to say the least, but she didn't care. He was home and whole, and it was all that mattered. She had been entertaining nightmares ever since he had ridden to join the other justiciars besieging Prince John at Windsor, especially after they heard about the savage acts of looting and rape around nearby Kingston. She knew the power of the Welsh longbow, and that his link mail was no protection against its arrows.

"There was," he said grimly. "I performed acts of *chevauchée* in the Young King's entourage when he was in rebellion against his father. I know all about looters and how to deal with them." He studied the grazed knuckles of his right fist, then opened his hand and Isabelle saw him gazing at the line of hard skin his sword grip had caused. "The ones we came upon have their piece of England now—their graves. The rest, if they have stopped running, will not venture from their own hearths for a long time. I lost a serjeant, six footsoldiers, and a palfrey. I gained thirty longbows from their camp, sundry weapons, and the things they had looted from the people of Kingston." A muscle worked in his jaw and she knew that he was not going to tell her what kind of things.

She unwound his leggings and he rose to let her help him out of the rest of his clothes. She gasped at an ugly burn on his wrist and hastened her maids to fetch salve for it. "A tipped-over cooking pot," he said with a shrug. "I've taken no wounds in battle."

"No? Yet I can see what it has cost you—"

He waved his hand in dismissal. "Mostly sleep," he said.

"There have not been enough hours in the day to accomplish all that needs to be done."

Naked now save for his braies, he crossed the room and parted the curtain to gaze upon his sleeping sons, one at either end of the cradle, small faces flushed with slumber. Will's hair was blond-brown, Richard's held a gleam of red like an echo of his de Clare grandsire. "All children should be able to sleep thus," he said to Isabelle. "In safety—untroubled." He shook his head. "I remember seeing Prince John sleeping just like this in Poitiers once, but somewhere he was ruined beyond redemption...I won't let it happen to my sons. None of it." He put his hands over his face. Isabelle wondered for a moment if he was weeping, but when he lowered his palms she saw that his eyes were dry and that the expression on his face was a glazed one of punch-drunk exhaustion.

"No, none of it," she said and gently led him to the tub. She stripped his braies and made him get in the water. She brought him the bread, capon, and more wine and, dismissing her maids and the squires, set about washing him herself. He stank of the camp, so she knew he'd been among his men and in the field. A marinated aroma of smoke and sweat clung to his skin.

As the food and wine began to work upon him, the colour returned to his complexion and the glassy look left his eyes. "Hubert Walter, Bishop of Salisbury, says that the ransom has been set, and he has confirmation that King Richard is very much alive."

"How much?" Isabelle asked.

William devoured the last of the bread and drained his wine. "A King's ransom," he said with a deep sigh. "One hundred and fifty thousand marks, to be paid in three instalments."

Her gaze widened in dismay. "Jesu! How is such a sum to be found?"

"God knows, and I hope that he tells me very soon because

doing so is in the hands of the justiciars and unless we achieve it swiftly, John's rebellion will renew itself and the country will descend into true civil war." He ducked his head under the water, swilled his hair, and came back up. "We cannot fail. What makes it more urgent is that Prince John and Philip of France will do their utmost to thwart Richard's release." He began to wash himself, his action more lively now. "I suppose there's the Cistercian wool clip, that'll account for some of the funds, and the Church has gold and silver that can be loaned." As he spoke his expression darkened.

"You are against the idea?"

"No, it has to be done, but it reminds me of my time in the Young King's service. Back then we stripped the Church of relics too—it was to pay mercenaries, not redeem a king, but it still leaves me uneasy." As he left the tub and tucked a towel around his waist and another across his shoulders, he sighed. "People will have to be taxed until they squeal. Individuals are to be asked to give as much as they can—with Richard's promise that they'll be rewarded for their fervour."

Gently Isabelle patted him dry. "And how much of a reward do you desire from Richard?" she murmured.

William exhaled and took her in his arms. "I have enough," he said, "and more than enough, but it is about keeping favour too. The Bishop of Salisbury hinted at a higher position in the Church for my younger brother—perhaps a bishopric. My loyalty, if it is unswerving and beyond the call of duty, will help to mitigate my older brother's support of Prince John. Besides, I swore my loyalty to Richard and it holds unto death."

Isabelle laid the palm of her hand swiftly to his lips. "Do not say that word," she admonished.

"Which one?" he asked. "Loyalty?"

She made to push out of his arms, but he held her fast against his body. "One is bound to the other," he murmured against her temple, "at least in my case it is. I cannot speak for Richard." He wound his hand around her braid and kissed her softly. "If it please you more, then I will say that it is the code by which I live my life, and while I know that God is entitled to end that life whenever He chooses, I pray He will grant me the boon of letting me see my sons grow strong and tall first."

Isabelle gave him another push, gentle this time, before swaying back into his embrace and silently tightening her arms around him.

John Marshal looked at the woman who had been his past and for whom his need still ached like a rotten tooth that he had never summoned enough courage to draw. And then he eyed the man standing beside her, dark-eyed, implacable, and quiet. Guillaume de Colleville was a minor Sussex landholder, a small fish for whom John could make life very difficult in his capacity as sheriff of that county.

"You want my blessing on your marriage?" John laughed sourly. "Christ, the last thing you want is a blessing from me!"

Reproach flickered in her eyes. The man's fists tightened. John was tempted to order him seized and imprisoned. He had been squeamish about such things at first but with time it had grown easier.

"I need neither your blessing nor your consent," Alais said, clasping her hands resolutely at her waist, "but I hope at least that you will wish me well. I came to tell you myself; it seemed the honourable thing to do…"

John swallowed against the sudden constriction in his throat. "Honourable!" He almost choked on the word and rounded on de Colleville. "She has told you her past?" John didn't know whether to sneer, speak man to man, be fair and just, or lash out like a wounded animal.

Grooves of muscle tightened and relaxed in de Colleville's

cheeks as he fought his own battle. "All of it," he replied with hard-won calm. "There are no secrets between us."

"Then take her." John gestured with his right hand as if throwing something away. "And may you derive more joy from her than I ever did."

Alais stifled a wounded protest and her eyes filled with tears.

"What do you want me to say?" John snarled at her. "What is left to say? You said it all at our child's graveside. If it was a sin to take you as my mistress, then I've paid a bloody price." He struggled for composure. "Does my brother know?"

"He has agreed to stand witness at our wedding," de Colleville said stonily.

John's stomach heaved. "I suppose my children have no objection."

"They are our children," Alais replied, her voice shaking, but still with a core of steel. "And they welcome it…I too have paid a price."

John swallowed. "I wish you well," he managed to say hoarsely. "I truly do, but ask no more of me than that because I cannot give it. I am not that generous of spirit."

They left soon after. In truth he had not expected them to stay. He folded his arms around his midriff, feeling as if someone had run a spear through him. Alais, Alais. It wasn't the pangs of love; it wasn't that he found it impossible to live without her. What did hurt was all the promise and sweetness of his once young life bleeding rapidly into sour old age. It was bitter regret and the knowledge that barren times lay ahead. It was the isolation and the betrayal. And that she had received from William the blessing he was not sufficiently generous himself to give.

"My lord?"

He looked up. His young wife's voice was hesitant. She never called him "John" although he had given her permission to do so. "What?" he snapped, straightening up. A headache had begun to pound at his temples and his eyes were hot.

White-faced, she stood before him, clenching and unclenching her hands. Seventeen years old to his almost fifty, God help him. "The visitors have not stayed?" she asked.

John gave a bitter laugh. "I doubt we'd have had much to say at the dining trestle. Perhaps you should leave too."

An expression of startled alarm crossed her face. "Leave, my lord? Where would I go?"

"As far away from me as possible…You don't snuggle up with a wounded boar, you take a spear and ram it through its heart."

"My lord?" Her voice was frightened.

"Christ, girl, get out, let me be!"

In the end he had to bellow at her and the sound of his own roar almost split his pounding skull in two. When the red mist had cleared from his vision, he saw that she had obeyed him and he was alone.

En route to the Marches to organise his own contribution to the King's ransom, William rode by way of Marlborough. His heart sank as he approached the castle on its great mound and saw that the walls were bristling with soldiers. The atmosphere, despite his having sent heralds ahead, was disturbingly hostile.

"Perhaps we should turn around," Isabelle said with a worried glance at the baggage cart carrying their two sons and their nurses.

William shook his head. He knew that whatever follies his brother might commit, fratricide was not one of them. "Even if he will not welcome the King's justiciar, he will extend hospitality to his own kin," he said grimly and heeled his palfrey on to the bridge.

John was waiting in the courtyard to greet him and William

was horrified at how old and ill his brother looked. His eyes were red-rimmed and watery, his cheeks mapped with broken veins. The tunic he wore was grease-stained and his chin was shadowed with heavy silver stubble.

"Have you come to wash your hands of me too?" he demanded almost belligerently.

A jolt went through William at the tone of voice. "If I were going to do such a thing, I'd not have brought my family and your son." He gestured towards the youth who had dark gold stubble of his own edging his square jaw. "He's almost of an age to be knighted, and he's shaping to be a fine man."

"Ever the diplomat," John grunted, making the words sound like an insult. "You had best come within."

"You know that the King will be returning as soon as the ransom is paid?" William said. The women had retired with the children to a chamber on the floor above, Isabelle murmuring with a gleam in her eye that she intended taking Aline in hand for a spot of spine-stiffening. William stretched his legs towards the heat of the brazier and rubbed his thigh, which was aching tonight.

His brother folded his arms and looked stubborn. "The Prince says that it is still uncertain that Richard's even alive."

"He lives, I promise you," William said curtly. "To deny it smacks of treason."

"It smacks of caution and common sense," John retorted. "And how in Christ's name are you going to raise a hundred and fifty thousand marks? It can't be done."

"Yes it can; open your eyes. The justiciars could have taken the Prince at Windsor. If a truce was agreed it was because no one wanted to humiliate him and he consented readily to yield the keep."

"On the understanding that you'd be able to raise the ransom and free Richard—neither of which is likely. If you fail and John becomes King, you will need to open your own eyes."

"We won't fail," William said harshly. "If John defies us then we'll do what we must. Ah God, brother, I don't want to come to Marlborough with fire and sword."

"Perhaps it will be me coming to Striguil instead," John snapped.

"Christ, this is no game. The Prince is leading you into dangerous territory. Look at this place—stuffed to the thatch with men and supplies. There can only be one outcome…"

"So you say, but it's a gamble, isn't it—as our father would have known. He wagered your life on King Stephen's weakness and he won."

"Did he?" William ran his palms across his face and thought of his father's ruined visage. "Did he win?"

"Yes, he did. Today he has a son in either camp. One way or the other the name of Marshal will survive. I hold Marlborough, which he always said belonged to us. He would be proud to see his eldest son holding it now—prouder than you will ever know."

"John…"

"Enough. I will talk to my son and in the morning you will go on your way. You and I have said all that there is to say. It is pointless to argue more." Rising to his feet, John Marshal left the room. William felt the cold air of his brother's leaving stir the hair at his nape and send a chill down his spine.

Forty-two

WILLIAM DREW ISABELLE DOWN THE VAST NAVE OF SAINT Paul's cathedral where, four years since, they had walked in procession to their wedding mass. Her eyes widened as she stared at the ranked iron-bound chests sequestered between the tall pillars supporting the vaulted ceiling, all bristling with padlocks, at the casks and barrels of silver pennies, the bolts of fine cloth and precious spices, donated in lieu of coin. All of this munificence was guarded by soldiers in full mail with shields and spears. To one side several officials were busy quantifying the treasure with weights and measures and tally sticks. They were speaking in German and using Latin to converse with their English counterparts.

Behind William and Isabelle, attendants in the green and yellow Marshal livery heaved Striguil's personal contribution to join the mass of riches waiting to be assessed and counted by the representatives of Emperor Henry.

"You have surpassed yourself, my lord," said Walter de Coutances, his gaze shrewd as he supervised the stowing of the Marshal donation.

William shrugged. "I have done my best," he said, "but it has not been easy. We mortgaged next year's wool clip and sold our finery. A man can only wear so many tunics and cloaks in a lifetime." He spread his hands to show that he wore but one ring—a fine sapphire cabochon. His fingers were bare for a man of his rank who would usually be dripping in gold.

"True," de Coutances said and looked at him quizzically. "Have you heard any news from Marlborough?"

"Not of late," William answered warily.

"I am told that it is well prepared for a siege, or to welcome rebels should they arrive at its gates." De Coutances shook his head. "These are wicked times when they set brother and neighbour against each other."

"I have no quarrel with my brother," William said evenly, "only a difference of opinion."

The letter from King Philip to Prince John was simple and succinct, carrying the warning words: "Beware, the devil is loosed." In point of fact it pre-empted Richard's release. The "devil" was still in prison, but likely to be free very soon. The first portion of the ransom had been paid and Queen Eleanor and Walter de Coutances were on their way to bring Richard back from Germany where he now dwelt under affable house arrest, holding his own court rather than languishing in fetters as his younger brother might have hoped.

William told Isabelle the details of the letter, a copy of which had found its way into Hubert Walter's hands. He had recently arrived back at Caversham from London where the news was already as rife as a plague of rats in a granary. A wild October wind was playing around Caversham's walls and the shutters rattled with each stormy gust. "Needless to say, John's fled England," he added.

Seated on their bed, Isabelle unwound her hair and looked at him. "You are not surprised."

"It is as much as I would have expected, given past behaviour," he said grimly.

Isabelle teased the ends of her loosened braids. "Does this mean he is fleeing the ship before it sinks, or hastening to fetch aid?"

William spread his hands. "Who knows? With John it could be either."

"What of his castellans?"

He looked bleak. "They'll have been ordered to hold out."

Isabelle bit her lip. She knew they were both thinking of his brother. She had watched William pace their chamber and the hall, playing a waiting game and suffering for it.

"He won't listen," he said. "He's like his master—he's gone too far down the road to turn back."

"You must try to talk to him though," she said with quiet conviction. "At least then you'll know you tried." She pressed her hand to her belly. She was entering her third month of pregnancy and nausea was a constant discomfort.

William chewed his thumbnail. "Do you think Richard will forgive John when he returns?"

Isabelle frowned. "Yes," she said slowly, "I think he will…not out of brotherly love. I don't believe they have that kind of affection for each other. And not out of duty, but perhaps because they have a shared parentage, and Richard knows himself so much above John that his plotting is no more to Richard than the meddling of a child. Besides, can you think of anything more galling to John than being magnanimously forgiven by Richard?"

William shook his head. "No," he said, "I can't."

Ralph Bloet, whose father was seneschal of Striguil, had brought William a gift from his father. "He thought it would suit your eldest son," he said, nodding smugly at the small dappled pony with shaggy mane and tail. "His steward won him from a dwarf at dice and sold him on. He's saddle trained."

"Ralph, I owe your father for this," William said with pleasure. "It's time Will had a pony but I've been hard-pressed to find one small enough without going to the big fair in London."

"Glad to help," the young knight said with gruff satisfaction. "You're avoiding London at the moment then?"

"No, not exactly avoiding, but preferring to be at Caversham—resting between storms," he said wryly. "Who knows, I might yet find the grace of time to turn Will into an accomplished horseman—and Richard too, the imp." He grinned at the thought of his younger son, only two years old but already lithe, co-ordinated, and getting into scrapes. "I…" He paused as a horseman trotted into the stable yard. The figure was familiar and filled him with a mingling of pleasure and trepidation. "Wigain?"

The little clerk dismounted from his blowing hack. Rubbing his buttocks and grimacing, he tottered bow-legged to William. "I swear the miles grow longer as I get older," he groaned, giving William a perfunctory bow. He eyed the pony. "You're breeding big dogs these days, my lord, if I may so."

Bloet scowled, "You are insolent," he growled. "If you spoke to me thus, I'd mend your manners with a whip."

"Let be, Ralph," William chuckled. "I've known Wigain since he was a common kitchen clerk and I was a landless whelp. Now I'm a royal justiciar with a countess for a wife and he's still common, but no longer a kitchen clerk."

"Sometimes I wish I were," Wigain said in a heartfelt voice. "Christ, the state of my arse, you'd think I'd ridden here on the haunches of a cow."

Bloet's nostrils flared. He was plainly unimpressed by their visitor but held to silence by William's dubious endorsement.

"You have news?" William sobered.

"From Archbishop Hubert Walter." Wigain produced a sealed packet from beneath his mantle.

"You know what it says?" William took it from him and started walking towards the hall stairs. A servant was sent running to fetch Isabelle.

"Yes, my lord. I wrote it myself from his dictation. You are not going to like it, but you will not be surprised."

William raised an eyebrow. There was grim relish in Wigain's expression. "You are not going to tell me that the ransom has been seized by thieves or that Richard is dead?"

Wigain shook his head. "Nothing as bad as that."

"It concerns Prince John then." William nudged the door open and strode to the hearth. Taking his belt knife, he slit the seal, opened out the vellum, and handed it to Wigain. "You might as well read it."

Wigain coughed meaningfully and William saw him furnished with a cup of wine. As he drank, Isabelle arrived from the private quarters and joined them, her expression questioning. Wigain bowed to her, wiped his mouth, and, clearing his throat, began to read.

The words made depressing listening. Prince John and King Philip had tried to prevent King Richard's release by offering a higher sum of their own for the German Emperor to keep Richard in prison or to turn him over to them. Letters had gone out to all of John's castellans in England, ordering them to stand firm and reiterating that Richard was not coming back.

"The Archbishop of Canterbury apprehended one of John's spies with a packet of letters," Wigain said. "There's no doubt of John's implication in treason. The Bishop fears that messages have still reached the castellans though."

William swore. "Has there been a response from the Emperor?"

Wigain shook his head. "It's too early for that."

"He won't agree to their offer," Isabelle said. "He's almost certain of receiving the ransom sum from England. His agents have been here and a part of it has already been paid. But where are John and Philip going to find such a vast amount of money? The French won't empty their coffers to keep Richard imprisoned no matter what Philip desires and John has few resources to milk."

William nodded; he had been thinking along similar lines. Philip and John didn't have the money, and matters were probably too far advanced to be changed anyway. But as to John's castellans...

"Archbishop Hubert's preparing to invest the Prince's castles," announced Wigain as if reading his mind. "I've seen the orders for chains and ropes and the ingredients for Greek fire. If they don't yield, they'll be stormed and suffer the consequences."

There was an awkward silence. Wigain helped himself to more wine. "I am sorry," he said with a shrug. "I am only the bearer of the message. If the Prince's castellans have any sense or care for their skins, they'll yield."

William shook his head. "My brother has neither," he said heavily.

At Marlborough, John Marshal listened to his clerk read out the instructions from his lord. Richard was not going to be released, the Prince was going to make a new agreement with the Emperor. The justiciars were likely to attack the Prince's strongholds in England and his castellans were to resist whatever the price.

Absently John paid the messenger and climbed laboriously to the battlements. By the time he reached the top, his lungs were straining and his legs were on fire. The castle had been built on a mound that some said was a burial place of the ancients. Occasionally, objects were dug out of the ground—arrowheads, beads, shards of pottery—that were nothing like the wares in current use. There was talk of spirits who walked through walls on gusty autumn nights, and footsteps heard on the wall walks on late June evenings, and a woman's laughter. He couldn't remember what a woman's laughter sounded like. Once, he thought he had seen his father walking the ramparts, one side of his face in shadow, the other showing a straight, hard profile. The sword at his hip was the same sword that John now wore at his own and his boots had made no sound on the boards of the wall walk. John had blinked and in that moment, the apparition, if such it was, had vanished, to leave John gazing in bemusement and fear at moonlit bare wood and stone. He had touched the sword hilt for reassurance and the pommel had been like a lump of ice in the cup of his palm.

Two riders were approaching from the town and he narrowed his eyes in the dusk. The black courser was very familiar, as was the roan cob. His stomach lurched. "Open the gate!" he commanded to the guards on watch and hurried down to the courtyard, arriving there just as William and his squire were dismounting from their horses.

"Have you come ahead of the besiegers?" he demanded. A crushing pain in his chest made it hard to breathe.

"What do you think?" William said, and John saw both pity and steel in his younger brother's dark gaze. "I have brought your son to see you, and I am here to plead with you to yield Marlborough before it's too late."

"Then you're out of time," John wheezed, "although perhaps you've done enough to salvage your conscience."

William recoiled and John felt a brief moment of satisfaction that his barb had hit home. He gestured towards the hall. "Come within. Let me offer you hospitality while I can." As he turned, he staggered. His son was the nearer and caught and braced him with a hard young arm. Close against him, John saw the smooth skin, the thick tawny hair, the features that mirrored his own. His child, his son. A man in his own right. Tears pricked his lids and his vision blurred.

He allowed himself to be aided into the hall and eased down on a bench. The strokes of his heart felt like a creature wallowing in mud. When William tried to send for a physician, he insisted he was all right, and indeed, after a cup of sweetened wine and a few moments of sitting down, the pain receded and the congestion eased. "You are wasting your own breath," he said to William, "unless you have come to offer me aid, or stand between me and what is to come."

"You know I cannot do that," William said quietly.

"You can, but you won't."

"As you can yield Marlborough to the justiciars but you won't," William retorted. "Did you know that Prince John has tried to bribe the Emperor to keep Richard in prison?"

John shrugged. "There are always rumours," he said wearily.

"It isn't a rumour," William said. "It's as hard a truth as the fact that Hubert Walter is on his way here now with an army. If you do not surrender Marlborough, then he will take it by force."

"It's true, sir," Jack said to his father. "I saw the Archbishop's letter."

John heard the deep voice, not a trace of boyhood in its cadence. "If Marlborough was in your charge, would you yield?" he asked the young man.

His son frowned and took his time to think before answering. "I might," he said after a while, "but not until I was forced. If I surrendered too soon, I would compromise my honour; too late, and I would lose anyway and be of no further use to my lord."

John looked surprised and then thoughtful. "Did you tell him to say that?" he asked William.

"No, he is his own man," William answered, looking thoughtful too.

"I cannot yield this place," John Marshal said, his expression tight and stubborn.

"You can," William answered, hoping that his voice held the right amount of encouragement and pleading.

John shook his head. "But I won't," he replied, and William knew then that he had lost.

They left the next morning as dawn cracked the eastern sky with streaks of yolk-gold. Looking back, William saw John standing in the gateway, arm raised in farewell. From a distance his grey pallor didn't show and he had made a visible effort to draw together the dissipating threads of his being. There had been no embrace, and even if eyes had acknowledged a final parting, expressions had not shown it. What John and his son had said to each other during their private time together, William had not probed. What would he say to his own son on the eve of such a final and sombre leave-taking? A part of William wanted to turn his horse, ride back, and embrace his brother fervently. They had never been close, but now that external distances yawned between them and the last bridge was about to burned, he felt both pain and guilt.

His nephew, who had been looking round too, now faced the road ahead and set his jaw. "He's going to die, isn't he?" he said.

The words flashed through William, making real what he was trying to keep to himself. "I am not a physician," he said brusquely.

"He is, though. His face was as grey as an unpainted effigy and you heard the way he was breathing."

William sighed. "Yes," he admitted wearily, "I fear he is."

Jack swallowed. "Do you think he listened? Will he yield if they come?"

The dawn widened and the sky became as bright as the lining of a seashell. "I know that he listened," William said. "But we both know he wasn't persuaded. He could have yielded Marlborough to me had he so chosen."

"He would never do that for the sake of his pride," Jack answered.

"No," William said wearily, "I suppose not." He took his eyes off the sunrise and studied the young man. "I have sent

Wigain back to Hubert Walter with a plea on your father's behalf. I know he must lay siege to Marlborough if your father refuses to yield, but I have asked him to be lenient—to tread lightly on your father's pride. I know it is not enough…"

The young man shrugged. "If your positions were reversed, would he do the same for you?"

William sighed. "You ask some hard questions. I would like to say yes, but in the balance I do not know. Nor does it matter now, save that in leaving him I feel I have betrayed him."

His nephew's jaw tightened. "The betrayal is Prince John's," he said. "Without his treachery, my father would not be in such a bind."

"Your father is right; he may yet be our future King," William murmured.

"That does not stop him being dishonourable," the young man flashed.

"No, but if he became King, we would be honour bound to serve him—as your father feels he is honour bound now." William grimaced. "Bound" was indeed the right word. Hog-tied and thrown in the fire.

Forty-three

MARLBOROUGH, WILTSHIRE, MARCH 1194

BREATH WHISTLING IN HIS THROAT, JOHN MARSHAL watched them come, the army that William had warned him about; the army who would take Marlborough from him and leave him in disgrace. There might be a pardon for his over-lord, the Prince, but John knew there would be none for him. One way or the other he was doomed. Bidding slow farewell to the rooms and corridors of his boyhood, he gave his wife the keys to the strongbox and such money as it contained. "If things should go ill, you are my deputy," he said.

She gave him a blank, frightened look. "I don't know what to do."

He returned her a dour smile. "Pretend you are the Countess Isabelle," he said. "No one is going to harm you. You're just an innocent pawn. Behave as befits a great lady and you will be treated like one." He went from her chamber into his own and bade his squires arm him. The weight of the mail hauberk dragged upon him as if the rings were fashioned of lead. The shimmer of the silk surcoat was too bright for his eyes; his father's sword was an encumbrance at his left hip, which was aching from the insinuating March damp; but the heaviest burden was that carried by his mind. Sweating, nauseous, he wondered how long he and the castle could hold out. Perhaps his son was right. Perhaps he should be prepared to compromise…but not yet. He had to make the enemy believe it was worth their while to do so, and he had to give himself credibility in his own and his lord's eyes. There was the rub. Something that William had possessed all his life without trying and which had eluded John no matter how he struggled.

"I have lived too long," he said to the startled squires. "Perhaps today is fortuitous."

At Striguil the March wind was bitter. Hugging her arms around herself beneath her cloak, eyes stinging, Isabelle went to look out over the palisade towards the lower bailey. William had been out schooling his horses all afternoon. Sensing his need for solitude and the disciplined concentration that left no room for a crowd of thoughts, she had kept to their chamber and told others to give him a wide berth, but as the hours drew on and dusk approached, she had thought it time to find out how he fared.

He was still at work with his new destrier, bought last month from the Earl of Norfolk—a powerful dark brown colt, dappled with chestnut on belly and rump. She watched him make the horse change leading forelegs at the canter and as always admired his straight spine in the saddle and his fluid understanding of the horse. In outline in the fading light, he could have been a lithe young squire and she felt both her heart and loins contract. His squires weren't there, so she assumed he had sent them to the guardroom and he was attended only by Rhys, who was blanketing up Bezant, preparatory to leading him back to the stables. Within her womb, their third child gave a confined kick. There wasn't much room these days.

Mindful of her advanced state of pregnancy, Isabelle moved carefully along the wall walk and descended to the lower bailey, her cloak flapping and her veil beating around her face so that she could scarcely see where she was going. By the time she reached the foot of the steps, Rhys had alerted William and he trotted the destrier across to her and drew rein.

"How is he shaping?" she asked, fondling the horse's plush muzzle.

"Very well," William answered, "although he still has much to learn." He glanced around and, lifting his right hand off the bridle, rubbed his face. "I hadn't realised how late it was."

"I knew you needed the time alone," she said, smiling but concerned.

William dismounted and handed the destrier to Rhys. Taking her arm he linked it through his. "You always do know what I need," he murmured.

A look passed between them and Isabelle lightened it by laughing. "I may know, but I cannot always give it." She laid her hand in emphasis to her belly. "I do not think it will be long now. I—" She stopped speaking and turned as the guards shouted warning of a rider and the porter made shrift to open the gate in the palisade. She felt William's grip tighten on her arm and from the way he stiffened she knew that he had not outridden his demons this afternoon, that they were still very much with him.

A messenger cantered into the yard on a sweating chestnut courser. "It's my brother's horse," William said hoarsely and a shudder rippled through him.

So, the news was here, she thought; the news they had been waiting for and dreading. The hooded figure that dismounted staggered on landing and turned towards them, and she saw that it was Wigain—a grey, exhausted vestige of his usual self, but Wigain nonetheless. The little clerk looked at William, all merriment quenched from his eyes. The evening wind whipped strands of grey hair at the side of his hood. "I've ridden from Marlborough," he said, "from my lord Hubert Walter…" He licked his lips.

"My brother is dead, isn't he?" William said flatly.

Wigain nodded and swallowed. "Yes, my lord. I am sorry. Archbishop Hubert sends his deep condolences…" He swallowed again, and coughed.

William ignored Wigain's exaggerated efforts to call attention to his parched throat. "Does he indeed?" he said, his nostrils flaring.

Isabelle swiftly took the initiative, reclaiming William's arm and tugging upon it. "It is cold and dark," she said sensibly. "We can as well listen in the warmth of the chamber as out here."

"Perhaps I don't want the warmth of the chamber for what I am going to hear," he growled.

She rolled her eyes. "But I do, and our unborn son or daughter."

It was an excuse below the belt and they both knew it. However, William capitulated and let her lead him up the stairs into the private chamber, pausing only to send a servant to the guardroom to summon his eldest squire.

As William entered his chamber, his sanctuary, his two sons ran to greet him. When the nurse would have called them back, he bid her let them come for he needed their joy and their innocent liveliness to steady him.

Isabelle took a seat by the fire and laid her palm on the shelf of her belly. Wigain drank the wine he was given with every evidence of wanting to make each swallow last so that he would not have to open his mouth and speak. Jack quietly entered the room, his gaze wide and wary. William bade him come to the brazier. The young man's eyes flickered toward Wigain.

"Your father is dead," William said gently.

Jack's expression did not change, although he stopped like a horse on a short rein.

Wigain ran out of wine to swallow. "I am sorry," he croaked.

The young man gave him a fathomless look and a small shrug. "It was expected," he said.

"Tell us." William sat his sons at his feet and set his forefinger to his lips, bidding them be silent. Will nodded solemnly. Richard copied his father's gesture and then exaggeratedly pressed his lips together and looked wide-eyed at Wigain, clearly expecting a story.

Wigain took the flagon from William's steward and helped himself to more wine. "Archbishop Walter brought troops to Marlborough and commanded your brother to yield the castle in the name of King Richard. Your brother refused and had his bowmen loose arrows upon our men. The Archbishop laid siege to the keep with vigour—you know the way of it, my lord. You have seen enough siege and *chevauchée* in service to old King Henry and his sons."

William nodded. "There is no need to give a blow-by-blow account," he said tersely. "It serves no purpose. He was killed in battle?"

Wigain tipped the wine down his throat. "No, my lord. It is true that he was directing the battle from the wall walk. I saw his shield and banner on several occasions…but it was during a lull that they took that banner down and then heralds came out to ask Archbishop Walter for terms."

Wigain saw a look flicker between uncle and nephew. "My lord archbishop desired surrender of the castle, and said he was prepared to let the garrison go free. But when the gate opened, it was Lady Marshal who brought the keys to him and told us that her husband was dead of a seizure." Wigain looked sombre, remembering. "She knelt before the Archbishop with the keys held out on the palms of her hands and begged his clemency…and he granted it. He had what he wanted. The garrison surrendered and he allowed Lord John's body to lie in the chapel while a coffin was brought and a cart to bear it away to Bradenstoke. There's to be a funeral mass in the cathedral at Cirencester."

William narrowed his eyes, calculating how soon he could be on the road. He felt leaden with sorrow and a deep sense of failure. How had it come to this?

Wigain took another drink from his cup. "There is more," he said.

William looked at him. "More?" The word was ominous.

Wigain licked his lips. "King Richard has landed at Sandwich. He's on his way to attend the siege at Nottingham and he bids you, as you love him, join him with all haste at his muster in Huntingdon." The clerk looked uncomfortable. "There were rumours that you were in Marlborough with your brother…that you had chosen to defy the King."

William clenched his fists and fought a powerful surge of fury. Turn your back and in an instant your enemies had their knives out. "But I wasn't, was I?"

"No, my lord," Wigain said, looking as ashamed as if he were the creator of the news and not just the bearer. "I am sorry. I didn't know which to tell you first…"

"Does a brother come before a king?" William asked with a bitter, humourless smile. He looked down at his sons. His youngest one was gazing up at him out of wide, dark eyes. He remembered his own father, who had been willing to put his ambition and a would-be queen before his family.

"Is that the end of the story, Papa?" Will asked. "I didn't like it."

"Didn't like it," Richard echoed, beginning to pout.

"No, it's not the end," William answered, ruffling his heir's hazel-brown hair. "Far from it, and for what it's worth, I didn't like it either."

"You'll like it even less when I tell you that William Longchamp is with the King," Wigain said. "Richard's revoked his banishment and welcomed him back to his side. He needs his money-grubbing skills and Longchamp has always been as slippery as an eel."

William felt revulsion churn his stomach. His hand remained on his son's head. "No need to ask who has been stirring the pot," he said. "I had better make haste before I'm accused of full-blown treason."

Riding hard, William met his brother's funeral cortège on the outskirts of Cirencester as it progressed towards the cathedral. Aline had hired a group of six professional mourners and they walked either side of the coffin, garbed in long dark-coloured mantles with voluminous hoods. Periodically they wailed and struck their breasts. Aline was as pale as a shroud and her eyes were smudged with exhaustion, but she had control of herself. Whatever grief and difficulty had come from her marriage to John Marshal, she had gained stature and maturity too. William dismounted from his courser to walk beside the bier. John's sword, their father's sword, was laid atop the pall of red silk. There was a grieving twist of regret in William's soul that he and John had not been closer in life, and now it was too late. Jack dismounted too and silently took his place among the mourners. The rest of William's knights followed suit.

"In the end he didn't have to surrender," Aline said to William and Jack as they walked. She too wore a dark mantle and hood, but beneath it her gown of costly red wool showed as a bright border with each step. "His body gave out and I am glad for him that it did—that he did not have to yield the keep and his pride." She bit her lip, remembering. "He came down from the wall walk to take a respite from commanding the men, and collapsed at the foot of the tower stairs. By the time I reached him, his soul had fled. There was nothing anyone could do."

"I am glad for him too, that he was still lord of Marlborough when he died," William said hoarsely, "although I would rather he had lived."

They walked in sombre and contemplative silence for a long time, but at last William turned to the wan girl pacing at his side. "What will you do now?" he asked.

She gave a forlorn shrug. "Return to my family…serve them by making another match and hope that it is a good one."

The grief and regret twisted a little tighter inside him. "I hope so too, my lady," he said.

Following the vigil and mass in Cirencester, William left his nephew and the majority of his knights to escort the coffin the rest of the way to Bradenstoke Priory, and prepared to ride fast for Huntingdon. In Cirencester too, he knighted young Jack Marshal. "Since you are your father's only son and a man, you should have the standing of knighthood," William said as he belted Jack with his father's sword. "Besides, you have earned it, and your father should have a senior member of his family and a sworn knight to lead his cortège." Guilt and grief bit at him. He knew that it was his place to ride to Bradenstoke with them, but he couldn't afford to.

Jack nodded, his jaw stiff with controlled emotion. William clasped his shoulder, man to man. "Join me in Nottingham when you have done your duty by your father," he said. "I'll have need of you."

Leaving the cathedral, he breathed deeply of the bitter March air and gathered himself for the next ordeal.

It was late morning when William rode into Huntingdon, having set out from Bedford at dawn. He and his three knights were stopped at the town gate and a messenger was sent running to inform the King of their arrival. As William waited on his sweating palfrey, he was aware of the speculative glances cast in his direction and he did not have to imagine hard what men were wondering.

"You ride light, my lord," said the captain of mercenaries who was in charge of the gate. He toyed with his sword hilt.

"The rest of my troop are following," William answered in a neutral voice. "They'll join us at Nottingham."

The mercenary nodded and said nothing, but William could sense him questioning on whose side. No one offered him hospitality, but William didn't cavil. He knew the game that was being played, and he was adept at it. He dismounted from his horse and threw a blanket over its sweating back, gesturing his knights to follow suit. He made soldiers' small talk and waited with an outward show of aplomb, although within himself he was fidgeting like a man sitting on a nest of red ants.

The messenger eventually returned with the instruction that William was to be brought to King Richard's pavilion. William Longchamp had accompanied the messenger, and there was a supercilious smile parting his full black beard. He was obviously bent on enjoying this moment and on paying back old scores.

"You're hanging in the balance, Marshal," Longchamp said, malice glittering. "I hope for your sake that you're in an eloquent mood."

William looked stonily at the Bishop. "I have hung in the balance before, and survived. Either the King knows me well enough by now, or he doesn't. Words, no matter how eloquent, will not alter that."

Longchamp's upper lip curled. "No, they won't," he said in an insinuating voice. "And the King is waiting to hear them and make judgement."

William gave his horse into the keeping of Roger D'Abernon. "I am ready," he said impassively, "and I do not fear to be judged."

"The garrison at Nottingham is still refusing to yield to the King," Longchamp said as he limped at William's side through the camp towards Richard's pavilion. "It's strongly held but no match for us. The pity is that the justiciars ever returned it to

John in the first place." His voice was bland, but since William had been the justiciar responsible for Nottingham's custody and subsequent handing over to John during peace negotiations, his words were neither innocent nor indifferent comment.

"I did as I deemed fit," he said curtly.

Longchamp gave a nasty smile. "You'll need to do better than that, Marshal," he said.

"Oh, I don't know," William retorted. "Others seem to have escaped lightly enough, when you consider the abuses they perpetrated in the King's absence, even down to forging documents and misusing his seal."

Longchamp glittered him a narrow look. "I committed no acts of treason. I cannot say the same for your brother and yourself."

William clenched his fists and held on to his temper by the finest of frayed threads. Mercifully they arrived at the King's pavilion and Longchamp ran out of baiting time.

William hesitated as he gazed upon the billowing canvas, painted scarlet and gold and crowned with a great bronze finial. Behind the guards, the tent flaps were drawn back to show an interior draped with hangings of Damascus silk. A fur-covered bed was positioned on the left-hand side in the tent and a long trestle surrounded by stools and benches on the right. In the centre was the King's chair, surrounded by an assortment of weapons, including his hauberk on a stand of beechwood poles. The floor was covered with a thick layer of green rushes, amid which spring flowers—cowslips and young daisies—gave splashes of colour. William's stomach turned over. Richard emerged from a curtained-off area at the far end of the tent, adjusting his hose. There was a frosting of silver in his apricot-blond hair and harsh lines graven into his features by sun, wind, and the privation of captivity. He was seven and thirty but looked ten years older. His shirt and tunic, open at the throat, revealed wiry auburn curls, but despite the dishabille, he still had the presence of a king. Swallowing, William entered the tent and knelt. The green smell from the rushes rose around him and he clenched his fists. It was more than forty years since he had played as a small boy in King Stephen's tent, innocent, unknowing, his life in the balance. If not for that long-ago day, he probably wouldn't be here now.

"Leave us," Richard commanded the servants and guards. "You too, my lord Bishop." He waved his hand at Longchamp.

"But, sire, you need witnesses and I—" Longchamp began, plainly desperate to remain and watch as his rival was humiliated.

"I said leave us," Richard said in a peremptory tone. "This is a private matter between myself and the Marshal."

Longchamp hesitated for an instant, then bowed and swept out of the tent, his cloak creating a cold draught behind him.

"You are late to the meet, Marshal," Richard said after a moment, gesturing him to his feet. "I had expected you sooner."

"I travelled as fast as my horse would bear me, sire." William resisted the urge to wipe his damp palms down his surcoat.

"But without your troop?"

William rose and faced Richard. His scalp was tingling. "My troop will come to Nottingham and be waiting. Currently they are under the command of my nephew and escorting my brother's funeral cortège to Bradenstoke."

Richard steepled his hands at his lips and paced the tent for a moment like a restless, hungry lion. "Your brother," he said at length. "Yes, I heard that he had died, and I am sorry for it. The pity is that it was in rebellion against me."

"He was loyal to your brother, sire."

"Who is fickle and does not know the meaning of the word loyalty. Tell me, Marshal, were your own loyalties strained?"

"Not beyond breaking point, sire."

Richard looked at him and William looked back without flinching. "I received letters in Cyprus, saying that you had betrayed me, that you had gone over to my brother's side. And I heard the same again when I landed in England."

"Whoever wrote them lied," William said with a meaningful look over his shoulder towards the tent entrance from which Longchamp had so recently flurried out. "I have never revoked my allegiance, once given."

"Yet you owe that allegiance to my brother for your Irish lands and your fief of Cartmel."

"But not for Striguil and Longueville, sire, nor for my post of justiciar. Yes, I supported the lord John when the Bishop of Ely overstepped his authority, but that was on the instructions of your lady mother and the Archbishop of Rouen, who were in turn acting on your authority." He made a throwing gesture with his right hand. "Either you have trust in me, sire, or you do not, and it ends here."

Richard grunted. Reluctant amusement curled his lips. "I have heard plenty of persuasion on your behalf from my mother and Walter de Coutances," he said. "In truth, enough to burn my ears off. And you have been eloquent in your own way if your contributions to my ransom are any statement of intent." Richard clicked his fingers and an attendant poured wine into two cups. William's glance flickered. For a moment it seemed as though there were two spectres in the tent with him and Richard: King Stephen, hollow-eyed and gaunt, beset by burdens but still finding a smile for a fair-haired little boy who looked not unlike William's own four-year-old son. The smell of the rushes under his feet rose in nauseating green waves.

Richard handed the brimming cup to William. "There are few people in the world to whom I would give my trust, and my brother is certainly not amongst them, although he has his virtues nonetheless and I can still use him. Whatever you think of my chancellor—and I admit that Longchamp is part weasel and part snake—he is completely dedicated to my service and

I find him valuable. But you, Marshal…" He paused for effect and William held his own breath. "You could have taken my life and you held back," Richard said. "You could have set the South-west alight by joining in rebellion with my brother. You put me before your own kin. Some say that it is all in order to serve yourself, my chancellor especially; but then he lost his skirmishes with you and he doesn't take kindly to being humiliated. My mother says that you are the most loyal man she knows…and that a king should value loyalty above all else."

William had known that the words were bound to emerge. He had borne the remembrance of his meeting with King Stephen in dreams for almost all of his life, and as well as memory it had been premonition; he realised that now. He waited to drink to loyalty in the wine trembling in his cup and hoped he would not be sick.

Richard nodded thoughtfully. "My mother is wrong," he said. "Or wrong in her choice of word at least…"

William stiffened. This was not how the scene was supposed to play out.

"I do value loyalty, but I value your integrity more. There's a difference of shade. It was integrity that kept you by my father and sent your lance through my stallion's chest…and it is what brings you here today. You will do what is right and just."

William wasn't so sure of that. True integrity would have seen him at Bradenstoke, burying his brother with all due ceremony, rather than attending a mass at Cirencester and cutting off to ride here. It was necessity and self-service that brought him to Huntingdon, but if Richard desired to give it a different word, then so be it. Loyalty, integrity, necessity. All were valid; all had shaped his life, and in different concentrations would continue to do so.

Richard raised his cup. "To the future," he said.

William forced a dark smile. "Whatever it may hold," he replied, thinking he could manage to drink to that.

Epilogue

PORTSMOUTH, MAY 1194

WILLIAM LOOKED DOWN AT HIS SLEEPING DAUGHTER IN her cradle. She was making small snuffling sounds and her little fists were like furled spring leaves. She had been born whilst Richard was besieging the now capitulated Nottingham Castle; arriving at Striguil to find mother and baby safe and well had been a gift beyond price to William.

She had been christened Mahelt and at almost six weeks old the furrowed, rumpled look of the newborn had been replaced by the pink and white rosiness of a healthy, well-nourished infant. Her hair was brown like his, and she had his eyes, too. Every time William looked at her, he was captivated. His sons were less enamoured. Will and Richard were more interested in their toy swords and hobby horses than their baby sister. Will in particular, being the eldest and most aware, was also wildly excited at the notion of a sea crossing.

William glanced from the cradle towards the open door of the long timber hall in which they were lodged as his sons ran past, giggling and playing chase, their nurse in hot pursuit. There had been some terrible storms at the end of April, and Richard's attempts to embark for Normandy had been thwarted by slanting rain and high winds that whipped the sea into a frenzy. Once he had put to sea and been beaten back into harbour. Today, however, the wind was warm, earth-scented and blowing towards Normandy, a perfect day for a crossing.

"My lord." His daughter's nurse curtseyed to him and then stooped over the cradle to lift the baby out and wrap her in a snug travelling blanket. Mahelt made a soft protest and her brow puckered a whim, but she did not waken. A serjeant-at-arms picked up the cradle and carried it away towards the wharf and the nurse followed him, crooning softly to the baby.

Isabelle, who had been outside supervising the carrying of the last pieces of furniture and baggage down to the ship, now poked her head round the door. "Are you ready?" she asked. She was wearing an Irish mantle of thick plaid edged with squirrel fur and a sensible wimple of heavy tabby-woven silk. There was amusement in her gaze and exasperation...and sympathy. She knew how much he hated sea crossings.

William secured his cloak pin and squared his shoulders. Warm or not, the breeze was still boisterous and would freshen at sea. He smiled at her. "Yes, I'm ready," he said and stepped out into the sunshine.

Isabelle looked up at him, her eyes layered with the blue tones of a summer sea. Placing her hand over his wrist in formal fashion, she secretly circled her thumb to his pulse beat and gently pressed, conveying deep affection and support.

Together they walked down to the ship, and despite being accompanied by an entourage of knights and squires, grooms and maids, children and nurses, they might as well have been alone—lovers, familiar but newly met in the bright spring morning.

A lone galley remained at the jetty, its wash strake lined with green and gold shields, and red dragon banners flying from the top of the mast and the deck shelter. The sea glittered in the bright morning and most ships had already embarked, including those belonging to Richard and Eleanor. A crowd had gathered on the jetty and William's own horse transport had just cast off from its moorings. By narrowing his eyes, he could see Rhys on the deck and his nephew, Jack, who had opted to sail with the horses and his new black destrier.

He inhaled deeply of the salt-tanged air and crossed himself. It was not so much the notion of the sea journey that made him do so, as the awareness that he wanted to enjoy his wife, his family, and their lands to the full, with all the vigour of the life that was surging in his veins as strongly as it had done when he was a youth at Drincourt. The shrouds he had brought from Jerusalem were packed at the bottom of his travelling coffer, but he hoped he would not need them until his children were grown, and his cup drained to the lees.

Author's Note

WILLIAM MARSHAL IS ONE OF ENGLAND'S UNSUNG HEROES and perhaps the greatest knight of the Middle Ages. He is a well-known character to academics and enthusiasts of the medieval world, but outside that circle few people are aware of this fourth-born son of a minor aristocratic family who rose from obscurity to become a champion of the tourneys, the confidant of kings, a great magnate, and eventually regent of England (saving the country from bankruptcy and an invading army at the same time). He might have been entirely forgotten were it not for a narrative poem commissioned shortly after his death which details the story of his life and which itself disappeared from knowledge for centuries and was only rediscovered in the 1890s.

I have wanted to tackle aspects of William Marshal's story for some time, but have only now found the space to write it. I said to my editor that William Marshal had stuffed so much living into the suitcase of his life that it bulges at the seams, and to cover every incident would probably take thousands of pages and still have moments left over. I have perforce had to streamline his tale and cover the most important incidents. *The Greatest Knight* explores the early part of this fascinating life. A second novel, *The Scarlet Lion*, is linked to the first but not dependent, and covers the doings of his later years (see excerpt from *The Scarlet Lion* on page 537).

I have filled in one or two gaps in William's life with my own imagination, but have tried to stay true to the spirit of his character. For example, it is not known whether William had a mistress, made casual arrangements with women, or was celibate before his marriage. However, the historical evidence suggests that he liked and respected women and that women liked him. The *Histoire de Guillaume le Maréchal* tells us that a woman helped him out when he was a wounded prisoner by giving him bandages inside a loaf of bread to bind his wounds. I decided to develop this character into Clara and to make her stand for the women William might have known before his marriage to Isabelle de Clare. The Histoire also tells us that he went to the aid of a woman in Le Mans whose house was burning down during Henry II's last stand to defend it (and the smoke from the quilt got inside his helmet and half-choked him!) so again I used Clara to bring the story thread full circle.

The jury is still out on whether or nor William had an affair with the Young Queen Marguerite. The general consensus is that it was possible, but unlikely. However, the rumours did seriously affect William's career for a time and led to his banishment. The more likely cause of his fall from favour was the fact that such was his charm and prowess that he took away the spotlight from the Young King who, by his nature, would have taken a very dim view of being eclipsed. Rather like the sporting heroes of today, the great tourney champions were much in demand and sponsors would pay vast sums of money to have them on their "team." The world of high earnings, transfer fees, hero worship, and celebrity that, for example, we associate with modern-day football was a concept already embraced by the followers of the tourney circuit in late twelfth- and early thirteenth-century Europe. William Marshal was the

David Beckham of his day! I should add here that William did have a destrier named Blancart and the incident with the stallion having too tender a mouth for the bridle is reported in detail in the *Histoire de Guillaume le Maréchal*.

No one knows what William did on his pilgrimage to Jerusalem. That part of his life is a mystery, although he almost certainly underwent a spiritual crisis following the death of his young lord and the robbing of the shrine of Rocamadour. His pilgrimage clearly affected him for the rest of his life. He did indeed bring home the cloths with which he intended to drape his coffin when the time came for him to die. The foundation charter for his priory at Cartmel has a curse written into it to protect against anyone plundering or desecrating the church. I can't help but think that this is in some way tied up with the looting of the shrine at Rocamadour and William's determination that nothing like that was going to happen to his own foundation.

There was an age gap of approximately twenty years between William and Isabelle de Clare, but they seem to have been very compatible. William seems to have valued his wife above and beyond her role of producer of children and keeper of the domestic hearth. As mentioned in the novel, he retained his own smaller knighthood seal and although clerks styled him an earl in their documents, he never called himself one until King John made him Earl of Pembroke in his own right. Having dwelt in the household of Eleanor of Aquitaine and remained her lifelong friend and confidant, William was accustomed to women with the ability to wield power and think for themselves and appears to have encouraged these traits in his wife. Incidentally, Striguil is better known today as Chepstow.

The character of Wigain is an interesting one. He is known to have been the Young King's kitchen clerk and he is also known to have kept tallies of William's wins in tourneys. However, he also ranged further afield and was entrusted with doing more than just counting the number of capons that passed through the kitchen door, for he is found hundreds of miles away from his master in the company of the Bishop of Norwich and the advocate of Béthune among others. What he was actually doing is not explained, but with such hints at other activities, I felt justified in giving him a wider role beyond the kitchens, and I enjoyed developing his character. I must confess that in the interests of keeping the character list within acceptable bounds, I gave Wigain the task of messenger to King Henry II on the death of the Young King, when the toing and froing was in fact undertaken by various ecclesiastical personages, including the Bishop of Agen and a monk of Grammont.

William's relationship with his eldest brother, John, seems to have been an uneasy one. When John inherited the Marshal lands from their father, he was in a position to help William out, but he didn't. Later, William took John's illegitimate son (also called John, but rechristened Jack in the novel for the sake of the author's sanity!) for his squire, and advanced the youth's career and standing, but when John Marshal was killed in rebellion against King Richard, William distanced himself from his brother and paid only lip service to the burial rites. Henry Marshal rose in the church to become Bishop of Exeter. Not a great deal is known about his relationship with William and they do seem to have led largely separate lives. Henry was involved in a deep quarrel with Henry II's illegitimate son, Geoffrey, who became Archbishop of York, but to feature the squabbling of these two contumacious priests in the novel would have made the story three times as long! Ancel Marshal disappears from the record after 1181. There is a strong suggestion that he joined the household of his cousin, Rotrou Count of Perche, following the tourney at Lagny-sur Marne, but that is all that can be said.

For readers who are interested in the story of William Marshal and would like to read further I can highly recommend Professor David Crouch's revised biography: *William Marshal, Knighthood, War and Chivalry, 1147–1219* (Longman, 2002, ISBN 0 582 77222 2).

Although I consulted a multitude of books and sources whilst researching the novel, here is a select bibliography of some of the most useful, aside from Professor Crouch's book.

Appleby, John T., *England Without Richard 1189–1199* (G. Bell & Sons, 1967).

Eyton, Revd R. W., *Court, Household and Itinerary of Henry II* (Taylor & Co., 1893).

Flanagan, Marie-Therese, *Irish Society, Anglo-Norman Settlers, Angevin Kingship: Interactions in Ireland in the Late Twelfth Century* (Clarendon Press, 1989).

History of William Marshal, Vol. 1: Text and Translation (II. 1-10031), ed. by A. J. Holden with English translation by S. Gregory and D. Crouch (Anglo-Norman Text Society, 2002, ISBN 0 905474 42 2).

Kelly, Amy, *Eleanor of Aquitaine and the Four Kings* (Harvard University Press, 1950, ISBN 0 674 24254 8).

Labarge, Margaret Wade, *Mistress, Maids and Men: Baronial Life in the Thirteenth Century* (Phoenix, 2003).

Meade, Marion, *Eleanor of Aquitaine* (Frederick Muller, 1978, ISBN 0 584 10347 6).

Painter, Sidney, *William Marshal: Knight Errant, Baron and Regent of England* (Johns Hopkins Press, 1933).

Tyerman, Christopher, *Who's Who in Early Medieval England* (Shepheard Walwyn, 1996, ISBN 0 85683 132 8).

Warren, W. L., *Henry II* (Eyre & Methuen, 1973, ISBN 0 413 38390 3).

As always, I welcome comments, and I can be contacted through my website www.elizabethchadwick.com or by email to elizabeth.chadwick@btinternet.com.

I also post regular updates about my writing and research on my blog: http://livingthehistoryelizabethchadwick.blogspot.com. There is also a friendly, informal discussion list at ElizabethChadwick@yahoogroups.com, which readers are very welcome to join.

An Excerpt from

The Scarlet Lion
by Elizabeth Chadwick

The Scarlet Lion *is the second of two stand-alone novels about William Marshal.*

"An extraordinary wonderful, true story…I really felt that I had walked with William Marshal, and that my own life was enriched."

—Richard Lee, founder and publisher
of the Historical Novel Society

William Marshal's prowess and loyalty as a knight in the English royal household has been rewarded by marriage to Isabelle de Clare, heiress to great estates in England, Normandy, and Ireland.

The couple's contentment and security is shattered when King Richard dies. He is succeeded by his brother John, who takes the Marshals' sons hostage and seizes their lands. The conflict between remaining loyal and rebelling over injustices committed threatens to tear William and Isabelle's marriage apart and ruin their lives. As the situation intensifies, William has to steer an increasingly precarious path that will lead him eventually to the rule of a country in desperate straits.

Fiercely intelligent and courageous, fearing for the man who is the light of her life, Isabelle too must come to terms with what the future holds.

AN EXCERPT FROM

The Scarlet Lion

*I*SABELLE STAGED AWAY FROM THE LATRINE SHAFT WHERE she had spent the last five minutes heaving. She felt drained and utterly wretched. 'It's going to be another boy," she said weakly to William.

Humour glimmered through his concern. "How do you know?"

"I'm always more sick when carrying the boys, and at all times of day." She took a napkin moistened with rose water from Sybilla D'Earley and patted her face and throat.

"Boys are always more trouble," Sybilla said with a knowing woman-to-woman look.

Isabelle gave a heartfelt nod of agreement. She didn't add that pregnancy was only half the reason for her queasiness, the other half being worry. William was about to depart for the English court, leaving her in nominal command of Leinster. This baby, above all her others, was truly going to earn the heritage of his ancestry.

Maeve, the Irish midwife, made her rinse her mouth with an infusion of ginger and bog myrtle to ease the nausea. Her maids robed her in a silk chemise and the saffron-gold gown William had stripped from her on a rainy spring evening when they had begotten this child. With her first babies, tight young muscles had kept her figure from ripening until the sixth month, but these days, she began to show at three…and to her benefit.

William wore his court robe of silver silk but instead of adorning it with the ornate belt of gold bezants, he had donned his plain leather swordbelt and his scabbarded blade hung at his left hip.

Elizabeth Avenel fetched a small pot of red powder from the cosmetic coffer and Isabelle suffered a tinge to be rubbed into her cheeks. She didn't want to resemble one of the painted women of the court, but from the way she felt she knew her complexion needed a boost—just enough to make her look robust and capable of governing Leinster while William was gone. Sybilla draped a wimple of cream-coloured silk over Isabelle's braids and pinned it at her throat with a circlet brooch of amber and gold.

William nodded his approval. "Beautiful," he said, "and regal..." His gaze dropped to her belly and a smile curved his lips. "And with child. Just the right note, I think. Are you ready to face them?"

She drew a deep breath and nodded. Somehow, she would ignore the nausea; somehow she would hold her head up and smile.

At a formal pace, William escorted Isabelle into the hall. She laid her hand over his in courtly fashion and walked with the grace of a queen, her spine straight, her expression imperious. Behind them came their children, Isabelle's women, and the knights of the mesnie, the latter all wearing their swords.

Isabelle and William halted at the centre of the dais and faced the company in the well of the hall at the feasting benches. Their children and Isabelle's women assembled to the left, and the knights stood on right.

Their gathered vassals had risen at William and Isabelle's entrance and all eyes had turned to the dais. Isabelle saw wariness, speculation, hostility, and the occasional spark of warmth. She and William would have to depend on the loyalty of these lords in the months to come. Most had not brought their womenfolk, although there were a few in evidence—for the most part older women, sure of themselves, and the occasional young wife whose husband preferred to keep her in his sight rather than leave her to temptation at home.

William waited for the scrape of benches and the murmur of conversation to subside, letting the silence draw out for just long enough to further embed the focus, then he drew breath and made full use of his rich, strong voice.

"My lords, her you see the Countess, whom I have brought by the hand into your presence. She is your lady by right of birth, the daughter of Richard Strongbow, who enfeoffed you all with lands once he had conquered them with his own sword." He gazed at Isabelle to accentuate the connection to his audience. "She remains among you, pregnant with his grandchild. Until, God willing, I return, I pray you all to serve and protect her faithfully, as is her right. She is your liege lady as well you know, and I have no claim to anything here except through her." Turning to her, he knelt in homage, putting his hands between hers as would a vassal. Isabelle felt a sweeping surge of love and pride. Her eyes welled with emotion. Stooping, she bestowed on him the formal kiss of peace, and then kissed him again, as her husband, her gaze tender.

One by one, the barons came to the dais, knelt, and swore their oaths of fealty to her while William stood a little to one side, now taking no part, emphasizing the fact that the right was indeed Isabelle's and that he was only present to support her. Everyone in the room made obeisance and swore, not one man demurred; but both she and William knew it was still play-acting.

Once the oath taking was complete, Hugh le Rous, Bishop of Ossory, blessed the food and the gathering sat to dine.

"I have done my best," William said as he served Isabelle and himself from a steaming dish of mussels. "I have appealed to their sense of identity and their loyalty to you, but it remains to be seen how many of them will abide by their word."

Isabelle looked out over the gathering below them, watching their guests setting to with industry—very willing indeed to take their bread and salt and drink their wine. "I know the value of the oaths I've been given and how they equate to the men who knelt in homage." She gave him a warm look. "Yours was made of gold." Her expression hardened. "But some I know offered dross. I have my eye on them."

While William was feasting his vassals and allies at Kilkenny, Meilyr Fitzhenry was in Dublin making his own final preparations to leave for England. He fastened his cloak with a large silver pin, stabbing it down through the thick red wool of his cloak. Smoothing his hair, donning a cap edged with gold braid, he turned to his nephew and the mercenary captain with whom he had been talking while he dressed. "You are clear what to do?" he asked.

"Yes, my lord," said his nephew, his dark eyes eager and bright. "We are to wait until you have been gone for seven days and then begin our work."

Meilyr nodded, then wagged a peremptory finger. "But not for a seven-day, be certain of that. Give me time to be away and Marshal too. He mustn't have the opportunity to turn back. And be thorough. I want that pride of his cut down to the size it should truly have, not the grand cockstand he flaunts at the world."

Meilyr's analogy met with appreciative grins from both men, and their good humour was further increased by the pouch of silver he gave each of them. "Go now," he said, "and I want to hear well of your endeavor."

"And good fortune go with yours, my lord," said his nephew as he headed to the door with a young man's swagger.

Meilyr smiled thinly. "I intend it to."

Acknowledgments

I WANT TO SAY THANK YOU TO SOME OF THE PEOPLE WHO have helped me to write *The Greatest Knight*, either by aiding me with my research, keeping me solvent, putting up with my moods, or just being there for me.

Academics are often accused of dwelling in ivory towers, but the ones I contacted while researching the often obscure details of the novel were most approachable and helpful. In particular I would like to thank Professor Gillian Polack for her contributions and for being my sounding board on various issues of medieval life, and Professor David Crouch for taking the time to reply to my questions. I would also like to extend my appreciation to Professor Crouch for writing such a superb biography of William Marshal to light my path. On the research front too, Alison King has been invaluable for her help in showing me hitherto unknown details of William Marshal's life. Any errors or misinterpretations are entirely my responsibility.

As always, the support and enthusiasm of my agent Carole Blake and my editor Barbara Daniel at Time Warner have been crucial. I'd like to thank them for putting up with me. I apologise to the lovely Richenda Todd for the massive amounts of copy-editing but would add in mitigation that medieval chroniclers do have a lot to answer for and it's not all my fault!

Also thank you to Sheena-Margot Lavelle, Rachael Ludbrook, and Cecilia Duraes at Time Warner for their supporting roles in bringing the novel to fruition. My thanks too, to my U.S. editor Shana Drehs for her enthusiasm, help, and inspiration.

I would like to thank my husband Roger (who, several novels on, is still doing the ironing) for understanding my obsession with another man, albeit one who hasn't been around for eight hundred years!

Appreciation also to Wendy Zollo for running my e-list at Yahoo groups and to various e-list friends who have lightened my life, given me food for thought, and offered their love and support when needed.

Reading Group Guide

By Elizabeth Chadwick

1. At the beginning of the novel, we discover that William Marshal was almost hanged as a small boy. William's father said that he cared not and that he still had the anvils and hammers to get better sons. How do you think William would have been a different man in adult life if this incident had not happened? How did this affect the kind of man he did become?

2. At the battle for Drincourt, William declines to take prisoners for ransom and finds himself impoverished. He had a revelation at this time, thinking to himself: "Fight for your lord, fight for your honour, but for yourself too." Did William maintain this new mind-set and act accordingly?

3. William was known in his youth as "Gaste-Viande" or "greedy guts." What part do descriptions of food play in bringing this period of the Middle Ages to life? Are the descriptions of medieval dishes what you expected people of the time to eat? Do any of the dishes sound particularly appetizing? Was there anything that stood out to you as being very strange?

4. William saved the life of Eleanor of Acquitaine when her enemies attempted to ambush her. Eleanor is so grateful, she pays his ransom and gives him a place at the head of her son's retinue. What does this tell you about Eleanor? How does Eleanor and William's relationship develop through the novel?

5. Other women appear in the novel, including Clara, William's mistress. Do you think William would have survived without her intervention when he was a prisoner? Would they have stayed together if Clara had borne a child? Women of Clara's status (courtesans) were part of a baronial household. Do you think William treated Clara well? How would you have felt in Clara's position?

6. William and his brother John are on uneasy terms throughout the novel. John says very early in the book, "You would find life as my knight dull after Normandy." Was John jealous of William? Do you think John felt that William was trying to rise above his station or his place in the household? If John had accepted William, would William have been content to stay at home and serve in his retinue?

7. William journeys all over Europe and visits the Middle East. When he went to Jerusalem, he bought his own burial shrouds. Did this seem morbid to you? What did it mean to William? Would you be comfortable choosing the trappings for your own funeral at William's age?

8. William was a champion of the tournament. Was there anything that particularly surprised, amused, or interested you about life on the tourney circuits? Are there any modern events that have parallels with tournaments?

9. At times, the Young King seems to have been a very difficult project for William. What life lessons did William learn from serving him? How did the Young King benefit from having William in his retinue?

10. William was accused of having an affair with the Young King's wife and was banished from court. The author has put forth one interpretation of this particular set of events, but historically, it is open to speculation. Do you think William did have an affair with Marguerite, or do you believe that he was set up by his rivals?

11. In his lifetime, William was renowned for his unswerving loyalty. Do you think William's intense loyalty was always to his advantage? Were there times when he would have been wiser to back off?

12. Henry II and his sons seem to have been perpetually quarrelling with each other. Do you think this was a case of incompatible personalities or the political situation? What qualities did William possess that allowed him to succeed in weaving his path through the politics? Do you think you would have been able to maneuver so well in his position?

13. When the Young King dies, William agrees to take his cloak to the Holy Sepulchre in Jerusalem. Why do you think he volunteered to go on a harrowing journey from which he might not return? Have you ever undertaken a distasteful or difficult task because of a sense of duty? Were there any unexpected benefits?

14. William took young Jean D'Earley under his wing on his return from the Holy Land. What do you think of the medieval practice of older knights raising and training adolescent youths to their profession? What is your impression of William's relationship with Jean, and Jean's relationship with William? Do you think any of William's responses were tied up with regrets about his former lord, the Young King?

15. William prevented Richard from attacking his father Henry II on the flight from le Mans by killing his horse and saying that he would leave Richard's taking to the devil. What does this tell you about William? What does it tell you about the relationship between Richard and his father? What would the consequences have been if William had indeed killed Richard? Have you ever been in a position where you have had to defend someone while knowing it might have repercussions for you?

16. When William marries Isabelle de Clare, there are at least twenty-one years between them in age. Isabelle and William seem to settle together very quickly and to be compatible. How would you feel, being given in marriage to someone you hadn't met, who was much older than you, and with no say in the matter? What do you think about the position of women at that time in history? Do you think they had any kind of power?

17. William calls Isabelle his "safe harbour." How important do you think having such grounding was? Was William a "safe harbour" for Isabelle? Who is the "safe harbour" in your life?

18. As soon as Richard is crowned, he goes on crusade. William is left as one of the co-rulers and has to try and keep a balance between the different factions. Was he successful? How would you have handled the situation?

19. The royal household moved around frequently, sometimes as often as every two or three days, taking their furniture with them. Do you think that being a part of the royal court would have been worth the constant upheaval?

20. *The Greatest Knight* is based on a true story from a detailed biography written in the early thirteenth century. Do you feel as if you know now what life was like in the thirteenth century? What surprised you? What did you want to know more about?

About the Author

Elizabeth Chadwick can remember telling herself stories from the age of three, but it was as a teenager that she fell in love with the Middle Ages and decided that she wanted to write historical fiction for a living. It took her the better part of fifteen years to attain her ambition, and during that time she married, began raising a family, and worked filling supermarket shelves to keep solvent. In 1990 her perseverance paid off when her novel *The Wild Hunt* was taken on by a leading London literary agency and

Charlie Hopkinson

then sold to a major UK publisher. *The Wild Hunt* went on to win a major UK award for romantic fiction, presented at Whitehall by HRH Prince Charles. Since then, Elizabeth's novels have gone on to become bestsellers translated into more than sixteen languages. She has been short-listed four times for the UK's Romantic Novelists Association major award. Richard Lee, founder of the Historical Novel Society, nominated her novel *The Scarlet Lion* as one of the ten best historical reads of the decade. Elizabeth has also had several historical short stories published in magazines and anthologies, and she was commissioned by Columbia Pictures to novelise the script of the film *First Knight*. She uses historical reenactments and visits to locations as part of her interdisciplinary approach to her research. She lives in Nottingham, England, with her husband, assorted animals, and itinerant adult offspring.